SHE.

SCONE

SCONE

A likely tale

ADAM FERGUSSON

SINCLAIR-STEVENSON
LONDON

To
James, Petra, Lucy and Marcus

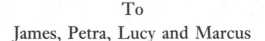
First published in the United Kingdom in 2004
by Sinclair-Stevenson
3 South Terrace, London SW7 2TB

ISBN 0-9543520-3-3

Copyright © Adam Fergusson 2004

Typeset by Rowland Phototypesetting Ltd., Bury St Edmunds, Suffolk.
Printed and bound in the United Kingdom by
St Edmundsbury Press Ltd., Bury St Edmunds, Suffolk.

SCONE

PROLOGUE

U NDER A starry summer night, that fine and solid edifice Scone
Abbey, for nearly two centuries an institution of high and
sober repute among the natives of Perth, rang with music and
mirth. Song dissolved in laughter. Laughter melted into song.
Wine flowed copiously in the refectory, an unusual indulgence
for the time of year, yet was the direct cause of neither the conviviality nor the merriment. And if the unrestrained rejoicing were
tinged with triumph among the brethren, who would blame them?
The forces of darkness had been made to look as silly as anyone
could wish.

Venturing to look out of his chamber window, Abbot Henry
smiled benignly on the brothers. Normally he would have put an
instant stop to any tendency to romp in the cloister, for that was
a practice on which St Augustine, the founder of the order, would
certainly have frowned. But the circumstances were exceptional.

By any ordinary standard the spring months of 1296 had been
depressing ones. Scotland's fierce forays against Carlisle and into
Northumberland had come to little, but the English counter-attack
would be devastating. The Border country was soon laid waste with
fire and sword – the Berwick garrison butchered and the town
lost at the end of March. The last days of April saw the rout of
the Scottish army at Dunbar and the reduction of the castle. After
a futile defence by James the Stewart, the stronghold of Roxburgh
fell in May. The same month brought news of King Edward's
march on Edinburgh castle, which impregnable fortress surrendered after a shamefully short siege. Stirling would be abandoned
even before the English army reached it.

In the first week of July came the crushing news from Kincardineshire that King John de Balliol, who had tried so hard to assert Scotland's independence and protect her liberty, had been obliged to perform the most humiliating feudal penance to the King of England. A white rod in his hand, and acknowledging the justice of the English invasion, he resigned the country, her people and their homage to his liege lord Edward. With that, all resistance crumbled. Edward forged his way northwards to the Moray Firth where, in Elgin Cathedral three weeks later, he received the sworn fealty of the Scottish barons in ceremonies conducted by dignitaries of the Scottish church; and by early August, with the reduction of Scotland complete, he was ready to go home.

Yet he had one more vindictive act of oppression to perform. As his army returned to cross the Dee and move south-west down Strathmore towards Perth, a swift horseman late one evening brought the urgent warning to Scone that a detachment of two score English mounted troops was hastening ahead on a secret and unexplained mission, and was only a few hours away.

The abbot needed no explanation, not doubting what was afoot. Unhesitatingly he gave the order to carry out his long prepared, meticulously rehearsed, contingency plan for averting the ultimate misfortune. Roused by the abbey bell, the tonsured sleepers in the dormitory struggled from their uncomfortable beds, donned habits and sandals, and hurried along the cloistral flagstones and out into the courtyard. Flaming torches were brought to light the scene as they pieced together a large and ungainly pine frame and mounted it on thick, wide oak skids appropriate for the transport of heavy objects over rough terrain. Meanwhile two canons were dispatched to the sacristy to recover from an iron-bound beech kist the strong leather cradle – three ox-hides sewn together in a treble thickness – which had lain there for four years awaiting this crisis. This was brought to the abbey nave, a little way from the high altar, where eight of the burliest monks were already assembled, equipped with two stout poles designed for the task.

The abbot bustled downstairs to supervise what was to follow. He carried a storm-lantern. As ever, he approached with awe and conscientious reverence the ancient sacred monolith, encased in its wooden frame to form a throne, fully aware of the significance of what he was doing but never doubting it had to be done. Except for the coronations which took place in the open air a few steps from the abbey doors the great stone had never been moved

2

from its resting-place here since its journey from Iona with Saint Columba seven centuries earlier – or from Ireland with King Fergus, or from Crinan with Kenneth MacAlpin (Who knew? The stories were legion). It was Scotland's palladium, the God-sent symbol on which her preservation depended, the legendary pillow on which Jacob once slept at Bethel when he dreamt of angels ascending and descending the ladder to Heaven.

Here was the Fatal Stone, the Stone of Destiny, flanked by bronze tablets bearing a mystic inscription, not in Latin, the *lingua franca* of the Dark Ages, but in the simple language and curious characters of the Dalriadic Scots whose capital Scone had been. Wherever the stone lay, they said, wherever it might be taken, that was where the Scots would hold sway and find safety. King John had been the last to be placed ceremonially upon it to receive, in 1292, the crown from the Bishop of St Andrews and take the oath – John who had now brought Scotland to a vassalage not even contemplated by Hadrian or Antonine.

Their muscles straining, the monks eased the throne out of its wooden casing and tilted it until it toppled over slowly upon the thick padding at the bottom of the leather cradle. The bronze tablets were placed on top. The legs of the oxhide had been firmly bound together, to form loops through which the poles slid easily. A moment later the immense burden was swinging from eight shoulders and borne out of the abbey. Abbot Henry led the way with his lantern.

As the new day dawned the monastery of Scone presented a scene of urgent commotion to the approaching English troop. Surmising that his arrival had been anticipated, its leader Corspatrick rode his knights forward at a brisk canter, but drew up short at the main gates just as they were slammed in his face. Along the walls to the left frenzied cries could be heard. The troop instantly wheeled and galloped round the monastery to the chantry gates, the evident source of the noise.

Two dozen monks were struggling with ropes to pull their heavy make-shift sled through the pillars. There it was stuck deep in a rut. The brothers were plainly in panic, not knowing whether to go forward or back. The gates could not be closed; and they ran this way and that. Once again Corspatrick halted his men, staring suspiciously at a bulky shape that lay on the sled covered

3

with hides. A canon came forward brusquely demanding to know his business. But the commander's eye was by then tracing the long, ugly gash which the sled had torn across eighty yards of turf all the way back to the abbey steps. Although he was not a clever man, he was astute enough to see what the monks were about. He directed an officer to seize and guard the sled while he rode through the gates, dismounted at the abbey door and ran inside, his sword drawn. There by the altar he found Abbot Henry alone at prayer. Beside him stood a partly dismembered wooden throne, its base gaping open. The stone for which Corspatrick had come was gone; and the pitying look on the priest's face as it turned his way signified that he had come too late. The commander looked out of the door and with a curt word beckoned him from his knees. The abbot rose and followed. As together they surveyed the scene outside, looking across the grassy mound known as the Moot Hill, his expression changed slowly from pity to incomprehension, then to dismay. Whatever his plan had been, it had evidently gone badly wrong.

Corspatrick laughed brutally, dismissed the abbot with a gesture, led his horse back to the gates, and signalled to his men to strip away the hides. A few monks moved forward to stop them but were quickly repelled, some falling on their knees to offer up prayers. Prayer was of no avail. The troop had found what they had come for: it even had large wrought-iron rings shackled to either end for easy handling.

But that had all happened early in the morning. King Edward arrived later in the day to satisfy himself of the success of the mission and to conduct such further ransacking as seemed desirable. Whereafter the great military caravan passed on across the Tay, leaving the monks otherwise unharmed and to their own devices.

Far into the next night their revels went on. Three boars, that ancient delicacy, had been roasted whole, and their severed heads now graced the long refectory tables, the last of the 1295 apples in their mouths. Their flesh, in liberal amounts, was eaten with a seasonal dish of oatmeal, cream, wild raspberries and honey. And when the long-preserved butt of good French wine was finished, the little monastery distillery gave generously of its bounty. It was another week before the brothers were able properly to go about their monastic duties again; and Abbot Henry,

4

perhaps aware that Scotland was facing the dark days of a long interregnum, and little peace, felt no inclination over-hastily to reimpose the ascetic disciplines of quieter times.

Meanwhile the massive stone which the monks of Scone had failed either to conceal or to protect was borne to the south, under close guard upon a bed of straw on a creaking ox-wagon in the train of King Edward's army as it trudged on its long march back to Westminster. It could look forward to a distinguished and turbulent destiny.

1

A SHROUDED shape hurried down the steps of St Stephen's Porch and through the murk of Westminster Hall before disappearing up the stairs in the north-west corner. The Grand Committee Room there had been privately booked for the winter's evening.

"That's Mr Macarthur," said the senior duty police officer, watching from the unobtrusive little cabin by the north door. "Unmistakeable."

A minute later, a head looked out of the central door in the eastern wall of the hall to determine that it was empty, and a second cloaked body scuttled over the stone-flagged waste of the largest single enclosed space in the Houses of Parliament.

"And that'll be Mr Montrose," the senior officer observed. "He always scuttles like that."

"More of a scurry," corrected the junior duty police officer. "It's because of his hip operation. And there goes Miss Ross, the Member for Minto Hill. Now she's a pretty girl."

"One of the Scottish Whips."

The junior officer sighed.

"Nor would I," agreed his superior.

A fourth, a fifth, then other shadowy figures stole across the hall. Whoever they were, whatever they were about, their apparent hope was to be unobtrusive, their demeanour conspiratorial and their purpose clearly secret. The duty policemen noted who was there, but only because it was their habit. They barely considered, and never commented on, the eccentricities of MPs. The vital thing was to recognise them under every guise, and to ensure their free, uninterrupted passage in the interests of liberty, justice and parliamentary democracy. Within ten minutes the stealthy transit of more than four dozen politicians duly went observed but unchallenged. As the duty policemen remarked to each other without further comment, they were from all parties and all represented constituencies in Scotland.

Privately, for policemen are only human, they wondered what was going on. The Scottish Grand Committee on which most of those members would once unwillingly have had to sit – service on it used commonly to be known as "the galleys" – had not met since the devolved Scottish parliament was set up in Edinburgh in the late 'nineties. Yet here it was reassembling, reconstituting itself as it were, voluntarily and in its accustomed place – but doing so for no official procedural purpose. The doors of the Grand Committee Room closed with an inadvertent crash that echoed to the ancient hammerbeam roof aloft. Nobody outside the room found it remarkable, and the attention of the Law turned elsewhere.

Campbell Macarthur surveyed the gloomy but expectant faces before him, and called the meeting to order.

"We are all, here, I think. Have you taken a count, Maureen?"

Mrs Findlay, the MP for Edinburgh Cramond, was still stabbing a finger towards the seats at the back of the room.

"Forty-eight, forty-nine, fifty, fifty-one, fifty-two. Then there's the two who are poorly, Jim Blair on the delegation to Abu Dhabi, and Betty McLellan with her appendix. And Graham Fraser. He didn't give me notice but we all know what he's up to."

"At least he has somethin' to do," said a voice at the back – that of Murdo Mercer, who sat for the Carse of Gowrie.

A few members chuckled. Graham Fraser, representing Inchcape Rock, was among those with some ministerial experience at Westminster from pre-devolution days, but the only one who had kept on his secretary full-time.

"Order, please," said Macarthur. "Anyone else missing, Maureen?"

"Aye, Andy Wedderburn – but that's tactical. He couldn't even pretend not to have been here."

"Quite so," Macarthur agreed.

"And I haven't counted myself."

"That brings me to the next points – before we start. None of you had written notice of this meeting: it was entirely arranged by word of mouth. So far as the press is concerned, it's not taking place, and won't have taken place. So far as our colleagues from the rest of the United Kingdom are concerned, but only if they ask, then a few of us may well have met informally – to discuss unspecified matters of mutual but passing interest. We have no written agenda. We shall have no record of who has attended. There will be no minutes. Any questions so far?"

Murdo Mercer rose, tall and craggy, his suit crumpled after ten hours on the train from Carnoustie.

"Ah'm unaware o' a full-scale committee meetin' in recorded history in the whole Palace of Westminster that didna leak like a cullender," he said. "Why wad this be different?"

There were mutterings of affronted dissent.

"The circumstances are exceptional," explained Macarthur. "None of us has anything to gain from letting the rest of us down. Anyway, since this meeting isn't taking place, it can't leak."

"Who cares what we say, anyway?" This came from James Doughty, MP for Glasgow Crawhall. "If anyone's interested, it'll be the first time. Look at the election figures."

The solution – the word will have to do – to the constitutional conundrum long known as the West Lothian Question had left the rump of Scotland's MPs at Westminster disenchanted and bitter. The creation of a parallel parliament in Edinburgh – a devolved government – in the closing years of the twentieth century had, as predicted, made their position and privileges anomalous and unsustainable, and no justification remained for Scottish over-representation in the parliament of the United Kingdom. The constitutional reforms implemented with the last general election duly culled more than a dozen from Scotland's seventy-two members; and much blood was spilt when sitting MPs fought for reselection to survive that unfeeling game of musical chairs.

However, the nub of the West Lothian Question, originally propounded in the 1970s by the wise and persistent MP for that constituency, concerned voting rights. If England's MPs could no longer vote on Scottish domestic matters – health, farming, education, transport, planning, to name a few – why should Scotland's MPs in Westminster be permitted to meddle in English home affairs? With their powers now duly truncated, south and north of the Border, in the areas critical for attracting votes in return for promises at election time, they wondered whether there was any political purpose left to their lives.

9

Doughty went on. "The turn-out in Cowcaddens was under ten per cent at dinner time and not much more at supper time. We were lucky to pass fifteen per cent when the polls closed. The counting was over even before the pubs shut. What kind of democracy is that?"

"It was still a record of a kind, Jimmie," said Mercer. "And ye gave the *Evening Times* a guid laugh wi' yer photie – comin' oot tae vote for yersel' when the polls opened at dawn. 'First of the few,' it said."

Doughty nodded. "Aye, and the headline 'Inertia lunges forward'."

"Onyway, nane o' youse did ony better. Didnae matter whit we tried tae get 'em oot their hooses." These were the glottal stops of the MP for Glasgow Lavery, Donald Mutwant Singh, another of the city's reduced contingent of representatives now collectively known as the Glasgow Boys.

Indeed, poor attendance at the polling stations was almost the only feature of the entire campaign to which newspapers and television in Scotland had paid any attention. Scottish reporters and commentators nowadays preferred to concentrate their time and space on the ever-unfolding misfortunes and scandals of the Edinburgh assembly beside the Palace of Holyrood, for which the public had an insatiable appetite. To Scotland's opinion-formers, the relevance of Westminster had waned to a sliver.

"They'd had four elections on the trot already," John Montrose who sat for Moray Firth reminded them, "not to speak of the referendum."

It was a fair point: in the course of eighteen months, candidates for local authorities, Europe, the House of Lords and Holyrood had claimed, strained and lost the attention of all but the most avid voters in Scotland. No one could even remember what the referendum had been about.

"And they all had bigger turn-outs, even the European ones," put in Doughty.

"Order, please," said Macarthur, and called on the Member for Merrick, Neil Buchanan, to open the discussion.

Buchanan was not the only MP present who had once served in government, but he had been on a front bench longer than any other, at one time in opposition, and so enjoyed some sort of authority and respect. In his sixties, beetle-browed and with a high complexion beneath his whitening hair, he rose and looked around with a contrived portentousness which, with audiences less inured to such devices, would have commanded immediate and sometimes lingering attention.

However, what he had to say deeply concerned every member there. They listened intently as he contrasted their present plight now with the heady days of Scottish political dominance in Westminster in the closing years of the twentieth century. That their numbers had fallen so drastically was the least of it. At the turn of the millennium, during the triumphal celebrations under the gigantic, useless dome in East London, every top government post had been held by a Scot: Prime Minister, Chancellor of the Exchequer, Foreign Secretary, Chief Secretary, Defence Secretary, Chief Whip, Lord Chancellor. Moreover, Scottish members had been ministers in the Treasury, the Board of Trade, the Department of the Environment, and half a dozen others. That had been the pattern for decades – for it had never bothered the English where their rulers came from – but it had reached a sort of apogee following the 1997 general election.

Today, apart from Andy Wedderburn, who almost for appearances' sake had been made Secretary of State for the Union, which nebulous cabinet position he clung to by his finger-nails, Scotland's representatives were like the Ulster members, all on the back-benches. Had the party leaders at Westminster wanted it otherwise, it would have been no more possible: now that Scotland had home rule, however limited and incompetent, English MPs were not going to let the part-time members from the North run their show any longer, or take away from them any of those government or opposition appointments every politician hankers for. What was true of the higher offices of State was no less so of the lower ones: to have a Scottish member in charge of any aspect of English education, just for example, would be a democratic absurdity. None had been given so much as a committee chairmanship. And what England's MPs felt was but a reflection of what was thought in their constituencies.

Further, Buchanan reminded his audience, before the Scottish parliament was finally set up in 1999, there had been five Scottish Office ministers in the British government serving under the Secretary of State for Scotland, in each case an opportunity for a Scottish MP to acquire extra status and an official car – Buchanan had been one of them. Now their tasks were performed by the twenty-two-strong Scottish Executive in Edinburgh. There were no Scottish ministers in Westminster. Dover House, so long the Whitehall base of the Scottish Secretaries, was occupied by the Secretary of State for English Rural Affairs. Andy Wedderburn was invited to cabinet meetings only when the agenda required it, lucky to be allowed to call himself Right Honourable. Scottish Question Time, that short fortnightly afternoon session which used to empty the chamber of any but the MPs seeking answers and Scottish ministers avoiding giving them, had been abolished. It had gone the way of the Scottish standing committees.

"I don't know about the rest of you," Buchanan said, "but my constituency letters – the ones I've actually to deal with myself – are down to about three a week. For the rest, they're about the usual things: schools, the health service, roadworks, so I have to refer my correspondents to their MSPs. There's nothing I can do for them. Nothing."

Doughty cut short the general murmur of sympathy. "That's why we're sharing our secretaries."

"Ither than on the Inchcape Rock," said Mercer.

"Robert, Janet, Callum and I have the one between us." said Maureen Findlay. "And she spends three-quarters of her time sending out little notes explaining that something's been devolved. Not that she's hard-worked otherwise."

"And the English members know it," Doughty added.

There was a long growl of agreement. The office expenses of England's MPs had been raised some time ago to accommodate the payment of three office staff each; but the Scottish Whips had not been able to justify anything similar for their own. What the Scottish members most resented was the loss of status such discrimination implied.

"Please let Neil go on," said Macarthur.

"No one in Galloway seems to care about foreign policy," Buchanan resumed, "unless it's Europe. But then it's about agriculture, and that's for the Department in Edinburgh; or fisheries, and so's that; or development grants, and it's the same story. Sometimes I have to refer people to their Euro-MPS. Imagine!"

"Anyway," grumbled Callum Geekie, representing The Monros, "that mob in Holyrood have had their own office in Brussels for six years at least, and they're adding to it. They deal directly with the Commission. They've got a European committee. There's a delegation swanning out to the Continental fleshpots twice a month. They're having language courses at the tax-payers' expense. French lessons! Bloody impertinence."

"What it amounts to," Buchanan added, "is that we've nothing to do that anybody cares about."

"He's right," observed the MP for Edinburgh Inchkeith, Robert Johnston. "My election manifesto was a disaster. Guess how many votes there are in overseas aid."

"Still, you got back, Bob, mind," said Ian McWhirter, the MP for Glasgow Hornel.

"That's because I put in a picture of our dogs and because the others were trying to excite the voters with global warming and works councils."

"Order!" called Macarthur. "Neil must finish."

"Thank you," said Buchanan. "And nobody's going to give us anything to do, either."

"The De'il aye finds work for idle hands," said Johnston.

"No question," said Buchanan. "Maybe you new members don't care yet, but you're facing life on the backbenches for as long ahead as you want to look, lucky if the Speaker calls you at Question Time so that you can talk about somewhere like Muscat or Madagascar –"

"No one knows the names of our constituencies, so effectively we're incognito," Montrose interrupted. "We're non-people, '*los desaparecidos*'. Moray Firth isn't even dry land. I've got an identity crisis."

"And mine sounds like a psalm tune," said Mrs Findlay. "And Jennie's just a weather station. And Ewan's a volcanic plug. Heaven knows why they had to change every single one. Most of them are landmarks, not areas. To avoid confusion, the boundary people said. The confusion is complete."

"Order, please."

"– ignored in committees," Buchanan continued, "but expected to stay on late at night to support your parties in difficulties, but only if it's nothing to do with Scottish affairs or English affairs as such."

The twelve MPs who had arrived at Westminster for the first time the previous autumn looked at each other aghast.

"That is just a shame," said Jennie Murray, MP for Rockall. Her gentle voice came from the West Highlands. "It is a cruel thing. I was still hoping to have a speech reported in the *Oban Times*."

"Worse than that, Jennie," said Buchanan, again engaging his portentous demeanour. "At Budget time – and we get to vote at Budget time: we can even speak – when the block grant to Scotland is cut down even more with no objections from anyone from England, you can guess who'll get the blame. We'll be lumped together with the others and accused of forcing the Scottish Executive to raise taxes at home. Holyrood has had it coming – and now they'll have to pin it on someone."

"But was I no' telling my voters I would fight for them every inch of the way?", wailed Jennie Murray.

"We all did, Jennie. So we shall. But they'll take no notice because Holyrood'll need scapegoats, and that's what we'll be."

Buchanan had finished and sat down. The gathering, whose initial mood had been gloomy, was beginning to simmer with indignation, and Macarthur judged it was time to move forward.

"An admirable summary of our situation," he declared. "Before we discuss what we are to do about it, are there any comments?"

"Certainly." This was a new voice, that of the MP for Ailsa, Ewan Cameron.

"Yes, Ewan?"

"I think you're missing most of the point."

The Members in front looked round while the others leant forward, all anxious to know what point they were missing. Cameron was a lawyer, and something of a constitutional expert.

"What is that, then?"

"It's the single issue – who ultimately speaks for the Scottish people. Is it us, or" – he gestured in a vaguely northern direction – "that circus? Is it Andy Wedderburn in his Union hat when he's not speaking for Wales and Ulster and the English regions too, or is it the clowns in Holyrood?"

"They think it's them," said Doughty, ungrammatically but succinctly.

"That's right," interjected Montrose. "They've said so. Their pretensions are intolerable. But this is where power is: they're only a *devolved* government.".

"It's a fine distinction," said Macarthur, "not easy to grasp."

"Maybe not," said Montrose. "The Scottish people certainly haven't grasped it. They've forgotten about us."

"And you've seen what the *Record* is calling us – Wimps. Short for Westminster MPs, more or less." This was Robert Johnston again.

"Order, please," said Macarthur. "Ewan?"

"The problem," Cameron resumed, "comes from trying to insert a federal unit – well, virtually – into a unitary state. It's an impossible contradiction. It's like trying to find a collective noun for hermits. You can't have it any more than you can have a square root of a minus quantity."

"Steady, Ewan," said Macarthur. "You may lose some of us."

"Can I no' have a square root of a minus quantity?" Jennie Murray whispered to Maureen Findlay. The issue had not come her way before.

"Seemingly not."

"That is just a shame."

"So?" Macarthur asked.

"Well, to put it simply," Cameron said, "we're in total conflict – constitutional, political, logical. Moral too, for all I know. We've been usurped. It's undignified. It's unacceptable. It's unstable."

"It's war," growled Mercer. "We shall resort tae desperate measures. Nae doot. If we can think o' some."

"Thank you Ewan," said Macarthur. "None of us finds our situation supportable. We don't know if we have a future. So it's unstable. That much is clear. Desperate measures, Murdo?" He smiled. "You're not considering violence, I hope?"

"Weel, ye hae tae fight fire wi' fire."

"Ah, well. We're not being fired at. That rules out shooting. It's a question of how to regain the hearts and minds of the people, of how to recover the – "

The sound of a throat being cleared at the back of the room stopped the chairman in mid-sentence.

"Is that you, Duncan?" he said. "You nearly caught my eye earlier, but I'm afraid I lost you. You have the floor. It's time we heard from your party".

Not everyone present would have agreed. Duncan Innes was the sole representative of the three-year-old Scotch Enlightenment Party. To everyone's surprise, this initially amorphous movement had won a respectable vote and captured twelveseats in the last

Holyrood elections. It had now made its first inroad at Westminster: moreover, its candidates had been runners-up in a dozen other Scottish constituencies. It found support in all quarters and all ranks, in town and in country. In a sense it was non-political, which is to say that its scorn for traditional parties of right or left, or for nationalist or unionist politicians, was evenly distributed. It therefore enjoyed an immediate bond with a public already cynical about or sickened by conventional politicking, a bond which had been smoothly translated into votes when the time came, as the older parties had discovered to their cost.

More significantly, the SEP was as much of a historic as of a patriotic tendency. Where others proclaimed, pursued and perhaps achieved a political correctness which vexed some of the electorate, amused others but convinced few, the SEP stood for historic authenticity. Its appeal was general, but also deep: for it reached down into that well of guilty ignorance of their own nation's true history that is sunk in most Scottish souls.

Innes, a tall, slender, personable man in his mid-thirties, his dark eyes peering from under rather shaggy hair, had chosen his moment well. Whether they would like it or not, his audience knew they would hear something either enlightening or unexpected, perhaps both.

"It doesn't seem possible to put things right unless we fully understand what went wrong, and when, and why," he began, and paused.

"Go on," Macarthur prompted.

"I must go back eight hundred years, to the wars of Wallace and Bruce which ended in Bannockburn."

Had Scotland's Nationalist members not withdrawn from Westminster – mainly out of disgust when they found what the boundary commission had done to their seats – they would no doubt have sensed a territorial trespass and bristled accordingly. It was left to the assembled MPs to eye one another in dismay. How long would this take?

"We won our independence then. Ever since, Scotland and her people have grown continually in stature and influence in these islands. Yes, there were ups and downs for two and a half centuries, battles and quarrels with the English – ".

"There was Flodden in 1513," muttered Buchanan, feeling an urge to contribute.

"– but one way or another the Scotch have made headway against extraordinary odds. After three hundred years, a Scotch king became monarch of England too."

"Jamie Saxt, 1603," Mercer explained, no less anxious to indicate a sound grounding in history.

"After four hundred years, the union of our parliaments in 1707 brought new opportunities to tighten our hold over the two countries. After five hundred years, the whole world was beating a path to Edinburgh where the Scottish Enlightenment was in full flower."

"It's true," said Johnston. "The Athens of the North."

"Then our learning, our literature, our philosophy, our arts, our science, our engineering and finally our manufacturing enterprise spread throughout the United Kingdom and through the British Empire. After six hundred years, despite our small numbers, there was nowhere in Great Britain, or in the world, where the Scotch had not made their mark and their name."

"Good," said Macarthur, a little impatiently. "But come to the point."

"I'm nearly there. I wanted to establish the pattern, the trend, the remorseless march of history, in your minds. Because after nearly seven hundred years we captured the political citadel itself. Neil Buchanan said as much just now. After the 1997 elections, there were more Scotch ministers in the very highest places in a British government than at any time in history. The Prime Minister, the Foreign Secretary, the Chancellor, the –"

"Yes, yes, Neil went through all that."

"Even the chairman of the Conservative Party was a Scot. He had a seat in Dorset. In those days the English didn't mind. Even the Liberal-Democrats were led by a –"

"Yes, all right."

"And so was Labour. Then the Director of Communications at Number Ten –"

"We don't need reminding. The one with the bagpipes."

"And the Speaker himself –"

"Your point is understood. And the manager of Manchester United, if I remember. Whatever else we needed, we didn't need self-government. Not when we were already running everything that mattered. And then Labour blew it –"

"Aye, but there's no need to name names," said Doughty. "We were pushed into it by –"

17

"Whoever it was," said Macarthur, cutting short any hint of partisan controversy. "But devolution! For people who didn't know what they had already, and weren't told, or wouldn't listen. That's why we're where we are today, nobody noticing our absence from anything. That's why 1997, with the new government committed to a devolved parliament, was the blackest hour for Scots in Westminster as well as the finest. Isn't that right, Duncan?"

"No. You misunderstand. The pass was sold already. By 1997 it was too late. A year too late. Think back!"

Scotland's assembled MPs thought back, a few brows knitted, others simply clouded, but no light dawning.

"Then think back seven hundred years exactly – the seven centuries I've been talking about."

The brows knitted again.

"1296?", asked the voices which had worked it out.

Janet Ross had not spoken so far. As a party Whip, responsible for herding the Scottish MPs in her charge through the voting lobbies, and thus privy to much personal information about many of them, a decent reticence was advisable in her relations with her colleagues. However, she saw no reason to restrain herself any longer. As well as the beautiful face and form that had earned the admiration of the duty policemen in the hall outside, she had a sharp mind that moved faster then most.

"The stone! That was it – the Stone of Destiny!"

"Thanks, Janet."

"They sent it back. Idiots."

"Seven hundred years of history undone in one reckless act of political appeasement," said Innes bitterly. "In the opinion of my party, it was a piece of vapid, dangerous, sentimental, self-serving folly. It impressed nobody. It meant the obliteration of a precious, significant episode in our island story. The link has gone. The coronation chair – the chair that Edward the First built for it – is empty. Here in Westminster, the stone meant something wonderful. Scottish kings sat on it when they became kings of Scotland. They sat on it again when they became kings of England, and then of Great Britain. It didn't just symbolise Scotland's influence here. It entrenched it."

"Did anyone else really think that much of it?" The question came from Callum Geekie, wondering rather than doubting.

"Well, yes," said Buchanan. "In 1940, when they thought Hitler would invade us, getting the chair and the stone out of Westminster and hiding them was one of Winston Churchill's top priorities. Just for example."

Innes nodded. "When our commissioners negotiated the Treaty of Union, they could probably have got it back. But they had the sense not to mention it. And now it's no more than a museum piece."

"Where is it now, please?" asked Jennie Murray. "I just can't recall where it was they put it."

"That makes my point perfectly," said Innes. "They keep it like a pet in a glass cage in Edinburgh Castle. Tourists look at it."

The meeting fell silent, considering what had been said. In 1996, in the declining days of a government, the Secretary of State for Scotland was alert to his party's decline north of the Border, and perhaps hoped to anticipate what, in a thoughtless moment, a Nationalist administration in Edinburgh might feel inclined to demand. He therefore announced that the seventh centenary of the theft of the Stone of Scone would be marked by its return to what he considered its rightful place – not Scone, for some reason, but Edinburgh. Can he have hoped for some personal credit? He was given little: like so many other things at that time, it looked like a gimmick, which of course was what it was. The Prime Minister of the day had been told in advance but had not understood the symbolic implications of the proposal. The cabinet were not informed until it was too difficult to back-track. The Dean of Westminster was affronted. No former Scottish Secretary was so much as consulted.

Neither the announcement of the stone's return, nor its prosecution with a ceremony at the Border in Coldstream and a somewhat self-conscious procession down Princes Street and up the Mound to Edinburgh Castle, where it was placed in the Crown Room of the Royal Palace there along with the Honours of Scotland, caused any lasting glow of satisfaction to suffuse the Scottish psyche. That psyche was bemused: few among the curious crowds knew what they were expected to feel, so most felt nothing. For, anyway, if the English didn't want the stone any more, what was so special about it?

"So need we ask how our humiliation began, or when?" demanded Innes.

"Has the stone so much power?" asked Macarthur. "So much that it dictates government policy? A barometer doesn't cause a change in the weather: it only records it."

"I can only point to a dismal coincidence," Innes said. "There was a much-quoted fourteenth-century Latin prophecy, which went

Ni fallat fatum,
Scoti quoncunque locatum,
invenient lapidem —"

There were instant protests from the committee. The more experienced members affected astonishment.

"That's unparliamentary language, Duncan. Give us the translation."

"Well, Walter Scott's version went

Unless the Fates are faithless found
And the prophet's voice be vain,
Where'er this monument be found
The Scottish race shall reign."

The meeting considered the message for a few moments, some making notes.

"Not much of a rhyme in the first and third lines – found and found," Montrose commented eventually. "I suppose vain and reign will do."

"It rhymes better in Latin," Innes said, "if you'd only let me finish."

"Better not," said Macarthur. "The meaning's plain enough. Was the prophet reliable?"

"Seems to have been right so far," said Innes. "Scotland is practically the only country in Europe that has never been conquered and held. I believe there's some doubt whether the stone's meant to give the Scotch dominance wherever it's found, or merely protection."

"At this minute," grunted Mercer, "we've got neither here, so it isnae relevant."

"So far, so good," Macarthur said. He looked at Innes. "Can you see the way forward?"

20

"Yes."

"Well?"

Janet Ross cut in quickly. "I propose," she said, "an all-party policy committee, which will set up an executive arm. That arm will take whatever steps it considers necessary in our joint interest. I do not think that this meeting, which, as you said, Mr Chairman, has not taken place, will wish to know in advance what those steps may be."

Macarthur nodded.

"Very well, Janet. Whom shall we have on the policy committee?"

"It doesn't matter, as long as there's someone from every party, so that we're all equally . . ."

"Implicated?"

"Committed".

"And on the . . . executive 'arm', you called it?"

"Duncan Innes".

"And –?"

"And me. It's enough."

Macarthur glanced at Innes, who was looking thoughtfully at Janet Ross.

"I think that'll do very well," Innes said quietly.

"Will there be expenses?" asked Macarthur.

"Yes. Not excessive, probably."

"You must let the policy committee know. We shall need a treasurer. Everyone will contribute equally."

"But of course no one here will know what the money is spent on."

"Exactly," Macarthur said. "No accounts. No one will know anything. If the meeting approves, I shall appoint a representative policy committee myself, to whom Duncan and Janet will no doubt report; and possibly I'll circulate a minute to that effect. But as we have not met there will be no minute. I shall convene another meeting when I consider it necessary. It will have no more substance than this one. Is everyone content?"

The general election, which had brought a greatly diminished number of disgruntled MPs to Westminster from Scotland, had had a predictable but unlooked-for constitutional impact on the conduct of affairs in the House of Commons. The new government had won a small but comfortable working majority of the seats in the United Kingdom, and could thus muster the party support to pass a budget, to approve fiscal policy, to ratify European laws, or to enact Bills on immigration, currency questions, telecommunications, air traffic control, environmental pollution and other matters of general national application.

Unfortunately, this working majority disappeared completely when it came to taking decisions of more immediate significance to the English electorate. The election had triggered the arrangement whereby MPs from Scotland, Northern Ireland and Wales were unable to vote on any issue devolved to their national assemblies, or on measures only applying to England. Such was the arithmetic of the election results, that the new British administration could not, without the opposition's consent, carry out in England any of its policies for the health service, or education, or transport, or pensions, or the social services, or anything else dear to its political heart. Arguably, in as far as election results reflect the balance of public opinion, this was to the net satisfaction.

"We're stymied," said the Prime Minister. "Snookered. Stalemated. Hamstrung. Hogtied. No one thought this thing through."

The cabinet secretary coughed.

"Well?"

"Prime Minister, you have always held that parliamentary devolution must be seen in the wider context of the regional assemblies –"

"Of course I have. We all came round to that view. But regional assemblies don't make laws –"

"They make by-laws, Prime Minister."

"I dare say, Matthew. But they're not parliaments. Just as well: you couldn't have a dozen little English parliaments behaving like the monkey-house in Edinburgh."

"No, Prime Minister."

"Meanwhile, look what's happened. We bring in a Bill to ban smoking in public places outdoors in England, in line with our manifesto, and it falls on second reading because we can't use the Scottish votes. Hartley practically burst a blood-vessel."

"It's certainly made it harder for Mr Blackman in the Whip's Office," agreed the cabinet secretary.

"Next, we successfully bring in the thirty-eight hour working week throughout the United Kingdom, thanks to our Scottish members. But they weren't allowed to vote on the opposition amendment which exempted England from its effects. So it doesn't apply in England after all. So the parliamentary party is furious. And the Scots are furious. What are we to do about it?"

"The simple democratic answer is for the English MPS to sit as an English parliament when English affairs are discussed."

"Absurd! I wouldn't be Prime Minister. We'd have a totally new front bench."

"As you said, Prime Minister: you're hog-tied."

"The whole thing's buggered."

"You could put it like that, too, Prime Minister".

"It's gone tits up."

The cabinet secretary shut his eyes. "Or like that, Prime Minister."

"How else would anyone put it?"

"Perhaps this should be on the agenda for the next cabinet? I'll put it there if you wish.

"You can put it – Yes! Why not? Something's got to give".

So the next cabinet after due deliberation commissioned a working paper from the Cabinet Office, and postponed further consideration of the question until the end of the year. It would find by then that the nature of the problem had changed beyond recognition.

Duncan Innes said: "I've never known a meeting stop as abruptly as that one. Why did you do it?"

Janet shrugged. "Campbell Macarthur got the message."

"Yes, but why did you do it?".

"Because you'd said enough. You were about to incriminate yourself."

"You know I wasn't. I'm not that stupid. All I told them was that I knew what had to be done, not what it was, or how."

"It was perfectly obvious what you were thinking."

"Probably only to you. So why?"

"Well – I believe passionately in what you believe in."

"Perhaps you do. But you don't know the first thing about me personally."

"You're wrong, Duncan. The Whips' offices know almost everything interesting about everyone."

23

"Only about everyone in their own parties."

"And in fragments of parties – like yours. They're not beyond exchanging hints with their opposite numbers."

"What do you know, then?"

"Thirty-four. Born Renfrewshire. Son of Professor of History at Edinburgh University. Superior degree in engineering at St Andrews; post-graduate course in classics and history at Edinburgh. Late entry Sandhurst. Eight years in the army. Retired with rank of captain acting major. Unmarried."

"You can get all that in Dod's *Parliamentary Companion*."

"All right, then. Served with the SAS. Secret missions in Montenegro, Kabul, West Africa, Basra, Fez. Highly regarded in regiment."

"That's all supposed to be classified."

"There's more. Torrid affairs with several women, all now concluded, names known but withheld for the present. Astute but politically inexperienced. Indifferent golfer. Chocoholic. Drinks moderately. Speaks well. Should not be asked to sing . . ."

"That'll do," said Duncan, "and it's intolerable. You've still to explain yourself."

"Can't you see – if there'd been any more discussion of means rather than ends at that meeting, it would have been all over the press lobby within hours. Murdo Mercer was right – committees leak like fishing nets. That's why I stopped it all. Not", Janet added with a modest smile, "without some success."

"You must have had some idea of what you're letting yourself in for."

"I once took a course in abseiling. One never knows when it'll be useful."

"Interesting but *non sequitur*, I think."

"And another making theatre props. I did it for a whole year. I'm pretty good at it – might be useful, too. Actually, I wanted to be an actress." Duncan waited. "So I decided to go into politics, where the opportunities are –"

"Will you soon be coming to the point?"

Janet looked at him levelly.

"All right, Duncan. You think you know what you're doing. Why d'you think the two of us will be enough?"

"I don't, particularly. *You* told them that."

"Yes, but you agreed."

24

"Well, I thought it would be more fun that way," said Duncan.

"I thought so too. That was why." She paused and smiled. "I hoped you'd say that."

"Janet?"

"Yes?"

"We must keep emotions out of this. Basic operational necessity. Otherwise it's just too dangerous."

"I agree. You keep yours under control. And I'll do my best with mine."

So they set about the operation with intense care and caution. Without neglecting their exiguous duties in the House of Commons and its committees, they spent three long weekends on reconnaissance in Edinburgh in late June and early July before parliament in London rose for its summer recess. Working out of Duncan's flat at the top of one of the tall Georgian houses in Drummond Place, and continually paying their way like common tourists, they stalked their quarry a dozen times. They meticulously cased the room where it lay, noting the Chubb locks on the massive metal doors, and marking the inconspicuous devices that secured the bandit-glass panels of the display case.

They dissected visually the ancient royal palace which housed it, noting every detail of the staircases, the doors, the ramps, the floors and the windows. They established the pattern of supervision, gauged the intensity of the security, marked the sites of the newly-installed closed-circuit cameras, checked on the alarm systems, probing at all times where the weaknesses and opportunities might be.

They explored the surrounding courtyards, paths, walls and terraces, observing gradients and sight lines. They marked dead ground where one might lurk momentarily with small risk of discovery. They calculated where there were shadows at night and where the artificial illumination would be strongest. They checked the hours of sunset and sunrise in the coming weeks, and when a moon would be present. They even bought the virtual reality interactive compact disc, thoughtfully purveyed by Historic Scotland.

Each time when they returned, they wore different clothes or altered their appearance in some way – a limp and a stick this time, spectacles and perhaps a moustache the next – so as to rouse neither suspicions nor anxieties. Sometimes they came with foreign accents. Sometimes they came singly, or bumped into each other with apologies.

Sometimes they behaved like lovers. Janet thought that was what they did best. Duncan said it only drew attention to them. Janet said she didn't mind, that it was in the line of duty, and that nothing must be left to chance.

Anyway, although the rehearsals were fun, the mission was clearly impossible.

"So we can't do it," said Janet. "Not without being caught."

"That's right," said Duncan. "We can't break in. If we were in, we couldn't break out. Especially at night, when the army take over. The alarm system is unbeatable. We can't use violence. No explosives."

"Can this be the SAS talking!"

"Dead right, it can. And no abseiling down sheer walls and swinging on ropes through shattering windows. Just in case you were thinking of it."

"It's what I was looking forward to," said Janet. "Eagerly, actually."

"We agreed to keep our emotions out of it. Eagerness is forbidden. That's still fundamental."

"I'm still doing my best."

"Me too."

They had walked down the High Street to the Deacon Brodie Tavern where, in view of the warmth of the evening, they were attending to their thirst. Edinburgh's summer visitors were all around, attending no less to theirs – as were the university students whose summer vacations were beginning. The walls of the Royal Mile were already hung with banners all the way down to the Palace of Holyrood. Coachfuls of holiday-making, culture-seeking humanity were blocking its upper reaches. A new "Museum of Porridge" was in preparation in the Lawn Market, and would soon be vying for custom with similar, neighbouring establishments celebrating the history of whisky, Highland dress and bagpipes. Tartan sprouted from a hundred shops selling all manner of costly tourist tat. Foreign voices, mystified, credulous, could be heard at every turn. In a word, the capital was throbbing with life although the Festival season was still three weeks away.

"Deacon Brodie?" asked Janet. "Should I know about him?"

"Under the circumstances, yes," said Duncan, frowning and

26

pointing over the street. "He lived across there. By day he was a cabinet-maker, and a highly respected town councillor. But by night he mixed with the dregs – a criminal, an inveterate gambler, a robber. And they caught him after he broke into the General Excise Office in the 1780s."

"I see. Just like us. Respectable by day . . ."

"Up to a point. His trial was one of the most famous in eighteenth-century Scotland. In fact, he was Stevenson's inspiration for *Dr Jekyll and Mr Hyde*."

Janet thought about that.

"We haven't done anything bad yet, and we won't do it by night, shall we?"

"We're not planning anything evil or for personal gain, at any rate. I hope we have a higher purpose."

"Our plans aren't going anywhere, anyway", said Janet. "What are we going to tell them in London when they ask? That we ran out of ideas?"

"Hold on," Duncan said. "Who's run out of ideas? I've just had a perfectly serviceable one. I only said we can't break in or out. And we can't do it at night."

"What does that leave? Walking in, in broad daylight?"

"Almost."

"How else?"

"There's the lift. And those ramps."

"Of course!" Janet suppressed a cry, looking round the pub and trying to turn it into a choke. "I'm with you!"

"Keep your voice down."

Duncan and Janet stared at each other with suppressed elation, their minds running in parallel.

"You were serious about your theatre props?" Duncan asked.

"Yes – I know where to get all the bits. Actually, a hot knife and the right spray paint are the main things. It'll only take a few days, and I've got the dimensions and the photographs. How's your practical engineering?"

"It'll get by. I can weld. We know the weight. There's a garage where I can work. It won't be very difficult."

"Shall we do a dry run?" she whispered.

"Why not? Tomorrow. I know where we can get a second-hand –"

"Keep your voice down, Duncan."

27

They wandered out of the Deacon Brodie into Bank Street, past the Bank of Scotland's head offices, and found an empty bench at the top of the Mound where, gazing out over the New Town towards the Forth and Fife in the distance, they picked over the operative details of their scheme.

"We'll need all our MPs," said Duncan. "We can't do it unless we have every single one of them here."

"Yes, they must be in it up to their necks too."

"Aiding and abetting, even if they don't know what's going on."

"Accessories after the fact. Conspirators. It'll guarantee their silence when they find out."

"Let's talk to Campbell Macarthur together," said Duncan, "just to tell him what we want of them. And I think I'll have to speak to Walter."

"Walter? Oh, your leader up here. Is that safe?"

"Better than safe. It could be an insurance. He won't want to be told what we're going to do, but he'll know one or two others who can be trusted. People who need part-time employment. For example –"

"All right. I don't need their names."

"We'll have to open the showcase. Not too difficult: I've army friends who won't ask silly questions."

They discussed the timing. If it were done when 'tis done, Janet argued, then 'twere well it were done quickly. In view of his Christian name, Duncan thought her remark in poor taste; but he did not demur.

"During the festival, then?" Janet proposed.

"We'll make it one to remember."

2

THE EDINBURGH FESTIVAL had come and gone, and with the school holidays over the Scottish parliament was reassembled in its expensive quarters at the foot of the Royal Mile. The First Minister sullenly pushed away his plate of organic clootie dumpling and stared through the parliamentary canteen's bomb-proof windows at the September rain drizzling down on Holyrood. He wondered idly why Salisbury Crags, now cloaked in a thin mist, were so called, and speculated on whether some political capital might be had from proposing to rename them. Bruce Crags? Wallace – Burns Crags? Too obvious. Billy Connolly Crags? Donald Dewar Crags? No. There was already a Donald Dewar Reading Room. They had better stay as they were. He wished he had gone back to Bute House, his official residence in Charlotte Square, where the refrigerator sometimes had something pleasant in it, left by his partner, that could be heated up.

He was tired and his mood was black. The Presiding Officer, that dignitary who in other parliamentary assemblies often went by the title of Speaker, had been too busy – so it had been explained to Craig Millar, his principal private secretary – to talk to him that morning, whatever the urgency or emergency. Millar's face, on passing on that information, had been sickeningly expressionless.

"A penny for them, First Minister?" said Morag, noting that his hair had ruffled.

"I was thinking that if I never had another helping of clootie dumpling – "

"No, you were not."

"What was I thinking, then?"

29

"That nobody gives a hoot who you are."

"Well, if you think you know what I'm thinking why do you have to ask?"

"It's good for you to recognise it."

"That's pure impertinence. You're my secretary –"

"Special adviser. I'm over-qualified to be your secretary. Anyway, no-one has secretaries any more. They went the way of stenographers."

"Why?"

"You're supposed to know how to use a PC yourself."

"Does Wee Dougie?"

He referred to the Presiding Officer, whose height made the epithet inevitable.

"Yes," Morag said. "Everybody does. Everybody else. And PDAs too for that matter."

"What's that?"

"Personal Digital Assistants. Crimsonhearts –"

"Crimson –?"

"Replaced Bluetooth and Blackberry. You know what they were?"

"This conversation is insupportable," said the First Minister, puckering an already rather pinched face. "I've enough on my plate today already –"

"Clootie dumpling," Morag agreed.

"God damn the clootie dumpling! I've got to see Wee Dougie."

Morag contemplated her employer, reflecting that his normal overbearing self-regard had for once given way to a more justified and healthier self-doubt. Or, as Craig Millar would have put it privately to her, having known him for longer, his delusions of grandeur had mutated into paranoia. That was why she had seized the opportunity to speak so plainly, for she pursued loyally her duty of smoothing his political path by coaxing him away from self-inflicted embarrassment whenever possible.

"You haven't told me what it's about. You haven't told your private office. And they're hurt."

"Listen, Morag," said the First Minister. "Just for once, this is serious. And I can't tell you even."

Morag's eyes widened.

"You mean – honestly? Something personal?"

"Of course not!"

30

"Well, is it another party scandal, like the time – "
"No, no, it's much more serious than that."
"Another budget overrun? The new visitor attraction?"
"No!"
Her imagination ran riot.
"The unisex hair-salon? – the creche? – the mosque?"
"No. It's nothing frivolous."
Morag's eyes narrowed.
"Like a State secret?" She saw that she was near the mark, and
her imagination sprinted towards breaking point. "In Scotland!
In *Scotland*? Do we *have* State secrets? And Dr Mackay won't
talk to you?"
"Nope."
She brooded.
"I'll away and have a word with him," she said.
"No, you won't. It's not your place."
"How d'you mean?"
"It's outwith your competence. You're not to."
"I will so. He's flesh and blood like anybody else. He can't
treat you like that."
"Why not?" grated the First Minister bitterly.
"Because it reflects on the dignity of your special adviser, and
she'll not put up with it."
Morag, a tall, striking young woman with long russet hair and
reputedly the finest legs in the Old Town, rose, put her mock-
bamboo tray on a trolley and left the canteen. Her progress was
followed by the wistful eyes of a dozen male MSPs and former
ministers coping morosely with kail brose, potted hoch, crappit
heids, chappit neeps, bannocks, bridies, smokies, stovies and other
traditional dishes which, because of a recent vote in the chamber,
were all the canteen supplied.

Intrigue came with difficulty to the leader of the Scottish opposition in Holyrood. Jock Hamilton was honourable, kindly and
conscientious; and although that was possibly why he had been
chosen for the leadership these attributes are not necessarily those
most practical in a politician. When dissembling or anything
approaching a political manoeuvre was demanded of him it needed
an effort of will in many ways foreign to him. When the need
arose, as it continually did, to initiate or implement some device

natural to the business of opposition, his demeanour became hesi-
tant, his shoulders a little slumped, his step uncertain. Then it
was hard to detect any elements of the ambition which had led
him into politics in the first place; and dejection was never far
away.

Yet fire still burnt somewhere in Hamilton's belly. One thing
that kept it stoked was his knowledge that within his own party
his leadership was being challenged, routinely and subtly, by the
apposite and snide questions put to him at every opportunity by
his deputy, Jean Murray Stewart. Mrs Murray Stewart had once
been a formidable party worker, a local councillor from Largs
with a legal training. She was a generously built woman now in
her middle years, whose proportions had long been enhanced
by a liking for the varied confections of Scotland's bakeries and
patisseries which are no less ubiquitous on the Ayrshire coast
than anywhere else. Hamilton resented her appearance almost as
much as her manner. He received notes from her, sometimes in
manuscript, sometimes by e-mail, sometimes by text messages
on his mobile telephone, sometimes through a third party, asking
whether he was aware of arcane developments in parts of Scotland
of which he knew little. She would communicate to his PA Sandra
dark intimations of trouble among the party faithful in Renfrew,
or Stranra'er, or St Andrews, without particularising and leaving
him to guess what was going on. In committee and without notice,
she would ask his opinion on inward investment ratios, on infras-
tructural networks, on policy initiatives for urban consolidation,
on the party position on biodiversity. Sometimes she seemed to
him to be the only person in the world who respected his position
as leader of the opposition – but he knew it was only because she
wanted it for herself. At every turn, she would make him feel
inadequate in a different way. She did it on purpose.

It was thus hard for the leader to share with his deputy his
immediate dilemma. He was under pressure, from the party, from
the press, to make the life of the Scottish Executive – the government – more difficult. No election to the parliament so far had
produced an overall majority for one party, but this executive like
its predecessors was able to coalesce loosely with a minor party
hungry to share power, or on most questions could usually find
an ally to help carry a vote. Hamilton considered that, although
a closer arrangement between his own troops and a minor party

unsympathetic to the administration might not bring it down, it would at least keep ministers uncomfortably on their toes most of the time. Everything depended, of course, on finding common interests against the executive.

The minor party whose support might most easily be solicited was that strange maverick band, the Scotch Enlightenment Party, about whom Hamilton had hitherto burdened himself with little detailed information. Unable to discuss an approach with his deputy, he struck up a conversation with one of the assembly clerks.

"Why Scotch? Why can't they say Scottish like anyone else?"

"Not authentic, Mr Hamilton. A hundred years ago everyone said Scotch. Scottish often meant like Sir Walter." The clerk wore a clipped black moustache which, its colour apart, reminded Hamilton of the topiary work in Princes Street Gardens.

"Oh? Ah. And what's wrong with 'Scots'?"

"All right if you pronounce it like Scotch. And only when it means the people or their language – or as an adjective sometimes, like when you're talking of the currency or measurements or regiments. By and large. You wouldn't say Scots whisky or Scots woodcock or butterscots."

"I suppose not. How d'you tell?"

"The SEP secretariat will tell you, but I shouldn't ask them unless you've time on your hands."

"It sounds like nationalism tied up in pedantry."

"Oh, they're not nationalists. If anything, they're unionists, but that misses the point. They want to get away from all that emotive, xenophobic stuff."

"Then what are they left with? Kilted posturing! Tartan affectation!"

"You've got them quite wrong, Mr Hamilton, if I may say so. They'd never be seen in a kilt outside the Highlands. And they'll tell you that most tartans are spurious anyway. You will recall what the late Lord Macaulay said."

"Not exactly."

"He said that before the Union, nine out of ten Scotchmen regarded the kilt as the dress of a thief."

"Goodness me!"

"Actually, the SEP are not that keen on Sir Walter Scott either."

"Oh? Why not?"

33

"He brought a false romance to Scotch history. Fine literature: dubious scholarship. The Enlightenment party doesn't like that."

"They sound like cranks."

"All politician are cranks, Mr Hamilton, and most sound like it. Present company excepted, of course. But the SEP are different in having no time for –"

"Why on earth did they want seats here in Holyrood?"

"They want to put Scotland back on track. They want to bring back lots of the genuine old traditional practices: they owe that to the past. But politically they want to go with the flow of history, not to fight against it, like some. Above all, they want to bring back the values of the Enlightenment."

"Of –?"

"You know about the Scotch Enlightenment?"

"Well, yes, of course. The – well, the Enlightenment".

"Exactly. And especially the internationalism Scotland stood for and the self-confidence and moral certainty she felt two centuries ago."

"I see. You seem to know a lot about them. You're not a member yourself?"

"Oh, Mr Hamilton, I have no party affiliations," protested the clerk. "I'm not allowed them in my position."

So Jock Hamilton asked Sandra to look up the SEP's manifesto from the last election, needing not so much to refresh his memory as to consider elements which he had previously discounted and so dismissed.

That unpretentious monochrome document had offered an astonishing political menu to the discerning voter. In respect of public order, miscreants were to be put to the horn – literally hooted out of the capital, as under the Stuarts; "persuasive justice" would be restored – the boot, the maiden, the pilnie winks; and the Act of 1757 which violated the Act of Union by abolishing Baron courts would be repealed. As a compensatory humanitarian measure, debtors would once again find sanctuary in the premises of Holyrood Palace and Abbey. As for the constitution, a priority was to ensure the adequate reconsideration and timely revision of new law. To that end, the counties and county councils would be reinstated; the power of the Royal Burghs would be reaffirmed; and the Thrie Estaites – as they were spelt – would be reconstituted as they had been until 1707, sitting together in the parliament

34

but voting separately. Agricultural proposals included opening up the old drove roads and relicensing some ancient abattoirs and cattle markets. Regarding the environment, tourism and the arts, there would be grants towards the restoration of castles and peel towers, and tax breaks for repairs to all buildings more than a century old; positive steps to propagate capercailzie, pine martens, otters, golden eagles, ospreys, voles and other endangered species; the reintroduction of wolves and wild boar to the Highlands, and bear and beavers to the lowlands; the razing of the St James's Centre, Edinburgh, and its replacement in the style of Adam, Craig or Playfair; and the rebuilding of the façade of the New Club in Princes Street to David Byrne's original designs. Transport improvements would see the reintroduction of trams in Edinburgh, Glasgow, Dundee, Aberdeen and Ayr; the privatisation of Caledonian MacBrayne; the encouragement of the breeding of Clydesdale carthorses to haul barges along the Forth and Clyde Canal; and the adjustment of the timing of traffic lights in Glasgow, Edinburgh and elsewhere to the real needs and patience of road users. In education, post-1314 Scotch history – including the creation of the Union, Scotland's part in building the British Empire and the Scotch contribution to international science, medicine, literature, the arts, engineering and philosophy – would be made a compulsory subject. The party's policy towards Europe consisted of applying the same positive proactivity and co-operation as, in the past three centuries, had permitted the Scotch to exploit the opportunities of belonging to the United Kingdom and maximising their control of it.

"Can any of this be serious?" Hamilton asked.

"Possibly not all of it," said Sandra. "But we want it all debated and put to a vote."

"'We'?"

"I mean the SEP. The electorate, you'll recall, had no problems with it; and the press reported everything with straight faces. Most people find it very refreshing."

"It's that. How did you vote last time, Sandra?"

"It's a secret ballot, Mr Hamilton. Anyway, if I'd been in your constituency I'd have voted for you."

"Thank you."

"Because of my job."

*　　*　　*

35

Morag found the Presiding Officer alone with a cup of tea in his office in Queensberry House, that fine seventeenth-century building forcibly incorporated into the parliament's uncompromising inventiveness. A tall man with a generous shock of grey hair, Mackay's long limbs made the modernistic armchair look inadequately small. He looked up from an order paper balanced high on his knees and smiled.

"Are you busy, Mr Presiding Officer?"

"It's always a pleasure to see you, Morag. Is there something I can do for you?" As a friend of her father, he had known the family for many years, and it had been on his recommendation that she had been given her job as a special adviser.

"Indeed there is. There's a girning, sandy-haired raincloud in my office that takes all the fun out of my life –"

"Oor Wullie?"

"Mr William McNish, the First Minister. And that's because you won't talk to him."

The Presiding Officer's attention fastened quickly on the order paper.

"Trivia, Morag," he said, tapping it. "Why don't you sit down? There's another fishery disaster on our hands and all the executive can come up with for the afternoon are its proposals for wholemeal bread for hospital meals –"

"Because they're not controversial."

"And dietary education for single mothers –"

"Scotland's top of the cardiac league. Highest blood pressure in Europe. We eat more sweet biscuits than anyone on earth. As well as fish suppers."

"I'm to waste my afternoon on cairry-oots!"

"Your predecessor used to get one of his deputes to –"

"What's more, they've a genuine crisis brewing down in Westminster, you'll have been reading."

"Scotland's MPs? I saw they've had their office allowances cut to pieces. I bet they're cross. I'm glad I don't work for any of them."

"Nothing to do with that. I'm talking about the government of England. No one in Holyrood ever thinks of that."

"True," Morag agreed. "They've other things on their minds."

"That's why government here is merely a farce –"

"Wheesht, Dr Mackay! Someone'll hear you!"

"– but running England has become an impossibility. They haven't got a majority for anything."

"Maybe that'll let people down there get on and run their own lives too for once?"

"That's the optimistic view," said the Presiding Officer flatly. "Where'll it end?"

"Don't you approve of our parliament," Morag asked, "or is it just the members?"

"What's Oor Wullie want?"

"You didn't answer my question, Dr Mackay."

"No. And I still have trouble bonding with a building that doesn't know what it's supposed to look like. What's Oor Wullie want?"

"Why won't you speak to him?"

"Because as like as not he's told the press first, and I'll read it there. It's happened before. All right, what's it about?"

Morag groaned. "I don't know. But he certainly hasn't told the press. He hasn't even told me."

The Presiding Officer took off his spectacles and looked at her keenly. "Maybe it's something important after all, then – if anyone in this place can tell the difference. Will the morning be soon enough?"

"I don't know."

"Well, I'll see him here for breakfast, you can tell him. The dining room's not open, but the canteen's never busy then, and I can be having something to eat while I'm listening."

Morag thanked him, returned to her desk and rang the First Minister's private office in St Andrew's House on the secure line.

"Yes, Morag?"

"That you, Craig? Would you tell Oor Wullie that Wee Dougie'll meet him for breakfast down here in the parliament canteen tomorrow?"

"Did you say 'eat him for breakfast'?"

"No. Not hungry enough."

"Right, Morag. What's it all about?"

"Don't know. He won't say."

"The police have been on to us again. That's twice now."

"The polis! Has one of the ministers done something silly –"

"For sure, but nothing the *polis* would worry about."

"What do they want?"

37

"Another word with the First Minister."

"You didn't tell me they'd had a word with him before."

"'Need to know'," Craig Millar explained. "I wasn't there. He was all by himself. No note-takers. But now he wants Wee Dougie in on it."

"To see the polis?"

"The Chief of the Lothians Police, Morag. And not just him. The Chairman of Historic Scotland. The two of them are coming along together – down there in the parliament. And so'm I. But that's for your ears only. Don't tell the First Minister I told you. Wait till he tells you himself. Stay in touch."

At eight in the morning, William McNish, Scotland's First Minister, was driven from Bute House to the Canongate where, having been deposited at the members' entrance of the Scottish Parliament, he dismissed his driver. The policeman on duty explained politely that the doors had not yet been unlocked, but that it should not be long now. He called him "Sir." The First Minister, who had had a wakeful night, mentally registered gratification that the policeman had paid the respect due to his office.

"Nasty looking sky, Sergeant."

"Police Constable, Sir."

"So you are. I'm sorry."

"No offence taken, Sir."

"Of course not." McNish scowled at his watch.

"You'll be having a busy time, Sir." The constable knew his place, and the remark was just short of a question.

"Trying to have one. I'm waiting for the Presiding Officer."

"That'll be Dr Douglas Mackay. A fine man. Well-spoken, a very civil gentleman. D'you know him, Sir?"

The First Minister's ego retired a little.

"Yes, Constable. I meet him from time to time. Professionally, of course."

"We'd be fine if there were more like him, Sir."

"I expect so. Nasty looking sky, Constable."

"So you were saying, Sir. Here comes the porter now. He'll let you in. May I see your I.D., Sir? Just a formality. Biometric's on the blink again."

"Biometric?"

"Iris recognition equipment, Sir. But your pass'll do."

His blood pressure rising, the First Minister fished in his pocket for his identity card and flashed it before the policeman's face.

"That's a credit card, Sir. Royal Bank – same as mine."

McNish remembered that he had left his identity card in his other suit. Having unlocked the doors, the porter was fastening them back.

"Look, Officer," he said. "D'you not know my face?"

"I'm new here, Sir. I expect you'll be one of the members."

"I'm the First Minister."

"Well, there you go, Sir."

"I said, I'm the First Minister."

"No problem, Sir. I just need to see your I.D. Otherwise we'll both be in trouble."

"The porter will confirm – "

But the porter had gone back into the building. For a full five minutes the First Minister could only breathe heavily and go uselessly through his pockets while the policeman refused to meet his eye. Relief came at last, but in the irksome shape of the leader of the Scotch Enlightenment Party, Walter Moncrieff, who strode up to the door, shook the constable's hand, and said: "Good morning, Jim. I thought you were in charge of the castle."

"They've moved me down here for a week or two, Mr Moncrieff. Good to see you again, Sir. You had my vote."

"I guessed that, Jim. Thanks." Moncrieff's ready smile changed to a look of concern as he spotted McNish. "Are you not coming in, Wullie? That's a nasty looking sky."

"Just what you were saying, Sir, wasn't it?", added the policeman, smiling and standing to one side. "That'll be all right Sir. Everyone knows Mr Moncrieff. Bring your pass next time, won't you, Sir?"

Ten minutes later the First Minister was sitting alone with a mug of coffee at a green formica table in the canteen while a piece of fish was being microwaved on his behalf. Moncrieff had gone off to a private meeting about which, when McNish asked him more out of sociability than curiosity, he would say nothing. There was no sign of the Presiding Officer who, now that McNish came to think of it, had not specified what time he enjoyed breakfasting. So he looked through *The Scotsman*, noting that his Minister for Tourism, Media and Cultural Exchange had a speaking engagement in Cleveland, Ohio; that his Minister for Biodiversity and Lifelong Learning was at a conference on ethnic values in Durban; and that his Minister for Social Convergence was on a fact-finding mission to Catalunya, wherever that was. He had no idea who had sanctioned those jaunts.

The plate was brought to him where he sat. As he took up a knife and fork, there was a step behind him.

"Hullo, Wullie. Is it Finnan haddock ye hae there?"

It was not the Presiding Officer. The First Minister recognised the voice of Alasdair McNab, a Glasgow MSP of his own party to whom he invariably grudged the time of day. He grunted without looking up.

"Finnan . . . puddock, for all I care. Do you mind? I'm reading the paper."

McNab, adjusting a thin sprig of white heather in the button-hole of his thick tweed jacket, considered those assertions. McNish, of course, was not reading his newspaper but eating his fish.

"Ah dinna think ye cuid smoke a puddock. At least Ah dinna think onybody ever has . . . Weel, mebbe ye cuid. Aye, mebbe . . ."

McNish managed a mouthful or so.

"Ah wadna wannae eat it, but. Nae personally."

McNish began to count ten to himself.

"Ah'm thinkin' . . . mebbe they French wad –"

"Could you not think to yourself instead of out loud?" the First Minister snapped.

"Aye, Ah micht. But wha'd profit from ma thochts?"

The First Minister had no civil answer, and relapsed into silence.

"Wee Dougie wis spierin' for ye."

"I'm looking for him. Where is he?"

"He wis in here, a hauf hoor back. Finishin' his parritch."

The First Minister knew in his heart that the Presiding Officer had eluded him again.

"How did you get in?" he asked McNab weakly. "The members' door was locked."

"In the front. The public door of wir excitin' new fledglin' parliament opens at seeven. Some o' us yins are nae sae vain-glorious."

"Vainglorious?"

"Big-heided."

McNish glowered.

"You know I can't use that door."

"Yon animal rights gowks? They dinna get oot their beds till the back o' nine." McNab considered McNish's face. "Ye look as if ye cuid dae wi' some mair sleep yersel, Wullie."

The First Minister pushed away the remains of his fish, which seemed to have gone cold.

That morning, the leader of the Scotch Enlightment Party, Walter Moncrieff, had a rendezvous with Jock Hamilton, the leader of the opposition. It took place at Hamilton's request, which was why Moncrieff had left McNish's earlier enquiry unrewarded. They met in the well-appointed members' bar known as the Cup o' Kindness which catered for the liquid and casual comestible needs of MSPs who spurned both the members' dining-room, called the We Hae Meat, and the anonymous canteen and cafeteria. It differed from the general bar (no less tiresomely named the Pint o' Wine) in enabling members and their guests at all times to drink what – to avoid affronting the wilfully affrontable – were designated as "stimulants" free from the critical eyes of journalists and parliament staff; while the press, duly offended, nursed its wrath but now made do with what it had.

The baffling array of beverages on offer in the Cup included barley-bree, birse-cups, brogat and deochandoruses, dispensed – in defiance of Brussels – in drams, willie-waughts, yill-caups and tappit hens (translated helpfully into Gaelic where applicable); but the two party leaders settled for coffee and shortbread.

Moncrieff, a lawyer, was one of the few politicians in Edinburgh who had stood for parliament not because he wanted to be someone but because he wanted to do something. His sense of purpose was therefore sharper than most. More accurately, in fact, he wanted to undo something. The devolution of power from Westminster to Holyrood, once acceptable to him in principle, was proving a lamentable experience in practice. Just as Scotland's media became ever more parochial in their concerns, thus reflecting the behaviour of the majority of the MSPs, so Britain's national press and broadcasting services seemed intent on withering Scotland's body politic with scorn, and were making a reasonable fist of that. Instead of the enhancement of Scotland's political position within the United

Kingdom, the trend was towards marginalisation; and Moncrieff knew that from marginalisation to separation could be a short step.

The wish for independence was neither widespread nor strong in Scotland these days: most of the electorate, when they thought about it, were not so impressed by the way the Scottish parliamentarians had exercised their powers to date as to want to give them any more. The very first of their concerns in the early days had been their own salaries, pensions and conditions of work, self-interested considerations which attracted almost uniform and universal disapproval and derision. The inclusion of land reform and the abolition of hunting in the initial bout of devolved legislation had been seen as vengeful and socially divisive – deliberately so in the view of many commentators.

Anyway, even when nationalism had been at its noisiest, the separatist wish had never been very deep. But now, far from pulling away from England, Scotland was being pushed: the political need for the Union, and even the expense of maintaining it, was no longer as obvious south of the Border as it still looked north of it to those capable of taking a hard-nosed view of Scotland's best interests. Britain's future might be in Europe, and the global economy might embrace Glasgow, Edinburgh and Aberdeen, and run all the way past Inverness to Muckle Flugga; but the place beyond Scotland's shores where she most needed economic influence and political clout – Moncrieff had no doubt – would always be London, just as her most important external markets would always be in England. Scotland sat geographically at the end of a European cul de sac, and her nearest neighbours were therefore by far the most significant ones.

It was no special objective of Moncrieff or his followers to dismantle the Scottish parliament: self-evidently there was room for improvement in both its practices and its inmates, but that institution's survival was an academic issue so long as it did not encourage any process of separation. If the problem were to prevent two nations from slipping further and further apart, the solution might well be to recreate the conditions under which, to both London and Edinburgh, and indeed to the whole British people, a solidly united kingdom was both desirable and desired. True, that might well imply a return to a single parliament or progress to federation, but the Enlightenment party was realist enough to recognise the difficulty of reversing a constitutional ratchet.

Moncrieff was therefore more amused by, than unsympathetic to, Jock Hamilton's proposal to form a voting alliance in the chamber. Hamilton's advocacy of that move had been characteristically diffident, but Moncrieff was perfectly prepared to take it seriously.

"You want to bring down McNish? Why?"

"Isn't that what politics are about? We all think we can do things better."

"We all think things can be *made* better, but being in government is not the only way to do that. And not necessarily the cleverest way."

"Isn't it?" said Hamilton, confronted by an unfamiliar idea. "But if we all think our own policies are more sensible, more practical, more – "

"What have yours in common with mine?"

"To be honest, I'm not sure," said Hamilton. "You want to bring back judicial torture."

"Oh, come! That's our romantic wing. It would be against the European Convention of Human Rights, even if it were a good thing. Half of your own party is for capital punishment. But they're for it because they're bloodthirsty. Our lot regard the pilnie winks and the boot as interesting historical traditions, along with trial by touch and witch hunts. They get the headlines. They're not serious. But the real point – "

"There's an ulterior motive?"

"Of course. This place has become a sickening cocktail of political correctness and historic distortion. All they do is ban things. Ridicule is the only antidote. It has to be pushed over the top."

"You want to bring back the Three Estates. Is that serious?"

"Oh yes, and why not? Institutionalised adversarial government is out of date. We should improve for improving's sake, not oppose for opposition's sake. And there's no revising chamber in Holyrood. The committee system is no substitute, not while a committee view can be ignored. The executive gets away with what's half-baked, time and time again. This is the most hit-and-miss kind of government since the Stewart regencies. If we have the MSPs and the burgh councillors and the lairds all voting separately, at least we'll get everything automatically considered

43

more than once. It worked satisfactorily three centuries ago. Why not now?"

"It'll mean enlarging the building again."

"Yes, so we've an alternative. We could have our MPs in London sit as an upper house for Scotch Bills. It would give them something important to do."

Hamilton blinked several times before moving to a new subject. "Your education policy doesn't seem to belong to the twenty-first century. History's all very well, but –"

"Unless you know where you've come from, you don't know where you are. And, if you don't know where you are, as sure as hell you don't know where you're going."

"I agree we don't know where we're going. The future's murky."

"That's because for most people in Scotland the past is even murkier. Bannockburn, Bruce, Braveheart and Bonnie Prince Charlie – that's about the sum of their awareness of their country's history."

"Stirring stuff, though," said Hamilton.

"You think so? Do you know how many major battles were fought between England and Scotland in the five hundred years before the Union? Forget the skirmishes."

"Up to 1707? There was Falkirk and Stirling Bridge and Solway Moss . . . and Flodden . . . and Killiecrankie . . . and . . ." Hamilton's memory faded out. "Well, let's say fifteen? Twenty-five?"

"Three hundred and fourteen. And do you know why the Union really happened, the final straw that persuaded both countries to get together?"

"Something to do with the Succession? Queen Anne –"

"Guess again."

"Burns said the commissioners were bought and sold for English gold –"

"Nationalist codswallop."

"Tell me what *you* think."

"Scotland and England were at each other's throats again – Scotland still plotting with France four centuries on from Robert the Bruce. England was destroying Scotland's international trade. Both parliaments were passing Acts against the other. Ships were seized or sunk on both sides. English captains were swinging in chains on the sands of Leith. Both countries knew that union was the only civilised alternative to war. And nobody's noticed or we've all forgotten this: unless you count the Jacobite rebellions, there's been peace in Great Britain ever since."

"True, it's taken for granted."

"That's the problem," Moncrieff said. "And you only have to go along to an international at Hamden Park to hear how the old hatreds have been revived again – quite deliberately, too. If that's the reawakening of Scotland's national consciousness, I'd like to put it to sleep again."

"I'm told," persisted Hamilton, "that you want Scotland to return to the values of the Enlightenment. Whatever it means, is that correct?"

"It's putting it broadly, but – yes, it'll do."

"How does all that history fit?"

"Two hundred years ago, the past was still fresh in their minds: Scotland under General Monck; the killing times; the Darien disaster; the Fifteen; the Forty-five – and the victory of Culloden and the relief it brought to the Lowlands, indeed the whole of Britain. The Highlands may not have liked it, but Butcher Cumberland was even made a freeman of Glasgow."

"Tough on the Jacobites."

"Yes, but after all that we took off. We grabbed the commercial, the political, the artistic opportunities the Union gave us. We looked outwards. We set about running it. The English were perfectly happy – and we flourished *because* of the Union. We led the world in the arts and the sciences."

"So?"

"Well, now history has gone into reverse. Some of us seem to think we'd do better with allies over the Channel rather than in London. We're sliding back into the quarrels and jealousies of the seventeenth century and before. Guess who'll come off worse."

"I expect you're right."

"I'm not against bringing McNish down in due course. I'm sure he does more harm than good. But there needs to be a good reason – and some idea of what comes next. In the meantime –"

"Very well," sighed Hamilton. "I'm prepared to support you on the history syllabus."

"Good! That'll be a start. You'll have a word with Jean Murray Stewart?"

Hamilton's face fell.

"Why her?"

"Isn't she your Education spokesman as well as your deputy?"

"Spokesperson. I suppose so. I'd forgotten."

"Well, tell her what we've agreed and then let me know when you want to ambush McNish. I'd be pleased to help. Hullo! What's the matter? Something I said?"

"No, no." Hamilton, red-faced, was standing up and fumbling for small change.

"Never mind the bill. I've dealt with it."

Uncomprehending, Moncrieff rose and followed the retreating figure of the leader of the opposition whom, almost visibly, a cloud of despondency had enveloped like a North Berwick haar. Although it might have been due to the bewildering design of the parliamentary building, in the manner of the Scots whom they had been discussing Hamilton hardly seemed to know where he was going.

"Mr Moncrieff?"

Moncrieff turned to find Ross Burton, the political correspondent of *The Herald*, unwrapping a Mars Bar. Burton was a small, cheerful man in his fifties whose deep professional shrewdness shone from his eyes. Politicians of all parties liked and respected him: confidences were safe in his keeping and his advice was good. Yet his daily column contained enough spice and political revelation to keep both his readership and his editor content.

"Mars Bars, Ross?"

"The indignity, the mortification, Walter!".

"What happened?"

"I was reported. And me a correspondent!"

"To –"

"To the Standards Committee."

"What were you doing?"

"Doing? Carrying a packet of cigarettes openly through a non-designated area. Not even smoking."

"Is that real? There are designated areas for cigarette packets?"

"Oh, yes. Out of doors in the landscaping, next to the water feature. Does Scotland need water features? Anyway, that's where the smoking goes on."

"So why weren't you out there?"

"It was raining. It's raining now. So it's Mars Bar time. And a fortnight ago I was caught using the disabled facilities. I've been

46

told one more strike and I'm out." He laughed bitterly. "It's this parliament that should have a health warning on it."

"Like 'contains nuts'?"

"If it could only contain them!"

Walter Moncrieff and Ross Burton looked at each other unbelievingly.

"Ha!" said Moncrieff at last, smiling. "You'll be put to the horn. Trumpeted off the premises."

"All right, Walter. A happy echo from the past. I'll work it into my column some time."

"Good! It's all part of the devolution experience."

But Burton clearly had something else on his mind.

"A quick question, Walter, if you've a moment."

"Go on."

"You're in touch with your colleagues in Westminster?"

"Ross, we only have one so far. Young Duncan Innes. Is that whom you mean? Yes, our lines are open."

"What's up, then? No one else is in touch. Relations are fractured. Communications severed. Half a dozen MSPs have told me they've had no correspondence from their MPs for weeks."

"They're all on holiday?"

"That's never stopped it before."

"Do they *want* correspondence?"

"Possibly not. It's mostly domestic stuff that shouldn't have gone to the MPs in the first place, or even to the MSPs for that matter. But that's by the by. Something's brewing. What is it?"

Moncrieff looked at Burton with a sad smile.

"Would you like to be one of those Scotch MPs in London these days, Ross?"

"Not many of them in office?" said Burton. "Not too much to do?"

"Mmm, but that's not the fault of anyone here. You might try asking another question. Who speaks for Scotland, when there's something to say? Or even when there isn't."

"Ah!" Burton said. "Thanks. I've got the point."

3

THE FIRST MINISTER looked in at Morag's small Holyrood office on the way to his own and snarled at her. Unless he planned to appear in the chamber he was more usually found a quarter-mile away in St Andrew's House where his larger private office, complete with press officers, did its best to keep him in touch with Scotland's administration and his government on an even keel.

"So you missed him," said Morag.

He snarled again.

"I heard you forgot your pass."

"I shouldn't need it in my position. I should be able to access my own parliament without being challenged."

"Never mind, First Minister. Wee Dougie telephoned a little while back to say you hadn't come to breakfast. He promised to drop in at half-past-nine if it suited you. And I said, yes, it would."

"All right."

"And your private office was looking for you."

"Craig'll be waiting for me up there. What do they want?"

"No, Craig's down here already. Three gentlemen are coming to see you at ten. He wouldn't say who they were, but he said you'd know."

The First Minister gave her a hunted look.

"Three? Who's the third?"

"I don't know. D'you want me to be there? You know I've signed the Official Secrets Act form, don't you? I'll have to know about it some time."

McNish looked at her dubiously for a few seconds. "You'd

better come in when Wee Dougie comes. He's got to know; and I'll tell you together. Then you can join me when I'm talking to the police."

"The polis!" Morag judged it tactful to sound surprised. "Has a crime been committed?"

But the First Minister only offered a further snarl, directed at the world in general rather than her; and Morag had to contain her bursting curiosity for another thirty minutes.

True to his word, the Presiding Officer Dr Douglas Mackay turned up outside the First Minister's office sharp at half past nine. Morag spotted him in time to knock on the door, announce him and lead him in.

"I'm sorry I missed you earlier, First Minister," Mackay said. "I hear you were held up somewhere. Tsk Tsk."

"Then I'm glad you were able to catch up with me finally," said the First Minister, smiling thinly. "Please sit down, and you, too, Morag. And I've decided to call in the head of my private office for this. There has been a serious development of which I must inform you. For reasons which I hope will be clear it mustn't be discussed outside this room."

McNish pressed the intercom button to summon his PPS from the adjoining room. Craig Millar appeared, a notebook in his hand, nodding politely at the Presiding Officer, then at Morag, as he put on his spectacles. Millar's pleasant, fresh face, neat appearance and air of quiet competence tended to cause McNish annoyance rather than comfort.

"No notes, Craig, I told you."

"Are you sure, First Minister? If there's ever an inquiry –"

"No one is contemplating an inquiry," McNish said testily. He had gone to the window and was wrestling ineffectively with the lever intended to open and close it. "Damn this thing. Why should they? Sit down there."

"Before you begin," said Mackay, "you'd better explain why I'm here. Is it appropriate to tell me what you can't tell the House?"

"I've asked you here because you represent the parliament. As to how far this should go, and when, I should appreciate your advice." McNish turned from the window and paused, swallowing. Mackay saw an unusual pallor on his cheeks and beads of sweat on his forehead.

49

"You've certainly aroused our curiosity, First Minister. Please tell us what it's all about."

"Would you get the window seen to, Craig? We need fresh air in this place."

Mackay prompted him again.

"Very soon we shall have a visit from the Chief Constable of the Lothians . . . McNish hesitated. "He's the polis."

Mackay thought he recognised the nervousness that many of his countrymen betray in the presence of the Law, not excluding politicians. "Then he'll be on our side," he said encouragingly. "Who else?"

"And the Chairman of Historic Scotland. You'll remember that Historic Scotland is funded by the executive and manages Edinburgh Castle among its other heritage sites. And I gather there's a third one, Craig. Who's that?".

"GOC Scotland – "

"The army!" whispered Morag.

McNish turned on her resentfully.

"Yes, the army! Why not?"

"A strange combination – tell us what's happened," demanded Mackay more impatiently than he intended. But he saw that McNish was not listening. His hair had become ruffled, and obviously something more serious than an encounter with the police was distressing him. "Look, Wullie – hadn't you better sit down as well? There's some water there. Morag, get him a glass. There! Take it slowly. You're under stress."

The First Minister recovered, drew a deep breath, glanced at the doors and lowered his voice.

"I'll tell you. It's kept me awake for two nights."

"What is it, then?"

"Just this. The Stone of Destiny" – the words came out slowly and quietly but without drama – "has been stolen."

McNish watched three jaws drop and six eyes widen before going on. Realisation that others, in whatever way, were as affected as he had been restored some of his confidence.

"It's true. They're coming to tell me how it was removed last month, in broad daylight – they think – at the very height of the Edinburgh Festival."

There was silence. Millar began to look through his pocket diary, his face puzzled. Mackay spoke first.

50

"You mean, they've only just discovered it's gone? But the festival's been over for three weeks."

"First Minister, I've just checked," Millar interrupted. "I took my children to see the Honours of Scotland and the Coronation Stone just before their holidays finished, as a treat. It was there on the twenty-eighth of August. I saw it myself."

McNish shook his head. "What you saw — so the Chief Constable tells me — is still there. It's an almost perfect replica. It's made of polysomething — a highly professional job, he said."

The telephone trilled once. Millar answered and looked at the First Minister.

"They're here. Shall I bring them up?"

"Go ahead."

"And shall I take notes when they're here?"

The Presiding Officer answered.

"You asked for my advice, First Minister. Well, for a start, I think you may need full notes. You may be right about an inquiry. But there will be a lot of people trying to duck the blame for this."

"Notes, then, Craig," McNish agreed, nodding his PPS out of the room. "You, too, Morag."

They were a sombre trio, seated opposite the First Minister and the Presiding Officer. Sir Hew Cunynghame, Chairman of Historic Scotland, white of hair, slight of figure and grim of countenance, was still deeply affected by the shock he had received only two days before. He explained that the discovery that the stone on display was a dummy was made during the routine maintenance of its bullet-proof glass display case. The senior castle steward, on being told that the stone had been distinctly seen to bounce, made a personal inspection and promptly swore the two junior stewards concerned to silence on pain of dismissal. He had then informed Sir Huw and, on his orders, called in the police.

"I'll naturally have to tell the other Commissioners of the Regalia," Sir Hew added. "When the stone was put in the castle in 1996, the Royal Warrant entrusted it to them. They include the Keeper of the Great Seal, the Lord —"

"Hang on," McNish interrupted. "Seal? Isn't that something to do with me?" He glared uselessly at Millar, who was assiduously jotting it all down, but Sir Hew answered.

51

"Yes, First Minister. That's why I have informed you. Perhaps you were unaware of your responsibility for the stone? In the days when there was a Secretary of State for Scotland – "

"Yes, yes, I know. It was all downloaded to the First Minister." McNish knew that his responsibility was even more official than he had feared.

"The others," Sir Hew went on, "are the Lord Justice Clerk, the Lord Clerk Register and the Lord Advocate. I shall have to keep them in the picture."

"I think those gentlemen shouldn't be told yet," said McNish quickly. The Lord Advocate sat in the cabinet, and if he knew the whole executive would know. "I haven't even told the Permanent Secretary."

"Then I'll leave it to you to tell them all," Sir Hew replied, his mouth hardening. He looked at Craig. "Perhaps that could be minuted?"

The countenance of GOC Scotland, the Governor of Edinburgh Castle, was no less grim. Major-General Sir Norman Brunstane, who had his headquarters in the handsome old building at the lower end of the castle esplanade, was having difficulty in suppressing his strong feelings that the fortress should never have been left in charge of a government agency. "Of course," he pointed out, "one must not blame civilians who do not understand the routines and disciplines of mounting guard," he said. "The trouble is higher up."

"If you are referring to me or my board," said Sir Hew acidly, "I must point out that we have over three hundred places to look after in Scotland and only seventy-five million euros a year to run them on. But no doubt you were thinking of someone else."

"The castle has been surrendered once or twice, but it's never been taken by force in recorded history," rejoined the general. "I don't count the time our own lot climbed up the side. My concern is for the prestige of the place. It's been pillaged – and the stone was sent there for safe keeping. It doesn't help that British troops were taking part in a military tattoo every night when this was going on."

"You weren't personally responsible for it, General," Sir Hew said with some generosity. "The security precautions were ours."

"Who'll believe that? It's a military establishment. I work there. We have detachments quartered in the castle. It's our piper on the battlements. Everyone thinks we fire the one-o'clock gun."

"We were advised, of course, by the Edinburgh police".

The countenance of Chief Constable Sir Andrew McCallum, hitherto benevolent and untroubled, fell abruptly. He had assumed he was there in a purely professional capacity. He had already given much thought to the sensitivity of the situation, but had neither anticipated nor expected the whiff of criticism detectable in the view suddenly advanced by Sir Hew.

"If I may speak, First Minister," he began.

"Certainly, Sir Andrew," said McNish, sensing that others were sharing the heat. "Please put us in the picture. We need to know what happened, when it happened, how it happened, who did it, why, and what you propose to do about it."

"Yes, First Minister. You've certainly asked the right questions." He glanced at the Presiding Officer. "Dr Mackay here will confirm that as First Minister you'll be required to give answers to all of them if this gets into the public domain.".

McNish's heart sank again. Indeed, that was why he had been losing sleep, never having thought his position better than weak. Here *par excellence*, in the *cliché* of any political thriller, was political dynamite. The Scottish Executive's failure to safeguard and protect the most significant symbol of Scotland's nationhood would be grist to the mean-minded mills of every other political party in the parliament. In the public mind, the executive must be the ultimate custodian of the Stone of Destiny, with its First Minister on top. He wouldn't be allowed to blame the police, or the army, or his fellow commissioners, still less Historic Scotland. The press would make not a meal but a banquet of it; perhaps two or three banquets.

"May we have your report, Chief Constable?"

It was probable, said Sir Andrew, that the theft occurred soon after noon on the third Saturday in August when the crowds of tourists and holiday-makers in Edinburgh were at their largest and visitors to the castle most numerous.

"Over a million a year at the castle," put in Sir Hew, "but August is much the worst. We have to take on part-time guides and stewards, and they're all run off their feet."

"How can you pin it down to that day?" the general asked.

The Chief Constable explained that that Saturday had brought a number of unusual and coincidental occurrences. The gang –

he assumed there were several robbers involved, possessed of a minimum physical strength – had taken advantage of the great crush of visitors recorded at the time. Indeed, the ticket sales revealed that just before midday an exceptionally large single group of tourists, male and female, were visiting the rooms where the Scottish Crown Jewels and the Coronation Stone were housed – so large that it had been necessary to hold up the introduction of further visitors until they had passed through. Even so, there had been a temporary but prolonged blockage of the flow.

"What sort of numbers are we talking of?" the First Minister asked.

"We know exactly." The Chief Constable consulted a notebook. "There were forty-three standard adult tickets issued to that group, plus fifteen concessionary tickets which go to women over sixty and men over sixty-five; and one more to a disabled person in a wheel-chair. Provision is made for the disabled to be taken up and down in a lift. That makes fifty-nine in all."

"Fifty-nine," the Presiding Officer muttered.

"The senior steward informs us that fewer than twenty is a more comfortable, a more manageable, number in any of those rooms."

"And no children?" This was the Presiding Officer again.

"No. All adults," the Chief Constable agreed.

Then at about five minutes past twelve – the Chief Constable resumed – it appeared that one of the visitors inadvertently set off an alarm in the double ante-room which held a display of the bronze replicas of the crown and sword of State as well as the great kist in which they had once been locked up. The two stewards watching over the crown jewels and the stone immediately went to investigate, and correctly suppressed the alarm while accepting the earnest and rather lengthy apologies and explanations of the erring tourist. The stewards only then realised that another alarm had been set off in the Crown Room itself. Unfortunately, they took almost ten minutes to fight their way back through the scrum to their usual places, a journey made the harder because some of the tourist group seemed to have been uncertain which way visitors were meant to progress. However, with calm restored, and just before the arrival of a duty police officer and an army detachment alerted by the siren, the group was then slowly shepherded past the exhibits, out of the room, down the stairs and into the courtyard below. Nothing seemed to be amiss: indeed, the police officer had reported as much to him personally.

"Leaving your post when on sentry should mean a court martial," interrupted the general. "Of course, I don't want to sound pompous."

"Our stewards are supposed to look after both rooms," said Sir Hew coldly. "That was in line with the advice we received. I don't think they're to blame for following it."

Sir Andrew made no comment and went on with his account. The group had had two guides. Both were part-time staff, employed for the festival season, and possibly unused to handling so many visitors at once. The police had not been able to interview them because, although their first names were known, they had not been traced.

"It sounds as though a lot of people know about all this already," said the First Minister. "How many have been questioned?"

"We've taken care not to explain what's behind the interrogation," said the Chief Constable. "The polystyrene stone is so skilfully carved and painted that only by touching it can you be sure what it's made of. For the present we've said that we're investigating an unspecified breach of security to do with the alarm system."

Sir Hew added that visitors were still filing past the glass case in the belief that what they saw was the genuine article.

"Our working hypothesis," said the Chief Constable, "is that the theft and the substitution took place during the minutes when the stewards were investigating the first alarm. The noise of one siren would have masked the noise of any other. In theory it would have been a simple task to effect an entry to the glass case with a master key, manhandle the stone on to a trolley, say, and complete the switch without the stewards' noticing. But you will no doubt ask how that could have been done in the presence of nearly five dozen members of the public."

The First Minister shook his head. "Your gang would have had to smuggle the false one in and the real one out without causing comment. It doesn't hold water."

"No," said the General, "it's stretching credulity, put like that. It would need an operation of *Topkapi* quality. You must have other reasons for fixing the time and the date so precisely."

55

"Yes, General. The security cameras. They were installed only a year or two ago, and they were functioning throughout the day in question. We have played back the tapes."

"Then you know how it was done and who did it!"

"Not with any certainty, because the cameras were tampered with. Until soon after half past eleven the recordings show good clear images of the two rooms, every visitor plainly depicted. Quite suddenly everything is out of focus – and it actually stayed like that until the next morning's check. We do not have a clear photograph of a single member of the group who were there at noon. You will appreciate that it's too late for fingerprints or any of that high-technology stuff."

"But the stewards must remember some of them!" said McNish.

"It's three weeks ago, First Minister. They have no recollection of any. They recognised nobody at the time. They said for all they knew they might have been a lot of MSPs. Oh, nothing personal, Sir."

Smarting again under the lash of official condescension, the First Minister wondered why the Presiding Officer's hand seemed to be concealing his mouth. But there were still questions to ask.

"The cameras must tell you something!"

"Yes, they do, First Minister. Everything is blurred, but the movement recorded immediately beside the glass case indicates that the transposition was contrived – we used to call it a switch-eroo when I was young – with the aid of some sort of chair on wheels. They were able to effect an entry to the display case. Then we can see a large but indistinct object being wheeled away with the crowd in the direction of the lift for disabled persons."

Sir Hew, Sir Norman, the First Minister, Morag and Craig all began to speak at once. Sir Andrew McCallum held up his hand to silence them.

"Yes, gentlemen. That seems to be how they did it. The fake stone – may we call it the ringer? – came in on the invalid chair. Perhaps it was stowed beneath the – ah – physically-challenged visitor. The real one left in the same way. It must have been a very strong chair, reinforced perhaps. The stone weighs as much as three adults. A very smooth operation."

"But, good God!" said Sir Norman. "Then the whole group of visitors must have been in the conspiracy together!"

"Precisely, General. That is our hypothesis."

"Well, what were they? Male? Female? What did the stewards say? Were they British? Germans? Indians? Japanese?"

"Oh, good heavens, General! We're not allowed to ask questions like that in Scotland!"

The general snorted in contempt.

"Have you no idea who was behind it?"

"No, Sir. Not yet."

"Or what they did it for?"

"No, Sir."

"A ransom?"

"Possibly, Sir. But no one has come forward with a demand. We would half expect the press to have been informed. If so, nothing has been divulged. Had it been a prank, perhaps by some of the young people at the university, they would have finished enjoying it by now – but, anyway, there were elderly people in the group. It is somewhat baffling. Meanwhile, a counterfeit stone is in place, and we must choose whether to let it lie there for the present, hoping that its secret will stay hidden, or make an announcement and start a hue and cry."

"Where d'you think it is now – the genuine stone?" asked Sir Hew.

"They've had at least three weeks' start, Sir Hew. It could be hidden next to the castle. But it could already be furth of Scotland if that was their plan."

"What is your advice, Chief Inspector?" McNish asked. "Silence or hue and cry?"

"We are investigating a crime, First Minister, in which perhaps five dozen persons were involved. In my experience, with such a number in on a secret, sooner or later someone will talk –"

"Not if they've gone back to Tokyo, they won't," the general muttered. "Not in English, anyhow."

"– so that I believe we should play a waiting game."

"But you'll be alerting the police across Scotland –?" Sir Hew began.

Sir Andrew pursed his lips and frowned. He remembered how in the international terrorist emergency a few years earlier Scotland's police security and intelligence co-ordination had been controlled from Glasgow.

"I would not propose to inform other forces yet, Sir Hew. We

57

must act timeously. Lothian CID have the problem in hand. I am working closely with my Detective Chief Superintendent. We would prefer to keep it in-house for the present. If Strathclyde police got involved . . . Obviously there is a certain sensitivity about these matters."

"There'll be more if the stone is being ransomed!" Sir Hew observed. "Won't people ask why we said nothing?"

"If it's a matter of a ransom, I'm sure we shall hear about it soon, and there will be little lost by holding our peace. But in that event, of course, a political decision would no doubt be required."

The First Minister avoided his eye.

"Sir Norman?"

"It will not help the reputation of the army or the castle if the story gets out – whosoever fault it was. Sir Andrew's advice is sound."

"Are you content with that, Sir Hew?"

Sir Hew looked glum.

"You are asking Historic Scotland to maintain a charade, with my staff in the front line. Very well. I hope Sir Andrew proves right. We want the stone back. We're very anxious not to lose the public's trust and respect as its responsible custodians."

"Presiding Officer?"

Douglas Mackay breathed in deeply before replying.

"If the Chief Constable turns his advice into an instruction," he said deliberately, "I must agree to it as well. Otherwise I should have to call on the First Minister to inform the parliament. However, I must make it clear that my agreement has nothing to do with saving anyone here from embarrassment."

He looked one by one at the faces of Sir Norman, Sir Andrew, Sir Hew and McNish.

"That applies whether the embarrassment may be military, or professional, or administrative, or political."

He turned to Craig and Morag who were still taking notes.

"And, like Sir Hew, I should like that to be on the record."

The uncomfortable silence that followed was broken by the First Minister. His vision of a feeding frenzy by the press, with himself as the main course, was developing in nightmarish detail. He thought back to the experience of one of his unfortunate predecessors, hounded from office for failing to come clean fast enough on a matter of constituency expenses: every newspaper in the country had spoken of the shame that the scandal had brought on the parliament and on Scotland.

"The real question," he said, levering his mind back to the stone, "is who took it."

The Presiding Officer dissented with a single shake of his head. "Well, no. I think the real question will be why they took it."

It was all he could trust himself to say. The seed of suspicion in his mind was still germinating. Yet he was already stunned by the enormity of what might have been done, and of who might have done it; and by the political consequences of its becoming public.

"What happened to Deacon Brodie?" Janet asked.

"He made a run for it. Took the stage. Went south."

"Just like us."

"Then he caught a boat in London for Amsterdam. Hoped to get across to the States – five years after the War of Independence."

"He never made it?"

"They caught up with him in the Low Countries, and brought him back."

"Then –?"

"He was shopped by his closest confederate, I'm afraid."

"No honour among thieves, of course."

"They found him guilty. He tried to get his death sentence commuted to transportation."

"West Indies? Australia?"

"Botany Bay itself. A lot of Scotch criminals ended up there."

"No good?"

"No. They strung him up in Edinburgh, at the Mercat Cross. On gallows he designed himself. In fact, Brodie had to show the hangman how to adjust the drop so that it worked efficiently."

"Hmm." Janet's face registered uncertainty.

"Cheer up. Ours isn't a capital offence."

"But I'm beginning to feel like Bonnie and Clyde, or Butch Cassidy and Sundance – one of those old road films, anyway."

"There's no comparison. We've struck a blow for the Union. We're not even on the run."

"Not yet. Anyway, it wouldn't feel much like Bonnie and Clyde with all our MPs on board too."

"And one or two others. Don't forget the temporary staff

at the castle, earning a little extra during the Holyrood recess."

"I remember that guide with the camp voice and the dodgy moustache, making sure the group was on its own. Is he reliable?"

"One of the parliamentary clerks. Yes, he'll keep quiet. Walter put us on to him."

"And the girl working the lift?"

"Sandra. She's Jock Hamilton's PA. One of our supporters. Sound as a bell."

"Have Enlightenment agents infiltrated every other party?"

"Isn't that something a Whip's office would know about?"

Janet laughed. "Anyway, we're the ring-leaders. You remember: we chose to be the executive arm."

"The rest appointed us."

"I suppose so."

"Bonnie and Clyde didn't have a white van."

"True," said Janet. "And incidentally, if you're really trying to avoid suspicion, you're not driving nearly fast enough."

"No?"

"Not for an unmarked white van in London."

"The number's traceable to Peebles, and we've a valuable cargo on board."

"Still, we don't want to be stopped and searched."

"They won't think of under the floor. What d'you want me to do? Look – there's a speed camera. We mustn't get photographed."

"Well, be a little more thoughtless. Get aggressive. Try cutting in on people. You've got to act the part."

If a Scottish police force had stopped and looked cursorily in the van before it crossed into England at Jedburgh, they would have seen little of interest inside: a rug, two suitcases and some smaller personal luggage, a well-used wheel-chair of slightly strange appearance, and two spare wheels. True, the block and tackle and the useful length of nylon rope might have raised an eyebrow, but not very far. The stone itself was stowed in the compartment, now discreetly strengthened and padded, where the spare wheels normally lived, with the top bolted down. These precautions might not have been perfect, but Janet and Duncan had had a clear run; and the journey down the motorways to the foot of the M1 was without incident.

The few weeks they had just spent north of the Border, although profitably used for some appropriate modification of the van's cargo compartment, had been a little wearing for them both. Each had had to put in token appearances in their constituencies – Janet in Lanarkshire, Duncan in Peeblesshire – but the public's appetite for political meetings with its Westminster MPs was weak, and they need hardly have bothered. In case of premature discovery and the setting up of roadblocks, they had thought it wise to stay in Scotland until mid-September, and safe so long as it was beyond the remit at least of the Lothian constabulary. Anyway, it was a relief to be four hundred miles further south.

Duncan and Janet entertained no wish to protract the second part of their plan; but that could not begin until the British parliament reassembled with its necessary Scottish cast in London in mid-October. However, Westminster Abbey would not go away, and their treasure was secure enough concealed in the white van behind locked doors in the anonymity of Central London. They could afford to relax.

Until this moment their emotions had been kept, as Janet later put it, unnaturally under control. That restraint was not to last – nor, perhaps, could it, now that operational disciplines were suspended. Strolling through St James's Park, whose trees betrayed the first signs of autumn, they discussed whether their provisional celebratory dinner that evening in a star-studded Mayfair restaurant could legitimately be charged – along with the two-month hire of the white van, the cost of welding equipment, diesel fuel and sundry other items – to the expenses to be borne by their colleagues in the House of Commons. The debate was over almost before it began.

"I think I want twenty-four hours which I don't want to have to account for to anybody," Duncan said.

"My feelings exactly. Or even longer."

"The human frame can endure only so much." Duncan's eyes roamed freely and admiringly over her figure.

"We've been astonishingly robust," Janet replied with a gaze equally uninhibited. "Under extreme provocation."

"You're overdressed."

"Yes."

"Is that you, Morag?"

"Speaking."

"This is Douglas Mackay."

61

"Mr Presiding Officer!"

"Can anyone overhear you?"

"No. I'm alone. Mr McNish is in the canteen."

"Why's he always in the canteen? There's a perfectly respectable members' dining room called the Winna Ding or something absurd. Same food, unfortunately."

"He likes people to think he's one of the boys. Able to mix with ordinary mortals."

"Oh, is that it? Listen, Morag – can you get away for a few minutes? I'd like a word with you in strict privacy. In my office, here in Queensberry House."

"With me! Right now?"

"At once. Immediately. This very minute. The noo."

"I'll have to let Craig know, in case anything crops up."

"Well, don't let on where you're going. And Morag –"

"Yes?"

"Would you bring your notes – of that meeting?"

"Sure, Dr Mackay. Anything else?"

"You have a copy of Dod? The Westminster one. Please bring that too."

William McNish was not in the canteen. He had been buttonholed on his way there by Ross Burton of *The Herald* and invited to have a pre-luncheon beer in the Pint o' Wine, the general bar. The Pint, as everyone knew, had been installed as an afterthought, under pressure from the press following an unseemly row. Some chipped old Cumnock pottery, dark brown with a cream slip and embellished with vernacular mottoes, a collection contributed by a sensitive member affronted by the otherwise soulless décor of that rendezvous, sat on the top shelf behind Margaret who tended the bar.

"Twa light ales, Maggie, please," said Burton.

"Margaret, Mr Burton, Ah've asked ye afore."

"This meenit, Maggie, if ye'd be so good. Hoo's Bessie?"

"Still waitin' for her treatment, Mr Burton, but when we get her into Paisley General, she'll be fine. Thank ye for yer enquiry." Margaret sniffed, and set about her duties.

Burton turned to McNish and whispered: "A former editor of my newspaper held that if you met anyone from Glasgow and asked after Bessie you'd always get a positive answer."

"The press has to have its fun."

"You're looking a wee thing weary, First Minister," Burton said. "Is anything troubling you?"

"Nothing out of the ordinary," lied McNish. "The cares of office." He tried to laugh airily, failed, and affected to clear his throat instead.

"I was wondering,'', Burton continued, observing McNish closely, "what you'd been hearing from your Westminster colleagues in the last few weeks."

"Oh? Well, nothing much: they're still in recess, aren't they? The Prime Minister has been in New York for the UN General Assembly – "

"You misunderstood me. I meant Scotland's MPs."

"Oh, that lot, the Wimps." McNish reflected. "Well, they're in recess too. One wonders where they've all gone. Ibiza? Cyprus? Bali? Three long holidays a year, fully paid, and what do they do for us?"

"Andy Wedderburn leads your party in the House of Commons. You surely have discussions with him?"

"What would we talk about? We're the government of Scotland."

"The block grant – what's left of it?"

"That would be between me and the Chancellor. If Andy interferes it does as much harm as good."

"Regional funds from Brussels?"

"None of his business. We've got our own lines to Brussels; and offices, too."

Burton resorted to a direct question. "First Minister, when did you last speak to Andy Wedderburn?"

McNish appeared to search his mind, his mouth pursed, but he was growing wary of the questioning. Instead of answering, he drank deeply from his glass.

"All right," Burton pursued. "When did you last talk with, or correspond with, any Scottish MP?"

But the question stayed unanswered. They were interrupted by the arrival of Alasdair McNab and his friendly concern for whether they were enjoying their beers. McNish, who as a rule never welcomed McNab's presence, reflected that there were exceptions even to that one.

"Stay with us, Alasdair, while we finish this, and join me in the canteen for a bite."

The purport of such an unusual invitation was hardly lost on Burton. It was not credible that any minister, least of all McNish, should seek McNab's company except *in extremis*.

"Good," he said, draining his glass, "and I'll join you both. How's Bessie, Alasdair?"

"Thank ye, Ross, she's quite cheery now, and it's hearin' aboot this place that keeps her laughin'. Were ye plannin' to pick ma brains, Wullie? Ah'll nae say ocht the press shouldna hear."

The First Minister's ploy had failed. While Burton settled the bill with Margaret the barmaid – who thanked him for choosing the Pint o' Wine – McNish led the way to the canteen, where for his benefit McNab compared the qualities of cabbie-claw and Kilmeny kail, the one a traditional concoction based on cod, the other a culinary escapade compounded of pork, greens and rabbit and served with oatcake. Neither dish appealed to McNish who, when Ross Burton appeared, followed *The Herald*'s advice to attempt the "howtowdie wi' drappit eggs", a recent arrival on the canteen menu. McNab followed suit, as he put it, in the interests of simplicity, and they carried their trays laden with garnished boiled fowl and glasses of water to a table by the window.

"I've often wondered," said the First Minister as sociably as he could, nodding towards the rain, "why those are called the Salisbury Crags."

Neither of his companions had any view on the question, nor indeed any interest in it. McNab speared a drappit egg with his fork and watched the yolk seep into the spinach below.

"Ah shoulda had the black puddin an' mince," he muttered. "Or brocht ma ain piece."

"The First Minister and I," said Burton to McNab after an appropriate pause, "were discussing Holyrood's relations with our MPs in London."

"It'll no' hae lasted lang, yer discussion, then," McNab rejoined. "They're no' talkin' tae us, and they dinna answer wir letters. A'body kens that."

"Is that what you were trying to tell me, First Minister," Burton persisted, "when you said you had nothing to say to Mr Wedderburn? It's clear there's a political crisis brewing. Can you give me some guidance on how you'll handle it –"

The First Minister pushed his howtowdie away. It had been a poor choice.

"– or are you saying it's not your business?"

"Just read over what you've got down about that group of tourists, Morag," the Presiding Officer asked. "There were fifty-nine in all, weren't there?"

Morag turned over the pages of her notebook.

"Uh-huh, fifty-nine. With fifteen concessionary tickets for the women over sixty and men over sixty-five. Isn't that a bit outdated? And one for a disabled visitor in a wheel-chair."

"Nothing about how many women. That's as I thought. But you've brought Dod?" She nodded. "And the Official Secrets Act applies to you?"

"Yes, Dr Mackay".

"I think that you and I are about to discover something which must be kept entirely secret from everyone – and that includes everyone who was at that meeting. Everyone."

"Even the First Minister? He's got lots of secrets."

"Especially the First Minister. This is so sensitive that it would be best if he didn't know. Do you promise?"

"Do I have to know?" Morag was torn between curiosity and alarm.

"No, Morag. We can stop right here. But I need you to help me. That would mean your solemn promise of silence, possibly for a very long time."

The struggle in Morag's mind came to an abrupt end, curiosity winning by a distance. In any case, she trusted Douglas Mackay not to ask her to do anything she should not.

"I promise, Dr Mackay. What must I do?"

"Check carefully on the ages of our Westminster MPs for a start." Mackay indicated the parliamentary companion and watched her as he added: "All fifty-nine of them, Morag."

She sat stock-still, staring astonished at him. Then for several seconds, as his words sank in, her mouth worked but nothing came out. Momentarily she looked positively alarmed, her eyes growing bigger and darker. She examined her notebook again, but the figures were right. Mackay, whose interest in her was normally of a paternal nature, fleetingly wished he were much younger. At last she found words.

"It must be a joke. Well, mustn't it?"

"See how many are pensioners. Go by their birth dates. Work

out how old they'd have been in August. Take your time."

While Douglas Mackay, looking outside, pensively contemplated the meaningless shape of the windows of the MSPs' offices – whose external oak lattices often made them feel like so many budgerigars – Morag opened the Scottish MPs section of Dod and made quick notes.

"I've finished," she announced at last. "Three women and twelve men."

"Fifteen. That's what I thought." Mackay turned from the window and held up his hand as Morag was about to speak. "Don't say anything! It proves nothing. It is circumstantial evidence at best. It could be pure coincidence."

"Well, it could be. But I don't believe it. What did they do it for?"

"I don't know. A serious crime has been committed."

"Dr Mackay, there must be a good reason. They're not natural criminals. They're only MPs."

"A reason, certainly. It may be a good one. But if the Chief Constable works out what we've worked out, he'll have to prosecute every one of Scotland's Members of Parliament, because in one way or another they must all be guilty – "

"Every one?" Morag struggled with the proposition.

"Every one of them from Andy Wedderburn down to the wee last from Uist. There won't have been a scandal like this in Scotland since – " He tapped his head.

"Bothwell and the Queen of Scots?" Morag pointed out of the window at Holyrood palace where Mary Stuart had married the Earl of Bothwell only three months after her husband's murder.

"That'll do. I was searching for something a little more recent. Anyway, we can't tell Sir Hew or Sir Norman, because they'd want the real stone back too fast. We can't tell Oor Wullie – I should say Mr McNish – it would answer all his prayers."

Morag was fully familiar with the First Minister's lively sense of self preservation when under immediate threat.

"He's feart of being blamed for losing the stone," she agreed. "And he'd love to be able to tell the world who took it."

"That's only half of it. Think of the political capital he'd make of it."

"Well, he's a politician."

"A politician, if I may say so, more than a statesman. He blames

66

everything that goes wrong in Scotland on our MPs – the cuts in the block grant, the new taxes he's raised, the low fish stocks, the high house prices. But the real trouble is he doesn't have the wit to see what a scandal like this would do to the Union. I told you before, Morag. There's a crisis coming again, and it wouldn't take much for the English to say enough is enough, because they need a government that works properly. The last thing we want is for Scotland's MPs to be made the laughing stock of Britain."

"But, Dr Mackay, you told the meeting that unless the Chief Constable ordered us all to keep quiet – these are your exact words – 'Otherwise I should have to call on the First Minister to inform the parliament.' You wanted it recorded that you weren't interested in saving anyone's face."

"It was true. And since they're all worrying about their own backs, it was good for them to know it. But the truth – can it really be the truth? – was only dawning on me. There's much more at stake. The parliament mustn't be informed by anyone, not if we can help it. Nor must the First Minister."

"I – I agree with that," Morag said.

"And in fact I'm at one with the Chief Constable. We should wait and see if it turns up."

"Will it turn up, Dr Mackay?"

"Well, it's been stolen before."

"Yes, by Edward the First."

"I mean in 1950, when I was quite young. It was taken by some eager but surely misguided young people who claimed to be patriots. And they raided Westminster Abbey where it was unprotected – sacred things were safer in those days – and took it out of King Edward's chair on Christmas Day. They pulled it across the floor on a raincoat or something like that, and bundled it into a small car. It turned up weeks later on this side of the Border, at Arbroath, I think."

"And?"

"Well, they'd made some sort of point. No one wanted to make martyrs of them – that would have been playing their game. All was forgiven. It was dismissed as a prank, and the stone was taken back to the abbey in time for the next coronation. Anyway, no one was blamed for *allowing* it to be stolen."

"So it'll be like that again?"

"As I said before – it depends on why they took it."

4

"YOU MAKE love better than anyone I've ever met," said Janet. Duncan considered the proposition with a smile. He ran his finger slowly and gently down her nose, her lips, her chin, her neck and on, studying her face closely. They had returned to Edinburgh the week before, and once again put in unrewarding appearances in their constituencies. No one had visited Janet's surgery, while Duncan had correctly referred both his visitors to their MSPs. This was a far pleasanter way to pass the time.

"I have no information," Duncan said after due consideration, "as to the quality or quantity of the competition. And I don't want to know."

"It must be all that practice," Janet went on.

"I can't think what you mean."

"But this particular episode will be edited out of your biography even before it is included. Have no fear. Your secret is safe with me."

"Does your Whip's office traffic in the same grotesque gossip about women members as about men?"

She ignored his question, and lowered her voice to a whisper. "Who were they all?"

"I thought you knew."

"Only their names."

"Let's leave it at that."

"Fine. Let's practise some more. And none of them'll know how good you've got."

"Dr Mackay, you said you wanted me to help you. Was it only to look up something in Dod?"

"No, Morag. I could have done that myself. But I needed to bring you in. You or Craig Millar, perhaps, but it would be even harder for him in his post. You were at the university here, weren't you?"

"Uh-huh, I was."

"Reading history, I think? Early Scottish history was one of your subjects. Alexander III, the Maid of Norway, John Balliol, the claims to the succession – all that?".

"Uh-huh," she assented again, guardedly in case her memory was about to be tested. "And a course in Scots Law in my fourth year, but I've forgotten most of it.".

"Useful, but not at the front of my mind. I need to know more about the stone."

Mackay missed Morag's momentary look of apprehension before her considered reply.

"Honestly, it didn't register much with me at the time. I suppose my tutor used to go on about it a bit."

"Ah! Who was that?"

"Professor Harry Innes."

"Ha! A luminary of the Speculative Society. Do you ever see him, or know how to get hold of him?"

Mackay turned to Morag, and to his surprise saw that she was colouring prettily. She closed her notebook and put it together with her copy of Dod.

"Dr Innes has retired. But he still lives near Edinburgh. I'm sure he'd be pleased to tell you all about the stone."

Wailing inwardly, and his hair ruffled, McNish had been driven to make a political comment. "If there's a constitutional crisis in Westminster," he said, eyeing his largely uneaten plate of how-towdie, "it'd hardly help for the Scottish government to interfere in it."

Ross Burton shook his head. "If it's a direct consequence of devolution, the constitutional crisis may be broader than you seem to think."

McNab had also finished all the howtowdie he felt inclined to eat. "Aye," he said. "The West Lothian Question's no' answered yet, for a' yer cairry-on in Lon'on last year. Restless – that's whit *The Scotsman* said the English were. Scunnert, *Ah*'d ca' it."

"And if it's exacerbated by bad feeling between Holyrood and Scotland's representatives down in London," said Burton to McNish, "you're not going to escape the storm. So what are you doing about it?"

"Storm? Me?"

"Perhaps you're the person best placed to bring a little common sense to bear, if you want to."

"Nae doot," said McNab, "but common sense is aye at a premium in Edinburgh. Sae is resipiscence, Bessie says."

"How d'you spell that, Alasdair?" Burton murmured, waiting for McNish's reaction to come to the boil.

McNish was thinking silently and angrily of the hurricane gathering invisibly over the theft of the stone. He wondered which storm would hit him first.

"If Andy Wedderburn and his bloody rabble won't talk to us, it's their fault!" he exploded. "I wouldn't lift my little finger to help them. What have we done to them? Hell, this is Scotland's parliament. We're the Scottish government, and they'd better not forget it!"

"Maybe *that*'s what you've done to them?"

"Nonsense! In the name of Heaven, who do they think they are?"

"That's a very relevant question, even if it's rhetorical. May I quote you, First Minister?"

McNish calmed down abruptly and looked at Burton, sudden suspicion in his eyes. "No!" he said, but immediately his indignation returned at the cost of his better judgment. "Aye! What the hell? Their attitude is quite unacceptable."

McNab coughed. "Wad ye be puttin' me in yer column tae, Ross?"

"Well, would you mind, Alasdair?"

"No' reely, but Ah'll hae tae tell Bessie. She disnae like me gettin' ma name in the papers."

"I could keep your name out of it. I could call you an influential back-bencher. Or I could call you a source close to the First Minister – "

"Naw, dinna fash yerscl.' Bessie'll jist hae tae thole it. Whit wad ye be sayin' Ah said?"

*   *   *

70

At the week-end, at about tea-time, a matter of three days later and accompanied by the First Minister's special adviser, the Presiding Officer called by appointment on Professor and Mrs Innes at their house in Inveresk, that little parish on the south-eastern fringe of Musselburgh which still preserved most of its eighteenth-century charm. Their pleasure at seeing Morag was evident and unreserved.

"It's been too long," said Mrs Innes, embracing her fondly. "And you look beautiful."

"A star pupil," the professor explained to Mackay as he shook his hand. "I could never have refused her request in any case, but it's an extra pleasure to welcome you, Dr Mackay. You can't have an easy task in that place. Sometimes it sounds more like a bouncy castle than a parliament."

"Maybe if politicians behaved like grown-ups it would be even harder," Mackay smiled.

"Well, we have one in the family ourselves, as Morag will have told you. So perhaps I know what you mean."

Morag quickly cut short any reaction Mackay might have been contemplating.

"The trouble is that I've forgotten everything you told me about the Stone of Destiny, Dr Innes. And Dr Mackay is interested in it, as I said. And I thought he'd better have it straight from the – the –"

"Horse's mouth?" Mrs Innes laughed. "Tea for everyone? Sit down. I won't be long. Get something else to sit on from the hall, Morag – you know your way."

"I was going to say 'the fount of all knowledge'," Morag mumbled, still a little flustered, as she brought in a chair, "or something like that."

Dr Innes dismissed the issue, waving Mackay to an armchair. "It's an odd coincidence," he said. "I've a new academic field project connected with the stone. I won't weary you with it, but the historic facts are still fresh in my mind. Tell me how I can help."

"The legend of the Stone of Destiny. Exactly how does it go?"

"Its origin?"

"Well, yes".

Dr Innes gathered his thoughts as he sat down himself.

71

"Murky. I think you can discount stories involving angelic transport, although if it was ever Jacob's pillow in Canaan – in Palestine – it must have got here somehow. No, the respectable account – not unchallenged – is that it was Saint Columba's altar in Iona, and that it was brought from there to Scone Abbey with long stopovers, as they call them nowadays, at Dunstaffnage and Dunkeld, reaching Perthshire perhaps at the end of the ninth century. Is that the sort of stuff you want?"

"Very much! Do you believe it came from Iona?"

"Not impossible, and in my view probable. It is not inconsistent with the notion that it came there with Columba from Ireland, or even that it originated in Egypt or the Holy Land – although geologists might be able to help."

"Good. Has it special properties?"

"Are you talking legend or geology?"

"Legend, I suppose."

"Well, it had all the aura and venerability of a sacred relic, or indeed an altar, when it was in use. The symbolism was enormous. But no miracles are specifically associated with it to my knowledge."

"Surely it's meant to protect Scotland from all ills: 'Where'er this stone is found,' and so on?"

"Ah, yes. The palladium of the Scots. Yes, maybe. But we must accept that there is no hard evidence for that piece of tradition before the 1380s, when John of Fordun – not the most reliable source, I think – wrote some hearsay in his *Scotichronicon*. It wasn't the last good story to start in Aberdeen. From an academic point of view, I'd say that the jury was still out. Nevertheless, personally – "

But Mrs Innes came in at that point with a laden tray and distributed tea and cake round the small company.

Morag had a question. "Dr Innes, you said that geologists might be able to help. I think Dr Mackay would like to know how?"

"Well, if we knew exactly what the stone was made of, we'd be able to guess intelligently where it – "

"Don't we know?" Mackay asked. "You're in no doubt, are you, Dr Innes, that the stone now – um – in Edinburgh Castle is the one that Edward the First removed from Scone?"

"No, no. I'm sure they're one and the same. Are we speaking

of that one? Oh, dear! I'm afraid we've been talking at cross purposes. Morag!" he said reproachfully. "Were you paying proper attention to my lectures?"

Mackay and Morag looked at each other, realisation dawning that their attention had been exclusively on what had been stolen. They waited as the professor thoughtfully put a piece of cake in his mouth and washed it down with tea.

"Never mind," he resumed, looking at Morag kindly. "You of all my students will recall that I'm of the school who believe Edward the First was sold a pup, and that the real stone is somewhere else."

"I certainly do, Dr Innes. But I wouldn't have been able to put the pros and cons to Dr Mackay as clearly as you can."

"Please go on," said Mackay. "I've heard that theory too, of course, but I'd like to know the arguments."

"Well, it has been observed for at least two centuries that the – let's call it – the artefact which used to be in the Coronation Chair in Westminster Abbey and is now in Edinburgh Castle is an ordinary, rough block of red Perthshire sandstone from the Scone area. It was exactly what might have come to hand if the monks of Scone were urgently looking for a credible substitute for what they treasured most – reputedly St Columba's altar, and by then the throne or seat used at the coronation of every King of Scots. They had ample warning of being plundered – and all they needed was a rock large and heavy enough to look credible in the space in the wooden chair that encased it. After all, very few people had actually seen the stone uncovered, and certainly not Edward and his soldiers. The monks' motives for deceiving him were extremely strong".

"But this is still speculation," Mackay said.

"Isn't most history intelligent speculation, even when the facts are beyond dispute, which is seldom enough? Didn't Carlyle describe history as a distillation of rumour? However, my point is that if it were red Perthshire sandstone its provenance would not be Saint Columba."

Mackay nodded. "I can accept that."

"And picture the scene. The abbot hears that the English are on their way back from Elgin. The first thing he must do is to hide the throne – well away from the abbey. But that's practically asking for the monastery to be sacked, so he has to stage some sort of charade. Perhaps he gets Edward's men to catch him in the act of making off with a surrogate."

"It can't have been easy to find something that looked as worn and venerable as the one they took – ring handles and all. Not at short notice."

"No? My personal guess is that the abbots of Scone had been using it to mount their horses for a couple of centuries. Talk about the patina of age!".

"A loupin-on stane!" said Mackay.

"Precisely. Look at it closely. It would explain why the corners have been knocked about like that. And the handles would be just right for dragging it out when it was needed. They're fixed in the wrong position for lifting: it would turn upside down."

"You're serious?"

"Oh, yes. It's surely a possibility."

"I agree it doesn't look like a throne, or even an altar."

"And not high enough. But there are other circumstantial pointers. Edward must have had his own doubts, because he made another raid on Scone two years later, in 1298, smashing the buildings and breaking down all the doors. They were looking for something, but there's no record that they found anything. Thirty years on in the Treaty of Northampton Edward the Third accepted Scotland's independence and actually offered the stone back. It was offered twice more, in 1329 and 1363. The Scots were never interested. They didn't even reply. Why not?"

"All right. What was the real one made of?"

"Was? Is? Well, whichever. I am no geologist myself, but let's say – some kind of marble. In that case, black marble. Possibly Irish, or from Iona. It could be merely basalt – and you find black basalt on Mull. Or it may originate much further afield. You asked about special properties. None that I can think of, unless it's something like lodestone – magnetite – which would make it magnetic. I certainly don't dismiss that. Again, the idea that it was shaped from a meteorite sounds fanciful – but not negligible if the stone genuinely originated in Palestine or Egypt where these heavenly objects were greatly venerated. After all, before Mahommet came along, the Arabs revered a sacred black meteorite which they kept somewhere in the Mecca valley." Innes laughed. "There is an obvious and attractive connection with the legend of an angelic air-lift. And meteorites come in all sizes and many compositions."

"Yet you said it was probably black marble."

"Most likely, and very big. Bigger, anyway, than the one in the castle. The thing is, there are contemporary descriptions, and most of them say it was marble. Some say it was black, and some say it had ornate carvings on it. But geology was a little primitive – let me see – seven, eight, nine centuries ago. Blind Harry who wrote the ballad about Wallace spoke of 'an ancient royal marble chair.' But 'marble' covers a broad field: the Greek word was *marmoris*, and only meant 'shining stone'."

"What a pity there aren't any pictures of it."

"But there are!"

"That's impossible! What do you mean?"

"Quite small," said Dr Innes, with a conspiratorial grin at Morag, "but compelling. I'll fetch them."

"I'll take your cups," said Mrs Innes, "unless you want more tea? Harry always gets excited at this stage."

"I'm just delighted when anyone's interested," the professor said mildly as he left. "I assure you I'll postpone any excitement till another time. Your cups are safe."

He returned, opening a small box, and showed them replicas of some of the great seals of the early kings of Scotland. In the first examples, the incumbent king – Alexander the First, David the First, Malcolm the Fourth or William the Lion – was shown clearly enthroned on what might well have been an altar: at any rate, the concave dip in the middle offered satisfactory accommodation for a sedentary monarch. In the latter, the altar was covered by a throne, apparently of carved wood, and the kings depicted were either equipped with footrests – Alexander the Second and Third – or, as with John Balliol, the last to occupy that particular piece of furniture, their feet were left swinging.

"So we know its shape, recessed almost like a chair," Professor Innes concluded. "In ancient times it was actually referred to as a chair. The people who made these seals wouldn't have got it wrong. And its size, if the kings were of average height, was roughly twice the height of the one in the castle: say, about twenty inches or half a metre."

"What about Robert the Bruce's seal, Dr Innes?" Morag asked. "If he was crowned on the real stone – "

"You're still coming up with the good questions," agreed the professor with obvious pleasure. "No – Balliol seems to have been the last in the line. The Bruce was crowned at Scone in 1306, but not on the stone. It was still hidden – I'm sure no-one wanted to tempt the English back for a third time. After that the stone seems to have disappeared from history."

"Why was that?" said Morag, seeing his brows knit.

"My guess is that no-one survived who knew where it was. There can't have been many in the first place. And Abbot Thomas, who succeeded Abbot Henry, was abducted and imprisoned in England, and certainly met an untimely death. If he was tortured, he didn't say anything helpful. The secret may have died with him."

"So the trail comes to an end," said Mackay.

"Well, Dr Mackay, this is where Duncan and I – Duncan my son, you know – have agreed to differ. He's a bit of a historian, too. He sees my point. But the disappearance, or let us call it the non-re-appearance, of the stone after 1296 has persuaded him that the sandstone version was the only Coronation Stone after all, that it's all there ever was, and that everything else is myth. It's a respectable point of view, and can't be disproved. Morag, I've always valued your opinions. You know Duncan. Which of us d'you think is right?"

Morag's confusion was evident to both men, and Professor Innes regretted having put the question.

"I'm certainly not going to choose between you on that one," she said. "And you know I wouldn't."

Mackay pressed his point: "The end of the trail, Dr Innes?"

"Not quite," the professor said reflectively. "There was a story that two children chanced on a landslip at Dunsinane, which isn't far from Scone, in 1800 or so. They found a vaulted grotto with what may well have been the stone inside."

"And was it?"

"Maybe. But they took fright – I suppose because they shouldn't have been there – and only spoke of their discovery years later. The grotto must have disappeared again, but there were reports of fresh sightings and diggings in 1818 and further stories of a marble throne. Not only that, but tales of round bronze plaques or targes beside it bearing interesting inscriptions. They related to the beneficial influence of the stone to which you alluded.

It's important, because there are round discs portrayed on some earlier royal seals. Look at this one."

"Go on, please," Mackay said.

"Well, the scene then jumps to London. According to the London newspaper which reported the discovery at Dunsinane, the real Stone of Destiny was shipped to the capital for examination by experts. Deliver us from experts, Morag!"

"Did they see it?" she asked.

"Who knows? That's the end of it. And no mention then of the targes. The trail disappears without trace."

"You mean the stone went to London?" demanded Mackay.

"My guess is that it did not," the professor said. "My feeling is that, if it really was found, it was as quickly lost again. The notion that it went to London could have been an intentionally false trail; and I think so for two reasons. The first is that I've found no sequel to the newspaper report. The second I'd attribute to the baleful influence of Sir Walter Scott."

"He knew the real stone had turned up?"

"He never wrote or spoke about it. And whoever had it in custody may have been determined to keep Sir Walter out of it. Note the date of the newspaper story: January 1819. Only the year before, Scott got the royal warrant to open up the kist in Edinburgh Castle that held the Honours of Scotland – the crown, the sceptre and the sword of State, all locked away since the Union in 1707. He was on a high. Heaven knows the trouble he'd have made if he thought the stone were lying about loose in Perthshire! But, if the secret was out, better to keep the stone hidden, and for safety's sake pretend it had already gone south."

"A pity, in some ways. If you're right it probably robbed us of another Waverley novel," said Mackay.

"Well, that's only one possibility. Perhaps Walter Scott knew all about the discovery and . . . well, it's all intelligent speculation at best," the Professor reminded him. "We shan't know the truth unless we find the thing. I hope we shall, one day."

"That would be thrilling," Morag said.

"Yes," said the professor, smiling at her, "and whatever other trouble it caused, it would certainly settle the argument between Duncan and me."

*　　*　　*

Driving back into Edinburgh from Inveresk, his tall frame squeezed awkwardly behind the wheel of a rather small car, Douglas Mackay quickly raised with Morag the question that had been troubling him for an hour or more.

"It was a surprise to me to learn that Dr Innes's son is one of our MPs in Westminster."

"Yes," said Morag evenly. "He was elected last time – for the Scotch Enlightenment Party. He's MP for St Mary's Loch."

"You didn't tell me."

"No."

"I knew the name Duncan Innes, of course, but I couldn't have guessed it was the same family." His tone now had a slight sharpness to it.

"I'm sorry, Dr Mackay. I should have told you. He's . . . he's a criminal now, I suppose."

"Surely not the ringleader, though, do you think?"

"I – I don't know."

"Yet it's curious that he seems to have strong views on the stone – and that they differ from his father's."

They considered that silently as they drove beside Musselburgh racecourse. Then Mackay spoke again.

"They're very fond of you, Dr and Mrs Innes."

"They've always welcomed his students. He makes history exciting."

"You went to their house quite often? Was Duncan there a lot – I mean, before he became an MP?"

"I suppose he was."

"Good. So you know him fairly well? Is he the sort of man who –?"

"I can't tell," she interrupted. "I haven't seen him for at least a year. Or so."

"Well, how well did you know his mind, then? Think back, Morag. This could be very useful."

They had just stopped at traffic lights. She was silent until he glanced at her to reinforce his question.

"I used to sleep with him, Dr Mackay. We lived together for a while. That well."

Mackay said "I see," and then was silent in his turn, embarrassed to have pressed her so far and so unfeelingly, but despite himself thinking: "Lucky bastard."

"What are you thinking, Dr Mackay? Dr Mackay?"

78

He closed his eyes and said "Lucky bastard."

To his relief, she giggled.

"Were you in love with him?"

"Oh, yes."

"Are you still?"

She thought about it. "Yes . . . a little . . . a little too much still. But it's over, I think."

"This complicates things."

"I'm afraid it does."

"Would you be prepared to be in touch with him –?"

"No."

"Or to ring him up and ask –"

"No."

The lights turned green.

"You're like a cat," said Duncan.

"Not usually the friendliest thing to say to a woman."

"You haven't a single position that is not totally elegant and utterly bewitching. Standing, walking, leaning, bending, turning, sitting –"

"Flat on my back?"

"Certainly. And sideways, and upside down."

"Mind if I purr?"

"No. But wait till you're stroked."

"I might scratch."

"I might like it."

"Duncan."

"Yes, Janet?"

"D'you really think they haven't noticed the stone's gone?"

They had been scanning the newspapers every day. At last, curiosity getting the better of them, Duncan once again disguised himself for safety's sake and returned to the Royal Palace in Edinburgh Castle as a tourist. He dallied in the rooms portraying the origins of the Honours of Scotland, well as he remembered everything in them, and finally strolled insouciantly into the Crown Room to inspect the glass case as closely as he could without seeming too interested. Janet had certainly made an astonishingly skilful job of the polystyrene: even the iron rings in the stone looked solid and real. He bought a postcard in the shop below and reported back.

79

"I really can't tell," he said in answer to the question. "It's still there, but it doesn't seem to be lying precisely as we left it. Of course, there was a good deal of bustling about before we closed the case again, so I can't be sure. It looks terribly heavy, though."

"It's possibly my masterpiece," said Janet.

"We're in no hurry for them to discover that. But we'd better assume that they know just the same."

"Then why don't they raise the alarm?" said Janet.

"Perhaps they don't dare tell anyone, out of embarrassment."

"Who'd be embarrassed? The castle people? The police?"

"Either. Or the government – the Holyrood troupe, I mean."

Janet thought about it. "Then they may be waiting for our next move."

"Conceivably. Well, we're not ready. But we could make a move to mislead them, couldn't we?"

"We could send a ransom note."

"Extortion is criminal. I'd prefer something cryptic – something tantalising but meaningless. Something that keeps them silent but guessing."

"Who'd we send it to?"

"Well, what about the First Minister? McNish."

"Goodness! Would he know what we're being cryptic about?"

"If he doesn't, it'll alert somebody. We've got to make him think we're coming back for more."

"Excellent! We'll play cat and mouse with him."

"And talking of playing with cats . . ."

"Yes, Duncan?"

Ross Burton was taking his morning coffee in The Auld Acquaintance. This sunless little establishment had been inserted adjacent to the press gallery above the debating chamber for the particular benefit of media people – inserted by one of the parliament's interminable sequence of architectural consultants as a diplomatic precaution. It had no windows of its own and borrowed its daylight from the so-called garden lobby. Plans were talked of to transfer it elsewhere when a space could be found.

Burton was there to check through his column in that day's *Herald*, a copy of which was always available in the Media Tower nearby. He was pleased with what he had written – an elegant little vignette from the previous day's debate on land reform during which the Minister for Public Resources had shown himself entirely ignorant of the provisions of the European Convention on Human Rights relating to the appropriation of private property. The episode had ended with the Presiding Officer calling for order because of persistent, barely suppressed laughter in the public gallery. As Burton folded his newspaper and sipped his coffee he noticed the uncharacteristic behaviour of the leader of the opposition on the granite flags below.

Jock Hamilton, shoulders bent beneath his cares, had been shambling unpurposefully across the lobby when he turned sharply towards one of the many planters which were disposed around its edges and contained subfusc shrubs of uncertain function. Now he was peering intently among the leaves of what might have been a rubber plant, and was settling down on the concrete rim of the planter, rapt in study. With all the restrained energetic curiosity of the political journalist, Burton finished his coffee, paid the bill and hurried down to investigate.

"What'v'you got there, then, Jock?" asked Burton.

"Wheesht, man! Watch."

Burton could see nothing but large dark green leaves.

"What is it?"

"Keep your voice down," Hamilton whispered. "That web – it caught the light as I was passing, and I'm watching the spider. It's still making it. Look!"

"Why are you whispering?" Burton demanded, wondering if he was being made a fool of. "Spiders can't hear, can they? Do they have ears? I've never thought about it."

"He's trying to spin a cobweb across to that twig," Hamilton explained, pointing. "And that's twice he's missed. But here he goes again." He leant forward with his mouth hanging open.

"It's a he? How d'you tell?"

"Go on, lad! Go on! Who dares wins!"

Witnessing the leader of the Scottish opposition pouring whispered exhortations into a rubber plant, Burton reckoned that perhaps he had now seen everything. He heard a footstep behind, and turned to find Hamilton's personal assistant Sandra approaching. He put a finger to his lips, indicating that this was no moment to disturb her employer.

"A spider," he told her, *sotto voce*. "A male spider, spinning a web."

"Lead on, brave heart!" Hamilton was murmuring. "You'll never walk alone!"

Sandra blinked in honest disbelief. "I thought he might have lost something." she said. "He's got a meeting to chair. Mr Hamilton!"

"There he goes!" said Hamilton excitedly, raising his voice at last. "Swinging in from the wing! Yes! What a shot! He's done it!"

"Done what, Mr Hamilton?"

"An inspiration to us all, Sandra! Never give up! Never lose heart!" Hamilton turned to look at her, his eyes alight, his shoulders braced.

"Mr Hamilton, you've better use for your time than passing it with insects."

"Or even with lobby correspondents, Sandra," Burton added mildly, "unless that's what you're implying."

"These are the papers for your meeting, Mr Hamilton," said Sandra, proffering a dossier.

"I've two things to say to you, Sandra," said Hamilton loftily, tucking the dossier under an arm. "The first is this: a spider isn't an insect – it's a . . . well, something else, anyway. The second – you're a Scots lass; so where's your sense of history?"

Sandra looked at him voiceless.

Hamilton's gaze met Burton's head-on. "And where's yours, Ross? What's it matter what sex a spider is? Haven't you bigger things to worry about?"

With that he inflated his chest, cleared his throat, turned on his heel, and marched off with a smile on his face, his head held high and, in his gait, a sense of purpose that neither Sandra nor Burton had ever seen before.

"Mercy me!" murmured Sandra, shaking her head slowly. "He's lost it. He really believes he's – "

"Just don't say it," said Burton, watching Hamilton disappear towards one of the feature staircases with a swagger and what might have been a flick of the hips. "In fact, don't even think it."

"All right," she said. "I just wonder what some of them would be doing in the real world."

For a fourth time Mrs Jean Murray Stewart, deputy leader of the opposition and front-bench spokesperson on education and culture in the Scottish parliament, read through the short Latin text on which her superior had scrawled the simple message: "JMS. What do you make of this? With AOB, I think – Jock." It was printed on a sheet of plain white paper, and bore neither address, nor signature, nor date.

Ad Ministrum Primum (it ran)
Apud Senatum Caledoniensium
Porta Canonici
Edinburgi EHXCIX ISP

Hic et nunc quaerant filii pictorum
Si sic facile palladium nostrum perditum est
Quo modo atri honores tuti manebunt
Et cui bono tandem et cui infamiae erit?

cc Hostium Dux

Mrs Murray Stewart's Latin belonged to her schooldays nearly four decades earlier. However, her frown indicated less a lack of comprehension, which was partial at best, than a suspicion that Hamilton was about to put something unwelcome across her. He had handed the text to her as the weekly private gathering of Scotland's twelve-member shadow cabinet began.

She had good reason for feeling a little tense as "any other business" approached. The meeting was nor following the normal pattern. At the start, without any warning of a change in the agenda, Hamilton announced the need – as he saw it, as party leader – to review the party's policy on culture and education. He would be bringing forward certain ideas towards the end of the meeting. This was all in stark contrast to the deference he was wont to accord her regarding her front-bench responsibilities. She challenged him at once; but he was ready for her, observing merely that his view was broadly shared that educational syllabuses were in need of enrichment. For the present she contented herself with correcting him twice in front of colleagues, once on a minor matter of fact and once to suggest – injudiciously, as it would turn out – that the plural of syllabus was syllabi. But he brushed those criticisms aside with a relaxed smile which caused her to flush angrily.

83

The piece of paper had come into Hamilton's hands that morning. Personally he had been unable to make much sense of it, and he had asked Sandra to include it in his papers for later consideration. Only as he left Sandra and Ross Burton in the concourse, his morale boosted by an unusual flow of adrenalin, had he perceived the advantages of consulting his spokesperson on education. If she could translate it, it would save him the trouble. If not, even better.

The main topic of the meeting was parliamentary tactics for a looming debate on public expenditure: its focus was the running costs of the parliament and meeting the backlog of bills for building it, all of which now fell on the Scottish taxpayer. Probably the executive's tenderest spot was taxation – the need to make good from Scottish taxpayers the growing shortfall of funds from the British treasury. Other forms of budgetary revenue remained obstinately unbuoyant: inward investment had slowed; Scotland's financial services industry had declined again; no amount of the climatic change which meteorologists had argued about for a quarter of a century had contrived to extend the summer even by a minute, and so the country's tourist season remained lamentably short. The ever-increasing financial demands of health, care, education and pensions, to which McNish's government, like its predecessors, invariably acceded for fear of political outflanking, were putting a burden on the exchequer which, again, only the Scottish tax-payer could meet if the budget were to balance.

As ever, but now with a commendable vigour which his colleagues noted, Hamilton charged them with attacking the executive's ministers in their several fields, concentrating on the fiscal implications of their policies. His social affairs spokesperson, James Maclean, remarked that successful challenges in the parliament had become much more difficult because those very ministers tended to spend so much time out of the country. When they were not on jaunts to distant continents they seemed to be in Brussels, whether they had any business to be there or not.

"And that," said Hamilton, slapping his hands on the table, "is why all the opposition parties here must join together, co-ordinate their tactics, and hold the executive properly to account."

"The trouble with that old idea," Mrs Murray Stewart put in coldly, hoping to dishearten her leader once and for all, "is that

84

the other parties are either in coalition with the executive or simply unwilling to co-operate with this one. Understandably, perhaps," she added tartly and with a sniff.

Raising her chins and looking down her nose at Hamilton, she was surprised to find him gazing levelly back at her, certainly with confidence, almost with hauteur. He was tilting his chair back and letting another lazy smile play on his lips.

"We shall come to your portfolio in a moment, Jean, if you'll be patient. In the meantime, I must inform you all that I've had some preliminary words – of an exploratory nature of course – with Walter Moncrieff of the Enlightenment party. Walter is not unwilling to examine means of mutual collaboration."

Mrs Murray Stewart could not let that pass. "I can't believe I heard that!" she exclaimed, looking round the table. "We couldn't be seen to associate with that bunch of crackpots! Good gracious! Did you ever read their manifesto?"

"Most carefully, Jean. I'm sure we all did. And of course I'm talking of co-operation – not of supporting their more far-fetched ideas. I think you may have missed the point – again."

Jock Hamilton checked the expressions of his shadow cabinet, none of which was showing any sympathy with his deputy's objections. It was time to strike.

"I was going to say something on the subject of education, yes, and Scottish culture in particular. I have been alarmed by how little knowledge of our own past is taught in our schools today. There may be a rudimentary knowledge of the exploits of Robert the Bruce or Bonnie Prince Charlie. But if you asked an average pupil doing highers to write about Scotland under Cromwell, or the Covenanters, or the origins of the Treaty of Union, or the significance of the Disruption – just to take some obvious examples – I don't think you would be handed more than a few lines at most, and none of them worth much."

He paused, satisfying himself with the apprehensive silence he had created before carrying on.

"How many could tell you which was the first lighthouse built by the Stevensons? Or which Australian city is called after a Scottish astronomer? Or how the Salisbury Crags got their name? Or – just for instance – how many pitched battles were fought against the English in the five centuries before the Union of the Crowns?"

Hamilton looked benignly around the table, noting with amusement the closed look of faces which, while admitting no ignorance, would have hated to be challenged on any of those questions.

Mrs Murray Stewart knew that she must make a stand. "All educational development these days," she began, "is incremental and structured to produce a higher –"

"If I may continue?" said Hamilton. "I therefore propose that in all our speeches in future we also take every opportunity to stress the value of cultural awareness, whether its purpose be to understand the merits of devolutionary government or to broaden our minds about the world at large. I might put it like this: unless we know where we've come from, we don't know where we are, and we shan't know where we are going."

He checked his colleagues' faces once more to be sure they had appreciated this shaft of homespun wisdom, then turned to his budget spokesperson. "There are no direct financial implications, I think, Gordon?"

"No, no," agreed Gordon Boyle, one of the "list" members. "Speeches cost nothing."

"Any other comments, then?"

"I have never heard such idealistic whimsy in my life," Mrs Murray Stewart protested. "And it will play straight into the hands of the Enlightenment party which makes such a virtue of –"

"No, the opposite will be true. It will cut the ground from under their feet. In fact, I propose to open the debate for the opposition in person." Hamilton looked at his deputy with a smile now tinged with pity. "Moreover, in view of Scotland's past reputation for learning and –" (he paused to indicate the entire parliament building with a wave of his hand) "– her crying need for better architects, home-grown if possible, I see good reason for insisting on a greater emphasis on the classics too." He leant forward self-deprecatingly, taking everyone into his confidence. "I'm afraid my personal knowledge of Latin was always rather poor. Only a short time ago, you will recall, I had to be corrected by my own shadow spokesperson on education. Syllabi! Well, bless me! How ignorant! For a moment I thought she'd said 'silly boy'!"

The shadow cabinet laughed dutifully while Mrs Murray Stewart's eyes went down to the table where lay the Latin text on which, she already realised, her leader was publicly about to ask her advice. She had sprung the trap herself.

86

"Jean," said Hamilton mercilessly, "you've had time to look at that document I gave you. It arrived in my office this morning and, frankly, because it's in Latin, I can't make head or tail of it. Perhaps we may benefit from your greater scholarship – ?"

Mrs Murray Stewart at that point knew she had no friend in the room. She stared furiously back at Hamilton, saying nothing and wishing he were dead.

"I think that makes my case perfectly," Hamilton said after a pause, gathering his papers together. "Jean, would you arrange immediately to have the piece professionally translated, then sent to me and circulated to everyone present, in case it's more important than it looks. Perhaps it's a joke. We can discuss it next time. If there's no other business, the meeting is concluded."

The shadow cabinet shuffled after him out of the room, making for their offices. Perplexed as ever by an architectural design which seemed to have been based on a random version of the chaos theory, a few of them paused to find their bearings.

"What's got into Jock?" asked Boyle. "Has he been at the cannabis?"

"God knows," said Maclean. "Maybe he hit his head getting up from his window-seat. But any more of that and we'll have to get rid of him."

"Don't be absurd, man. Think of the alternative."

5

WILLIAM McNISH, the First Minister, too, was preparing for the debate on the cost of running Scotland's world-class parliamentary building. He had called his press officers and his speech-writers to his art-deco office in St Andrew's House to address once again what, ever since the devolution settlement, had remained Scotland's single most vexed question. He was now considering the preliminary draft they had submitted to him.

There should be no harking back – this was their advice – to the scandals revealed by the first public inquiry into Holyrood's financial and timetable overruns. No one in Scotland had forgotten how the White Paper proposition that a new legislature might be had for as little as ten million pounds had quickly climbed, over the long years of construction, from twenty-five to forty to sixty million, then to two hundred, three hundred, four hundred million and beyond. Allegedly there had been 15,000 design changes even before the fitting out began. The extra expense in wasted time and material had all been borne by the Scottish taxpayer, either by new taxation or by foregoing other benefits normally covered by the treasury's block grant. Official occupation of the Holyrood building had taken place more than three years late in 2004.

With luck the opposition parties would steer clear of all that history. None wanted to remind the voter that the figure of a hundred thousand pounds per MSP at which the parliament had once been commended to the Scottish public had risen to well over three million. That was enough, as was pointed out, to buy each of them a sporting estate or a luxury island off the west coast, and still leave room for a handsome pension.

The First Minister fell into a reverie, remembering what this serial spending disaster had done to his predecessors – indeed, to everyone who had attempted and failed to put a ceiling on the costs, the blame flowing on as from a leaking tap, the buck stopping here and there but never for long.

McNish was still looking disconsolately at his draft speech when a knock on the door heralded the entry of Craig Millar.

"I think we've got the ransom note for the stone, First Minister. Have a look at this."

The anonymous Latin lines which humiliated Mrs Murray Smith had been dealt with more expeditiously by the First Minister's private office, whose resources were greater. A translation had been supplied by a classical scholar in the education department, and Craig had already classified it "top secret."

"Just the occasion for a ransom note," McNish said flatly, shoving his speech away. "Let me see it."

"It came in Latin, but I've had it construed," Craig ventured. "Which version would you like? They're both somewhat cryptic."

"Give me both and I'll make up my mind," said McNish frowning. He spent no time on the Latin and turned to the translation.

To the First Minister (he read)
The Scottish Parliament Canongate Edinburgh EH 99 1SP

Here and now the sons of the painted people ask,
since their palladium was so easily lost,
whether their other honours can be safe; and who
will benefit and who be shamed [blamed?]

cc Leader of the Opposition

"What sort of a ransom note is that?" McNish demanded. "You're certain that's what it is? And why've you sent it to the leader of the opposition if it's top secret?"

"No, that's part of the translation. So Mr Hamilton's probably got it too."

"Anyway it doesn't mean anything," McNish grumbled. "Painted people? And what's palladium? Sounds like a cinema."

"One of the elements, when I was doing science," said Craig. "Has some been stolen, then?"

89

"Perhaps you should reconvene the meeting of insiders, First Minister. The Chief Constable might know."

"I doubt it," said McNish. "But we need a report from him in any case. Yes, we'd better have them all back as soon as possible. First thing tomorrow, if you can arrange it. And for safety's sake it had better be in Bute House. Same cast as before. Stress that it's top priority."

The party conference season in the United Kingdom was about to begin. The party of government that year had chosen to go to Brighton again, whereas the main parties of opposition would be boosting the economies of Bournemouth and Blackpool.

The Prime Minister of the United Kingdom was looking with concern down the list of conference motions sent in from the constituencies. Many of these, he knew, had been drafted by the MPs themselves – the member would be the main floor speaker for any selected for debate. Most were genuinely framed by the constituency parties, and fairly reflected their feelings. It was generally easy to tell the difference, because MPs' own motions often congratulated the Government on its achievements before paraphrasing official policy on the subject chosen.

On education, health, defence and crime the submissions were in no way extraordinary. Of course, they came exclusively from English constituencies, as these matters were devolved to Edinburgh and Cardiff. More striking were the motions dealing with finance and the constitution. The Prime Minister was startled by the virulence of some of the language employed.

This conference (ran a typical proposal) *demands that English taxpayers cease to be milch-cows for other parts of Great Britain; and that the devolved assemblies be given full powers to raise what they wish from their own taxpayers to spend as they please without further recourse to English pockets.*

This conference (ran another, more moderate and so more dangerous), *resenting the burden of Scotland's demands on the common exchequer, calls on the Government to reduce the block grant for public expenditure in Scotland to a per capita sum precisely equal to the average spent in England.*

"The English backlash goes on and on," he said to the national party chairman who had come to Downing Street to express his alarm. "Cutting the number of Scottish MPs and removing their powers over English business should have been enough. But it's about money just as much." He turned to the constitution section and scanned it.

This conference (he read aloud) *takes note of the difficulties experienced in carrying out a coherent political programme in England, and calls on the government to use its United Kingdom majority to initiate such constitutional changes as may rectify these anomalies.*

"Good God!" he exclaimed. "We all know the opposition is making a monkey of parliament – but how would we get a measure like that through? If we let Scottish MPs vote on English affairs again, the country would rise against us."

"I've been able to see some of the motions tabled by the opposition parties for their conferences, Prime Minister," said the party chairman. "If it's any comfort, they are just as resentful of Scottish claims on the budget as these ones are."

"Comfort isn't quite the word, I'm afraid. Our politicians on both sides are playing to the gallery, and it's a nasty sight. The parliaments are drifting apart on a tide of mutual distrust. Quarrels over money are the most pernicious of all."

The party chairman had more bad news.

"Have you looked at the European motions, Prime Minister? Page twenty-five of the proof. Look at this one – it's quite subtle."

This conference proposes that clocks in the United Kingdom be permanently aligned with those on the Continent, while respecting any decision of the Scottish, Northern Irish and Welsh Parliaments to maintain present arrangements locally.

"Yes it's ingenious. Of course there's nothing to stop farmers in north-west Scotland getting up to milk their cows an hour later than other people if they really must do it by daylight. The cows wouldn't mind. But it's asking for trouble."

"And there's a lot suggesting in different ways that UK relations with the Commission in Brussels should be conducted strictly by government ministers and their departments."

"Well, I agree with that," said the Prime Minister, having glanced through a few of them. "What's so special about it?"

"The trouble is that in every case these motions have been tabled by a Scottish MP."

"What's that imply ?"

"Not a single one from a Scottish constituency association. I've spoken to the Scottish party chairman: he says the MPs are the only people who mind. It's natural, because most European policies which affect Scotland are administered through Edinburgh."

"And the Scottish members in Westminster object to that? Well, they would. Could we get one or two to introduce a suitable resolution to conference? Give 'em a platform? Not the same as a place in government, I know, but . . . any good?"

"Not much," said the party chairman unhappily. "In fact, there won't be a lot of Scottish rank and file party members at Blackpool at all. There's no interest. And, frankly, Prime Minister, I don't think they'd be very welcome if they did come – not in the conference hall, still less at the fringe meetings. Look at the tone of the constituency resolutions."

There was silence around the table in the First Minister's office in Bute House while Sir Andrew, Sir Hew, Sir Norman and Dr Mackay studied the Latin and English texts before them. Once more Morag Macleod and Craig Millar had their notebooks ready. Craig had passed her a copy of the documents which she, too, now saw for the first time.

McNish broke the silence. "*'The sons of the painted people ask, since their palladium was so easily lost, whether their other honours can be safe.'* Sir Andrew? Is this the sort of message we have been waiting for? Somewhat cryptic, you could call it."

In his opening report to the meeting, the Chief Constable had admitted that his force's enquiries had revealed nothing new. Now he stroked his chin abstractedly and said it was difficult to say.

McNish turned to the Chairman of Historic Scotland.

"Sir Hew?"

"Palladium," he said, looking at the text. "Yes, the Greek word is palladion. That takes me back to my school days. It was the sacred statue that protected Athens – or was it Troy? Both, perhaps. Anyhow, I think it's a fair description of the Coronation Stone."

Mackay was nodding, recalling that Professor Innes, too, had used the word.

"In which case," Sir Hew said, "it's obvious that whoever wrote this knows we've lost it – and probably knows where it is."

"It's not exactly a ransom note," said the general. "More a threat than a demand."

"And 'honours'," said Sir Hew, "clearly refers to the Honours of Scotland – the crown jewels. We keep them in the same place, after all."

"Good Lord!" said the general. "Then it is a threat. They're coming back for more!"

The Chief Constable looked alarmed. "We can always advise on extra precautions, First Minister – "

"Like when to lock a stable door?" the general said sourly.

"It's a perfectly good literal translation," Sir Hew resumed, ignoring their interpolations, "but 'pictorum', the painted people, surely means the Picts. Scone was their capital, the capital of Dalriada."

"Of who?" asked McNish.

"It's not important, First Minister. The note is obviously genuine, in the sense that it comes from the gang who raided the castle. Heaven knows why it's in Latin."

Mackay, who had been wondering the same thing, glanced at Morag and saw her sitting stock-still, her pen idle.

"I detect another threat, at least by implication," Mackay said quickly. He tapped the paper in his hand. "Look. It talks about shame or blame. Now who would that be about?"

Sir Andrew, Sir Hew, Sir Norman and McNish were all examining the table.

McNish looked up first and changed the subject. "Time for hue and cry yet, Chief Constable?" he asked briskly. "What's your advice?"

Sir Andrew was thinking coherently at last.

"They may believe that the theft is still undetected – but I don't think so. More likely by now they suspect the truth, that it's been discovered and we're keeping quiet about it. So if we'd started a hue and cry last week, I doubt this note would have been sent at all."

"I don't see what you're driving at, I'm afraid," said McNish.

"Well, I do," said the general with approval. "The note is to

93

goad us into action, to make it public. Well, we don't know why – but we won't be their catspaws! Let's hang on longer and wait for their next move. We've got them guessing."

"I thought they'd got us guessing," said Sir Hew. "I don't really understand. But all right: we can hardly decide whether or not to pay a ransom if none's been demanded. What's to be lost by waiting?" He looked at the Chief Constable. "Though it won't stay secret for ever. Nothing does. It can't. Especially" – Sir Hew tapped the Latin text – "if Mr Hamilton works this out."

Sir Andrew blew his nose, playing for time. "I propose, however," he said, "at this stage to widen our net somewhat. I shall activate SPICC – that is to say," he said responding to the First Minister's look of bafflement, "the Scottish Police Information and Co-ordinating Centre. It has direct links across the UK. It's not impossible that the invalid chair will be employed again nefariously, either in this city or elsewhere, so I'll put out a general signal to all forces in Scotland and England to be alert to and report on any suspicious activities involving invalid chairs in heritage sites. It's a routine police exercise, although in a slightly unusual form. Of course, I shan't mention what we've lost."

"Mr Presiding Officer?"

"Is that you, Morag?"

"I need another word with you."

"I could tell. I'm in my office now. There's no one else here. Can you get away?"

She tapped on his door a few minutes later, and came in looking unusually distraught.

"Duncan wrote that note," she said miserably.

"That was his Latin?"

"I'm sure of it. We used to write secret messages – well, short ones – to each other in dog Latin as a joke. He did classics, and I remembered some of mine. The whole thing is exactly what he'd do, and how he'd do it."

Mackay sat her down and returned to his own desk.

"What was the note for?"

"Just for a tease. Just to confuse the issue."

"Well, it worked. We were confused."

"The general's quite wrong. They're not coming back for the

Honours. They've taken all they want. That's just Duncan laying a false trail."

"Is he the ringleader? Surely Andy Wedderburn or Campbell Macarthur –"

"Perhaps, but I bet he had the ideas."

Mackay considered the facts. Scotland's Westminster MPs had jointly conspired to steal the Stone of Scone. A few of them – probably not all – knew where it was now. Other persons may have been involved. Presumably none knew the theft had been discovered. One MP, Duncan Innes, appeared to have a special interest in the stone as a historian, and might have taken the lead in making off with it.

In Edinburgh, the police were on the case. Otherwise, of those not part of the plot, only six people – or nine including the stewards who had discovered the theft – knew that the stone had gone. Only two people – he and Morag – had so far guessed who had taken it. The rest, not least the police, were baffled.

"Do you know why they did it, Morag?"

"No. Unless Duncan put them up to it. He's always thought the stone should never have come back to Scotland."

"Why not?"

"Well, two reasons. One, it had more historic symbolism where it was at Westminster: it was there longer than anywhere else – seven centuries. That's quite powerful, isn't it? Two, he's convinced it works."

"Works?"

"Yes. He believes it has mystic – magic – powers, important for Scotland. As far as he's concerned, London's where it benefits us most. He says look what happened after it came north – we've no one in the British government any more."

"Well, that ties in with the mood of our MPs. They're all disgruntled and resentful. No one listens to them any more, and they've nothing much to do. So d'you think the idea's to make a fool of the Scottish Executive?"

"Maybe. But Duncan . . ." Morag hesitated, searching the floor, the walls, the windows with her eyes.

"Go on. What's really driving him?"

"Haven't you guessed, Dr Mackay?"

"No."

She thought for a few seconds, then spoke in a low voice.

"It's because of his father. You were listening to Dr Innes. The two of them have been arguing about the stone for years. Duncan says the one in Edinburgh's genuine – Alexander the Third's throne and all that. Dr Innes says it's rubbish, that Edward the First was fobbed off with a fake, and that it has no special properties at all."

"Is it a serious quarrel?"

"Mmm. Academic disputes outside a family are bad enough. Inside, it can get quite unpleasant. But sometimes I think they enjoy it. For myself, I couldn't bear it."

"You mean that's what you and Duncan split over?"

"I told him I hated that kind of bitterness, and that he was causing it, and that until he sorted out his relations with his father . . ." She fell silent.

"I see." He wondered what else she had to say.

"Well, of course that wasn't the only thing. There was another woman after Duncan, and I told him he had to choose. She's gone now, but it took too long. The quarrel with his father was bad – but I suppose it was more of an excuse."

"You never took sides?"

"I've been very careful not to, in case – "

"Yes?"

" – in case . . . well, it wouldn't help anything, would it?"

"What would Dr Innes say if he knew that Duncan – ?"

"It would be awful. He would be terribly shocked. You mustn't tell him!"

"Where d'you think Duncan's taken the stone? Westminster?"

"Very likely, if he's trying to prove something either to his father or to the other MPs."

"King Edward's chair is still there, empty, waiting. The stone is supposed to be taken down and put back there each time there's a coronation."

"There'd be no point in putting it in the chair right now. It'd be found and brought up to Edinburgh again. That wouldn't prove a thing."

"It might make the Scottish Executive look silly."

"Duncan'd only call that a useful by-product. No – he'll hide it somewhere clever. His project would need time."

"What are we to do, Morag?" asked Mackay. "Of course, we could just do nothing, wait for the hue and cry to begin, and see whether so many people can keep a secret and for how long. That would sort things out."

"It certainly would," said Morag gloomily. "The Chief Constable was right. Someone's bound to talk. And Duncan's going to end up in prison."

"Not alone, though!"

"I wouldn't be so sure. Think of the damage it would do if fifty-nine Scottish MPs were locked up in Barlinnie. Duncan knows that. It'd be like him to take the entire blame for the lot of them, and I bet they wouldn't stop him. Anyway, it wouldn't get the stone back – for Duncan the stone's the one thing that can keep the Union together, so long as it's at Westminster."

"Would you mind if Duncan went to prison?"

"Yes."

"All right, Morag. What are we to do?"

"We've got to find the stone before he hides it, Dr Mackay."

"How? I could confront Andy Wedderburn – have it out with him – threaten to expose him unless he puts the stone back."

"There's a problem with that. And now the press are on to it, Oor Wullie – Mr McNish – says. None of our Westminster MPs is talking to the Holyrood ones."

"Not even to me?" asked Mackay in surprise. "I hadn't noticed." He reflected. "Yes, it could be true – I haven't heard from any of them for weeks and weeks, and that's unusual. Still, Andy's an old friend –"

"So you're going to clype on him?"

"Confront him, I thought."

"It won't get you anywhere. Duncan's a professional –"

"Professional thief? Gangster? Blackmailer? Extortionist?"

"Of course not!" said Morag, shocked. "He's a soldier! He's trained in special operations. No one'll know anything who doesn't need to know. It wouldn't be safe to tell someone in Mr Wedderburn's position where the stone is now. And it wouldn't be fair."

"Goodness me!" said Mackay. "Oor Wullie's surely lucky to have you as his special adviser. Well, have you a better idea?"

Distress had returned to Morag's face. Her better idea was why she had come to see the Presiding Officer.

"Yes. Duncan. I suppose I'll have to get in touch with him after all."

Mackay nodded. He had been waiting for her to say that. "Would you mind very much?"

"We decided we wouldn't make contact with each other for three years. That was two years ago."

"I won't put any pressure on you, Morag."

"I know, Dr Mackay. I'm grateful. But you know this is too important."

Janet went to her party conference in Brighton in early October, along with the dozen or so other MPs from Scotland of the same political persuasion. None of them enjoyed it. The silent criticism from their English colleagues was no doubt irrational. They were not responsible for Holyrood's continued incursions into British affairs, nor for the tendency of a regional government to introduce measures from which it alone drew the benefit but for which, as often as not, the entire nation was expected to pay. Yet resentment was growing; and Scotland's MPs were found guilty by association. And that was only half the story. Whereas the members from north of the Border felt deeply their lack of consequence or recognition on the Westminster scene, those from south of it looked on them with scorn because of their limited power and with irritation because of the capriciousness of their voting capability.

That poor regard was reflected on the conference platform. The motions they had tabled, for example on European affairs, were not called. The Scots were not acceptable as suitable speakers from the floor in any of the main domestic debates, because as usual these were about devolved matters. They felt no great inclination to speak in the lesser debates, chiefly because so few of their constituents had thought it worth while to come all the way to Brighton.

They met in a private room where Campbell Macarthur, after double-checking the security measures, and assuring everyone that the meeting was not happening, enquired on behalf of them all whether Janet had anything she would have wished to report to the policy committee, had it been convened. She replied guardedly that all was under control and running to plan; and that she knew she could rely on the continued patience, confidence and silence of everyone present. Macarthur then wound up the meeting and, without actually saying so, left no one in any doubt that there would be another all-party meeting of Scottish MPs early in the next session of parliament. Janet went out to the sea-front and rang Duncan on her mobile telephone.

"It's terrible here, Duncan."

"All party conferences are terrible."

"Brighton in October!"

"Better than Blackpool."

"They hate us," said Janet, coming to the point. "They won't let us speak. They think the constitution has been ruined and that Scotland is the only place that benefits."

"They're right. Their patience is running out. We always said that would happen. Why don't you join my party?"

"Would that help?"

"Well, it would double our MPs in the Commons at a stroke."

"Yes, but the entire membership could still get on one motorbike!"

"Or even better, into one bed. Why don't you come back to Edinburgh?"

"I'm a Whip, so I'll have to stick around till it's over. Only a couple of days. But we'll have another week before the House goes back."

"Good," said Duncan. "Because I've worked out when we deliver. It's full of symbolism."

"Symbolism?"

"The historic kind. What were you thinking of?"

The First Minister sat in an armchair in his office, editing the third draft of his speech. The debate was tomorrow. His ball-point had dried up again, probably because of the angle at which he held it. He was resentful that his Minister for Public Affairs, properly responsible for the record-breaking run of the parliamentary building farce, was visiting one of the Baltic states, leaving him alone on the battlements reviewing his options.

The opposition parties, he still hoped, would pull their punches, first, in respect of capital costs. Even after so many years, the parliament's construction was still incomplete; but all MSPs, evidently enough, must benefit eventually from the half-finished new extension, a generous extra reception facility in which visitors would be able to admire holograms of every member, buy mugs with pictures of the Holyrood parliamentary complex on one side and individual MSPs' portraits on the other, and perhaps listen

99

to edited recordings of their chosen speeches before being ushered into the public seats in the chamber.

Nor had he too much to fear from critics within the Holyrood compound of the constantly rising current expenditure. This embraced the recently "improved" salaries of members and their secretariats and of the assembly staff; the wages of the security officers, porters and cleaners; the subsidies going to the bars, restaurant and canteen; the massive, recurring printing bill; and the travel expenses of MSPs throughout Scotland and, for that matter, Europe. More controversially and to the public's disgust, it included the huge supplementary pensions and severance payments made to former ministers, including First Ministers, who had been forced to retire from the executive or sacked either for incompetence or for the financial misdemeanours commoner in local council affairs.

The executive was more vulnerable regarding ministerial cars. However, it had long since been recognised that the only practical way to cut down on them was to reduce the number of ministers, which meant trouble in cabinet. Anyway, the rules governing these outgoings had been decreed by the original Scotland Act, so that only Westminster could put a stop to them.

The new problem, McNish realised, was that a second front was expanding on which disaffected MSPs could with greater impunity assault the executive for financial imprudence – the things that were going wrong. That would produce rancour enough.

The first batch of the new parliament's technological teething troubles turned out to be what any cynic (and there were many about) could have predicted – the electronic voting system which invited impassioned complaints from MSPs who believed, often correctly, that their votes had been misrecorded; the smart pass cards – for use when biometric devices failed – which made fuses blow and passage impossible; the monitor screens in members' offices which could not be seen either from their desks or their daybeds; the climate control system which, delivering a range of atmospheric conditions from the Arctic to the Saharan, inexplicably concentrated on those extremes. For the past two years, hardly a month had passed in Scotland but the public was scandalised by stories of parliamentary luxuries or electronic novelties replaced because they did not work or – like the desk-top minibars

– were deemed inadequate for members' needs. In those cases, the executive was criticised not only by the press but by MSPs suffering both popular obloquy and physical inconvenience.

Now there were instances of granite cladding coming loose from the concrete fabric in the main concourse; of flooding in the members' carpark; of suspected dry rot in Queensberry House. The landscaping had been an aesthetic catastrophe. Controversy was growing over the provision of facilities for oecumenical worship, in particular the proposed mosque to be located discreetly behind the twice-replaced amenity trees in the soft landscape – the necessary corollary to the Chapel for Reflection installed in the MSPs' building. On top of other misfortunes, the arrangements for wheelchair access to these amenities had been overlooked. Traffic congestion in the Canongate, which aroused the ire of ordinary citizens who lived or worked locally, was a further problem, intermittently compounded by bomb scares. It was aggravated by the growing number of tourist buses short of parking space, and would provide ammunition for those who, even at this stage, still argued for a move to the old Royal High School on Calton Hill where the congestion would probably be much worse.

It was no use to lay these failings at the door of the opposition, or to reproach the dead architect, or to turn the problems over to the all-party committee which was supposed to monitor the progress of the works. If he blamed the builders – those which had not gone into liquidation – they would probably sue. McNish considered the traditional resort of heaping coals of fire on the Westminster administration which had wished the Scottish Parliament into being and cut its funding when it most needed it. But that was a ploy favoured by the Nationalists. Better to parade his regrets that Scotland's MPs in the South had exerted so little influence on the British exchequer to ensure the well-being and dignity of Holyrood. They had not lifted a finger – at least no such event had been reported – to prevent the reduction of the block grant to Scotland. They did not protest, so far as anyone in Scotland discovered from her national press, when English MPs criticised the Scottish Executive for exceeding its theoretical remit. In fact, the more he thought about it, the more the MPs looked like a soft target. Had not Ross Burton, the man from *The Herald*, more of less asked who they thought they were? Or put the question into his mouth? Maybe it was someone else. Anyway, the question had come up.

The First Minister made circular scribbles with his pen to get it writing again, and put down some more notes which he hoped Morag would later be able to decipher and the speech writers to incorporste. Here was a rich vein to exploit. Especially when the opposition were calling a vote of no-confidence, he saw no reason to use a debate like this to restore any of the love lost between Scotland's representatives in Holyrood and Westminster. After all, there was more than the poor performance of the parliamentary fabric for which the Scottish Executive would find a scapegoat useful. However, exactly how he could blame Scotland's MPs for the loss of the Stone of Scone he could not imagine.

Anyway, as well as stirring up the MSPs against their own countrymen he would throw them a bone – one that wouldn't cost too much. Every member was already awarded a parliamentary medal as a matter of course: what about a bar to it for each term served? Or, better, some new facility for their comfort.

It was late on Thursday afternoon. Duncan gazed round his flat in Drummond Place. He was fond of it, having had it since his days as a mature student at Edinburgh University; and he reflected that nothing much had changed in it since then, not even the carpet. The sitting room was of generous proportions, the single bedroom big enough for a large double bed, and the kitchen sufficient for a dining table as well as the usual necessary appointments. An estate agent would have claimed that the property benefited from a fine view to the north over the Forth; and might have mentioned, too, the exceptional luminescence of the rooms – for bright daylight shone straight through from the south, at any rate when the internal doors were open. Its worst features were the ageing wallpaper and hangings, the unremarkable furniture, and – for the unfit – the high ceilings of the floors below, characteristic of that part of Edinburgh, which necessitated an exceptionally long climb up the stone staircase to reach his door. When he had visitors, they often arrived panting and with their hearts beating fast.

The doorbell rang, signifying a caller in the street below. Duncan went to the telecom at his flat door, pressed a button and said "Hullo? Who is it?"

"Duncan? It's me."

"Morag! We said –"

"I know. But this doesn't count. I've got to see you."

"What's it about?"

"I'll tell you in a minute."

He paused before saying "All right, come up" and pressing a second button which buzzed. It would take Morag at least a minute and a half to climb the stairs. He used that time swiftly to clear newspapers from the sofa and crockery from the table and to check on his own appearance too. He had no idea what had brought her here, and waited for her footsteps, opening the door as she reached the top steps.

Duncan knew the sight of her would upset him. Her colouring was always striking, but now, with cheeks lightly flushed from the climb, her face no less than her figure was set off to perfection by the high-necked black sweater she wore above her fawn jeans.

"Hullo," he said. "Did you have to come looking like that?"

"Like what? Oh. Well, you still look pretty good yourself." Her eyes roved quickly round a room long familiar to her, then turned to meet his. Both were wary, and neither allowed any emotion to show.

"Tell me why you're here, then."

She put her bag on the sofa. "The stone."

"The what?"

"You've to put it back. Now."

"I don't know what you're –"

"You've never told me a lie in your life, Duncan, so keep it like that, please. Where is it?"

He looked at her. She had moved to the window where she stood in silhouette, the sinking sun lighting up a russet halo round her head. He found it hard to maintain any coldness in his voice.

"Safe," he said at last. "What d'you know about it?"

"Everything, except where it is."

"Everything? How did you find out?"

"If you send silly messages to the First Minister in Latin with your fingerprints all over them, someone's bound to guess where they come from. You probably didn't know I'm his special adviser."

"I didn't. Oor Wullie! Why on earth d'you work for a man like that?"

"He must need me, d'you think?"

"So he knows the stone's gone?"

"Yes, they know. They know the one there's a fake. And they know how you did it."

Duncan considered that, his brow knitted.

"So why haven't they told the police?"

"They have."

"Well, why hasn't it been in the papers? Why haven't we been arrested? What are they playing at?"

"What are you playing at? What did you do it for, Duncan? You and all you other . . . politicians!" She spat out the "p." There was a catch in her voice. "You'll end up in prison!"

Duncan took a step towards her.

"No," she said sharply. "Stay where you are. How did you persuade them all to steal it?"

"We haven't stolen it – not in that sense. We're relocating it where it should be."

"You're like children! Suppose the press discover that fifty-nine MPs have – "

"Now I understand." said Duncan. "You know who did it. But no one else does. Am I right?"

"No, you're wrong, so it'll be no use gagging me and putting me in a cupboard. But Oor Wullie doesn't know who did it. And the police don't know. And the castle people don't know. So you can still put it back and I can promise you no one'll say anything."

"And if I don't put it back? Will you tell Oor Wullie it was me?"

"No. Nor the police."

"Thank you, Morag."

Her eyes narrowed. "But I'll tell your father."

For the first time, Duncan looked alarmed.

"Morag! You couldn't do that."

"No? Where is it now?"

"Not here. It's in London. Look – this isn't reversible. It's going ahead. Anyway, it isn't just me."

"Of course not. Somebody else made the fake stone. Who was that?"

"I mean we were all in it together. The decision's not only mine. It's not coming back to Edinburgh. Anyway, you know how I feel about it. I'm doing this because it must be done."

The door bell rang from the street below.

"And that's why I'll be speaking to your father," said Morag. Duncan was about to protest again, but she inclined her head towards the bell. "Hadn't you better answer that?"

Duncan gave her a long, angry look before crossing to the door and pushing the telecom button.

"Who's that?"

"It's me. Janet." The voice was disembodied but clear. "It ended a day early, thank God, my darling. Let me in."

"Oh. Right. Um –"

"Well, press the thing . . . Okay . . . and I think you'll need to help me up with my case. It's full of conference papers I haven't had time to dump."

Duncan looked round warily, knowing Morag had listened. She was watching him steadily, her mouth slightly pursed.

"I'll be down in a moment," he said into the telecom, then turned back to Morag.

"Go on then," she said. "Help the lady up with her case."

"Morag – it's a colleague –"

"It sounded just like one. Don't be embarrassed."

"Would you like to –"

"No, I'm not going to be hustled past her down the stairs. But I'll leave as soon as you get back with her."

"You'd no business coming here without warning." His tone was defensive.

"I told you this doesn't count. I'm not prying into your private life. Carry on with it. Sounds fun."

He went to the door, stopped and looked back.

"And you must keep my father out of this."

"Not me. Only you can do that. And I'll tell you how long you've got when you come upstairs again."

She heard his quick steps going down the stairs, and an impatient exclamation down the stairwell from the hall. She took a deep breath, walked unhappily towards the familiar mantelpiece and looked at herself in the glass above it before doing some quick work with a comb. Her eyes then moved curiously along the shelf, taking in several outdated invitation cards to political functions, a stopwatch, three bars of KitKat, a service medal, and a jumble of knick-knacks including some she had once contributed herself. They stopped and opened wide on encountering a little mound of assorted keys. Two of them had tags attached and were on a single key-ring.

On reaching the top of the stairs, followed by Duncan with her suitcase, Janet walked straight through the door and stopped short. Whatever whispered briefing Duncan had given her on the way up, she had not expected to find there anyone with such obvious animal attraction as the tall, slim, long-legged woman standing by the window with the light on her. Morag, no less displeased and disconcerted, and for the same reason, recovered her poise first and came forward.

"How d'you do? I'm called Morag. I'm . . . well, a family friend."

Duncan confirmed that, and tried to explain that Janet Ross was the MP for Tinto Hill, contriving to make it sound like an excuse.

"I'm sorry," said Janet, managing a thin smile, "if I've interrupted anything private."

"Not at all. I'm on my way out anyway, aren't I, Duncan?" Morag smiled back at Janet and glanced at her suitcase. "I know you'll be comfortable here."

She picked up her bag from the sofa and went to the door.

"What we were talking about, Duncan: let's say the end of October, shall we? Nearly three weeks. But, of course, if I can be of any further assistance in the meantime, please don't hesitate to be in touch. As they say," she added.

She smiled brightly at him, closed the door behind her, and ran all the way down the stairs and out into the street. There she burst into tears.

6

SPARSELY POPULATED, the press gallery looked down on the half-dozen semi-circles of seats reserved for Scotland's ruling classes. These, too, were thinly occupied, it being that stage in the afternoon when it was credible for MSPs to plead that they were keeping an eye on and an ear to the proceedings through the closed-circuit monitors in their offices. That it was also possible to tune those monitors to everything from CNN news reports to feature films, football, golf, quiz games and other entertainments was not a consideration likely to occur to enthusiasts for Scottish politics thronging the public gallery. In fact there were none there; and the nearest approach to a throng was a small party of school children for whom a visit to Holyrood was something of a treat. They had smuggled in packets of crisps and were passing them to and fro along the glass balcony, causing a thin, intermittent shower of roast potato crumb to fall to the chamber below.

Despite weak public interest and professional absenteeism, the debate, as McNish had expected, was a rancorous affair. Against predictions the building costs over the years were raked through again, though briefly. That entailed a short wrangle between the front benches over whether, so far, the aggregate bill had exceeded the original estimate by forty times (as the opposition alleged) or by only six times (the executive's calculation). The Presiding Officer, interrupting, pointed out that it depended on which of the several original estimates you chose, adding jocularly, but in McNish's opinion unhelpfully, that whether or not the parliament was a world-class building it was incontrovertibly a world-class price.

Jock Hamilton, however, leading the main attack with unwonted vigour, eschewed any reference to costs. He quickly deplored the

107

lengthy list of technological and constructional failures which still featured regularly in the press, then turned to a stinging criticism of the whole design. He condemned it on grounds of utility – the debating chamber was positioned in the complex as far away from members' offices as it was possible to be; on grounds of taste – although its ungainly sprawl, he said, could only be seen in its entirety from Arthur's Seat, which he would avoid in the future; on grounds of culture – for it disgraced its historic setting; and on grounds of professional inadequacy – no architect with a classical training would have dared to assemble so many amorphous, meaningless hulks in one place, pointing in every direction, and then to present them as a coherent creation. The result lacked shape, proportion, probity, dignity, compatibility, and memorability. If the Scottish people tried to visualise their parliament, he maintained, a litter of hungry piglets at supper time would swim into their mind; or perhaps a fishing harbour after a hurricane. If this was a signature building on a world heritage site, it was one that no one could read.

This was old ground: the aesthetic merits and demerits of the building had wearied its critics and admirers into silence soon after its opening. The dozen or so backbench members who hoped to intervene against the executive later paid small attention to Hamilton's words until they became conscious of a strange drift in his rhetoric, sensing the discomfort of having their own cultural shortcomings challenged. After a short discourse on forgotten episodes in Scottish history, the leader of the opposition began to drop the names of remembered or half-remembered architects in ever-larger packets too turgid to mean anything.

What a reflection this bleak story cast, Hamilton ventured, on the noble tradition of Thomas Hamilton – he who built the Royal High School (but not a relation, he insisted modestly) – and of "Greek" Thompson, and of Charles Rennie Mackintosh! What a slur on the legacy of Robert Adam, of Robert Hutchinson, and of Robert Lorimer! It must already be disturbing the last sleep, he opined, of giants like William Adam, William Atkinson, William Bruce, William Burn, William Chambers, William Playfair and William Wilkins. Who would answer, he wished to know, to the ghosts of James Adam, James Craig, James Gibbs, James Gillespie, James Milne, James Smith, James Stuart, James White or James Wyatt?

Sandra had come into the public gallery when her monitor revealed her employer to be on his feet in the chamber. She had expected him to expatiate on the virtues of at most three of the Scottish architects from the alphabetical list of names with which she had been at some pains to supply him. Now she put her hand over her face. Somewhere in the chamber a voice said it thought it was falling asleep. The Presiding Officer took note of the growing restlessness of the members present and called Hamilton to order, requiring him to address the subject of the debate, the parliament's finances.

"This sorry saga", Hamilton persisted, "illustrates the lamentable state of Scottish education today. Our culture, our history, our values – the values, for example, of the Enlightenment – have all been sacrificed on the – "

The Presiding Officer called Hamilton to order again. But the peroration was ending, with only a concluding thought to come.

"Is it too late", Hamilton demanded, his eye roving round his expressionless audience, "even now to abandon a building whose construction promises no end, to remodel it as a hotel and conference centre, and to move back where we came from – to the old Scottish Parliament in Parliament Square beside St Giles'?"

He sat down. In the press gallery Ross Burton, looking in on his way from the Pint o' Wine to a cigarette outside at the water feature, marked the friendly nod Hamilton's speech earned from the SEP leader Walter Moncrieff. James Maclean and Gordon Boyle, recalling the views of the shadow cabinet, stared at each other dumbfounded. A move to the old parliament had never been discussed: their leader was making policy on the hoof. Meanwhile, an impromptu eruption of applause seemed to come from the public seats. Hamilton looked up in gratification, only to see that the party of schoolchildren, fatigued beyond endurance by the proceedings, had all blown up their now empty paper bags and were bursting them in a protracted *feu de joie*, sending clouds of potato crumb into the air above the balcony. Parliamentary staff were already hurrying along the gangways to admonish and eject them.

"I know it's hardly six o'clock, Duncan, but I think I need a drink."

Duncan poured some whisky for both of them, each with a splash of tap water.

"That conference was ghastly," Janet continued, lowering herself onto the sofa, kicking off her shoes, leaning back and putting her feet up. "A horrible atmosphere for us. I got a lift to Gatwick, and hadn't time to ring. My mobile's flat. Sorry."

There was silence until Duncan, his back against the mantelpiece, addressed what they were both thinking about. He tried to keep his voice matter-of-fact.

"Morag works in the Scotch Parliament – for McNish, in fact, though I wasn't aware of it."

"Morag McLeod, isn't she?"

"How d'you know that?"

"I told you, Duncan. We had all their names in the Whip's office. Wasn't she your last bidie-in? She's certainly very attractive. I thought your affair with her was over."

"One: it's over, so don't get brittle about it. Two: she came to tell me –"

"Tell you what?"

"To put the stone back."

"How does she know?" said Janet, sitting up. "Well, never mind: that can wait. What does she want?"

"What d'you mean?"

"I mean, where she's coming from, what's driving her. Why does she mind about the stone? What was that about the end of October?"

"A sort of deadline. Look: it's like this. They know the stone's gone. McNish knows. The police apparently know how we did it, too, and when. Those alarms going off, I imagine: they'll have worked that out. But they don't know who took it, so we did a good job on the cameras."

"I thought you said –"

"Yes, Morag knows. She seems to have guessed. I don't know how. She may be acting on her own, but I'm not sure. Anyway, she's not telling anyone she can't trust – yet. That's why she was here."

"You mean she's blackmailing you!"

"No. That's not right."

"Isn't it? Well, is she working with the police? And why haven't they told the world? If they know it's been stolen, they should be looking for us. Why aren't they?"

"I can't imagine, Janet. Perhaps your fake stone is so realistic they think they can afford to play a waiting game. Perhaps they hope someone talks. I suppose the chances are pretty good, with so many involved. How long they wait doesn't matter to us so long as our lot keep their mouths shut, and so long as Morag doesn't tell them – and she won't."

"Can you keep her quiet?"

"No. Perhaps. I don't know. Anyway it's not relevant."

"Well, what do we do?"

"Our plan was – is – to hide the stone permanently somewhere in the Palace of Westminster or the precincts of the Abbey as soon as parliament starts again. There are several possible places. And we'll have to do it alone."

"What about the others? I left our people in Brighton in no doubt they'd be hearing from us. They're quite jumpy, so we ought to involve them."

"Well, we can't use the same method as before," said Duncan, thinking aloud, "because we don't want fifty-seven others knowing its final resting-place. But we could use them – a large crowd of visitors whom nobody recognises, creating a diversion."

"I'd like that," said Janet, "so long as they don't get arrested and identified."

"Agreed. But it's not such a big deal this time. Nobody guards against the return of stolen goods."

"When do we move?"

"I'd thought of November 13, the day before the Queen's Speech."

"Why?"

"It's the anniversary of when they took it away in 1996."

"That was your historic symbolism?"

"Yes. But the secret isn't safe any more. So we'll have to move faster, at any rate to get the stone off our hands. We'd better go south next week. Sunday, if possible."

"I must get out of these clothes and have a bath," said Janet. "You could bring me another whisky while I'm having it. Then let's go and have supper somewhere. Then let's sleep on it."

So they did, but Duncan's heart wasn't really in it.

As voting time approached – hardly a threat, for the opposition would take care not to carry the vote of no-confidence because that would only bring the parliament further into disrepute – two or three dozen more MSPs drifted into the chamber from their offices and from the bars and coffee counters devoted to their refreshment. They had read, mostly with scorn, a note circulated earlier by the executive to say that plans were being considered to increase by half a dozen the parking spaces available for members – First Ministers never forgot them when times were hard, and it would only mean another small turn of the screw on business rates.

The press gallery, too, had become slightly more populous, for it was generally possible for political correspondents to concoct a readable story out of a minister wriggling on a hook, even an old one, and the public liked that sort of thing.

Rising to wind up the debate, and long irritated by the harangues of his enemies, William McNish had resolved to make no more promises about when the parliament would finally be completed: its Catalan architect, after all, had held that works of art were never finished. He would give no more guarantees that the voting electronics, the air-conditioning or the very lavatories would work. Nor would he be drawn on the ultimate cost. Contumely had been heaped on the building as on the executive, but nothing new had been said, and no more polished or original insult had been delivered than had been heard a few years earlier at the Fraser Inquiry and, indeed, the one that followed it: the only difference was that, then, the nightmare was merely in prospect, whereas now this derided, increasingly dysfunctional extravagance was a reality.

McNish, without consulting his officials, had sharpened his chosen line of attack. He would create a diversion, introduce controversial assertions to set new hares running and the press pounding in pursuit. And he would thus take the heat off himself and his ministers by channelling public anger against that body of men and women who had most failed the Scottish people in their hour of need, bringing ridicule on their elected leaders. That would strike a note to which the whole parliament, surely, would warmly respond.

Oratorically he stalked his prey, perhaps less like a leopard than a hyena, circling round those who being absent were in no position to reply, putting questions which raised suspicions but admitted of no answers, dropping hints which stoked the imagination while withholding any evidence that might have lent them substance.

That, at any rate, was his intention. For a time, his listeners wondered whom on earth he was talking about.

It became clear. The parliament building, its site, its size, its pretensions and its architect, had been wished on Scotland by Westminster. Unable to dictate the terms of the contract, presented with a bill which no one had contested, the Scottish taxpayer had been required to sign the cheque. It should not be supposed, McNish contended, that this represented a new English perfidy. Far from it; and he would leave it to politicians of a nationalist bent to pursue divisive, xenophobic arguments of that nature. No one needed reminding, he said, but he would remind them just the same, that the government who drove through the devolution of power to Scotland consisted largely of Scots.

"And more power to them!" he cried. "Their hearts were where hearts should be."

"Aye, i' the Hielans, a-chasin' the deer," came a suggestion from the back benches.

"Chasin' the deer's bin banned!" came an objection from opposite.

"Order!" commanded the Presiding Officer, quietening the rising titter. "The Minister has the right to be heard."

However, if the First Minister were to hold members' attention it was time to name names, or at least to hint at them. Scotland's quarrel, McNish asserted, was not with the government of the United Kingdom. No – it was with those who had failed, and were even now failing, to persuade that government to see the thing through. Scotland's enemy was within, he declared. Her representatives in Westminster – all of them, irrespective of party – had conspired to withhold the resources essential to launch and sustain a devolved parliament (but he did not explain how he knew that). The block grant had melted like an iceberg in the Gulf Stream, and they had done nothing to salvage it (but he did not suggest what they might have tried). Both individually and collectively, they had forsaken their roots – in fact they had gone native. It was the most poisonous and damaging accusation that any politician could level at another.

Notwithstanding the grotesqueness of these charges, there was an audible groundswell of approval from the chamber, now more than half filled. Here was a line of argument with which few MSPs would wish to quarrel. All who had Westminster counterparts were experiencing icy relations with them. The correspondents in the press gallery leant forward in the confident expectation that the First Minister would soon say something even sillier. Television cameras had him in their sights. Ross Burton feared the worst.

The First Minister's voice was rising. If a reason was sought for the physical shortcomings of Holyrood, he challenged, if blame had to rest anywhere for the lack of funds and the levy of taxes, why look further than to the MPs who, in pursuit of some unspecified agenda of their own, daily stabbed their electors in the back?

"This is Scotland's parliament!" he thundered. "This is the seat of Scotland's government! When Scotland speaks, it must be the voice of Holyrood!" There were cheers and desk-banging from all parties, except the SEP who looked on wearily. "We won't have our position usurped by a few dozen assorted time-servers with long holidays and too little to do, living it up in London and giving themselves airs at our expense! They are not only out of touch with us: they are out of touch with the people!"

Members began to beat their desks in approval. It was the sort of oratory – aggressive, cumulative and spiteful – that McNish excelled at, for on his day he could rouse a rabble as effectively as anybody.

"None of them has been given as much as a junior ministry to look after," McNish spat contemptuously. "They have nothing to contribute. We've heard the stories about their private lives. We know about their expense accounts. We've seen them posturing on television. We've had enough! So this is the question all Scotland is asking – "

He paused for the maximum effect, while the whole chamber and all the journalists in the press gallery – apart for Ross Burton, who had guessed – wondered wildly what enquiry could be on every lip. The First Minister spoke again. He lowered his voice to a slow Churchillian growl and said: "Who do they think they are?"

McNish sat down. For a moment there was silence. Then loud applause erupted from his own benches, with murmurs and nods of agreement from others. He had successfully switched the minds of the chamber from affairs of substance to matters of prejudice; and when the Presiding Officer called for the vote to take place, there were too few opposition MSPs present to make a contest of the result.

"Right!" thought Ross Burton, looking down at the executive front bench in disillusion bordering on disgust. "I warned you. You've asked for it, and you have it coming."

The telephone was trilling when the Presiding Officer returned to his office, relieved to escape the laminated oak beams and stainless steel nodes of the debating chamber and stultified by two hours in the chair. Today's performance had been reprehensible; and having to pay professional attention to a combination of the parochial, the predictable and the petulant, he had discovered, stretched his patience to the limit at the best of times. Had he been a drinking man, he would have kept brandy in the cupboard in his desk with frequent recourse to it. Now he eyed the telephone with mistrust, but finally picked it up.

"It's a Professor Innes," said his secretary. "He rang earlier. Can I put him through to you?"

Mackay brightened. There was a real world outside, and it had not forgotten him.

"Of course!" he said, ignoring the poverty of her syntax. He waited for the ethereal pips and clicks which characterised Holyrood's state-of-the-art switching system. "Dr Innes?"

"Dr Mackay? Forgive my disturbing you in parliament. Something very interesting has come up. Have you a moment to talk about it?"

"My time is yours, Dr Innes. And, frankly, it's a relief to hear the voice of sanity. What is it?"

"When you came to see me with young Morag McLeod not long ago, I mentioned an informal academic project I was engaged in, in connection with the Coronation Stone. Oh, it was only an exercise to explore an idea, but . . . well, these kinds of activities sometimes have surprising results."

"I'm hanging on your words."

"I've been working with two young graduates at the university, one a geologist and the other an archaeologist, who like me have long been curious about the stone. We thought we would test out one of the theories which I think I put to you – the romantic notion that it was brought from the Holy Land and that it may once have been part of an asteroid, in fact a meteorite. You will

115

recall that heavenly objects which landed were much venerated fifteen hundred years ago."

"I remember you said that."

"Meteorites, if they fall to earth without being vaporised on the way down – they're travelling at forty times the speed of sound when they catch up with us, and then have to decelerate – are pretty hard to find if you don't see them fall, even the big ones. But there are two areas where it seems to be much easier."

"Oh?" said Mackay. "Where are they?"

"The polar regions are one: in Antarctica, old falls of meteorites become exposed from time to time. In the Arctic you can pick them out on frozen snow. The Eskimos – we are supposed to call them Inuits these days, aren't we? – have carved things out of them for centuries. This is what my geological associate tells me."

"You can carve meteorites?"

"Yes – the stone ones. The metal ones are a different story. But I'm coming to that. The other good hunting ground is the desert – anywhere from Australia to the Middle East, it seems, you can see them against the sand, so long as they aren't buried. The wind uncovers them. That's mere circumstantial corroborative detail, of course, but not unimportant."

"It's certainly very interesting. Please go on."

"Well, there's a third general class of meteorite composition, neither pure stone nor pure metal but something in between, called 'stony-iron'. It's fairly rare. But, now, if we were looking for a large lump of meteorite, carved into something like an altar or a chair and polished to look like black marble, it is clear that the stony-iron variety would meet the bill. Even in Roman times, tools were well up to that sort of thing."

Intrigued as he was, Mackay wondered where all this was leading.

"I'm most interested, Dr Innes. But tell me, what would be the significance if the stone were made partly of iron?"

"I'm afraid I'm trying your patience!"

"Of course not. But you said that something had come up."

"I wanted to take you through the argument. D'you know what I mean by a magnetometer?"

"Isn't it for detecting things under things?"

"Exactly. It's revolutionised archaeology. You can even use it for underwater surveys. Now, if a large buried object has a significant ferrous component –"

"– such as a stony-iron meteorite –"

"Yes! And especially if it happens to have acquired magnetic properties too – then new opportunities open for us. My archaeological associate has one – a magnetometer. We were out last week-end. Funnily enough, the first clue we had was when my own pocket compass began to point the wrong way."

Mackay was convinced that the detail could wait. By now only one question needed answering.

"Just tell me, Dr Innes – have you found the stone?"

"No."

"No?"

"But we think we know precisely where it is."

"Where?"

"I'd better not say over the telephone. And, of course, we could be entirely mistaken. Dr Mackay, this is Thursday – can you make yourself free this weekend? I have a rendezvous with my collaborators on Saturday about two hours' drive from Edinburgh. They'll have the equipment we need."

"I want to be there."

"I thought so. I think I can promise you, at worst, a bracing walk to one of the finest panoramas outside the Highlands; and at best – well, perhaps the archaeological discovery of our lives!"

"I need no more persuasion! When do we start?"

They agreed on an early departure on Saturday morning in Innes's car, since he had further to come. Mackay believed he could pledge that Mrs Mackay would provide a picnic for four. They would both swear their wives to secrecy about what they were up to. They would take boots and warm clothes.

"One more thing," said Innes. "I'm sure our young friend Morag would be interested too, and would know how to keep quiet about it. There's room for her in the car if she'd like it. And she could bring her camera for the record. It would mean a picnic for five. She works there in Holyrood, doesn't she? Would you like to ask her?"

Although Mackay had barely considered the implications of this adventure for the theft from the castle, he was happy to have Morag fully involved.

"No one else must know," said Innes before ringing off. "For one thing, we may be making fools of ourselves."

Mackay tried Morag's extension but was connected with the First Minister's private office. Craig Millar answered.

"Morag? No – she went off early this afternoon, not feeling too well. Would you like to call back tomorrow?"

Friday morning brought *The Herald* to the Mackays' breakfast table. Mrs Mackay was nearly as tall as her husband, a handsome woman whose congenial preoccupation was the national heritage and the work of the National Trust for Scotland in particular. She had once held important positions on the various official bodies set up to safeguard Scotland's inheritance, but these had disappeared with the spectacular bonfire of quangos staged a few years earlier by the Scottish Executive against whom, with others, she consequently nurtured a grievance. It was thus with some satisfaction that she passed the newspaper over to her husband, tapping Ross Burton's front-page political column. "Look at that. 'FIRST MINISTER: PUBLIC FIGURE OR PUBLIC SPECTACLE?' Oor Wullie won't like that much."

William McNish, Mackay read, was never a man to let duty stand in the way of expedience, or to put prudence before self-interest. Petty and self-important, his understanding was confined to the small but tortuous field of Scottish poltiics, beyond which his range of interests was narrow, his information uncertain, and his mind cramped. A minister armed with these dangerous limitations had thus tackled yesterday's vote of no confidence, which he had been in no danger of losing, by declaring war on his country's MPs and holding them at fault for every ill that came Holyrood's way. Who, he had asked, did they think they were?

"Whereas wise men poured oil on troubled waters," Burton's assessment continued, "we are burdened with a First Minister who cannot see a bush fire without dousing it with petrol. He does so not only out of malice and fear, but out of stupidity. He has neither the courage of a statesman nor, except in respect of his own survival, the astuteness of a politician. Yesterday, ducking responsibility for the executive's managerial and budget short-comings, and laying it squarely on Scotland's members in Westminster, he purposely fanned the sizzling bitterness between Scotland's two disparate sets of parliamentarians. Sooner or later there will be a whirlwind to reap".

"It's the truth," Mackay said, forbearing to read the rest of the article, "though it'll be water off a duck's back. And the shame is that it was exactly what most of the MSPs wanted to hear. The ill-feeling against our MPs is building up all the time. The Enlightenment party is the only one left on speaking terms."

"Oor Wullie! I'll never know how he got the job."

"He can stir: and anyway there was no one else. He was the parliament's nominee – that is, his party's, which was the same thing."

"Surely his own cabinet can see through him?"

"Of course. But they trust each other even less. That's why he's there. And he stays there because he knows how to play on their pride and weaknesses – he learnt that when he was leader of his regional council. "

"You'll be better off for your day in Perthshire, Douglas," Mrs Mackay said, "whatever it is you're up to there."

That reminded Mackay to repeat the invitation to Morag to join the expedition. But she had telephoned McNish's private office to say she thought she was getting 'flu. They did not expect her back till early the following week.

A question formed momentarily in Mackay's mind, but he did not challenge what he had heard.

The remains of Macbeth's Castle lie on the steep conical summit of Dunsinane Hill, a few miles north-east of Scone at the southerly end of Strathmore. It is a site of notable beauty: the path up the hill from Collas village skirts a small pinewood before passing through abundant heather; and from its higher slopes one looks back north to Blairgowrie and the Highlands and south-west to Perth. From the castle itself the spectacle is fully panoramic. To the south the River Tay may be seen winding and gleaming all the way down to Dundee; while, to the west, with the aid of a map, one may locate Birnam Wood and, with a little imagination, conjure in oneself some of the foreboding with which Shakespeare endowed his villain and his wife.

The castle, like the more northerly one where Duncan met his fate, has a pleasant seat, but little else is left of it. Traces of the entrance gate and a track through it are obvious enough. There are earthwork arcs where the outer defences of fosses and ramparts stood. Inside them the space is not great: if the castle were large and strong enough to resist, as Macbeth hoped, ten thousand

English troops, it must have been built high rather than wide. Some foundation stonework is visible, but most of what is left is now covered with turf or reeds. There is no sign of a well which might have made it feasible to withstand a siege. The south face of the hill is much steeper than the north.

On a beautiful, still October Saturday morning, two grey, uncovered heads were working their way up the heather track that led to the summit. Dr Innes and Dr Mackay had left their car beside the old canvas-hooded Land Rover which they found as expected in a lay-by below. Burdened with their picnic, they were both panting a little, but they had excuses to stop and catch their breath. They paused to listen to the strange accelerating pipe of a whaup, and again to sympathise with a lame ewe tottering along the edge of reedy drainage ditch. Then they disturbed a single grouse – a declining species on Scotland's unkeepered moors – and watched it whirr angrily into the distance pursued by a couple of hen-harriers. At last they struggled to the top and into the castle premises. Their fellow treasure-seekers, Tom the archaeologist and Ian the geologist, were there before them, seated with various pieces of equipment on outspread mackintoshes and contentedly surveying with binoculars the splendid expanse of Perthshire scenery below embellished by the alternation of yellowing woods and larch and spruce plantations.

"Dr Mackay," explained Innes introducing them, "will be a useful witness to whatever we find. I hope he won't be able to believe his eyes – but we both have cameras in case. What are the chances?"

"A month ago," said Tom, "I'd have said we were cranks. Today – well, I'm not speculating." He cast a polite but dubious glance at Innes's pocket-sized camera, and patted a canvas bag beside him. "Although I just thought I'd borrow the department's new digital box of fun in case we needed a picture."

"A month ago," said Ian, "I wasn't speculating. I still think we're cranks, but harmless ones. That's progress of a sort."

"Professor Innes," Mackay said to them, "only promised me a fine view. He wouldn't say where he was bringing me, un-til half an hour ago when we left the car. What's changed in a month?"

Innes relented. The story of the 1818 discoveries in Dunsinane Hill had been too nebulous to follow up methodically. But, two weeks before, he had come across a reference to a further attempt at excavation in 1857, when the owners of the estate had found a small vaulted room not far below the summit. It had been empty save for a bronze ring shaped like a double-serpent; but might this – Innes had wondered – have been the same cavern as before, from which the stone had been removed and reportedly, but not very credibly, sent south to London? If it were the same, and if the surmise were right that in 1818 the stone had been quickly reburied to conceal it from Sir Walter Scott, then it might not be very far away. It was worth a try.

"But they didn't find it in 1857," Mackay pointed out.

Innes pointed to a hold-all Ian was now opening.

"In 1857 they didn't have what we have now. What's that thing called again, Ian? GPR? Ground Penetrating Radar, isn't it? You can hire it. It's like echo-sounding. Excellent for detecting cavities. Well, we found the vault just like that. Last week-end."

"Your compass was doing odd things, Dr Innes."

"Yes, it showed us where to start."

Mackay was wide-eyed. "You know where the vault is?"

"We'd better show him." Innes said to the others. The professor's usual urbanity, Mackay saw, was disappearing: there was no doubting his excitement, much as he tried to suppress it. "Bring the instruments and the lamps," he said to the younger men; and to Mackay: "Come this way."

They scrambled a little way down the south face of the castle mound, where Tom and Ian pulled away heather-covered turfs which hid a dark hole in the rock face, large enough to climb through.

"We had to burrow a bit to find this," Innes said.

"No one's disturbed it," said Tom. "I'll go first with the light."

As he disappeared, Ian passed him a powerful lantern which immediately lit up the cavern below. Two minutes later all four men were standing on the damp earth at one end of a small, oblong stone chamber. Its outside wall, through whose remains they had climbed, had long since collapsed, perhaps under the weight of rock and earth above. However, the remaining three walls were in good enough order to support the vault above, and towards the back of the chamber the floor was flagged and dry. Thin lime stalactites hung from the ceiling, in whose crevices nestled large, white, silky spiders' eggs.

"You see?" Innes smiled at Mackay, whose height obliged him to stoop a little. "There's life in the old castle yet."

"But not much else," said Mackay, looking round the walls. "Are we to dig up the floor?"

"Not the floor," said Innes. "I think you'd like to see the magnetometer working. Ian? It's your toy. Let's show Dr Mackay what we saw last weekend."

Ian had unpacked from the hold-all a small black metal box with knobs and dials and a folding tripod. He set it up in front of the rear wall of the chamber, turned a switch, made some adjustments, and stood back.

"That's it," he said. "We already know the vault continues back into the hill below the castle. The GPR showed us that. It must be part of the original foundations. Now, if you look at that needle as I turn the scanner from left to right, you'll see it register a substantial mass as it passes the central point. It's called a spike, or a high intensity anomaly. There! D'you see it? I'll do it again."

"Yes! What is it?" asked Mackay.

"It has to be metallic, otherwise we couldn't pick it up. But this signal's so pronounced that there's likely to be magnetic content, too. Not necessarily very strong – but it was enough to interfere with Dr Innes's compass last weekend."

"And that's all we had time for then," Innes said, "except for one thing. The walls look very old: they could date back to Macbeth himself quite easily. And you can see every stone is dressed to the same contemporary standard. They all look as though they've never been disturbed. Anyway, it was enough to fool the Victorian diggers. But we scraped away some of the mortar in each wall, just to check – and on the back wall here you can see it's not so old as on the sides: there it's just lime and sand, but here it's more like Portland cement – anyway, early nineteenth century."

"You're suggesting," said Mackay slowly, examining the mortar with the torch Innes had handed him, "that the Stone of Destiny was walled up behind this in 1818?"

"Or thereabouts."

"To stop Walter Scott finding it?"

"Possibly. But mark this: Scott's next spectacular after rediscovering the crown jewels was to organise George the Fourth's visit to Edinburgh in 1822. That was only a year after George was crowned in Westminster Abbey on King Edward's chair with the traditional stone underneath it."

"Yes," said Mackay, seeing the point, "and with Queen Caroline beating at the door of the Abbey demanding to be crowned with him. London was in riot."

"Exactly," Innes said. "The king needed a triumph in Scotland. But if what was demonstrably the real Stone of Destiny had turned up at that point, it would have cast doubt on the validity of his coronation. Scott wouldn't have dared! So maybe it was he who got it walled up again after all."

"We may never know."

Their musings were interrupted by polite throat-clearing from Tom and Ian.

"Dr Innes, we got as far as this when the light was going last Saturday," said Tom. "Shall we –"

"Yes, Tom. I think it's time to make fools of ourselves. Get the crowbars out. I'll take a photograph of the wall as it is. Dr Mackay? Would you put your hand on that stone to show the scale?"

Mackay paused. "Are we entitled to dismantle –"

Innes had anticipated the question and interrupted quickly. "I think this wall once belonged to Macbeth," he said, his voice tenser than before, "even if someone else – a Mr Nairne, I believe – may have rebuilt it almost two centuries ago."

"I see," said Mackay.

"We'll put it back again of course. I don't propose to do anything I know to be illegal. Anyway, there may be nothing there."

Mackay mentally pushed his qualms about legal niceties on to a backburner. He knew Innes's interest was as purely academic as, under normal circumstances, his own would have been. Although uncertain how discovery of another Coronation Stone might affect the political scandal he hoped to avert, he had no inclination to stand in the way. Indeed, like Innes beside him, he was already experiencing something of what Sir Walter Scott felt before opening the kist which held the crown jewels.

The first stones, levered with difficulty out of the end wall, fell to the flags below. Within ten minutes a dark void, two feet across, appeared at waist level and five minutes later had been extended upwards and downwards far enough to allow a reasonable inspection of whatever lay beyond.

"Put a lamp through, Ian," said Innes, his voice now taut with emotion. "Then tell me what's there. Nothing, I expect. You, too, Tom. Take a look with Ian, if there's room."

Innes raised his gaze to Mackay and their eyes met. In the artificial light of the large lamp in the outer chamber Mackay thought he saw fear, the fear of disappointment, in the professor's face. He tried an encouraging grin but the tension stayed unrelieved. They heard Tom's voice first, a little muffled.

"It's pretty dark. There doesn't seem to be much here – just fallen stones and – "

"No – at the back there" – this was Ian – "where's your torch? Yes! Good God!"

There was silence. Tom and Ian, the archaeologist and the geologist, pulled their heads slowly out of the hole, and two faces turned as one to Innes. They wore the broadest grins Mackay had ever seen.

After a little more work with the crowbars, it was possible to step easily into the small inner chamber. Innes went first with the large lamp, setting it down where it lit up the entire space. He stood gazing in wonder at the grey throne a few feet from him, uncertain how to react. He hardly believed what he saw, half fearing it would disappear.

"Dust!" he said suddenly. "That's what's wrong! Tom – there's some cloth in the knapsack. See what you can do."

Ian retreated to the outer chamber and returned with a towel. Innes waved him on. A few moments later the grey cubic mass had been turned into the glistening black marble chair of the ancient legend. Innes now went forward, slowly, and at last touched it himself, letting his hands slide over it, sinking to his knees – perhaps to see it more closely. He turned to look at the others.

"The Stone of Destiny," he said, his voice quavering a little. "Here it is. Here it is. The Lia Fail. At last, after seven centuries – here it is." He quickly became self-conscious and stood up, as it were to make way for Mackay, Tom and Ian to share his feelings. There were tears on his cheek.

The stone stood some fifty centimetres above the floor. It was a chair in so far as it had a marked depression in the top, sufficient to provide a seat, and a raised edge round three sides. At each corner was fixed a metal hook, discoloured and corroded but firmly secured. For all its squatness, it had a strange majesty which

124

commanded attention. The four men crouched down to examine it. Ian, the geologist, shining a torch on the surface, was the first to comment.

"Meteorite," he said, matter-of-factly. "Stony-iron, as we thought. Look – these are iron-nickel particles. Meteorites always have nickel in them. But it's quite unusual – so dark! – though some of that may be fusion crust. I'd like to see it in daylight. A mesosiderite, I suppose: that's basaltic achondrite."

"Oh? A little on the technical side," Tom said mildly.

"Well, it would pass for marble if you didn't know better."

"Good, and look at the tool marks," Tom said. "Metal on stone. Water-polished, I wonder? And you see the carving down the sides. Certainly done with metal, though where, I don't know – Ireland, Egypt, Palestine? Not exactly ornate: primitive but effective. It's beautiful."

Mackay, not trusting himself to comment sensibly, borrowed Innes's torch again to look behind the stone. His gasp of astonishment brought the others to their feet.

"What's there, Dr Mackay?" asked Innes. "More surprises?"

"I'm amazed by everything I've seen, Dr Innes. Tell me if those aren't the bronze targes you spoke about in Inveresk."

They were tucked down behind the throne. Tom brought one of them out and shone a light on the surface. Using a small soft-bristled brush, he cleaned its surface carefully, dislodging a cloud of dust.

"There's writing here," he said. "It looks like Gaelic, but I don't know any. Dr Innes?"

"And I don't know much," said Innes, squinting at it, "but I think I know what it'll say. It's where the prophecy comes from – 'the kingdom lies under the stone's protection until angels carry it back to Bethel' – that sort of thing. I've a friend in the Royal Museum who'll help."

"What now?" asked Mackay. "We can't take the stone home. I suppose we could take a targe, or both of them." He thought about it. "Why would we do that? In fact, are we allowed to?"

"You said 'What now?'" said Innes. "I propose lunch, and in the open air. Then Tom must take some proper photographs."

The concept of treasure trove remains firmly enshrined in Scots law, so that nowadays the fate of archaeological discoveries may not be the same north of the Border as in the rest of the United Kingdom where for some years past the Treasure Act has applied instead. The treasure trove system in Scotland differed substantially in any case. For example, all portable antiquities have been regarded there as treasure irrespective of their composition – gold, coin, stone, metal, glass, horn, or even wood. The law recognises no distinction between what has deliberately been concealed for later recovery and what may have been lost inadvertently. Furthermore, the proprietors of the land where an antiquity has been found and excavated have no more rights of ownership than anyone else.

In Scotland the Latin maxim pertains, *quod nullus est fit domini regis,* which is to say that what belongs to nobody belongs to the king or queen. In other words, objects whose original owner or rightful heir cannot be identified – known as *bona vacantia* – are the property and prerogative of the Crown. Although treasure trove now comes under the aegis of the Scottish Executive, operational responsibility rests with the Crown Office. And it is to the Crown that all archaeological finds must be reported.

Professor Innes finished explaining the finer points of the law of treasure trove to Dr Mackay as the four men drank hot tomato soup from the large thermos Mrs Mackay had supplied.

"So sooner or later we'll have to tell the Crown Agent in Edinburgh what we've found," said Innes. "I fancy it'll cause something of a splash."

"It will that," Tom agreed. "The archaeological implications are stupendous. It'll establish Macbeth's Castle as a major mediaeval historic site. So far it's been more legend than fact."

"Oh, sure, that's interesting enough," Ian said. "But it's going to send the meteorite boys back into the stratosphere. If any other fragments have been picked up from the same shower somewhere in the world, we may find out where it really came from. My money's on the Middle East. After all, remember Sodom and Gomorrah, the cities of the plains – "

"Archaeology after all, then?" Tom prompted.

"Not a bit. There's a widely-held theory that they were hit by meteorites. Fire and brimstone look-alikes."

"Good heavens!" said Innes. "We all have our priorities – but just for once you can't put archaeology and geology before history! Think what's down there in that vault. It's the real throne that

Edward thought he'd stolen! What does that say about every coronation held in Westminster for eight hundred years? What does it say about that lump of sandstone in Edinburgh that people have actually venerated – venerated! – since . . ."

Innes stopped, his face lengthening. He looked at Mackay who had listened solemnly to the enthusiasms of his three companions.

"I wish . . . I wish that Duncan had been with us today. I must tell him before anybody. He mustn't hear about it from anyone else. He'll be – "

"Thrilled?" asked Mackay. "I think you said – "

"He won't mind being proved wrong," said Innes firmly. "It's been a matter of a little contention between us, as I think you know; sometimes rather heated. But he'll be pleased that it's out of the way. And, yes, I hope he'll be thrilled by what we've found. Who wouldn't be?"

Mackay could guess. He could well believe that Scotland's archaeologists, geologists and historians might soon be turning cartwheels in their excitement; but her politicians would surely have very mixed views, starting with Innes's own flesh and blood. The Presiding Officer's one aim, shared with Morag McLeod, was to avert one of the most explosive political scandals ever to threaten Scotland and perhaps the Union. He did not know where Morag was, nor where the stolen stone was, nor where Duncan Innes was. All he knew was that a grotesque new ingredient was about to be added to the political witch's brew, one which might well cause it to boil over. Something of a splash? That was something of an understatement.

"And of course we must tell Morag," Innes went on, his expression softening. "She'll certainly be thrilled. And we must finish these sandwiches. Ian? Tom? Where's your appetite?"

They munched in silence. Tom handed round coffee in plastic cups.

"What we shall do," said Innes, "is wall up the stone again before we leave, to keep it secure. But we'll take the targes with us for examination – "

" – and translation?" said Tom.

"Yes, and also to substantiate our story, although of course we'll have the pictures. Then it'll be up to the Crown Office to decide how to proceed."

Mackay knew this was the time to grasp the nettle.

127

"I'm here as your guest, Dr Innes, and yours, too, Ian and Tom. But I must ask you, most urgently, to consider the political consequences of this extraordinarily exciting discovery. When the news bursts on the world, well, of course it'll make a splendid story in the press; and, as you have pointed out yourselves, academic interest will be simply enormous. But –" He hesitated.

"You're not telling us to keep it quiet, Dr Mackay, are you?" asked Tom anxiously.

"No, no. But it's a matter of timing – of preparation. For reasons which I can't go into at the moment, it mayn't be the best time – indeed, I know it isn't – to show that the stone on display in Edinburgh Castle isn't what it's supposed to be." For that matter, Mackay thought to himself, it wasn't even the stone that wasn't what it was supposed to be.

Ian said: "I'd have thought the Scottish Executive would be delighted. Oor Wullie would have something new and cheerful and fascinating and wonderful to tell people. It's a long way from the routine horror stories and lame excuses coming out of Holyrood most weeks. Where's the harm?"

Mackay reflected, not for the first time, that politicians made things complicated for themselves simply by being politicians. What was the harm? He could not explain the political dangers without admitting that the stone had disappeared from the castle.

"Please believe me," he said. "I'm not asking you to keep it quiet for long. Perhaps a week or so, while you look at the targes. If I may, I shall talk to the First Minister. I'm certain that high-level decisions must be made before the discovery is public knowledge. Not just the executive in Holyrood but the Prime Minister in London will expect to be informed and forewarned. This is a major event for Scotland. The first announcement of it would properly be to the parliaments – Westminster as well as Holyrood. I suspect the Queen herself will require to be consulted. And – consider – there are English sensitivities involved: after all, as Dr Innes has just said, the stone, the old stone, lay venerated in Westminster Abbey for eight centuries . . . ."

Dr Innes held up his hand. "Say no more," he said. "I'm sure you know better than we do. It's been a huge privilege to have you with us. None of us'll speak of this until you give the word. The Crown Agent'll just have to wait."

Mackay tested his luck once more. "And your son Duncan?"

"No, I'll have to tell Duncan. It'll be just between him and me. He's entirely discreet."

Mackay could not press the point. He suspected his luck had run out.

Professor Innes telephoned his son next morning, a Sunday, to ask him to lunch. He could not make contact with him. Duncan had already left Edinburgh, taking the train south from Waverley Station with Janet Ross early that morning.

The following day, the Presiding Officer, Dr Douglas Mackay, having learnt that Morag had still not been well enough to return to work, was put through to her home number. He was able only to talk to an answering machine. His brief, guarded message invited her to what she would understand to be a council of war.

7

"I'VE ASKED Campbell to convene our members tomorrow week," said Duncan after lunch, as they left the basement restaurant in Horseferry Road and walked along the Embankment towards the Houses of Parliament. "That's the day after parliament's recalled, so they'll all be there. We'll need a credible action plan for them – something to boost their morale a bit."

"Yes," Janet said. "The recess must have sapped most of it, even before the party conferences finished it off. What's on your mind?"

"I'm not really happy about using the invalid chair trick again," said Duncan. "The Edinburgh police know about it – we must assume they do – and it's just possible that security people are on the alert for one that looks too heavy – even here in London."

"Good thinking," Janet agreed, "but do we have a choice? We can hardly trundle the thing around on a fork-lift truck, or in a wheel-barrow."

"Well, the first thing is to decide where it's to go. Then we can work out how to put it there."

"Just run through your criteria. It's got to be here in the seat of government, in the Palace of Westminster or in the abbey precincts – is that right?"

"That's the idea. It's how it worked before. Next, nobody must find it – or at least recognise it for what it is – for a very long time. I mean a century or so. That would spoil the entire exercise."

"Fine. Can we bury it?" They were walking across Palace Green, that useful sweep of greensward where, with the Houses of Parliament as a backdrop and traffic roaring past, dyspeptic or disaffected MPs like to give instant interviews to television personalities on the controversies of the day. Janet pointed to the grass. "There, for instance, deep down?"

"Perhaps, with a bit of deft spadework. We'd have to put the turf back very carefully."

"Would it matter which way up it was – the stone, I mean? Could we put it in vertically?"

Duncan laughed. "I don't know. Let's look at the alternatives."

There were several. Below the old Treasure House, opposite the Lord Chancellor's door to the House of Lord's, was one: Duncan suspected that the Stone of Destiny might well be inserted undetected among the massive blocks which lined the dry, sunken moat which once protected the palace on its upstream side. They strolled along the path between Westminster Abbey and St Margaret's Church, where MPs are permitted to hold their memorial services, and considered a position against the church wall – behind, but conceivably below, the herbaceous border that decorated that short walk. They passed, with the usual crowd of visitors, through the north door of the abbey, wandering anticlockwise round the aisles and up to the choir, examining each little chapel to see if it could offer a secure and permanent hiding-place. At last they gazed at the gaping, empty shelf below King Edward's chair where, except for the episode in 1950, the Coronation Stone had lain barely disturbed for exactly seven hundred years.

"That's where it really belongs," said Duncan gloomily. "Anything else is second best."

"There's nothing we can do about that."

"No."

In silence they left the abbey by the south door and walked slowly through the cloister, inspecting there the potential of each vaulted stone room now used for the exhibition of important relics of the abbey's past. In one corner they found the replica coronation chair made for Mary the Second of England so that she and William of Orange could be crowned together. A panel was fixed over the corresponding space reserved on King Edward's chair for the stone. Duncan shook his head.

"Why not?" asked Janet.

"Tempting but too speculative. It might collapse. And too short-term."

At length they worked their way round to the beautiful, tall octagonal Chapter House where Simon de Montfort's parliament, England's first, met thirty years before Edward Longshanks began to hammer the Scots. If there were anything in the conceit that the Westminster chamber was the mother of parliaments, here was their grandmother, its splendidly ribbed stone roof supported by a single central pillar, fluted and columned. The knights and the commons had not sat there for long, because the monks of Westminster objected to the noise they made, and complained that their stamping was damaging the slip-decorated clay tiles of the floor. The tiles had thus survived into the twenty-first century, when visitors were still forbidden to tread on them. As they climbed the few steps from the cloister, Duncan and Janet instantly recognised that here would be an appropriate resting place for the Stone of Destiny if only a prolonged stop in it could be guaranteed.

They were then alone in the building, for the last visitors had walked out as they entered and no one from the abbey staff was normally posted inside. Duncan surveyed the walls, the buttressing, and the worn stone benches, now lined with warm pipes, below the high, leaded windows. Quickly he saw the opportunity he was looking for.

"There!" he said quietly to Janet. "The grilles. That's the place. There's enough room under them. I'd need ten minutes only."

"Understood," said Janet. "And our friends can create their diversion out there in the cloisters to make sure we're not interrupted. And they won't know exactly where you've put it. But we'll have to use the chair after all."

"Afraid so." He thought for a space. "The ideal moment would be just before twilight, to give the cement a night to dry before anyone's about again. We'll check on the closing time."

They sat on a stone bench from where, no doubt, thirteenth-century burgesses had once tried to catch de Montfort's eye.

"We did a dry run in Edinburgh," said Janet.

"So let's do another," Duncan agreed. "We'll get the chair out now and practise tomorrow with it empty – apart from you sitting in it. If they're looking out for wheelchairs and they stop us, there'll be no harm done."

"Should we be in disguise?"

"Yes, why not?"

"As lovers again?"

"Difficult if I'm wheeling you. And not in the abbey, perhaps."

Feeling more positive about the operation, they left the abbey precincts through Dean's Yard, walked to Palace Yard and recovered Duncan's car from the members' carpark underneath. They drove westwards along the river, crossing at Lambeth Bridge, and came shortly to a stretch of the south-bank railway arches which since Victorian times have been used in pursuit of their trade by every discipline from warehousemen to coachbuilders, and from vintners to smugglers. Duncan stopped the car opposite the short row currently hired out as lock-up garages.

"Number eight," he said to Janet. "Here are the keys. I'll open my boot."

"The key won't go in," she said a few seconds later. "Neither of them goes in. You try."

He tried. He checked that the number on the lock-up key-tag tallied with the number above the doors. Then he compared both keys with the make of the padlock, and knew he had a problem.

The Presiding Officer's telephone trilled.

"It's Morag from the First Minister's office," his secretary intimated. "I'm putting her through."

There came the expected disembodied beeps, then silence. The teething troubles of the parliamentary telephone system had never cleared up. Mackay put his receiver back and sat drumming his fingers. In ten minutes' time he would have to resume his seat in the chamber for Question Time. In due course the telephone warbled again.

"I'm sorry, Dr Mackay, I was going through a tunnel,"

"Morag! What's happened to you? They said you were poorly. I've been trying to find you ever since Thursday."

"Och, no, I've been perfectly well. Under a bit of pressure, that's all."

"Where on earth are you? In a tunnel? On a train, you mean?"

"No, Dr Mackay, I'm on an airport bus. At Heathrow. I've something to tell you. I've got it."

Mackay recalled with difficulty what "it" was. "Morag, you haven't! How did you do it? Where is it?"

"How? I hijacked it. Now I want to know what to do with it."

"Have you it with you?" Mackay vaguely visualised a little tubular-metal trolley with a huge paper parcel strapped to it. The notion was unlikely, but he could think of nothing better to say.

"Not on a bus! It's in a safe place. I'm catching a flight and I'll be in the office tomorrow. Can we meet then?"

"Yes, Morag. But there's a debate. It'll have to be when it's over."

"There's no hurry. I'll have work to do for Mr McNish."

"Good. And –"

"Hullo? Dr Mackay? Are you still there?"

"Yes, I'm here." He decided against trusting an insecure telephone line. "I'll have something to tell you, too."

Mackay leant back in his chair as they rang off. Whether the plot was thinning or thickening he could not guess, but he dared to hope that its elements were better disposed and that prospects were improving. The bell ringing outside the chamber brought his secretary in with his papers for the afternoon's business. It would be harder than usual to keep his mind on it.

Duncan pointed down the arches to a small wooden cabin with large bright yellow signboards and said "We'd better go to the office and see if they'll help."

The proprietor acknowledged that the key-tag was his but disclaimed the key attached to it. Grumbling and insisting on seeing, first, the lock-up hire documentation, then Duncan's driving licence – precise identification which he was anxious not to give – he unwillingly walked back with them to unlock the padlock with a duplicate of the original key retrieved from a safe. Wooden-faced, Duncan pulled a door open, certain even before he looked inside that the van would not be there. Instead, there was a small, plain white envelope drawing-pinned to a shelf on a side wall. Duncan pulled it off and drew a piece of paper out of it.

"*Epistolas mysticas et puellae scribere possunt,*" he read. "*Petra panis relocata fuerit. Administratio incommodum factum quodcunque dolet.*"

"Morag," he said, passing it to Janet.

After a quick glance, Janet refused to puzzle over it. "What's it mean?"

Duncan studied it again, his face a mask.

"She says that even girls can write mysterious notes, and that the stone of – well, *petra panis* is the stone of bread, literally – I like it – will be relocated."

"Stone of bread. A bit juvenile?"

134

"Is it? Well, all right. You sound peeved."

"What's the last sentence?"

"Loosely? Something like 'The management apologises for any inconvenience caused.'" Duncan, biting his lower lip, looked down at the keytag with the address on it. "There's no other way. She must have switched the key for the right one in my flat when I was . . . when you were . . ."

"I remember the occasion," said Janet briskly. "Look. That isn't the proper key of the van either. What are we going to do?"

"Well, we'd better pay the bill here. They'll want something more for losing the key."

"Yes, but after that?"

"We can hardly report a stolen van."

"No. Think harder, Duncan. We're meeting our MPs next week. What'll we tell them?"

"A week's a long time in – "

"Come on. You know the – the woman. What'll she do?" Janet was doing her best to keep the acidity out of her voice.

"She's not easy to second-guess. But she probably thinks she's outsmarted us, which she has, I suppose. Anyway, she's not going to shop us to the police."

"Are you sure?"

"Yes."

"Because she's in love with you?"

"That's over, I told you. Now you've interrupted my train of thought."

"You were saying she wouldn't shop you."

"Us. We must try to negotiate. And the point is – she's got hot goods on her hands. She can't just turn up at the abbey, or back at the castle for that matter, and produce the stone without facing awkward questions. So let's make sure they'd be really awkward."

"How?"

"Time to put the cat among the pigeons. We'll make sure the Scotch media hear that the stone in the castle – "

"– has been stolen?"

"No. Too simple. It would let the cat out of the bag too quickly."

"So many cats!"

"It's the same one. The world deserves simply to know the stone in the castle is a fake. No more. The rest will follow."

135

The political scandal which duly gathered and broke over Holyrood like a thunderstorm that week began as a rumour in the tabloid offices, among whom, as every politician knows, seeds of suspicion may be most rewardingly planted: Tuesday's diary in the Glasgow *Evening Times*, ever ready to poke fun at Edinburgh, first made the rumour public. Yet journalists working on the broadsheets do not hold themselves apart socially from their populist *confrères*, and the story gained substance the same day with a routine enquiry to the castle from *The Scotsman*, which was rewarded with a categoric assertion by the press officer of Historic Scotland that nothing was amiss. That rebuttal was innocent enough, but Sir Hew Cunynghame, to his chagrin when confronted with his press officer's statement, and having no time to consult those who knew otherwise, said that he could neither confirm nor deny it. Sir Hew's mystifying words were duly broadcast on the later Scottish radio and television news bulletins. It was unfortunate that Sir Hew, who had been well prepared to limit the damage from a revelation that the stone had been stolen, additionally and inappropriately chose to refer further enquiries to the Lothian police. Taxed with these, the police refused to comment, other than to say that the authentication of antiquities was not their business but a matter for the Scottish Executive. After that, with so little straw to build a story, media interest quickly became avid.

At some moment in the course of these developments, Morag slipped into the Presiding Officer's Holyrood office to make her report. The sun had set, and about half the members, having registered their attendance at the parliament for personal administrative purposes, were leaving. Others were making for the places where, fed by the journalists and broadcasters they found there, skeletal rumours about some unspecified fraudulence in Edinburgh Castle, coupled with a serious security lapse, were acquiring flesh.

"Now that the press are on to it, the game's changed again, Morag," said Mackay, having divulged news of the growing speculation in media circles he had heard earlier and privately from Ross Burton of *The Herald*. "But perhaps we're still ahead of it. Tell me what you've been doing."

So she told him how she had taken Duncan's keys, flown south and removed the unmarked white van complete with contents from the lock-up garage in Lambeth. It had been a relief, she said, to find the stone intact under the floor because, at first sight, there was no sign of it. However, the loose spare wheels had given the game away. She had spent a day trying to find another lock-up garage anywhere in London to keep it, but all the offices were closed at the weekend and nothing was available on the Monday. She had suspected the van was not insured for her to drive and hoped that – apart from appropriating it without permission – she had done nothing illegal. Anyhow, she had now left it in the best alternative hiding-place she could think of.

"Duncan won't forgive me," she concluded.

"If Duncan doesn't admire your enterprise as much as I do," replied Mackay firmly, "he'd be a damn fool."

She smiled and shook her head. "I told you. He believes what he's doing is right."

They were silent for a while.

"Well," said Mackay, "I told you I had something to tell you. If you're ready for it, this is still the closest secret. I'm letting you know on the same terms as before."

"All right," she said. "Tell me."

"Last Saturday, while you were driving that stone round London, Duncan's father, Harry Innes, found the real one."

Morag looked blank. "What d'you mean 'the real one'?"

"Just that, Morag. The real thing. The real Stone of Scone, practically as he described it to us. Black, shiny, like marble. Large." He spread his hands to show its height and width. "Meteoritic, so I gather. And beautiful. I was there. He wanted you to be there, too."

He paused to let her consider it.

"My God," she said quietly. "Where?"

"Perthshire, not far from Scone. Macbeth's Castle on Dunsinane Hill. What will Duncan make of that?"

"I – I don't know, Dr Mackay. You said it's still a secret. Who knows about it?"

"The four of us who were there. There were two of Dr Innes's young university friends with us. And now you. That's five. Because of what happened at the castle, I swore them all to secrecy until – well, until the Crown Office could be informed. Technically it belongs to the Queen. They kindly agreed – except that Dr

Innes felt he should tell Duncan first and at once. That was understandable, but – "

"That's why you asked what he'd do."

"Yes."

She considered the question. "I hope . . . No, I just don't know."

"I also told Dr Innes that the First Minister should be among the first to be told. He perhaps expects me to tell him."

"Oor Wullie!"

"But that was more to emphasise the need for secrecy. I don't want to tell him yet. I think I know what he'll do when he hears of it. He'll look on it as a gift from the gods – so that he can escape the flak about the theft from the castle. He'll think he can just declare the old stone, the traditional stone, as much a fake as the – the polystyrene one. If I know him, he'll go straight to the press. This has to be played much more carefully."

"That's how his mind would work," Morag agreed. "Self-preservation's always at the top of his agenda. He can only think things through about half way; but if he goes for the main chance as usual he won't get any support from his cabinet."

"I agree. The real stone could let him off the hook eventually. But he's got to face today's problems first."

"You were talking to him when I left his office ten minutes ago," said Morag diffidently.

Mackay, himself far from certain that he was acting for the best, let alone dutifully, in keeping the First Minister in ignorance of what lay in the vault on Dunsinane Hill, was aware again of the conflict of loyalties he was imposing on her. Her work for the office of the First Minister was no less confidential than what she heard from him, and her relationship with Duncan Innes certainly increased the stress. However, he felt sure she could handle it so long as none of her allegiances was tested to breaking point.

"I told him he must make a full statement to the House – tomorrow. He'll be having a word with the Chief Constable first."

"Poor soul. He's frightened."

"That goes with the job. You're too kind-hearted. What frightens me is that he was thinking of suggesting the theft was an English conspiracy. I forbade him, as well as I could, to say anything so daft. If he knew the truth!"

"I'm afraid his first resort is always to find someone to blame."

"Well, politically that's usually a boomerang. This time he's responsible, but it's not directly his fault – enough people will see that. It'll be much easier for him once it's out in the open."

"Can you help him, Dr Mackay?"

"As much as I can. Collectively our friends in that place have no more sensitivity than a wallie dog. Presiding over them is like being a referee at Murrayfield without being able to send anyone off."

"Yes, you said the game had changed."

"I suppose someone talked."

"Mmm. Or someone made sure we couldn't put the stone back quietly where it was without the public noticing," said Morag, thinking aloud. "Or without having to explain where we found it."

"What are you saying?"

"I'm saying that Duncan knows I've taken his van, and he's daring me to give him away."

"You mean he told the press? Are you sure?"

"About ninety-five per cent."

"And you still won't give him away?"

"No. That's the rules."

"You certainly each know how the other thinks."

"Uh-huh."

"So what'll his next move be?"

"He'll ring me up and try to negotiate. That's against the rules, but he's got no choice. And I broke them first."

"And what'll you say to him, Morag?"

"Not a problem. I'll tell him his father wants to speak to him. That'll terrify him, because he won't know what it's about."

The First Minister, William McNish, had come to understand beyond a peradventure that he would be held accountable for the disgrace of losing the stone, unless he could convincingly point a finger elsewhere, which he could not. The Presiding Officer had roundly informed him that the House would expect a statement forthwith. It was not possible, Mackay had argued, to keep the theft secret any longer. At this stage any dissimulation by the executive would make things worse, in parliament, with the press and with the public, and the consequences would be even harder to unscramble.

139

McNish's mood now modulated from self-righteousness into one of angry truculence against the world. He agreed with Craig Millar that Sir Andrew McCallum must be instructed now to alert all the police forces in the United Kingdom; but he turned down contemptuously his private secretary's offer to draft, for general consumption, a careful exposition of the circumstances of the raid on the castle. Instead, recognising that he must inform his ministers before anyone else, he summoned them to an immediate cabinet in Bute House. It proved a trying experience.

Although he knew few had any liking for him, he tried to elicit from them what sympathy he could. He mentioned the row blowing up over the award of a new parliamentary maintenance contract to a company which, it had just been revealed, were significant donors to the party. He mentioned the barrage he suffered daily from the animal rights lobby, determined now to add trout and salmon to its other trophies by stamping out fly-fishing on lochs and rivers. He mentioned his domestic difficulties, especially his partner's refusal to stay in Bute House at night because the security devices frightened her. He even managed to mentioned the latest turbulence in Scottish Opera, of which he had mistakenly become a patron, before passing on to the terrible reception the press had given to his speech in the chamber the week before.

The ploy was singularly ill-judged. It is an axiom of successful political leadership never to tell your followers of your troubles: half your listeners will not care, while the other half will be glad you have them. When into the sullen silence that followed this catalogue of woe McNish dropped the bombshell of the missing stone, they reacted with anger and resentment. How long had he known? Why had they not been told before? None, of course, had better cause for anger at being kept in ignorance than the Lord Advocate, who remembered that *ex officio* he was one of the Commissioners of the Regalia and thus a custodian of the stone; but he instantly saw the advantage of allowing responsibility for its loss to continue to encumber the First Minister's shoulders.

McNish did his best to explain that the Chief Constable had insisted on silence in the certainty that someone would talk. He hoped that the executive would now support him loyally in his determination to bring the culprits to book, and in rallying the

parliament and the people to that cause. His colleagues unhesitatingly replied that they could not be expected to take the blame
for such a disgrace after being kept by him in the dark so long.
He was on his own.

McNish scowled with loathing at the faces around him. Two
ministers were still missing at unspecified assignations overseas.
Of those present, none was a crony in the sense that McNish's
predecessors had promoted obliging friends either to their cabinets
or to Scotland's most powerful quangos. However, his scrupulous
rejection of cronyism – for which he had been given some credit
by the press – meant a reduced choice from anyway limited talent
and narrow experience; and the toils of Scotia Nostra (a term
coined by an unfriendly journalist some time back) were still heavy
upon Scottish government. Half of McNish's appointments bore
the awful taint of past careers as local councillors. Three had
actually undergone the rigours of the law courts and punishment.
One was under investigation over a new expenses irregularity.
The partner of another had been held on a drugs charge. Two
of the women were having extra-marital affairs with other MSPs
which the press would probably get wind of shortly. A third, his
Minister for Single-Parent Families, was suckling an infant beside
him, a practice permitted anywhere in the parliament although it
had not yet occurred in the chamber itself. McNish trusted none
of these people further than he could have kicked them but, as
they all hated each other, knew there was little danger of their
forming cabals of any size or strength against him. In that event,
anyway, he would reshuffle his pack once more, a resort employed
so frequently these days that it hardly drew headlines. He rose
with gritted teeth and made for his car and Holyrood.

When the MSPs reassembled there for the afternoon session,
the duty of raising the issue of the Coronation Stone fell to the
member for Glasgow Burrell. Alasdair McNab would not have
been the First Minister's first choice for the task of asking the
Presiding Officer to call for an official statement, but the Executive
Whip had its favours to distribute and felt that the Glaswegian
MSP could do no great harm.

"Dr Mackay," McNab began, "the Hoose is alive wi' a rumour
that the Stane o' Destiny sittin' in its glass cage up at the castle
isnae the genuine article at a'. Ah've heard tell there are even
doots aboot its composeetion."

A buzz of astonishment arose from those MSPs whom the rumour had not yet reached. They sought enlightenment from those near them who were better informed. The Presiding Officer called for order. McNab, enjoying his moment of glory, waited until he could make himself heard again without strain.

"For masel'," he continued with deliberation, "Ah never gi'e credit tae ony tittle o' that kind 'til it's bin offeecially denied, but what wi' yer obfuscation fae Historic Scotland and yer prevarication fae the Lothian polis it's startin' tae seem that way. Sae wad wir First Meenister be guid enough tae pit wir show-piece parliament oot o' its agony? Forbye, if it's nae the real thing, wad he min' tellin' the Hoose whaur he thinks it's went? That is," he concluded reasonably, "gin he kens onything aboot it."

The First Minister rose as the Presiding Officer quelled the tittering in the public gallery. He expressed his gratitude to McNab for giving him the opportunity to make a full and frank statement to the parliament on a most serious development. He had, he explained, been in constant touch not only with the Chairman of Historic Scotland and the Chief Constable of the Lothians but with GOC Scotland, Sir Norman Brunstane, whose troops were stationed in the castle. They were all in agreement about the facts. For example, they were uniformly persuaded that the stone now in Edinburgh Castle was not what it appeared to be. In fact, it was not stone at all. Experts had examined it. It was made of some quite different substance. It was nothing very heavy. His honourable friend, Mr McNab, would be able to lift it himself, unaided. If he wished to, he added.

"Get oan wi' it, Wullie!" called a voice from the government benches. "Whit's it made o', then? Stookie?"

"Naw, it'll be yon organic muck the Co-op can't unload," another added helpfully.

In the official gallery, the First Minster's private secretary sunk his face in his hands. Having waived Millar's proposal to prepare a carefully constructed statement McNish had now lost the plot. In the chair, thankful that he had not so far been included openly among the initiated, Mackay realised that McNish was not merely searching for a word but was in a state of panic. What the fake stone was made of was completely immaterial. He stood up, obliging the First Minister to yield the floor.

"Order! You explained to me earlier, First Minister," he said,

142

"that the object was made of polystyrene. I consider it perfectly proper for that word to be used in this chamber".

The chamber buzzed incredulously.

"Order!", commanded Mackay. "You also made it clear to me," he went on, coaxing McNish back on to the rails, "your belief that the Coronation Stone – that is to say," he corrected himself, "the stone lately in Edinburgh Castle – has actually been stolen." The chamber buzzed again. "Order! The House will wish to know when that was and what steps are being taken to recover it. First Minister?"

Regaining his composure somewhat, McNish thanked the Presiding Officer for his guidance. Then, to members now convinced that he had something to hide, he agreed that the real stone had been removed by a person or persons unknown; and that he was not aware of its exact whereabouts for the present. He was, however, acting on the advice of the Chief Constable. The situation was being carefully monitored. He was able to confirm that all the police in the United Kingdom were on full alert. He announced his willingness to offer a reward in return for information leading to the recovery of the stone and the arrest of the thieves. He simply forgot to say when the theft had taken place.

Hamilton, the leader of the opposition, smelled blood, a strange and heady experience for one of his temperament. Although some of the executive were present, the seats on either side of the First Minister were empty, and his isolation was glaringly apparent.

"Will the First Minister now come clean?" Hamilton demanded, jumping up. He switched from third to second person, addressing McNish directly. "When did you first know about it? How long has the pantomime been going on? Why have you withheld a scandal of such enormity from the House and from the people of Scotland? We shall have answers!" He stayed on his feet until his target, shifting unhappily in his seat, at last rose to give them.

"The events at the castle were first brought to my notice three weeks ago," McNish ventured, adding daringly: "Since criminal enquiries are being pursued I cannot for the present give any more details of the affair." He glanced at Mackay. "Nor shall I be drawn on who the culprits might be, or who is behind them. I will leave that sort of speculation to others."

Hamilton simply warmed to the fray. "Three weeks! Three

weeks! By what right have you kept the House in ignorance? It has been a conspiracy of silence – no more, no less. Will you confirm unequivocally that it has been shared by your ministers?" Hamilton looked at some of them, noted the shaking heads, and raised his voice. "Well, if not, why not?" He was determined that McNish should have it neither way. "What have they to say? We shall have answers! We must have them now!" He went over the top, intimating that the executive would pay for this and that heads must roll.

The MSPs of the opposition parties beat their desks in approval – all except Jean Murray Stewart who glowered at Hamilton sullenly, indicating that public display of emotion was beneath her.

Mackay intervened again – this time to announce that, because police enquiries were continuing, he deemed it unwise and unsuitable to call the First Minister to answer further questions on the issue that day. There would of course be a debate when the time was ripe. In the meantime he would give the floor to others who had signified their wish to comment.

The First Minister, grateful enough for the respite, cringed lower in his chair as the other party leaders poured their several and collective scorn on the entire executive. No more than Hamilton did they show interest in what the police might have advised. Even the identity of the culprit or culprits was to them an academic matter. The circumstances of the theft of so sacred an object was not their concern. If they had grasped, they certainly did not refer to, the historic import of what they had heard. No, their fire was concentrated on McNish's cavalier treatment of the parliament. One by one, they shook with unconvincing indignation. For each, having been kept in ignorance of the loss of the stone was a gross personal affront for which the First Minister would answer and take the blame.

As leader of the smallest party, Walter Moncrieff was the last to be called. Silently, the press and the television reporters in the gallery prayed that he, at least, would say something to save a potentially splendid drama from lapsing flatly into Holyrood's habitual competitive parade of wounded egos. They had their story – and what a story it was! – but they still needed a spin to put on it, some emotive phrases to embellish it, and a headline to trumpet it.

They were not entirely disappointed. The shame, announced

Moncrieff, was not the Parliament's but Scotland's. Since the days of the Bruce – apart, he agreed, from an unfortunate but brief and isolated incident in 1950 – the stone had rested secure in Westminster Abbey, venerated at last by English and Scotch alike, a potent symbol and guarantor of the enduring position of Scotland in British history. The stone . . . but he would come to the meaning of the stone. It had spent seven centuries in London. It had survived barely a decade in Edinburgh. And there it had at best been a curiosity for visitors to pay to gape at, at worst a joke: for hardly one in twenty of Scotland's schoolchildren knew what it was, and hardly one in fifty of the population cared.

"Yet here," Moncrieff declaimed, "is the single most precious symbol of our Scotch nationhood. Here is the throne on which the kings of Scotland, then of England, then of the United Kingdom were crowned. Here, its origins lost in the mists of time yet rooted in the beginnings of Christianity in these islands – here, neither more nor less, is Scotland's palladium –"

In the front row of the government seats opposite, McNish's head jerked upwards in recognition. He remembered the word, although he was still perplexed about its meaning.

"Our palladium," he mouthed, nodding.

"And, not for the first time in history, we have failed to take care of it!"

The Presiding Officer, his face expressionless, watched Moncrieff with curiosity. He knew him to be an honourable man. He assumed him to be – unlike the other party leaders – on close terms with his representation in Westminster. Therefore he could hardly be unaware that Duncan Innes was the leading spirit in the theft that he had all but condemned – or at least appeared to be about to condemn.

"Our palladium has slipped from our hands. But is it not possible," Moncrieff postulated, looking round the assembly, "is it not possible that history is trying to tell us something? I am one of those who, a decade ago, asked not only what the Stone of Scone was doing in Edinburgh, but what it was doing out of the Coronation Chair where it lay for seven hundred years. No one had asked to have it back. There were thousands who thought as I did. I cannot pretend to be overly concerned that it has escaped from our keeping again."

Mackay realised that condemnation was far from the speaker's mind. On the contrary, he was trying to soften up parliamentary feeling to accept what had occurred. If Moncrieff had condoned what had taken place, then these were deep waters indeed.

"We do not know with certainty where this mighty rock came from," he resumed. "Palestine, Spain, Ireland, Iona – it seems to have moved like the wind, blowing where it listeth. We may find it again one day, or we may chase after it in vain. However, wherever it has settled now, we can be confident, it will give its protection to the Scotch people. It will," he concluded, looking hard at McNish, "protect us better than we have protected it."

The chamber had listened with awe, the press with attentiveness, and the First Minister with doubts about whether he had been attacked or not. Here was a politician, they all perceived, whose concern was not for personal dignity – enough had been heard of that – but one who entertained a clear distinction between the trivial and what was momentous in the world. Even though most of the MSPs present would have preferred to see the rolling heads which Hamilton had called for – but mainly for the human interest – they all judged Moncrieff's to be the more competent histrionic performance. Mackay, however, reflected on its purport with growing discomfort. Whatever lapse of security the leader of the Scotch Enlightenment Party seemed to be publicly excusing, he recollected that all fifty-nine of Scotland's elected MPs had actually aided and abetted an act of prodigious and felonious larceny. He had begun to understand from Morag what Duncan Innes's motives were. He had long known about the disgruntlement among Scotland's MPs. He now felt sure not simply that Walter Moncrieff knew what was driving them but that he shared their aims and their agenda.

The time allotted for the First Minister's statement and the opposition responses was over. The Presiding Officer rose and announced the next business before leaving the chair to a deputy. The press galleries emptied even quicker than the chamber. Sensational headlines were soon being composed for the evening newspapers announcing to the world the raid on the castle and the theft of the stone. The evening radio and television bulletins rapidly took up the story, relaying the salient points recorded in the House and unfailingly emphasising Moncrieff's cry that the loss of Scotland's palladium, the most priceless and revered symbol of her nationhood, was part of its rolling history. By the following morning the technical details of the daring castle burglary by a huge gang of now untraceable visitors at the height of the Edinburgh Festival had been prised from Historic Scotland's stewards, and the front pages of daily newspapers from Shetland to Sussex exploded in a joyous celebration of wonder and concern, sometimes of a patriotic though more often of an ironic nature. Comparisons were made with the Westminster theft of 1950. Parallels were drawn with the Elgin marbles and the Benin bronzes, and the doubtful wisdom discussed of returning looted artefacts to their former owners. Fingers were gleefully pointed and blame liberally allotted, while the names of William McNish, Sir Hew Cunynghame, Sir Andrew McCallum and Lieutenant-General Sir Norman Brunstane featured just as they had feared, censured by some, pitied by others; and the noble institutions they represented were variously calumniated and admonished. Within forty-eight hours no sentient person in the United Kingdom could have been unaware of what had befallen the stone, of its ancient and modern history, or of what it stood for. Pictures of it were flashed around the globe, accompanied by recent views of Scone Palace, of Edinburgh Castle and even of the First Minister, so that the hue and cry rapidly spread across the face of the earth. And quite soon almost everyone in the English-speaking world knew what a palladium was.

Meanwhile, as he withdrew from the chamber to his office, the Presiding Officer considered what he had just heard. Duncan Innes, he realised, had not yet informed Moncrieff that, like the aforesaid wind, the Stone of Scone had again moved on to settle where it listed.

"Morag?"

"Hullo, Duncan. I thought you'd be calling."

"Is anybody listening?"

"You mean the secret police? I don't think we're at that stage yet in Scotland. There's no one with me, if that's what you're asking."

"What did you do with the van?"

"Didn't you get my note? It's been relocated, along with contents. You know the number. Why not tell the press that as well?"

"Look, Morag, may we meet and talk?"

"Who?"

147

"Just the two of us. You and me."

"What about your friend?"

"I don't think that would help."

"No? Well, no, anyway."

"All right. What are you going to do?"

"What are *you* going to do?"

"That's not being helpful."

"Why should I help you? But I will. When did you last talk to your father? He's been trying to get in touch with you."

"Morag? You said you wouldn't – "

"Not this month. Ring him up, then, and you may learn something to your advantage. Well, of interest, at least. My advice is to do it when you're alone – "

"Why? What's it about?"

"– and sitting down. Bye!"

The deputy leader of the opposition in Holyrood had nursed her current resentment against her leader for more than a week. When she felt aggrieved, which was frequently, she found relief, first in sending harassing text messages suitably illustrated to the object of her disaffection, and secondly in food, especially carbohydrates. Thus while MSPs streamed out of the chamber after the First Minister's statement, some to committee rooms, some to their offices, a few to position themselves where they might be easily buttonholed by media people, Jean Murray Stewart sought the Cup o' Kindness and the therapeutic comfort of its cakes and pastries. These tea-room delicacies, in conformity with the gastronomic dialectic of the all-party catering committee, included broonies, cookies, parlies (a species of gingerbread allegedly fancied in the old Scottish parliament before the Union), shortie, Tantallon cake, Abernethy biscuits, and the fly cemeteries whose ingredients are reconstructed every Hogmanay into black bun.

Mrs Murray Stewart had left the chamber with a furrow on her brow as well as rancour in her heart. The furrow signified a burgeoning and singular realisation. Now, beside a plate of shortbread, potato scones and a cup of tea, she scrabbled through the papers in her briefcase, searching for the Latin text with which Jock Hamilton had so humiliated her ten days earlier. With it was a copy of the passable translation speedily supplied by a university friend and which, without comment, she had immediately forwarded to Hamilton; to whom, she guessed, knowing nothing then about the disappearance of the Stone of Destiny, it could have meant as little. She read it through again and saw now that, whoever had sent it, the reference was implicitly, even explicitly, to the castle burglary. Her eyes narrowed as she thought back to the speech with which Hamilton had, for a time, gripped the attention and, more annoyingly, dictated the mood of the House. So much for his hypocritical complaints about keeping MSPs in ignorance of the crime! So much for his sanctimonious indignation about a three-week conspiracy of silence! Hamilton himself, who had belaboured McNish for neglecting his duty to the House, had been given personal intelligence by the thieves at the same time as the First Minister. Moreover, she could prove it. It was time to release this new information on her own account, and to let the media draw condign conclusions about the character of her leader. She rose and looked out into the foyer.

Ross Burton was standing not far away, a mobile telephone pressed to his ear. She beckoned him over.

"Mr Burton, I'd like your advice on something I have here. You'll see – it's a note about the stone sent a little while ago to Mr Hamilton as well as the First Minister. I think you'll be very surprised that neither of them mentioned it in the chamber just now."

Burton put away his telephone and studied the paper she held out. Like other political journalists in Scotland he was well aware of the antipathy which governed relations between her and Hamilton. Though obscure in meaning, the words he read were obviously relevant to the issue of the stone; but he was too experienced not to suspect Mrs Murray Stewart's motives in showing them to him.

"What sort of advice were you after, Mrs Stewart?"

"It's up to you, Mr Burton."

"Then I think you shouldn't show this to a journalist like me. You should have shown it to the police. I daresay Mr Hamilton already has. He realises a serious crime has been committed."

Mrs Murray Stewart was palpably taken aback. "I thought it might make an interesting story – "

"It will, it will, Mrs Stewart, thank you. The way members tell stories on each other never fails to amuse my readers."

He left her open-mouthed and made his way to the Pint o'

Wine, considering what he had just seen but concluding that it added little to what he knew. It was time for half a pint of beer.

"Margaret, please, Mr Burton," said Margaret before he could speak and noting that he was deep in thought.

"You know, Maggie, you couldn't write a novel about this place."

"Why ever not, Mr Burton? And you a writer."

"Because the reality is beyond belief."

They both considered the proposition while Margaret filled a glass and put it on the counter.

"Sometimes you think you're in a kindergarten," Burton went on.

"Whiles Ah hae tae pinch masel' tae see if Ah'm asleep," she agreed.

"And sometimes it's like Edinburgh Zoo – "

"Aye, weel, the public come traipsing through often enough."

" – but without any big beasts."

Douglas Mackay and Professor Innes were having lunch in the New Club in Princes Street, of which both were members, at Mackay's invitation. Had the story of the raid on Edinburgh Castle not broken and cascaded over Scotland the previous day, Mackay would still have found it difficult not to take an early opportunity to explain more fully his request for discretion about the secret of Dunsinane Hill. Now it was easier; and the club's oak-panelled dining-room, hung with oil paintings of kings and eighteenth-century Scottish celebrities, provided the calm he needed and time for the topic to come up naturally.

"I was less than candid with you and your helpers, Harry. You must forgive me. The police were supposed to be on the trail. I'd been sworn to silence." The two had been on first-name terms by nightfall in the euphoria of the previous Saturday as they drove back across the Forth.

"On the contrary, I'm grateful to you, Douglas. If this had happened while we were still explaining and proving what we'd found it would have spoilt all our fun. Now we can wait till it's out of the way and we can choose our own moment. I wouldn't want to wait too long, though."

"The timing is what we must discuss, if I may make it my business again. It could be a big political issue. I've told Morag about it, as we agreed. No one else. McNish is still in the dark."

"And I've told my son Duncan."

Mackay noticed the hint of flatness in his voice.

"Oh? Then he wasn't . . . thrilled?"

"Well, no, not exactly. Mind you, it was only on the telephone so I couldn't see his face. He's in London. He was, well, rather silent. Perhaps I hadn't realised how much faith he had in the other stone."

"Didn't he say anything, then? Surely he believed you?"

"Oh, yes. He conceded he'd been wrong." Innes laughed a little uncomfortably. "But perhaps he stopped short of congratulation. Maybe that'll come later."

"You told him exactly where we found it?"

"Of course."

Mackay concentrated on dissecting the half roast grouse, of necessity a native of Yorkshire, which still complemented the New Club menu at that stage of the autumn.

"We've had some work done on the targes in the meantime," said Innes more cheerfully. "You remember you were the first to spot them. My friends at the museum – oh, acting under the strictest promise of secrecy: the targes are in a safe – confirm that they are a fine bronze, Celtic, probably of the eighth or ninth century, but carbon-dating of the wooden elements will confirm that. The bosses have tiny traces of gilding which was apparently characteristic of the Celts. They're still deciphering the inscription on the bigger one. It's in a kind of old Gaelic, with unusual lettering, but they came up with a phrase about a 'protective shadow over the kingdom' without being prompted."

"It sounds conclusive."

"Adequate, I think, although nothing's conclusive enough for some people. But Duncan'll accept it."

What else would Duncan accept, Mackay wondered? If the reception he gave to his father's news had been grudging and ungracious, that was not due merely to academic disappointment. Once more he had to be less than open with his guest, partly to respect his feelings but more to honour an unspoken pledge to Morag. If Innes ever learnt who was behind the knavery at the castle, it wouldn't be from him.

"There's been a lot of talk about palladiums, Harry. The word seems to be in every mouth. What happens if a palladium is replaced – superseded? I'm sure you follow me. Does the old one lose its magic?"

"Of course it does! And for you politicians I'm sure it'll be the crux of the matter. It's a question of what symbol or totem or superstition people respect. There can only be one Stone of Destiny. The one they've lost will soon be indisputably what it always was – no more than a very interesting historical relic. Its interest is that it made a fool of Edward the First and a lot of other people since – including whoever stole it from the castle."

"You mean it's no use to anybody?"

"You could use it as – well – what about a mounting block again, a loupin-on stane for bicycles?"

"I mean, as a palladium."

"No, I think it'll be no good as a palladium any more. Whatever powers it had will have gone. So whether the police find it again is comparatively unimportant."

"There's a reward out for it now."

"Well, I expect it'll turn up, then. But who'll care, much?"

"And would Duncan agree with you?" Mackay asked the question as casually as he could.

"Oh, yes. He'd see it the same way."

Their luncheon finished, they walked together along Princes Street and up the Mound, and so by way of George IV Bridge to the premises of the Queen's and Lord Treasurer's Remembrancer in Chambers Street. There they began the process whereby treasure trove is duly reported to the Crown Office by the finder; and whereby, after consultation with the appropriate panel of experts, the Crown either formally disclaims it or, if it wishes, appropriates it before allocating it to a worthy institution. The Q&LTR (as that official is known), a woman of obvious intelligence and good sense, listened to Professor Innes's story and grasped its import at once. She gave him forms to complete, instructing him to describe the dimensions and composition of the find without speculating in writing what it might be. Although he had to record on paper exactly where the object had been found, she counselled him to refer publicly to a location merely "somewhere in Perthshire."

That task completed, Mackay and Innes discussed how best to acquaint the governments of both Scotland and the United Kingdom with the latest twist in a seven-hundred-year-old story, agreeing that both had an equal right to know. Innes fully under-stood at last, even though as a historian he regretted, the political sensitivity of his discovery. Mackay would liaise with the Speaker of the House of Commons to ensure that, if possible, Westminster and Holyrood were enlightened simultaneously. He hoped that his influence with the First Minister was great enough to restrain him while a joint statement could be agreed with the Cabinet Office in Whitehall. It would be up to the Prime Minister to inform the Sovereign. Professor Innes would make a presentation in Edinburgh as soon as the parliamentary statements were over. There would be a press conference at the Museum of Scotland in Chambers Street. Ian the geologist and Tom the archaeologist would be present and given the credit due to them. The photo-graphs that they had taken, especially Tom's digital holograms, would be the evidence and illustration of what had been found. Mackay reluctantly agreed to be there too, yet only as a credible witness to their story: he wanted none of the glory. But in the meantime, from Prime Minister and First Minister, from parlia-ments, press and public, the palladium's hiding place in Dunsinane Hill had to kept a tight secret. Incontestably, the stone concealed there was the most significant antiquity ever found in Scotland.

8

M PS RETURNED to Westminster to wind up the session's business in advance of prorogation and, come November, of the annual re-opening of parliament. Scotland's members were privately convened once more by Campbell Macarthur in the Grand Committee Room off Westminster Hall to discuss together for the first time the electrifying reports from home. Many had been in their constituencies when the news broke of the daring August raid on Edinburgh Castle. Some – those who doubted their ability convincingly to feign surprise, shock or horror – confined themselves then to tut-tutting to their local party officials over the Holyrood reports. Others offered to give their outraged views on the episode to the press and their local radio and television stations; but their eagerness to ask rhetorical questions about whether the Scottish Executive could be the trusted custodians of anything was in vain. Media attention was on Edinburgh as ever, and their opinions remained unvalued, unsolicited, unaired and so unnoticed.

Any resentment the MPs might have felt in regard to a familiar slight was already forgotten. The Prime Minister's statement the previous day to the House of Commons, coinciding with an identical one by the First Minister in Holyrood, had altered every perspective. The same evening, throughout Britain, the subsequent press conference given in the Museum of Scotland by Professor Innes and the team who discovered the authentic Stone of Destiny had monopolised the news and comment programmes on television. There had been three-dimensional colour photographs of the throne and live pictures of the targes – these with the inscription on the larger one satisfactorily translated to confirm the full import for the survival and ascendancy of the Scottish people. Now the morning newspapers which the MPs brought to the Grand Committee Room carried excited and more extensive reports of the event, tricked out with hastily assembled views of archaeologists and historians anxious to add their tuppenceworths. Interest was concentrated on what was still a mystery to the world – where the discovery had been made. The only clues from the photographs were the stone vaulting and walls and earthen floor where the throne rested. Although its location had not been divulged, the site was now stated to be under a twenty-four-hour police watch, as though it were the nest of a golden eagle.

Macarthur called the meeting to order and, as before, explained that it was not taking place, that there was no agenda and that therefore there would be no minutes.

"Are we all here, Maureen? I'll rephrase that. Are all of us not here?"

"All except Andy," said Mrs Findlay. "And he'll join us if I 'phone him. Then he won't be here, too," she added to make it clear.

As with the gathering in June, Wedderburn had stayed away so that his position in the British cabinet should be uncompromised by the possession of awkward intelligence. Apart from him there were no absentees, not even the Member for the Inchcape Rock: the MPs' interest and involvement in what, when strictly necessary, they referred to simply as "the business at the castle" were both mutual and several. If any felt qualms or guilt about it, those doubts were happily outweighed by a burning sense of injustice and a no less sharp instinct for self-preservation. They needed to know what was going on.

"Those of you who were not in the chamber yesterday will all have had copies of the Prime Minister's statement," Macarthur began. "I must first thank those who heard it for keeping silent afterwards as requested. That restraint was admirable. The questions from the English MPs affected nothing."

It was true. Most of England's MPs had assumed that, for once, their Scottish colleagues would want and be given the floor. Their comments had been ironic rather than substantial.

Macarthur continued. "I'm sure we have all appreciated that any previous efforts that may have been made – or not – to improve our circumstances have been overtaken by the events the Prime Minister described. I've talked with our policy committee, and we agreed that I'd first ask for a report from our – ah – executive arm. These, of course, are non-existent functional groups – but I don't have to say that again. Duncan? Would you like to speak, or Janet?"

Duncan and Janet were decided that nothing useful would be served by telling the meeting that they had lost an object which had ceased to have any symbolic importance. The embarrassment of their failure would have been too great. The advantage of candour would have been too small. It was true that the loss might have added to the risk of the exposure and perhaps the punishment of everyone present, so perhaps they had a right to know. Yet what good would it have done to make such a confession at that stage? Had circumstances not changed so completely, they might have met leading questions with assurances that the venture was proceeding *ad hoc* yet more or less according to plan. However, for the present, that the plan had been derailed might as well remain the concern of the executive arm. As Duncan had casually reminded Janet, a week had again proved a long time in politics. He accepted Macarthur's invitation.

"Thank you, Campbell. There are two issues here, one old and one new. As to the old – plainly, whatever we may have achieved together so far has been superseded by the new development. Till not long ago your executive arm were making excellent progress with the previously agreed programme, in which we were all intimately involved. Now we'll do our best to contrive that the restoration of the *status quo ante* attracts the least possible attention – quite how, I don't yet know. Nor do I know if further general assistance will be needed. It isn't easy at present to gauge the remaining press or public interest in the business we have in mind."

"All right, Duncan. Our confidence in the executive arm is complete. You'll tell us what you want. And the new issue?"

Duncan took a deep breath, his eyes straying momentarily to the back of the room where Janet had propped herself against a desk.

"Perhaps not all of you noticed that the man who discovered the – the real, the genuine, stone has the same name as mine. Well, it's because he's my father."

Macarthur nodded encouragingly at the small knots of MPs to whom this came as a surprise. Duncan, who realised that he had been frowning, managed to smile.

"I'm very proud of that, of course. He is a historian, and it's a great triumph and excitement for him. But I can't deny that it wasn't the moment I'd have chosen for it."

Apart from a short outbreak of self-conscious throat-clearing, there was silence in the room. Duncan looked at Macarthur.

"Campbell, I believe this in no way changes what I said when we met in June. The best place, the right place, for the Stone of Destiny is here."

Duncan leant back in his seat to show he had finished, and again there was silence.

"That's grand," said Murdo Mercer, breaking it abruptly. "Let's gae an' get it again."

Callum Geekie caught Macarthur's eye. "I've been looking through the statement," he said. "It says the stone is Crown property, and that the Queen may be expected to take advice from her Privy Council about its future."

"What's that imply?" The question came from Robert Johnston.

"Easy," laughed Neil Buchanan who had been a minister. "It means they don't know what the hell to do with it."

"That's what I thought," Geekie said. "I've been looking at the Scottish papers too. The main interest is on where they found the stone. But a few are speculating on where it'll go. They don't leave much doubt about their preferences, and London isn't one of them."

"Hae ye seen the *Record*, but?" asked Donald Singh, holding it up. "They're nae askin' whaur tae pit it. They're offrin' a reward fur onyyin wha can fin' it! Ye'll min', naebody wis lettin' oan. Sae's a matter o' seein' whaur there's unexplained polis."

"Good point," said Ewan Cameron who had been reading over Singh's shoulder. "It means, whatever we do, we've got to move at once."

"Ah'm tellin' ye, ah'm no' gonny catch ma death hingin' aboot in the castle again at this time o' year," said Jessie Lambie, the MP for Glasgow Guthrie. "Ye'll hae tae think o' somethin' better."

"Aye, but until they tell us where they put it, that'll hardly be an option," Johnston pointed out.

"It is the gentlemen on the *Daily Record* that will be telling us," said Jennie Murray brightly. "There is two rewards offered now. One for the old stone and one for the new one. It is just a pity that – weel, no, it would no' be for us to . . ."

157

"Hold on!" said Graham Fraser. "Duncan? Your father will have told you where he found it – hasn't he?"

No one spoke. The silence was disturbed only by the low-frequency rumble through the double-glazed windows of buses accelerating through Parliament Square. All eyes turned on Duncan. Janet came to his rescue.

"Mr Chairman, Murdo's proposal to go and get the stone wasn't serious, was it, Murdo? No," – Mercer had turned to look at her with his eyes twinkling – "I thought not. It would be a bad mistake to try the same trick twice, even if we knew where to pick it up. Jessie's right. We'll need to think of something better."

"I have three names who've asked to speak," Macarthur said, glancing at the pad in front of him, "and I'll call them in order. Ewan Cameron?"

"Mr Chairman," said Cameron, "I'd like to refer to what I said here in June – and since there were no minutes I'll just refresh everyone's memory. I said Holyrood was a constitutional contradiction – a federal unit inserted in a unitary state. The question has never been answered – who ultimately speaks for Scotland: her representatives here or her representatives there? If we can't establish our supremacy in the last resort, then it's futile to be here at all. I fully accept that the future of the Stone of Destiny and what it symbolises is central to our endeavours. So this is our chance."

There were murmurs of approval.

"Ewan's right," agreed Jock Montrose, called in his turn. "It's now or never, while the main interest is on the discovery and where it happened. It's time to force the issue – both with Holyrood and with Downing Street. Edinburgh can have the old stone back, and the Government must take steps for the real one to be brought down here – permanently."

The approval became enthusiasm. There was a chorus of hear-hears. Knuckles drummed on desks.

"That requires a simple decision endorsed by the Crown," Montrose explained. "An Order in Council perhaps – just as was done in 1996 when the old one was sent to Edinburgh. Anyway, it wouldn't need an Act of Parliament. Holyrood can't stand in the way."

"In theory," Neil Buchanan said, "but unfortunately nobody's told them up there, and they've got some passable lawyers."

158

"Aye, braw fighters, sae we'll hae the mither and faither of a' legal battles," said Mercer.

"Callum Geekie," said Macarthur, nodding to him.

"I'm beginning to see some light," said Geekie. "It's a matter of solidarity. The business at the castle was a rehearsal for the main show ahead of us. But this is something else. This is power politics. We'll win if we stick together. There are enough of us, after all."

Power politics!" repeated Mercer. "Aye, Ah kent ye'd come roond tae ma way of thinkin'."

"But it'll need close collaboration, complete unity, no back-sliding. And all three Whips operating as one – Janet, Maureen and Jock. It'll be like one party." Geekie looked at them one after another, the dispensers of discipline to the Scottish sections of the three main Westminster parliamentary parties. "Can you handle it? It'll sometimes be in defiance of your own Whips' offices. That'll be true for you especially, Janet. Can you stand up to Hartley Blackburn?"

The question caught her by surprise, but she rallied quickly as the meeting's eyes turned on her. "He's only a Chief Whip," she said. "If he doesn't like what I do, he can appoint someone else."

"Very good." said Macarthur. "Now, if we're re-constructing the non-existent executive arm we can't have Duncan there left out – at least, not simply because his party's too small to need a Whip." The MPs signalled their assent again. "So who wants to speak? Duncan himself! Are you happy with all that?"

"Yes, Mr Chairman. And I'm sure an approach needs to be made to the Prime Minister as soon as possible. We mustn't give him time to come up with alternatives. I propose we call Andy Wedderburn in right away to put him in the picture. We'll depend on him to explain the circumstances to the Prime Minister now, and to the cabinet later on. He'll do it well."

Five minutes later the policemen on duty at the north door of Westminster Hall spotted the Secretary of State for the Union, his face hidden in a scarf, stealing across the five-foot-square flagstones towards the committee room steps. "It's Mr Wedderburn finally," said the senior duty officer to his companion. "That makes fifty-nine. Full house!"

*   *   *

159

The insistence with which Wedderburn lodged his request perplexed the Prime Minister at first. He took the point readily that
Scotland already owned one Stone of Destiny and had been care-
less enough to lose it; but that seemed insufficient reason for
insisting that the new-found stone should come to London, especially as the other had turned out to be a counterfeit. Like everybody
else in the country, he understood almost to the point of exhaus-
tion the symbolic importance of the ancient relic to the Scottish
people. The national newspapers based in London may have
regarded the raid on the castle more as a good story than a serious
scandal; but they had not held back on the historical any more
than on the political or criminal detail. Public interest, boosted
by the announcement of a handsome reward in the first instance,
had spread to Scots around the world; and now the discovery of
the authentic stone was fanning that interest to a new intensity.

The previous day, while the Prime Minister was considering
the text of his joint statement to the House of Commons with its
intimation of further decisions to be taken later, it never occurred
to him that the real stone would not be retained in Scotland – in
a cathedral, perhaps, or a museum, or in a castle. He wondered
afterwards why the Scottish MPs had not followed the leader of
the opposition's question about the Royal Prerogative with more
searching supplementaries of their own: it was so unlike politicians
to keep silent about their own patch, given half a chance to cause
a disturbance. Evidently, though, as Wedderburn's visit showed
him, that reticence had not been for lack of concern.

Now the Prime Minister recalled what the party chairman told
him before he went down to Brighton earlier in the month: the
minuscule attendance by Scottish party rank and file at the national
conference; the difficulties which Scotland's MPs had at home
in raising the barest interest in Westminster business; their resentment of the arrogance of Edinburgh in dealing directly with
Brussels; and his own rejected suggestion that some of them should
be given a good conference spot just to boost their morale. He
had sympathy for them, and his inclination was to help them now
if they really cared so much. As Premier, after all, it was his duty
to consult Scotland's MPs and to give heed to their requirements
in such cases. If all the Scottish MPs were in agreement for once,
there was nothing more to be said.

"Very well, Andy," he assented. "If you assure me it's what

Scotland wants, I can't see a difficulty and I won't stand in your way. Where d'you want to put it? Westminster Abbey?"

"That would be traditional and correct," said Wedderburn. "And it'll need to be properly secured. King Edward's chair may have to be adapted."

"We'll speak to the Dean," said the Prime Minister. He turned to the cabinet secretary who had been sitting silent throughout the meeting. "Make a note of that, would you, Matthew? And we'd better check what the procedures are – the same, I suppose, as when they sent the other stone to Edinburgh ten years ago. Royal assent, of course, but that should be a formality if our advice is clear."

Wedderburn rose to leave.

"My colleagues will be very pleased, Prime Minister. They are a bit dispirited these days, as you must have noticed. Re-establishing the stone in the precincts of Westminster will be a vast encouragement to them."

"Hmm," the Prime Minister said. "Meanwhile, I'll have to tell McLeish – "

"McNish."

"I should say McNish – what I've decided. Make a note of that as well, Matthew. I dare say it'll have to be jointly announced too."

"Then it would be appropriate," rejoined Wedderburn immediately, "to explain that you've carefully consulted Scotland's MPs on the matter, and that they are unanimous. I'm sure that would avert any possible accusation of highhandedness on your part."

The Prime Minister saw the logic of that. Wedderburn in due course informed Macarthur of what had been said; and Macarthur passed it on to those who required to know.

As members of the non-existent executive arm, Duncan and Janet were among them. They left Macarthur's desk in Dean's Yard together – apart from Wedderburn himself, no MP from Scotland had been allotted one of the plush modern offices in Portcullis House in Parliament Street – and made their way back to the House of Commons and found a bar there, unfrequented by members because it was still too soon in the evening even for the early drinkers. There they sat side by side, drinking ginger beer, on high stools reviewing developments in low voices, while the barman occupied himself polishing glasses in the background.

They were far from dissatisfied with what they had heard but were well aware of the rocks on the Prime Minister's path. Almost certainly, contingency plans would be called for.

"Of course," said Janet, "Murdo may be right, and we'll have to go and get it again."

Duncan laughed. "You and me? At least twice the weight of the other one, the police watching it and the world's cameras focused on it?"

"No, they're not. Not yet. Where is it, Duncan?" Their eyes met, and Duncan looked away first. "I'm genuinely interested. You can tell me."

He shook his head. She laid a hand gently on his lap.

"I got you off the hook when Graham Fraser asked you. Now I want to know."

"Curiosity killed –"

"Another of your cats? Tell me!"

"Janet – you can see there's a family angle to it."

"You once told me to keep personal emotions under control. An operational necessity, you said." She moved her hand a little.

"They're under control."

"It doesn't feel like it. Tell me, Duncan. Whip's honour. It won't go any further. The secret, anyway, I mean."

For William McNish, the chief relevance of the discovery of the original Stone of Destiny was that it took the heat off him in respect of the stolen one. He recognised no other significance. It had not excited him: excitement was for historians, possibly for the newspapers. The most urgent step, as he saw it, was political: while the police hunted for the lost stone, to produce the new one and display it in some suitable place with as much razzmatazz as possible.

That might not be straightforward. His statement in the Holyrood parliament, carefully co-ordinated with the Prime Minister's in the House of Commons, had gone well. The opposition parties, totally unprepared for his revelations, could immediately think of no way to turn them to their advantage. His cabinet, whom he had informed of the burden of his announcement at the last possible moment – so that none of them could leak it in advance to the press – glumly observed his triumph. He was pleased, too, with his responses to the questions that followed, their content carefully rehearsed with his head of strategy and his press office. When he explained to the assembled MSPs that he was not at liberty to divulge where the stone had been found, no one could have guessed that he did not know himself. When he was asked when it would first be on public view, the house accepted without question his assurance that there were inescapable formalities involving the Crown Office to be completed, and invincible reasons for not divulging an answer, although the display would of course be delayed no longer than necessary. On the question of where the Stone of Destiny would finally rest – there had been an innocent enquiry, not a challenge – he simply said that the house would be told as soon as a decision could be made. Yet the decision, it seemed to his listeners, judging by his tone, would be none but his.

Two more days had gone by when Morag came across him in the parliamentary canteen, pushing away an almost untouched plateful and staring balefully at the space it had occupied on the formica table. His presence there was, of course, his customary paternalist display after a morning stretch in the chamber declining adequately to answer "First Minister's Questions". Not all who were gratified to notice him were aware that his chauffeur would be driving him to St Andrew's House a little later.

"Good afternoon, First Minister," Morag said brightly. "What's the matter now? Shall I bring you some coffee?"

"This is the last time anyone will see me here," he said, pointing at his plate. "That's inedible, tasteless."

She looked at the dismal white and grey lumps swimming there in a yellowish liquid. "What is it?"

"Cabbie-claw. The small print on the menu says it's wind-blown cod in an egg sauce. It can't be meant to taste like that – or even look like it." He picked up a fork and stabbed it.

"Well, it's no use taking it out on a fish. What's the matter?"

McNish regarded in her in silence.

"You'd better tell me," she prodded.

"The Stone of Destiny. The new one. I've given instructions for it to be produced at once. My private office is handling it. I'm going to have it placed here – in the parliament. Possibly in the concourse. It'll bring a new dignity to the building. It's the right answer."

Morag looked at him, concealing her despair. His capacity for self-delusion was sometimes astounding. He was half conscious of it himself. It was what had brought the latest cloud of gloom upon him.

"You know where it is, then?"

"No," he said after a pause. "That's not my business. My business is where it's going to be."

"Has the Crown Agent done the report on it?"

"I've no idea."

"Who's going to fetch it for you?"

"I'm First Minister. I've limitless resources at my disposal."

"What if it needs the army?"

"What if it does?"

"Defence isn't devolved," said Morag.

"Then we'll find another way."

"The thing is," said Morag, "that Downing Street's been in touch. It's to do with the stone. You'll have to talk to the Prime Minister when you're back at the office. Craig Millar's in a state about it – he's just been on."

"You'd better come back with me, Morag. Something tells me we'll need a cabinet. And maybe the press officers afterwards."

McNish was coming down to earth. Millar met them on the steps as they got out of the car and walked with them into McNish's office.

"The cabinet secretary was on the secure line. The Prime Minister wants to speak to you, First Minister. He's made a decision about the stone."

"Oh? What sort of decision? What's it to do with him? He can't." McNish's bravado was unpersuasive.

"Shall I put a call through? They're expecting it."

"Very well."

Millar lifted the receiver on the First Minister's desk and spoke to an assistant. "Get Number Ten, please, Deirdre."

"Meanwhile," said McNish, "have you located the stone? Did you find the professor, whatever he's called?"

"No, First Minister. The information's classified. They were your own instructions. The need-to-know principle."

"Well, don't I need to know?"

Craig Millar, drawing breath for a difficult reply, was saved by a warble from the telephone. He picked up the receiver again and, having acknowledged a question, passed it to McNish. McNish pointed silently to the monitor ear-pieces so that Millar and Morag could listen and take notes.

"This is Willie McNish speaking. How can I help you?"

A female voice asked McNish to hold for the Prime Minister. Some moments later a disembodied recording asked McNish not to ring off, assured him that his call was valuable to it, and thanked him for waiting. He was about to bang down his receiver when the Prime Minister came on the line.

"Ah – er – William! Good afternoon! Are you keeping well?"

"Thank you, yes, Prime Minister. And yourself?"

"The Coronation Stone," said the Prime Minister, wasting no more time on the courtesies. "I know there are still some formalities to be gone through – well, with the Palace for one – but I don't want to delay the provisional announcement about its future. Otherwise we'll invite speculation and confusion."

"Yes," agreed McNish. "I'm of the same opinion."

"Good, William. Bill! May I call you Bill? You'll have been in touch with your MPs, then. I understand they're all of one mind – "

"In touch with my MPs?" McNish sounded puzzled.

"MPs. Members of Parliament."

"Yes, I know."

"The Scottish ones."

"You mean . . . You mean, the Westminster ones?" McNish's eyes turned in bafflement to meet Millar's and Morag's.

"Of course. I've been speaking to Andy Wedderburn, too, and I've no problem with that proposal. None at all. Hullo? Hullo? Have we been cut off?"

McNish forced his attention back.

"No, I'm here. What proposal was it, Prime Minister?"

"Well, to have it installed in the abbey. If you like, we could make simultaneous statements, like we did before, to show we're in complete accord. I think we should. All right? Or we . . . Hullo?"

McNish was thinking of abbeys he knew of. He seemed to remember there were ones in Dunkeld and Melrose; and Arbroath where that Declaration had been signed some time ago; and of course the abbey ruins at Holyrood. Those ruins would be a dramatic setting for a block of black marble. Rather exposed, admittedly. Or perhaps the Prime Minister had had St Giles' in mind all along, Edinburgh's High Kirk, forgetting it was a cathedral.

"Yes. Which abbey, did you think, Prime Minister?"

"Well, Westminster, of course, where the old stone was." There was irritation in his voice. "Look, er – Bill, haven't you spoken to the Scottish MPs about this, even the ones in our own party? We seem to be at cross purposes. I'd be grateful if you'd get that straightened out, otherwise we'll both look fatheaded. All right?"

McNish had the sensation of being on a runaway horse. Morag and Craig watched him control his panic and attempt to resist being hustled.

"As a matter of fact, Prime Minister, I'd been thinking of making an announcement about it myself."

"Excellent! Then our offices must co-ordinate both statements. We must sing off the same song-sheet. Thursday's a good day, if it suits you too. I'll have cleared it with the Palace by then. Tell me – how are you coming along with the other one?"

"The other one?" asked McNish weakly. Was he speaking about legs being pulled?

"The Coronation Stone you lost. Are you any nearer to finding it?"

"No – but as we've found the original – "

"Well, you wouldn't want two, anyway, William, would you? Let me know if you need help recovering it. It can't have gone far. And, by the way, it occurred to me that the people in the Tower of London know a thing or two about that kind of security if it would help you in the future. Of course, it might be a bit insensitive to offer advice unless it was asked for."

"Aye, yes, it might be a bit."

"Good to talk to you, then, Bill. We must have another word about bringing the thing south, but perhaps you and Andy should fix that up together. As early as you can, I think. We'll need a date. All right? Our people must get in touch. Goodbye."

A hounded look on his face, McNish handed the receiver to Millar and said: "That was the Prime Minister."

A less fraught, more academic telephone conversation was taking place between Professor Innes and Ian the geologist. Ian had let his usual urbanity slip, and the words tumbling out of him betrayed his excitement.

"Settle down," said Dr Innes, "take a breath and try again. Where d'you want to start?"

"Jerusalem."

"Ah!"

"I've been on to the geological department's web-site there. The print-out's come through. You remember about meteorite showers?"

"Go on."

"Well, fragments – a substantial spread of them – have been found and collected over the years in a belt running east-west about ten to fifteen miles north of Jerusalem. Near a place called Beiten, formerly known as Luz."

"And –?"

"Basaltic achondrite. Stony-iron. Dark, like the stone. Some pieces are magnetic – only slightly but, then, they're small and they've been knocked about."

"And they match up?"

"As close as it's possible to judge. The composition seems pretty well identical."

"Well, well, well!" said Innes. "Anything else?"

"Yes," said Ian. "Tom's just pointed it out to me. The old name for Luz was Bethel."

"Jacob's pillow!" Innes said softly. "How extraordinary! Everything falling into place. And I still think it must have been a most uncomfortable thing to sleep on. We might ask the opinion of the Moderator sometime."

"The shower points towards the 'plains'."

"You're surmising that this was the fall that destroyed the cities there?"

"Just a working hypothesis, Dr Innes, to keep Tom amused. Me, too, actually. It's only circumstantial evidence, of course: it'll never be anything more, but still . . . Should we say anything about it all yet?"

He considered. "Well, probably not, Ian. There's enough hullabaloo already, don't you think? I hear one of the papers has a reward out for its hiding place. But I'll have another word with Dr Mackay. He thinks it'll have to be brought to Edinburgh once all the paperwork's done. That'll be another big event, I suppose. So let's keep quiet about its origins until then – if you can bear to."

"Fine, Dr Innes. I'll tell Tom."

When briefing his cabinet on his talk with Number Ten Downing Street the First Minister understandably put his own gloss on it. He had, he explained, stood up robustly to the proposition that a decision on the future of the stone should be taken anywhere but in Scotland: indeed, he had told the Premier that he was about to make a decision himself. And he had expressed astonishment that any account had been taken of the wishes of the Scottish MPs in such a case. They were to talk again later. None of that was unreasonably far from the truth, and McNish quickly believed it himself. At any rate the ministers – the dozen or so who could be brought together hastily for an urgent meeting – considered that outrage was an appropriate response, although it would directed less against the Prime Minister than against Scotland's tribunes in the south who had so obviously nobbled him.

"I don't propose to let the Stone of Destiny leave Scotland without a fight," McNish informed his colleagues sternly. "This seems to me a point of the highest principle, and I invite your views." He shifted himself away from the puking infant on the lap of the Minister for Single-Parent Families next to him. "You, Christine? Is our constitutional position solid?"

The Solicitor-General said it was uncertain. Treasure trove was certainly a devolved area. She had examined the Scotland Act once more, but could not see how it entitled the Scottish Executive to appropriate treasure of whatever provenance against the wishes of the sovereign expressed in Council. The subject was not covered. It was not clear whether it was reserved. "On the other hand," she said, "if the Queen's and Lord Treasurer's Remembrancer decided to allot the stone to a Scottish institution for safekeeping – "

"Such as St Giles'?" asked the Minister for Arts, Science and Lifelong Education.

"Yes, if it had registered status."

"Or Edinburgh Castle?" suggested the Deputy First Minister spitefully.

"Precisely. And backed by a royal warrant. Then it might be held there on the same terms as the stolen one."

168

"How do we square this remembrance person, then?" McNish demanded.

"I can't think what you mean, First Minister. However, the Treasure Trove Advisory Panel is appointed on the advice of the official arts committee –"

"Fine!" said McNish. "So who's on the committee?"

The Solicitor General turned to the Arts Minister for an answer.

"There's a number of *ex officio* members," said the minister, consulting a file. "The chairpersons of the Historic Buildings Council and the Ancient Monuments Board for Scotland, for a start. And someone seconded from the Royal Fine Arts Commission."

"Excellent. Those are all executive appointments, aren't they?"

"Yes, but there's a problem."

"You mean the Standards Commissioner?"

"No. You'll remember we had the bonfire of the quangos a few years back. It was supposed to be a vote-winner."

"What's that to do with it?"

"We abolished the Historic Buildings Council."

"Ah, yes."

"And the Ancient Monuments Board."

The First Minister frowned. "Well, that's only two."

"And we wound up the Royal Fine Arts Commission. And the Advisory Commission on SSSIs."

"What's that stand for?"

"The scientific site people. And the Royal Commission on the Ancient and Historical Monuments of Scotland. That makes five out of the committee."

"They were fuel on the flames." The Deputy First Minister suppressed her glee unsuccessfully.

"Who does it leave, then?" asked McNish uncomfortably.

"Really only the chairperson of Historic Scotland," said the Arts Minister. "Sir Hew something. The genius in charge up at the castle. A worthy man, for sure, but maybe not the best one to say who should look after another stone. We haven't got round to appointing a full new committee, or even discussing it."

"How long would it take?"

"I suppose, if you were thinking of appointing – well – some of our friends again, a week or so . . . but the policy was to avoid putting our friends on quangos unless it was absolutely necessary."

"Well, isn't it?"

"We thought it was a vote-loser."

"You're the minister," said McNish sullenly. "I'll leave it with you. And even a week could be too late."

He looked round the cabinet faces, knowing that so far as packing the panel was concerned he had struck an impasse. They were waiting for a better plan.

"What we are left with," he said grimly, "is to move before the Prime Minister does. I propose making a simple announcement to the House on Wednesday that the newly discovered stone will be installed in a suitable place in Scotland – and that that will be confirmed later by a free vote of the elected representatives of the Scottish people in their own parliament. That is the challenge we shall throw at them!"

To McNish's satisfaction there was no dissent. To the new Minister for Local Government, the latest of a long succession to hold that poisoned chalice, who asked where the stone was now, he regretted that he was still not free to say. To the Deputy First Minister's enquiry about where he would place it he replied that he was still taking advice. The Solicitor-General asked what he would do if his action were declared *ultra vires*.

"*Ultra* –?"

"Christine means if you're not allowed to," said the Lord Advocate. "What would you tell them?"

"Easy," McNish said. "Finders keepers."

The real reason why the First Minister withheld from his ministers his plan to put the Stone of Destiny in the middle of the parliamentary concourse was the usual one – his fear, born of experience, not that they would object to it but that one of them would leak it to the press first. He could trust them, just, not to divulge his intention deliberately to pre-empt what the Prime Minister might announce to the Commons; but he would give them the shortest possible notice of the full contents of his statement to the House. They wouldn't enjoy being bounced, he expected, but running a tight ship – whatever that meant exactly – was never easy.

The more McNish thought about his idea for the stone, the more he liked it. He might get the Queen or one of the royal family to perform the unveiling. A household name, anyway. He might do it personally. There would be a plaque to record it. The stone would have to be securely fastened down, of course; but at all times there were security guards in the building, twenty-four-hours a day every day in the year, not to speak of a police presence. He would have a word about that with Sir Andrew McCallum as soon as the Chief Constable could drag himself away from the pursuit of the castle thieves. Never mind: those were details. What was pressing more uneasily on his mind was his being kept humiliatingly in the dark about the stone's whereabouts. He had dissimulated to his cabinet as well as to the public. Morag's questions to him had been pertinent. True, he had personally ordained that no one should know who did not need to know. It was a sensible enough order: a mass public excursion to a possibly sensitive site had to be averted – if it was still on site: he was uninformed. He had forgotten to say who would take the need-to-know decisions, and it was intolerable that no one had thought to put him in the picture. The secret seemed to be the property of a small clique of academics and, of all people, Wee Dougie the Presiding Officer.

Wee Dougie would have to be tackled, not only to extract the secret from him. He was the authority to whom notice had to be given him of any ministerial intention to make a statement – a task he now entrusted to his principal private secretary.

"The stone, Craig. I'll make my announcement to the House on Wednesday. Would you notify the clerk and the Presiding Officer?"

"We haven't finalised the wording with Downing Street yet, First Minister – and, anyway, you agreed to do it together on Thursday."

"No. Look at your notes. The Prime Minister said Thursday would suit him. It doesn't suit me. Leave it like that, please."

Millar, meeting McNish's eyes, immediately saw rough weather ahead. "Shall I show you the draft as it stands?"

"As you please. I made no promises to agree to it. I'll have my own text."

"Would it be prudent – as the Prime Minister suggested – to have a word with Mr Wedderburn?"

"I can't see the advantage, Craig. He'll find out soon enough what I'm going to do. The paella – what's that word?"

"Palladium."

"Yes. The palladium will stay in Scotland. The ministers are all behind me."

The rough weather was suddenly closer than Millar feared.

Morag had already warned him privately of McNish's off-the-cuff plan to keep the stone in Holyrood, but he had thought it too nebulous to worry about. Now storm cones were hoisted in his head."I am certain, First Minister," said Millar, "that we should let Downing Street have the text of your statement before you tell the MSPs. We've been working on a joint one in good faith. If we don't warn them, you'll be accused of bad faith, and that'll make future communication very hard."

McNish saw the sense in that. "Very well." He thought for a moment. "But I'll be damned if I warn Andy Wedderburn or any of those baboons with their three-day weeks, long lunches and parties every night."

It was a pity, Millar thought, making a note, that he had not said as much to the Prime Minister. The explosion might have cleared the air usefully.

"And get David up here. We'll draft the text together, and a press release." Millar made another note: David Cadell, the First Minister's chief press officer, was a difficult character whose approach to constitutional matters was mischievous rather than actually irresponsible.

"Yes, First Minister. And, meanwhile –"

"Meanwhile," said McNish, "I need full information about the stone. Where is it? Who's got it? I must be told!"

"You'd best speak to Dr Mackay," said Millar. "Maybe he'll tell you. I'll be in touch with his clerk right away."

When they met briefly by arrangement outside the chamber, the Presiding Officer would add nothing to the First Minister's knowledge of the stone's location. That, he assured him, would no doubt be disclosed in due course when the Queen's Remembrancer's decision was published. In the meantime he could not reveal what he had learnt wholly by courtesy of a friend.

Craig Millar had conveyed his worries to Morag, and Morag with his encouragement had spoken to Dr Mackay. She could not tell him directly what McNish had in mind to do, but she had been able sufficiently to indicate that a crisis was brewing, without breaking confidentiality, to cause him to question McNish carefully.

"You're making a statement about the stone, are you? About its future?"

172

"That's why I need to know where it is."

"But not from me. Until the Crown Agent has – "

"This is a matter for the people of Scotland. For this parliament. I have discussed it in cabinet."

"I suspect what you're doing is *ultra vires*."

A troubled look passed across the First Minister's face.

"You're aware," said Mackay, "that my office has been in touch with the Speaker's office in the House of Commons. The two statements were to be made simultaneously."

"Well, now mine'll be first."

"Does the Prime Minister know that?" asked Mackay.

"I've spoken to him. He'll have the text in advance."

"I'd like to see it, too, if I may. Have you consulted the other party leaders here?"

"I don't have to." McNish began to sound peeved as well as defensive.

"It might be sensible. It would certainly be civil."

"I'll let them have the text before I speak. If I propose to keep the stone in Scotland, what can they say? 'Let's let the English have it'?"

Mackay looked at him. His rising anger was evident but he disguised his contempt.

"Do the English want it?" he asked. "Is it the English who bother you?"

"Will you tell me where it is?"

"No."

"Then will you join me at a press conference after I've made my statement?"

"Certainly not. And if any journalist releases your statement before it is made to the House there'll be no statement to the House."

"Then it'll be on your head and my conscience will be clean."

Mackay forced himself to keep his temper. "What do you mean by that, Wullie?"

"You'll see, Dougie."

At noon on Wednesday the Prime Minister was in his drawing-room in Downing Street discussing with the American ambassador the latest dismal twist of events in the Middle East. They were interrupted, not by the Foreign Secretary who was to join them, but by his own agitated principal private secretary bearing the proposed text of the First Minister's statement to the Holyrood parliament. With it was an apologetic notification, drafted by an agonised Craig Millar, that it was to be delivered at half past two that day.

"You must excuse me, Ambassador," the Prime Minister said, taking the documents and adding to his private secretary: "I hope it isn't trivial."

He read it in growing puzzlement, then handed them back. "It makes no sense. Wedderburn must have got it all wrong. You'd better get him here as fast as possible. And ask for sandwiches to be sent up when he comes."

The Secretary of State for the Union arrived soon after one o'clock when the ambassador had gone. He was shown what the Prime Minister had seen and asked to explain it.

"He can't do that," said Wedderburn firmly. "He isn't within his rights."

"What I find disgraceful," said the Prime Minister, "is that McNeish and I –"

"McNish".

"Didn't I say McNish? He and I were in full agreement on a joint statement. It was to be on Thursday. And the stone was to come to the abbey here. We're waiting for the Queen's assent. What's he playing at? I've never met him. He doesn't sound too bright."

"He isn't."

"The man's a plonker. Has he discussed it with you yet?"

"Well, no, Prime Minister. Communication is very . . . uncertain."

"You told me that this was what Scotland wanted. You said it was the settled opinion of her representatives."

"That's correct. We're a hundred per cent behind it."

"And in Holyrood –"

Wedderburn spread his hands. "You spoke to McNish."

The Prime Minister brooded, realisation dawning. He poured himself a glass of water, took a sandwich and passed the plate to Wedderburn.

"In other words, it's another turf war, is it? Here we are well into the twenty-first century, and you're squabbling over a symbol. Squabbling? Not even on speaking terms! And you're asking me

174

to risk the integrity of the United Kingdom over a thing like that by supporting the Scottish MPs down here."

"It's not a 'thing'."

"Yes, it's a totem! Face it – you'd like me to stop the Scottish parliament doing what it wants with an old lump of meteorite, because you want to stuff it somewhere in Westminster Abbey. Is that it?"

Wedderburn, always a man of fair judgment as well as steely calm, considered that as a proposition. At one level it was true. But what risked the integrity of the kingdom was the uncertainty of who ultimately spoke for Scotland within it. The devolution legislation, incomplete and ambiguous on too many points, had never clarified that central issue. Some matters were reserved, some devolved; but the gut question was unanswered because it was unanswerable. The future of the stone was as significant – indeed, as potent – an issue as any. If the MPs lost this turf war, if their every power were neutered, if they really had no *raison d'être* beyond constituting a formal presence in Westminster, the Union of the Parliaments, three centuries old, would be at an end. Its Scottish members might as well go home.

Wedderburn thought it a bad moment to debate the finer points of the devolution settlement. There was still a chance that the unfortunate rift between Scotland's politicians could be prevented from widening irreparably, but – he looked at the clock on the Prime Minister's mantelpiece – there was not much time.

"Even if it were a lump of any old meteorite, which it isn't," he said carefully, "what you are threatened with is a huge new assertion of power by the Holyrood executive. Whether the whole parliament there will support it, we don't know – but it's in the nature of all parliaments to push continually at the limits of what they can do."

"A huge new assertion of power?" The Prime Minister was doubtful.

"Yes." Wedderburn tapped the First Minister's text. "This is like a hijack, an act of piracy. It is the conscious, politically-motivated misappropriation of Crown property. It is *ultra vires*. It is certainly a deliberate challenge to Scottish MPs and a wilful act of defiance against you personally."

"Perhaps. What if the Crown Agent agrees with it?"

"That might be another story. But we're talking about power.

175

Please don't underestimate the mood of our members down here. They've been sidelined. Their strength has been sapped – and Holyrood is claiming it. The sapping goes on."

"If you say so. It won't have escaped your notice that my government here is just about castrated. Every time I try to pass an English Bill I lose my majority. There's devolution for you!"

"Exactly," said Wedderburn. "We're in this together." He looked at his watch again. "It's nearly half-past one, Prime Minister."

"What should I do about it?"

"There's still time to telephone the First Minister or get a message to him. You must say that, as he has made it impossible to agree on a common statement, he must postpone any announcement until the Queen's and Lord Treasurer's Remembrancer – from the Crown Office in Edinburgh – has reported."

"What if he says no?"

"You are Prime Minister."

9

R OSS BURTON, who received and read his time-embargoed copy of McNish's statement a little after two o'clock, encountered the Presiding Officer while on his way to the press gallery. He indicated the paper he was carrying.

"Good God, Dr Mackay," he said as their eyes met.

They stood to one side as the party leaders Walter Moncrieff and Jock Hamilton walked past together, making for the chamber, earnestly discussing the same document.

"Good God, Ross."

"Our people in London are expecting the statement tomorrow."

"So I understand."

"Can he do this?"

"No. The stone belongs to the Queen."

"Can't you stop him?"

"No. He has followed the parliamentary procedures correctly. He can say whatever he likes."

"Won't it be challenged?"

"I don't think he's interested in my advice."

They passed on to their destinations.

Observation of the oecumenical, multicultural or possibly simply agnostic ceremony known as Time for Reflection being over in the chamber, the Presiding Officer rose to say there would be a statement from the First Minister.

The two previous statements about stones – one about a loss, the other about a discovery – had been virtually on Mackay's instruction. This one he would have prevented if he could. When he saw the text he had difficulty in believing that Downing Street could have accepted it without protest. Its content reflected McNish at his blinkered, expedient, self-deluding worst. Its tone was both crowing and inflammatory. There seemed to be a swagger to the First Minister's mien as he stood up and surveyed the House, conspicuously taking in his own party, the opposition members, the public gallery and the press.

"The people of Scotland are anxious to know what is to be done with their Stone of Destiny," McNish declaimed. "They demand that their ancient and revered palladium" – he made two stabs at the word, neither precisely on the mark – "be installed in a place and a setting fully worthy of their reverence. That is both natural and justified. They could scarcely ask for less."

He paused to permit a demonstration of approval from his own ranks. It was slightly delayed, but it came.

"It falls to the government of Scotland to take the decision on their behalf. It has done so without fear, for no one else could take it for us . . ."

He paused again, nodded, and received another short burst of approval.

". . . though they might try! Though they might try! It has done so without favour, for that is how we conduct our business."

"Or claim to," thought Burton in the seats above. His eye went round the gallery rail to where he saw Morag McLeod, the First Minister's special adviser, and Craig Millar, head of the private office, sitting together listening in patently sombre mood. Here were two whose duty it was to cope with the succession of personalities assumed by the First Minister often in the course of a single day. At one moment he would be bending without resistance beneath a storm of assumption and presumption from the quicker-witted operator in Downing Street. The next he would be countering with spirit the unwelcome advice and ill-concealed dislike of his ministerial colleagues in cabinet. And, now, here he was posturing as Scotland's populist champion, egomanic, knowingly short-circuiting civil service procedures and wilfully defying the Prime Minister. This alternating display of erratic judgment, cravenness, narrowness of interest, pusillanimity, self-delusion, opportunism, hypocrisy and bravado were offset by the high degree of political astuteness he showed when his career depended on it. Oor Wullie's watchword was expedience.

"We are agreed," intoned McNish solemnly, "that its permanent home must be in Edinburgh –"

This time there were cheers and slapping of desks, led by members from Edinburgh and the Lothians. They were interrupted by the inevitable cry of "Whit's wrang wi' Glasgow? It's still Scotland's city o' culture, innit?"

"Order, please," commanded the Presiding Officer. "The First Minister will take questions later."

"– Edinburgh, because it's the capital of Scotland. But where in Edinburgh should it be placed? Different possibilities have been discussed in cabinet."

At least two cabinet ministers could have been seen to blink, but they were soon enlightened.

"They included Edinburgh Castle – but we've just had the unfortunate experience there. And St Giles' Cathedral too – but this is for all Scots, not only the few. So I'm sure that members will warmly approve the decision that the Stone of Destiny – the real, authentic stone – is to rest permanently here at Holyrood, within the very precincts of Scotland's own parliament –"

McNish paused to appreciate the stunned silence which, as he expected, greeted his idea.

"– where the people of this country, regardless of creed – yes – and of colour, class, age, party or gender –"

The Deputy First Minister hissed something at him.

"– or sexual orientation, naturally," he continued smoothly, "perhaps whilst exercising their democratic right and privilege to come in person to hear laws that are being debated and perfected in their name, can glory in the presence of their" – he hesitated over a word –" of the symbol of their nationhood. And tourists, too, of course," he added, spoiling the effect.

"There'll be a small charge, then?" The intervention was not loud, but it was audible enough to raise a chuckle and puncture McNish's pretentiousness.

"And I propose," McNish went on, his voice rising, "that the Stone of Destiny be placed in the very centre of our parliamentary foyer." He pointed to the doors of the chamber. "It will bring a new dignity to this institution and everyone who works here. It will be a permanent reminder of the high respect Scotland enjoys within the United Kingdom" – this largely meaningless aspiration had been suggested by McNish's speech-writer to remove any flavour of a nationalist rant – "and above all it will remain a majestic assertion of the primacy of this House in speaking and acting for the people of Scotland."

Pretentious or not, it was a sentiment which his followers could welcome, and they did so loudly. There were more muted but positive noises of assent from other quarters, but not all. The First Minister raised a hand as though to calm some unseemly excitement.

"Although my executive has given a courageous lead on this occasion, this is not a party matter," McNish informed the MSPs unconvincingly, looking at the scowling faces of Jock Hamilton and Walter Moncrieff in front of him. "No, it calls for the support of the whole parliament. And I therefore propose to put the implementation of this decision into the worthy and capable hands of our Presiding Officer. We shall ask him to appoint and chair an all-party committee, and to ensure that the Stone of Destiny is brought here as soon as possible – which he is in a unique position to do – and to have it installed with whatever ceremony he judges fit."

He turned to the chair with the suggestion of a bow, and then sat down. There was prolonged applause in which all parties, conscious of the cameras above, eventually joined in. McNish had made, by his lights, a clever move; and a permanent enemy of Mackay.

While MSPs were still rising to comment on McNish's plan, word came to the Prime Minister in his room in the House of Commons that his demand for the postponement of any statement to the Scottish Parliament had been ignored. Both his press officer – formally known as the Director of Communication – and his permanent private secretary, who had taken the call from Downing Street, were with him. The PPS at once sent for Wedderburn who, for want of anything better to do, was sitting on the government front bench in the chamber where Question Time conducted by the Chancellor of the Exchequer was pursuing its usual quasi-informative knockabout course. Yet he had guessed he would be summoned.

"Andy? What does that bloody idiot in Edinburgh think he's doing?"

"He's gone ahead with it, then?" Wedderburn sat down on the

green leather chair the Prime Minister's finger indicated. "I thought he might."

"Well, what now?"

"You can't accept it, Prime Minister. It's a deliberate act of defiance."

"You pushed me into it, Andy. And I told you – it's not worth a confrontation over a lump of rock which nobody'd heard of a month ago."

"If it isn't this, it'll be something else."

"I'm inclined to let it go."

"I shouldn't do that in your position, Prime Minister." Wedderburn's voice had hardened, and both the Prime Minister and his PPS looked at him quickly.

"No?"

"It would upset our Scottish members here. You know the mood they're in. They want the stone in Westminster. You need their support."

"Are you saying what I think you're saying?"

"Yes. And if I may say so –"

"What?"

"The Scottish press will want a reaction from you very soon. They'll know McNish has jumped the gun, even if the MSPs don't."

The Prime Minister turned to his press officer. "Can you stall? I can hardly make the joint statement now, flatly contradicting what that bugger's said. But" – he looked sternly at Wedderburn – "I can't concede anything, either."

"In that case, Prime Minister," said the press officer, "we can say that Downing Street is studying carefully what the First Minister has said."

"Pretty weak," said Wedderburn. "They'll want more than that."

"We might add that we were still in discussions about a joint announcement," the PPS suggested, "and that the statement took you by surprise. That will put McNish in the wrong."

"Why not tell them that the stone is Crown property," Wedderburn said, "and that in due course the British government and no one else will be offering advice to Her Majesty on its future?"

"That's not stalling. It's confronting."

181

"It's what you're going to have to say sooner or later. Why not now?"

The Presiding Officer, still boiling inwardly, was working his way through the names of the MSPs wishing to question the First Minister. Jock Hamilton, conventionally bound as leader of the opposition to question the executive's wisdom, thought of several alternative places where the stone might suitably be installed, none of them with the political overtones of Holyrood. McNish's reply verged on the coarse. Hamish Wu, one of Paisley's Nationalist representatives, introduced the abrasive consideration that until the stolen stone was returned to the castle the people of Scotland would entertain no realistic hope that a parliament led by the present executive could keep it safe. Fortunately, said McNish, popular confidence in the executive had never been higher than now. There followed the predictable jeers, but no hostile questioner had seized any solid partisan advantage from what appeared to be the unassailable general position occupied by the First Minister. Even Walter Moncrieff, for the Scotch Enlightenment Party, confined himself to putting on record his willingness to consider McNish's proposal and asking for the parliament to be given a chance to look at it thoroughly later on.

Mackay of course marked the reticence of Moncrieff's intervention. His comments when the theft from the castle was revealed to the House had been of a different order, advising the parliament in almost as many words to overlook the crime because all would be for the best. Mackay guessed that SEP policy on the Dunsinane stone must still be developing, perhaps in tune with whatever plot the Scottish MPs might be hatching in the South. On the other hand, Moncrieff alone among the MSPs could have been aware that the Prime Minister in London had had very different plans for it.

The First Minister had caught his political opponents on the back foot and was having an easy time. He continued to respond with varying degrees of ill nature to questions he found unhelpful, to others with good humour bordering on the patronising. When Mrs Murray Stewart harped back to the stolen stone, asking whether in view of the changed circumstances the Scottish taxpayer was still expected to fund the reward for its recovery, he told her that her party must drag itself out of the past and look forwards. When James Maclean, the shadow spokesman on social affairs, asked what the opinion of the Queen's and Lord Treasurer's Remembrancer had been, and whether it had influenced the executive's recommendation to the chamber, he was congratulated on the appositeness of his question. But neither he nor Mrs Murray Stewart received, or had indeed expected, a straight answer, so when the Presiding Officer finally recognised the MSP for Glasgow Burrill, willing as ever to give audible evidence of his presence, Alasdair McNab scorned to put a question of any import.

"It's guid," he said, "that the embellishment o' wir grand new landmark Edinburgh parliament continues unabated and regardless of expense." He pointed towards the chamber doors as McNish had done earlier. "Yon's the biggest sitooterie in Scotland nae coontin' Glasgow Central Station. But there's naebody sits oot in either o' them, because there's been naethin' tae sit on."

"Order!" interjected Mackay. "Does the honourable member actually have a question in mind?"

"Aye, Mr Presiding Office. Wad oor First Minister confirm that pittin' the Stane o' Destiny oot there wull be the start o' a proper furnishin' an' fittin' programme for wir concourse?"

It was time to move on. The Presiding Officer allowed McNish his brief, unpleasant answer – to the effect that McNab had never come to terms with what happened to Rangers in 1967, the year Celtic won the Champions' Cup – before announcing next business, a private member's Bill extending the right to education in minority languages to Urdu, Hindi, Punjabi and Gujarati. Mackay vacated the chair for one of his deputies and marched purposefully out of the chamber. Ross Burton, hurrying down from the press gallery, buttonholed him.

"Dr Mackay, there's a press conference scheduled right away."

"So I believe, Ross. He'll be on his own."

"I think you should be there, Dr Mackay. He's landed you in it, hasn't he?"

"He has a right to ask me to chair a committee, even in public like that without warning." Mackay laughed humourlessly. "For some reason he told me his conscience was clean! I think he meant 'clear'."

"If it's clean, it's only because it's never been used."

"Well, I've a right to refuse, and for your information I shall."

"That's why you ought to be there, Dr Mackay. There's trouble coming."

"Something new?"

"Aye. Number Ten has put out a statement. One of its own, repudiating McNish, and he'll only just be hearing of it now. I've had a copy from our people in Westminster." Burton indicated Craig Millar beside the stairs leading to the press room, speaking urgently to the First Minister, who was shaking his head vigorously. David Cadell, chief press officer at Bute House, stood beside them wearing his usual expression of detached amusement.

Mackay could always subordinate his anger and pride to the requirements of his office. "Thanks, Ross. Maybe I'll slip in at the back."

The First Minister surveyed the gathering with a pleased smile. The entire Scottish political press corps seemed to be there. He nodded at Joe Hunter from the *Press and Journal*, Arthur Ferris from *The Scotsman*, Ian McCafferty from *The Sunday Post*, Mary Andrews from the *Scottish Daily Express*. He saw the Edinburgh correspondents of *The Times*, *The Daily Telegraph* and the *Independent* breaking up from a huddle. He noted the usual television cameras, and beside them the political editors of BBC Scotland and the various regional stations probably hoping for individual interviews afterwards. He must remember to congratulate Cadell: the press room had never been so full. It would have been madness to have taken Craig's advice to postpone a press conference like this. True enough, the Prime Minister's statement sounded like a complication, but some such reaction was predictable and could be dealt with in due course: first things first.

Whatever doubts anyone had once had about devolution, McNish reflected, Edinburgh had certainly become an important political centre in its own right. For the first time since the middle of September, he felt that the world was appreciating his personal importance too. Here he was, Scotland's First Minister, with the national media about to eat out of his hands: he had given them a story about a bold Holyrood initiative for their front pages, and he would welcome their questions with answers that would give it wings. Cadell had settled the press in their seats and was now beckoning him to his own. As he sat down he caught sight of Douglas Mackay sitting at the back of the room. Near him and standing next to one another were Morag and Millar from his office. Good – he would ask them later how they thought the conference had gone.

"Thank you for coming, gentlemen," said Cadell. "We have forty minutes, which should be enough. The First Minister is ready to take questions about his statement to the parliament – I think you have all had copies."

McNish rose to welcome his friends from the press personally, told them of his pride in arranging provisionally for the real Stone of Destiny to share the Holyrood site with Scotland's parliament – provisionally, because there were details to be worked out. Then he signalled to the first questioner, Peggy MacShane of *The Guardian*. "Ladies first," he said, risking a smile.

"Thank you, First Minister. Will you confirm that you made your statement to the House just now in the face of an urgent request from the Prime Minister to postpone it?"

This was not quite the invitation McNish had hoped for to expatiate on the historic relevance of his proposal.

"I'm sure we all want to speak about the future of the stone," he said. "Any discussions between the Prime Minister and myself are naturally confidential."

"Is that Yes or No?" Peggy MacShane demanded.

"As you will be aware, Peggy, treasure trove is a devolved matter, so that the future of any object found in Scotland will – "

"I know about treasure trove. Would you answer my question?"

" – will naturally be decided here – "

"You are saying Yes, then? There was to be a joint statement in Holyrood and Westminster tomorrow, and you went ahead today by yourself without telling them? Is that correct?"

It had been an uncomfortable start, but McNish had not forgotten how to duck and weave. "Not correct, Peggy. Downing Street had an advance copy of my statement. Someone else, now? You, Mary?"

The political editor of the *Scottish Daily Express* willingly took up Peggy MacShane's baton. "That was when the urgent request came then," she said.

"What's your question, Mary?"

"On the statement from Number Ten – "

"I have nothing to say about that. You must ask Number Ten."

"Very well, First Minister. Treasure trove. The Crown Office in Scotland hasn't made its report on the stone. Why didn't you wait for it?"

"I am First Minister."

"That doesn't entitle you or anyone else to appropriate Crown property. Our lawyers say it's *ultra vires*."

"Lawyers are paid for their opinions," retorted McNish injudiciously.

"Are you above the law? What does the solicitor-general say?"

"Naturally I have discussed it with the solicitor-general. Someone else's turn? Yes, Jim?" McNish signed to the *Daily Record*'s correspondent.

"Did you answer Mary's question, First Minister?"

"I hope so, Jim. I'm waiting for yours". McNish was actually gaining confidence. He knew that the press were probing every weak point, but he was giving as good as he got, and believed he had managed to stonewall or respond convincingly on each one. He had forgotten that when journalists scent blood they are adept, at least while it matters, at concealing their growing hostility.

"Well, I was in the press gallery just now with everyone else," Jim Bell said. "Nothing was said about the objections from Downing Street – and the plan for a joint statement tomorrow. Did the MSPs not know about that?" He paused and, as no answer came, added a supplementary question. "Did your Cabinet know?"

"I never agreed to a joint statement," McNish said, firmly and truthfully. "I must make that quite clear."

"That wasn't my question, First Minister. I am wondering why you have given everyone the impression that you can act on your own and no one will mind. Do you accept that the statement you did make would not have been agreed by Downing Street?"

"You must put that one to Downing Street. Yes, Ross?"

Burton had not intended to intervene, but had been driven too far. He stood up to be sure of everyone's attention.

"No need to ask Downing Street, First Minister. You have the answer already in your hand, haven't you? No? Then I've a copy and I'll read it out. Downing Street's reaction to your statement. The third paragraph. 'The British Government and no one else will be offering advice to Her Majesty about the future resting place of the Stone of Destiny. They will do so when other formalities are completed and after duly consulting the opinions of Scotland's Members of Parliament'."

The room was silent apart from the low buzz from cameras. The story was improving by the minute. Burton paused, then pressed on.

"That's pretty clear, don't you think?"

McNish weighed it carefully. "If you say so, Ross. As far as I'm concerned the advice to Her Majesty will come from the Scottish Executive."

"But I understood you were leaving that to an all-party committee."

"Well, yes," McNish agreed. "It shouldn't be a party matter. The executive will act on the committee's recommendations."

"First Minister," Burton went on relentlessly, "you have kept the parliament ignorant of the requests and warnings from Downing Street. You have failed to discover whether you have a constitutional right to dispose of the stone. Will you now tell us if the Presiding Officer has agreed to chair the committee, as you announced?"

There was silence again while Scotland's political press waited for McNish's answer. His eyes went to the back of the press room where Mackay had tried to position himself out of harm's way. McNish wriggled once. "As you heard, I've invited the Presiding Officer to conduct this matter. There he is. He can speak for himself."

All faces turned to observe Mackay. A tall man in any case, when he slowly rose to his feet on the highest tier holding the media desks, his shoulders hunched and his eyes flashing under heavy brows, he had something of the towering aspect of an Old Testament prophet about to call a she-bear from the woods to devour unruly children. An apprehensive hush descended once more, but when he spoke his voice as ever was gentle.

"This is not my press conference. As a servant of the parliament I don't give press conferences. However, since I am here, it may be helpful to you all if I correct some impressions that may otherwise masquerade as fact. First, I have not agreed to chair any committee, all-party or otherwise, to consider where or how to install the stone. Nor shall I agree."

Some correspondents breathed in deeply. Some held their breath. Others exhaled sharply and loudly. Mackay waited until the noise stopped.

"Secondly, although treasure trove is indeed a devolved matter,

I believe that gives no right to the Scottish parliament, or to its executive, and still less to its First Minister on his own, to anticipate a decision due to be made by the Queen's and Lord Treasurer's Remembrancer. I have already brought this to the attention of the First Minister himself."

The susurration of gasps and whispers resumed until the room saw that the Presiding Officer was not finished.

"Last," said Mackay, his voice becoming quieter but no less compelling, "while I have your attention, I should like to say something about the Stone of Destiny. As you all know, I am one of the few who have so far been lucky enough to see it. It is a beautiful, historically wonderful object, for many a venerable one. Its interest and importance extends beyond Scotland to the whole of Britain. I believe it would be a tragedy if political expedience, ambition or short-sightedness – on anybody's part, north or south of the Border – were to lead to the stone's being made a deliberate cause of contention, jealousy or unhappiness between our peoples. That is not the destiny to which any of us here should subscribe. Rather, it would have been better had it remained undiscovered. I hope the press will agree with me. Thank you."

Mackay gathered the bundle of papers he had brought in with him, nodded bleakly at McNish, who was still standing at the podium in front, and walked out.

"Are there any more questions to the First Minister?" Cadell asked breezily.

There were no more questions.

Every November in the Houses of Parliament in Westminster, the British government's programme for the year ahead is outlined in the Speech from the Throne, delivered by the Monarch in the House of Lords with the members of the House of Commons admitted to listen. The chief surprises in it are generally the omissions, the policy proposals dropped through lack of time or hope of success or because of a change of heart. Occasionally there are new proposals, too, but conventionally they must accord with the manifesto on which the government won power. Bland as the Speech may be, it is always closely studied for its emphases and its nuances.

The Prime Minister sat in his usual chair at the middle of the long table in the Cabinet Room at Number Ten Downing Street.

Opposite him was the Cabinet Secretary. They were alone. Between them lay some of the day's newspapers whose headlines, with that heavy wit irresistible to headline-writers, rang the changes on a single theme:

CORONATION STONE A POLITICAL FOOTBALL

POLITICS FOR THE STONE AGE

THE STONE OF CONTENTION

DIALOGUE OF THE STONE DEAF

SCOTLAND'S ROLLING STONES

But the newspapers were not their immediate concern. Each had before him the draft of the short paragraph in the Queen's Speech with which Wedderburn had earlier presented them; and both were silent, doing simple addition sums with ball-point and paper.

"Blackmail, then," growled the Prime Minister at last. "Already we cannot govern in England. Now, unless we do what they want, we shan't have a majority in the United Kingdom either."

"Mr Wedderburn said you could rely on fifty-nine Scottish votes every time for a motion of confidence, Prime Minister. That would bring your overall majority up to forty-nine."

"There's more to running a country than surviving votes of confidence."

"Well, at least you'll win all the votes on the Queen's Speech – "

"Formalities!"

" – and all the procedural ones."

"And lose every Bill we bring forward. Thanks. Bouncers up, that's what it's gone. Ask Hartley to come in, would you? And Junc Bates, if she's here yet."

The Cabinet Secretary gave some instructions to a telephone. A few minutes later, the Chief Whip and the Deputy Prime Minister were apprised both of Wedderburn's arm-twisting and the consequences of refusing it.

"Bloody Scots," Hartley Blackburn said.

"They've an argument, though," said June Bates. "What would you do in their place?"

"They're shafting us," said the Prime Minister. "In ordinary circumstances we'd resign and have a general election rather than let ourselves be buggered about like this. You could argue that we should go to the country anyway: we can't govern except by universal consent – and we don't have it. However, we must be realistic about the outcome, mustn't we, Hartley?"

"Yes," said Blackburn. "Certainly lose any election in next nine months,"

Mrs Bates nodded. "Nothing's coming forward at the moment. The hospital programme's stalled. The new school schedules – "

"Exactly," said the Prime Minister. "So we lose, and what does the next parliament look like? That's the point. For the first time the governments here and in Scotland will come from different parties. And if Holyrood goes on spending its way out of trouble – "

" – and it will," said Mrs Bates.

" – the English'll never pay for it. It was hard enough to get the block grant through last time, pared down to the core."

Blackburn pursed his lips. Scotland's finances tended to test his whipping skills to destruction. "Might not be a bad thing. Got to face reality one day."

"D'you see the UK surviving?" said the Prime Minister.

"Not in its present form. Bust-up first. Far worse than bouncers up."

"Quite. I don't want that."

"The trouble," said the Cabinet Secretary, "is what we mentioned before, Prime Minister. We've still got no proper regional parliaments in place. And no one wants them, not seriously."

"Of course they don't, Matthew. There'll all afraid of blowing half a billion each on the buildings and fittings, just like those frigging Scots."

Mrs Bates said: "Andy Wedderburn wouldn't want us to fall – not if the country were to break up. Couldn't we call his bluff?"

"He's their spokesman, whether he agrees or not," the Prime Minister said. "And he says they're in earnest. I'm sure they are."

"Me, too," Blackburn said. "Had words with the Scottish Whips – ours and the others. Quite open about it. There's Janet Ross in my office – "

"She's that very attractive – "

"That's the one," said Blackburn. "Says the Scottish MPs are a bloc – monolithic. New glint in her eye: likes to get what she wants."

"Anyway," said the Prime Minister, "I'm not going to the country for at least two years." He turned again to the text in front of them.

My Lords and Commons, in due course, in accordance with advice I have received on the disposal of Crown property, and in willing response to the expressed wishes of the members of the House of Commons representing the people of Scotland, my government will effect the installation of the Stone of Destiny permanently in the Abbey of Westminster, there to await the crowning of future sovereigns of our united nation.

"You could cut out 'willing'," said the Cabinet Secretary.

"Involves crown in politics, of course," Blackburn pointed out.

"No more than when the other stone was sent north," Mrs Bates said.

The Prime Minister tapped the text. "Andy says that, properly speaking, any decision on treasure trove is made by someone called the Queen's Remembrancer in Scotland. In theory it might be overruled by the Lord Advocate in Holyrood, but that's never happened."

"Can't rely on either decision going our way," said Blackburn.

"No," Mrs Bates agreed. "And if not –"

"I suppose we could take action ourselves," said the Prime Minister. "Of course, the notion that the British Government might step in as the ultimate power – we could, after all, amend the Scotland Act or even repeal it – has never been tested either. Yet."

"Amend the Act *again?*" groaned the Chief Whip.

"A one-line Bill specifically extracting the stone from the jurisdiction of the Scottish Executive won't take any time," said the Prime Minister. "I've Andy's word for it, Hartley. We can give notice of it in the Speech. Maybe that's the best way."

"And the House of Lords?"

"Not a factor these days, is it? I think the trick is to shoot first, just as McNeish – is that his name? – tried to do, and answer questions afterwards. If we can't answer them we'll change the rules until we can."

The Cabinet Secretary shook his head slowly, but said nothing.

*   *   *

Craig Millar held the First Minister's full attention for the sole reason that, for the first time in his life, McNish conceived himself to be something on the international scene. A message from the Israeli ambassador in London, still unacknowledged in its electronic form but confirmed by ordinary post, now demanded a response. Tel Aviv was making a claim on the stone on the grounds that in some previous epoch it had been unlawfully removed from what was now Israeli territory.

"Tell the ambassador," said McNish, "to go jump in the Dead Sea."

"I could," said Millar, "but I think that would be for the Foreign Office. We've had this telegram from Madrid."

"Madrid?"

"Capital of Spain."

"I knew that, man, for Christ's sake. What's it about?"

"The stone, too. It may have spent some time there in the fifth century. They're claiming it as well."

"Tell them to go jump in the – the – "

The First Minister searched his mind for an appropriate stretch of Spanish water.

"Somewhere off the Costa Brava, First Minister?"

McNish snorted. Millar produced a third document.

"And the Irish. Saint Columba appears to have escaped with the stone from Ireland when he brought it to Iona."

"It's staying here," declared McNish. "Israel, Spain, Ireland – that's three more places it isn't going. I don't care who tells them."

"Then there's Scone Palace."

"What about it?"

"It's where the stone was removed from in the thirteenth century. The Earl says the Countess would like it back, and so would he. Perhaps they have a point."

"Thank ye for chuisin' the Pint o' Wine," said Maggie.

"It's for yourself, Maggie. If you were to move to the Cup o' Kindness, to a man we'd all – "

"Margaret, please, Mr Burton."

"There's no barmaid in the entire Old Town with your peerless touch – "

"Barperson, please, Mr Burton."

"Aye. Right. A light ale, Maggie, please. Make it two, one for Mr McNab here."

"Thanks, Ross."

"Did you ever think it would come to this, Alasdair? On the one hand, the First Minister in the Scottish parliament declares – "

"Oh, aye, but Bessie says – "

"And on the other, the Prime Minister's going to bring in a Bill – "

"Weel, he wis pit up tae it, mind."

"It's confrontation, Alasdair, with a capital C."

"Aye, it cuid be. Maist of wir people'll gang alang wi' Oor Wullie if it comes tae a fight. We widna like tae lose wir seats no' supportin' Scotland's rights."

"The opposition?"

"They'd aye fight wi' their ain taes, but they'd be on dangerous groond takin' Lon'on's side."

"But the Enlightenment party – ?"

"Aye, weel, they micht dae somethin' daft for their ain inscrutable purposes."

"Everyone knows it's only the Scottish MPs down there who want the thing back in Westminster. Don't you think they have an argument?"

"Aye, but it's nae a guid yin."

"They represent the broad interests of Scotland, don't they?" Burton asked the question mainly as a tease.

"There wis a time," said McNab after considering it, "when Ah micht hae concurred. But that wis ere Ah heard the ca' o' Fame's imperious bugle."

"Its what?"

"Weel, as the poet pit it."

"You're a romantic, Alasdair."

"Aye, mebbe. Ye've tae be a bit weird onyway tae want tae bide in a place like this."

Major-General Sir Norman Brunstane, GOC Scotland, stared in dismay and disbelief at the letter, marked for his eyes only, that had just been delivered to him in a sealed envelope personally by a senior official from the Ministry of Defence in London. Sir Norman had, of course, assiduously applied himself to the Scottish newspapers, noting their deeply cautionary approach to a crisis induced (so they all agreed) by the devious and ill-judged initiatives and declarations of a First Minister whose single priority was to preserve the hegemony of his party in Scotland with himself in control of it. He was fully apprised – for he had watched on television some of the recent exchanges in Holyrood – of the strong language flowing in the chamber. Age-long distrust of Westminster and suspicion of the claims of Scottish members there had fanned those feelings to a white heat – a heat that, though with some exceptions, had fused parliamentary opinion into one. The passage in the Queen's Speech which seemed to assert the right of Scotland's MPs to speak for Scotland appeared to have robbed most MSPs of their reason. In a word, Sir Norman had grasped the political sensitivity of the moment, and how easily crisis might develop into catastrophe. Still, he was astonished to have intimation of an operation which would pre-empt the course of action foreshadowed in the Queen's Speech, and therefore received with the gravest misgivings the order to give all possible assistance in achieving the secret objective set out before him.

The nature of that assistance was at first uncertain. He was not being asked to supply either equipment or personnel. The commando to be mobilised for the occasion would not come under his command. Army helicopters deployed in Scotland had their headquarters in Wiltshire; and if anything more powerful than a Lynx were required – an Apache, for example, to carry heavy equipment – it would have to be flown up from the south. No specific facility, not so much as a landing area, was requested. In due course, however, as he read the brief through, the truth was revealed to him. Allowance had been made for operating on every kind of terrain – anywhere, indeed, from a Hebridean island to a city centre. In short, Sir Norman realised, the ministry had no information about the stone's location, and was relying on him to supply it. But he no more knew where the newly-found stone might be than where the old one was.

However unwise the ministry's plan, it was not Sir Norman's to reason why. An ingenious way immediately occurred to him for at least finding the stone's hiding-place. Recognising it was a slim but sporting chance, he had his secretary telephone the office of the Chief Constable of the Lothians. As it happened Sir Andrew McCallum was available and came on the line.

"No luck yet with your investigations, Sir Andrew?" Sir

Norman began. "We're still guarding a lump of polystyrene up here at the castle, and there's a steady flow of visitors coming to marvel at it. Actually, Sir Hew tells me it's drawing more sight-seers than the old one did."

"Information on the robbery is still a little slow coming in, General," Sir Andrew admitted cautiously. "But, of course, there's been a lot of public interest in the new discovery. The First Minister has asked me to make preparations for its security when it's moved to Holyrood."

"Ah! And when's that expected to happen, Sir Andrew? It's what I wanted to talk about. I say, would you like to come round here? I think we should have a chat."

The Chief Constable was happy to oblige. He had been under strain for some weeks, aware of having failed to provide the results expected of him. His officers had wasted fruitless hours following up hoax information, often with credible corroborative detail, about probable hiding-places all the way from Dunstaffnage to Arbroath as well as in Glasgow and Edinburgh. The general might turn out to be a useful ally, or at least sympathetic to his difficulties. An hour later, the two were together drinking army coffee.

"Like you, I'm sure," said Sir Norman, "I've followed what's been going on between London and Holyrood. We're in a very sensitive situation, you'll agree. Thank God, the press are behaving themselves for once."

The Chief Constable looked doubtful. "True, General, but we're not exactly expecting riots, are we?"

"Still, we can't afford to be complacent," Sir Norman said. "You may need help. I was going to suggest the army might give you a hand watching over the stone – the real stone, that is. To relieve some of your force for – for – well, for tracking down the old one, for example."

"Watching over the stone?"

"Yes – I understand you've got it under a twenty-four-hour guard now, until it's moved to Edinburgh. It was in the papers. It was in case anybody, well, interfered with it."

Sir Andrew looked levelly at Sir Norman. "No, General. No such decision was taken. It's true that an announcement was made to that effect: the idea was to dissuade the public from looking for it – with a reward having been offered and so on."

"Hmm. Well, perhaps it's time to review that policy? As I

say, the army could undertake a chore like that without drawing unwanted attention to the site. Where is it, incidentally? Maybe we have an installation close by."

"Ehm – I'm not in a position to say where it is, at any rate not at this moment in time," explained the Chief Constable. "Need to know, and all that."

Sir Norman stared at him aghast. "You mean you don't know where it is, either!"

"Well, no, not really."

"Good God!" said Sir Norman, putting down his cup with a clatter. "Who does know? McNish knows, doesn't he? He gives everyone the impression that he has it under lock and key."

"I asked him a week ago, General, whether he'd passed information about it to any of his colleagues. I explained it was a question of security. He was adamant that he was not at liberty to do such a thing. So, no – he doesn't know any more than I do."

"Well, Wee Dougie knows, because he was there." Sir Norman cleared his throat. "I mean the Presiding Officer, of course."

"You'll have read in the press, General, what Dr Mackay thinks of Mr McNish's plans. You won't get anything out of a man like that. He's quality."

"What about the archaeologists who dug it up?"

"None of them'll speak."

"What are they waiting for?"

The Chief Constable and GOC Scotland gazed at each other, bemused. The former reflected on the difficulties of guarding an object in an unknown place; the latter on the problem of directing a detachment of Royal Marines or one of the Special Services to find it. Sir Andrew stood up to leave.

"I'd appreciate it, General, if you'd regard our talk as secret. The First Minister remains unaware that the stone is not under police surveillance – and of the very good reason I have given you for that."

"Supposing he orders you to produce it?"

"Then I'd have to explain my difficulty, and he would have to admit that he didn't know either. It wouldn't get us anywhere. I can't guess what would follow."

Sir Andrew left, while Sir Norman started to work out how to word his reply to the Chief of the General Staff.

*   *   *

The Defence Secretary, the Home Secretary and the rest of the Civil Contingencies Committee were already installed in Cabinet Office Briefing Room "A" – known as COBRA – when the Prime Minister joined them. He had convened them in the evening under conditions of unusually tight confidentiality, because it was unclear how much of the information coming from Scotland could be trusted. Under exceptional circumstances such as a fuel crisis or a terrorist emergency threatening the entire United Kingdom, members of the Scottish Executive might have been required to attend a CCC meeting in COBRA. Not this time. The report simply did not hold water that the Chief Constable of the Lothians, though charged with guarding the authentic Stone of Destiny, had no idea where it was. That officer's further allegation, dutifully relayed by GOC Scotland, normally a reliable source, that the First Minister was similarly ignorant was even more quickly dismissed. No, the stories coming out of Edinburgh had all the hallmarks of a clever disinformation campaign calculated to forestall and avert any kind of intervention, constitutional or legal, in advance of a *fait accompli*.

"Wedderburn says none of his MPs seems able to help," the Defence Secretary said. "I'm sure they would if they could. McNish is obviously playing this very close to his chest."

"Home Secretary? How do you stand with the Edinburgh police?"

"We only have co-operative arrangements, Prime Minister, and they're usually very good. But the police service is devolved. We've no locus. They report directly to the Justice Minister in Holyrood. And if we start asking questions they'll start wondering why we're concerned."

"CGS?"

"Better to hold back in that case," the Chief of the General Staff agreed. "We shouldn't lose the element of surprise in this sort of operation. But we can be fully prepared for action – wherever it may be." He glanced at the Director Special Forces. "Your people are ready now?"

"Yes, sir. If it's a rural or coastal site it shouldn't be a problem. If it's an urban environment – as we assume – with a lot of civilians present it'll be delicate but perfectly feasible. It may be necessary to cause a diversion. We'll work something out."

The Prime Minister frowned and rubbed his chin.

197

"Are you happy with that?" This was to the Defence Secretary who nodded the ball on to the CGS.

"Short of reliable data on the stone's location, Prime Minister, we can't really do anything except wait."

"How long?"

"Until McNish makes his move, I suppose," said the Defence Secretary.

"I'll talk to Wedderburn again," said the Prime Minister. "Bloody Hell, they're all Scots, those MPs. Someone must know something."

Andy Wedderburn, Secretary for the Union, being leant on heavily by the Prime Minister, consequently informed Campbell Macarthur that unless someone could tell the Government where the stone was hidden it would have to stay where it was and there was nothing to be done. Macarthur sent for Duncan Innes and put the facts before him.

"It isn't our problem," Duncan said, "as long as we keep the pressure on the Prime Minister. He can bring in his Bill for a start."

"Yes, but he's making it our problem, and he has a good case if we're looking for a clean surgical operation. You with your – ah – background will see that."

"I must consider what to do," Duncan said, "and perhaps make a telephone call. Give me twenty-four hours."

Jock Hamilton and Walter Moncrieff had sought a corner of the Cup o' Kindness where they could discuss the crisis in privacy, away from their aides and secretaries and, in Hamilton's case, away from the eye of Jean Murray Stewart whose office was next to his.

"You used to speak about bringing McNish down," Moncrieff said.

"Regime change. And you couldn't see the purpose."

"I saw no purpose in change for change's sake, if it didn't change anything at all. But I never thought the likes of McNish could be dangerous. He's become like a bus driver hurtling along a street when he can't see through the windscreen."

"With Scotland the bus."

"If he was a Nationalist, one might understand."

Ever since his assumption of high office, they recalled, when McNish considered that the actions, policies or the budgetary provisions of the British government fell short of satisfactory, or if he sought simply to deflect attention from his own problems, he had habitually blamed Scotland's MPs for failing to fight successfully for Scottish interests. True to that form, since the bombshell in the Queen's Speech, every utterance, every metaphor he mixed, was directed at the treacherous nest of vipers in the South who had stabbed their country in the back. Stoking those fires assiduously whenever he could, he was now playing the separatists' game as they would have wanted. His message was that Scotland had no use for the charlatans in Westminster, who might as well come home. In that matter, the Nationalists had already shown the way.

"He's got to go," said Moncrieff. "He's driving us all to a disaster. He sees no point of view but his own. His patriotism is sham. His motives are base. He doesn't understand what our MPs are on about – not even the ones in his own party."

"He hates them too," Hamilton said. "Their standing's at rock bottom in Scotland, and he'd like it even lower. So what'll we do?"

"It all comes back to the Stone of Destiny, doesn't it? I've been speaking with young Duncan Innes in London. They've no other way to assert themselves. We've got to help them."

"Good God!" Hamilton exclaimed, blanching, "and let the English have the stone?"

"Not the English. Our MPs. It has to be their decision, and if they want it down there, why not?"

"It sounds like suicide. Three-quarters of Holyrood have swallowed the McNish line. And the rest are wobbly. We'd be digging our own graves."

"Nonsense. We'll get McNish to make a fool of himself. The press have no sympathy for him. His own members support him only because they're afraid of losing their seats. The people may be behind him and his patriotic claptrap, but mostly they're bewildered."

"All right, Walter. How do we go about it?"

"Let's encourage him. We'll call for immediate action. We'll demand that the stone is installed this very month – anyway, before the Government can pass its Bill to take it away. We'll dare him to do it. Let's rush him! Tell your members and I'll tell mine."

Hamilton suddenly noticed one of his own, the approaching bulk of Mrs Murray Stewart. She had spotted him and was bearing down on them, exuding suspicion. He lowered his voice and rose to go.

"I don't understand how that'd help, exactly."

"Rely on me. Do what I say, and wait and see."

"You said you have to know what comes next."

"Yes, but sometimes you've to take a step in the dark. We must keep in close touch."

10

"MORAG MCLEOD, private office," she said.
    "Morag? It's –"
"Yes, Duncan. Goodness! These calls are becoming a habit".
"Could we have a civilised conversation without the sarcasm? Please, just for once? Is anyone listening your end?"
"Not so far as I know. And yours?" Her voice was still flat.
"No. I want a word about both the – um – objects."
"I expect you do. Which one first?"
"Well – call it my father's one."
"You know as much about it as I do."
"Do I?"
"You know where it is."
"Yes. When are they going to move it?"
"Who?"
"Well, anyone."
"Why d'you want to know?"
"I hoped you could give me guidance on –"
"On what, Duncan?"
"Well, the plans for putting the thing in Holyrood. The executive's plans. Next week? Next month? Next year?"
"I don't know when, and if I did I couldn't tell you. Anyhow, what about the government's plans for putting it in Westminster? Your plans, I mean, of course. How are they coming along?"
With Duncan silenced by that question, the truth dawned on her and some warmth at last came into her words.
"Oh, I see why you want to know! You mean it's safe where it is as long as it stays there. Well, I'm glad about that, Duncan." She thought about it some more. "All right, if it's so important

why don't you ask your father? No one's going to move anything until he tells them where to find it."

"Oh, aren't they?"

"Or unless he's let down by someone he trusts."

He was silenced again for a few seconds. "You needn't have said that."

"Sorry. Well, whatever you're thinking of, you'll ask your father first anyway, this time, won't you, before you do it?"

"Morag, no one's contemplating anything illegal. It's a constitutional issue now."

"Oh? Well, let's talk about the other one. It must be costing you a lot of money in hire charges. That van, I mean. And, for your information, it's running up a lot more in parking fees. Wherever it may be. How will you explain that to your friends? And have you told them you've lost what's inside it?"

"Listen," said Duncan. "We don't need what's inside it any more. It's time it was returned where it came from, even if no one there wants it much either. I guarantee to get it back somehow."

"Good," said Morag pleasantly. "That'll be a great boost for law and order."

"You're being sarcastic again. May I have the van key? And an address?"

"Yes, and the ticket to bail it out – they'll be in the post to the House of Commons tonight. Plain brown envelope, with small bulge."

"Thank you, Morag."

"And, Duncan, don't use a wheel-chair again. The police are still searching them."

It was the kindest thing she had said to him for two years. "Well, thank you for that too."

"Just one other thing. I meant what I said about your father and what he discovered. Personally I don't care where it ends up. But you're not to do anything about it yourself without telling him first. Is that a promise?"

"Or –?"

"No keys. The CID are on your trail: they'd love to have them. And, as I said, the costs are going up all the time."

"It's a promise – made under duress, of course."

"Blackmail, probably. But don't worry – it doesn't affect your statutory rights", said Morag reasonably. "You can have me prosecuted, if it would be any help."

"Send me the keys, Morag, please. If I got the object back to Edinburgh Castle, would that restore me to favour a bit – in your eyes?"

"D'you care about my eyes, Duncan?"

"Guess."

Duncan and Janet met in the statue-lined Members' Lobby which guards the south end of the Commons chamber. He had just collected his post, and was pleased to find among the circulars, charity appeals and other junk mail that constituted the bulk of the correspondence sent to Scotland's MPs the plain brown envelope which Morag had promised. He opened it and examined the contents.

"Heathrow!" he exclaimed, looking at the ticket.

"What?"

"It's the key of the van. That's where she hid it – in the long-term carpark. Not a bad place, was it?"

Janet said nothing. He looked up at her and saw that her face was expressionless.

"It's no use to us any more," he said, "so we'd better take it home."

"You take it home. Was that your idea or hers?"

"How d'you mean, Janet?"

"It was her hold over us, wasn't it? She could have turned us in any time – the police would have traced the van to Peebles and that would have been it."

"I told you – she'd never have done that."

Janet smiled thinly. "I know, because she's –"

"Because nothing."

"She wrecked that entire exercise." There was real anger in her tone.

"So what? It was the wrong stone. We're after the real one now."

"Are you sure? When did you speak to her? Why, if it comes to that?"

"Does it matter? Yesterday, after I'd seen Andy."

"Just tell me, Duncan. What did she want in exchange?"

"Exchange for what?"

203

"That key. And the ticket. All right! You've compromised yourself. You needn't say, because I can guess."

Duncan could think of no useful reply to her in that mood. He therefore said he was going to see Campbell Macarthur to discuss the next move, and he was sure she would be welcome. She merely turned away, her eyes blazing and her lips pressed tight together. He left, passing through the Central Lobby and stopping in St Stephen's Porch to construe the little manuscript note in dog Latin, unseen by Janet, which had been stapled to the carpark ticket: "*vestra iura legitima non affecta sunt.*" Smiling, he walked past Westminster Abbey towards his rendezvous with Macarthur. He found Wedderburn there as well.

"I haven't come up with any new ideas," he admitted. "I really think all we can do is watch and wait."

"Did you find out anything?" asked Wedderburn.

"All I'm sure of is that McNish doesn't know where it is – yet anyway. Perhaps he never will."

"You know where the stone is, Duncan?" Macarthur prodded gently.

Janet Ross walked into the room in time to hear the question.

"Of course he does," she said airily. "Don't be silly about it, Duncan. Everyone knows you're bound to have been told."

He regarded her with a mixture of puzzlement, hurt and annoyance. Her face had relaxed. She was smiling but looked entirely businesslike.

"If I did, Janet – if I do – I couldn't say anything. Well, I can't can I?"

Her reply was unkind. "It depends what you're trying to achieve."

"The question is," Macarthur interrupted, sensing the tension between the two, "what shall we tell the PM?"

"Sooner or later the stone will go on show, won't it?" Duncan argued. "That'll be our moment. And I still don't see why we should help the PM out of his difficulties."

"He's trying to help us, now," Wedderburn pointed out.

"Listen, Duncan," said Janet. "Be practical. If we want the stone down here in London, this is the time to get it, before the public see it. You know we can't have armed forces storming the parliament, if that's really the plan. Edinburgh would explode."

"And you know," replied Duncan firmly, "that I can't betray a trust."

"Fine," said Janet, coldness in her voice, "and all our MPs here trust us to do what's right for them. Your making us – and me – part of your moral dilemma."

"You mean," he said slowly, "if you knew what you think I know, you'd sacrifice your –"

"I'd have to think about it, too, wouldn't I, Duncan? – and try not to get my emotions involved." Her scornful undertone was as obvious to Wedderburn and Macarthur as to him.

"What about Whip's honour?" he asked as evenly as he could.

"It only applies in one's own party. I expect I should have mentioned that."

"I see. The Deacon Brodie shopping list after all."

She shrugged, gave a little laugh and walked out. Duncan stared after her, his mind churning.

"Well?" asked Macarthur.

"I can hardly tell the PM that we know and won't tell him," said Wedderburn.

"I agree," Macarthur said. "And we can't have you two falling out, Duncan."

"No," said Duncan, although he realised that the rift between them was already a gulf. "But Janet's right about storming Holyrood. I'll have to think of something better."

"Shall I fetch you a cup of tea, First Minister? Would that help?"

"What good would it do? And I thought you said you weren't paid to get me tea." McNish's thin sandy hair was ruffled again. Morag had noticed before that it seemed to be self-ruffling. Anyway, it generally reflected the state of its owner's mind much as crinkly seaweed may be used as a weather gauge.

"Quite right, I'm not, but I can make exceptions when they're needed. It's your own fault."

"What is?"

"That you're in that condition. You're always too proud to admit you don't know something, and look where it's got you. Have you seen the papers?"

"I've never said I knew where it was."

"You've never said you didn't. Everyone thinks you've got it tucked away somewhere. Even the cabinet think that. Well, don't they?" she said, seeing him about to protest.

"I don't care what they think."

"I was in the gallery watching. You walked straight into it. Now you've got to produce it! Saint Andrew's Day! That's next week!"

"I was thinking of Burns Night. I thought I'd a couple of months in hand."

"Scotland's First Minister can't tell Burns Night from Saint Andrew's Day! I'll get you a cup of tea just the same."

"Send Craig in, would you?"

"Please."

"Please, then," growled McNish, wondering why he let Morag talk to him like that.

In fact Morag was wrestling with her own soul. Her sharpness with her employer was due in part to the pressure she was herself experiencing. Before her eyes, McNish had solemnly – if that was the word: he had been on one of his usual self-deluding ego-trips in the chamber, spurred on by the cheers of his own members and the jeers of the opposition – assured the parliament that the Stone of Destiny would be installed on a plinth in its concourse on Scotland's national day; and, no better, that it would first be brought ceremonially to the esplanade at Edinburgh Castle before being taken in procession down the Royal Mile to Holyrood, escorted by members of the Royal Company of Archers, the Queen's Bodyguard for Scotland. The procession had been suggested by Walter Moncrieff, Leader of the Enlightenment party, whose highly unlikely gesture McNish, thinking on his feet but as ever not for long enough, had welcomed with enthusiasm. The employment of the Royal Archers had been Jock Hamilton's inspiration, a helpful piece of garnish from the executive's political opponents. The media had interpreted the proposition as a mailed gauntlet thrown at London's feet, the endorsement by a united Scottish parliament of the First Minister's constitutional challenge to the authority of Westminster.

All in all, Morag realised, Scotland's parliamentary affairs were heading for a seismic débacle. The challenge to Westminster might easily lead to a dangerous rupture between the two parliaments; but it was just as likely to end in laughter and mockery on a global scale. No part of the display that McNish had promised could be carried out in the absence of the stone itself, and the stone would remain absent until its hiding-place was known to the appropriate authorities. She, Morag, was the only member of the First Minister's entourage who had that knowledge, yet could hardly admit to it, even were she asked. Only three days earlier she had forcibly reminded Duncan of his duty of trust towards his father. More, she had threatened him with exposure if he betrayed that trust. Walking down the passage, she decided she must talk to the Presiding Officer: he knew what she knew, had the same obligation of silence to Dr Innes, and must be sharing her thoughts though not, possibly, an identical conflict of loyalties.

Craig Millar was taking notes from the First Minister when Morag returned with a plastic mug of tea from the Cup o' Kindness.

"The architect at the office of works," Millar was saying, "wants to know what you want the plinth made of, and how high."

"Tell him it's up to him."

"And where to position it."

"Right in the middle, like I told them. But nowhere near that desk."

"And he wanted the dimensions and weight."

The First Minister glared. "Find out," he said.

"Yes, First Minister. I've got them."

"You've seen the stone!" It was as though an albatross had fallen from McNish's neck.

"No, Dr Innes gave out the measurements in his news conference last month."

McNish's neck resumed its burden. "All right," he said, "we'd better get this show on the road. Find out who the right people are. There's the logist – I mean, the transport problem. And the ceremonial: I don't know who that would be. We've got to involve the university people who found the stone in the first place. McCallum will be in overall charge of security, won't he? He's got a guard on the thing already. You may have to speak to the Remembrance person, whatever he's called."

"She," said Millar.

"Whoever. And the press arrangements. I'll want a word with Cadell. And a brief on my desk in – let's say – forty-eight hours. Earlier if you can. If there are problems, let me know at once. Is there anything new from London?"

"Not a word, First Minister. But you've read the papers, and you remember the radio this morning. And the *Holyrood* programme on Sunday."

McNish looked at Morag, recalling something she had said to him a few days earlier.

"Best keep the army out of this, Craig. But perhaps you'd better get the Chief Constable here right away, so I can tell him what I expect of him. Can you do that?"

"Yes, and I can call spirits from the vasty deep," Millar murmured, leaving.

"What's that?"

"Henry the Fourth, Part One, I think," Millar said, closing the door behind him quickly to avoid explanations which could only baffle the First Minister further.

By the time the Civil Contingencies Committee met in COBRA for the second time, they were convinced of the deviousness of Scotland's First Minister. His plan to parade the Coronation Stone down Edinburgh High Street all the way from Castle Hill to the Canongate confirmed the committee in the belief that the previous reports from GOC Scotland were misinformed. The members had before them the relevant excerpts from all McNish's recent statements, either in the Scottish parliament or on television. It was easy, at least for the military, to conclude that no astute politician – indeed, no sane one – in McNish's position would make such commitments without being a hundred per cent confident of being able to fulfil them. The Chief of the General Staff double-checked in his diary when Saint Andrew's Day fell: otherwise, with little more than ten days to go, the political risk would be too great.

"So McNish has made his move," the Prime Minister said grimly. "Until now I've thought he was thick. But he's cunning. He's allowing the shortest possible time for things to go wrong, but just enough to stage a spectacular to win public support."

However, the committee now had what was more useful than a timetable to work on. The Home Secretary notified them of new intelligence on the current location of the stone. True, it was little better than the grid reference of a desolate hill site in Perthshire; but, if it was accurate – and his sources were confident of that – then it would be a simple matter surreptitiously to invest the area before moving in as circumstance dictated.

"Where did this come from?" the Defence Secretary asked.

"Since you ask," said the Home Secretary, "I had it from

Hartley Blackburn. The Whip's Office often has information our other friends don't pick up."

"No identity?"

"I pressed him, but all he would say was 'Civilian, Scottish, female'."

The Prime Minister smiled, recalling the recent conversation he had had with his Chief Whip. "Enough said. I can guess the source."

"It seems that the stone hasn't been moved from where it was found," the Home Secretary finished, "but the site has been a secret. Known to very few, though, I expect."

"Clever of McNish," said the Prime Minister. "Nothing to draw attention to. Well, it may be a long shot none the less, but no harm in trying. CGS?"

"DSF?" said the CGS.

The Director Special Forces had taken out a map. "This is only small scale, sir. The location seems to be north of the Tay, a few miles east of Perth."

"How quickly can you move?"

"DMO?" said the DSF.

"I'll need a day's reconnaissance, sir," the Director Military Operations responded. "There's a Lynx at Leuchars with a spotter and equipped for long-range high-definition digital transmission. We'll get that up tomorrow."

"Good – and you'd better have a team on hand right away, just in case."

The Prime Minister turned to the Attorney-General whose presence in COBRA is to ensure that no domestic military operation infringes civil law. "Any problems yet, John?"

"No one's done anything wrong yet, Prime Minister."

"It's Crown property, after all."

"True."

"All we can do," said Dr Mackay, having listened to Morag's account of the First Minister at bay, thrashing about in an unreal world, "is to put it to Dr Innes himself. Anyway, it's unfair of me to ask him to keep the stone out of sight any longer. He's due his real academic triumph, and he won't have one if he doesn't have it now."

"I'm sure he knows the political implications, Dr Mackay."

209

"Of course. And he'll see that our moronic First Minister – you'll excuse my language – has done nothing to avert a crisis. On the contrary, he's created it. But it'll be good for us to hear the opinion of a wise head that hasn't been turned by this place."

Morag looked at him with raised brows: she had long regarded the Presiding Officer as the most sensible voice in Holyrood. "Yours is turned, too, Dr Mackay?"

"A little Morag, I'm afraid. By anger, by disappointment and perhaps by more worry than it warrants. Frankly, I haven't the least inclination to help McNish out of his difficulties again. He deserves everything he gets. But it won't do much good for the parliament, or the country or the Union. It's hard to know what's the best course."

"If he doesn't find the stone before Saint Andrew's Day he'll certainly look a fool," said Morag, "and I'm sure that's what Mr Moncrieff's up to, egging him on like that. He'll know that Mr McNish hasn't got it."

"How would he know that?"

"Because – because Duncan will have told him," Morag said, looking at the floor.

"You're speaking to Duncan again?" Mackay smiled.

"I had to. Last week, for one reason and another. Well, he telephoned me."

"I see."

"Dr Mackay, I've got him to promise to return the stone they stole. I've sent him the keys of the van. I know he will."

"If you trust him, so do I, Morag. So do you think he put Walter Moncrieff up to –"

"No, he wouldn't interfere with what his party does here. But I think Mr Moncrieff's misjudged Mr McNish."

"How?"

"The First Minister can't afford to be made a fool of," said Morag.

"What'll he do?"

Morag considered it. "When he finds out that even the Chief Constable doesn't know where the stone is," she said, frowning, "he'll panic. He'll send out press releases, blame everyone except himself, go on TV, attack our MPs in London again, and let all hell loose. He might offer another reward. He might get the Lord

Advocate to instruct the Crown Office to release the information it has,"

"Can he do that?"

"I don't know, but he'd try. And he'd certainly twist Dr Innes's arm with bogus patriotic appeals – making him responsible for Scotland's shame and all that nonsense. He's quite subtle enough when his back's to the wall."

"Quite myopic enough. But it'll buy him some more time, it's true, and then we'll be into another downward spiral. I'll just ring up Harry."

That same evening, with the day's business finished and a warm invitation received, Morag again set off with the Presiding Officer in his car to Inveresk. Rain made the night darker and the home-ward-bound traffic slower, so that it was nearly seven o'clock before they rang the door-bell. Mrs Innes greeted them with a command that they must stay for supper, the assurance that she had already informed Mrs Mackay, and a promise of an unexpected treat later if they were lucky.

Having put a glass of whisky in Mackay's hand, and a gin and tonic in Morag's, Innes sat them down and heard with close interest about the turmoil in Holyrood and their need for guidance on the immediate future of the stone.

"The public good must always be considered," he said at last, "but unless that's at risk I don't usually go out of my way to save politicians from embarrassment – any more than to cause it to them, however tempting that may be."

"Excellent," said Mackay. "I hope I've made that my precept, too."

"Now, as you've been good enough to ask me, here's my answer. In my academic hat I'm indeed in favour of bringing the stone into the sunlight, in public, as soon as possible. Maybe it'll get McNish out of the pit he's dug for himself. However, as a citizen and a voter, I'd say that whether we do that before or after Saint Andrew's Day is neither here nor there. Sooner or later I'm afraid our politicians are going to fight over it: they're mad, but what can we do? We can't keep the stone hidden for ever. And I should tell you that our good friends Tom and Ian are bursting to show the world."

"That's what I wanted to hear, Harry," said Mackay. "I'm not surprised. I won't stop you any longer. Are you ready to move?"

"We've been ready for a fortnight. We've only to warn the farmer of an incursion as a matter of courtesy. The museum's lending us lifting gear and a pick-up – a Land Rover, I think. We can have the stone in Chambers Street before anyone knows. Ian's got some work to do on it – just a little composition analysis – and Tom wants to look at the carving in a proper light."

"Then another press conference?"

"Well, a suitable presentation of some sort. The press, of course. There's more to say than before. The geologists from the Natural History Museum will want to be there, and a lot of academics. And other people. Duncan, for instance."

The doorbell rang. Mrs Innes called from the kitchen that she would answer it.

"You've ten days in hand, Harry. Is it long enough?"

"Why not, if we move fast? What about November the twenty-ninth – so McNish can have it for the thirtieth? Incidentally, I've heard informally that the Crown will appropriate it, which doesn't amaze me. They're not notifying anybody – it's too important. So when we've finished in the museum it'll be for McNish or the Crown Office to take care of it, and good luck to them both."

Mackay nodded. "Or it'll be between Holyrood and Westminster. That's the showdown we're really facing, isn't it, Morag?"

But Morag had frozen at the sound of Duncan's voice in the hall. Innes looked at the door and got up.

"Ah, splendid!" the Professor said. "Here's the politician himself, earlier than we thought. He'll be delighted to find you here again, Morag. Duncan! Come in – we've a surprise for you!"

Mackay rose from his chair as Duncan came in. Young Innes's surprise was more than evident to him, for he stopped in the doorway and gaped at Morag for a moment before recollecting himself.

"Hullo, Duncan," she said pleasantly, sitting firmly where she was. "I thought you were in London. You drove up, then?"

"Duncan, this is Dr Mackay," said his father, "the Presiding Officer at Holyrood. He and Morag have come to discuss what to do with the stone. We'll certainly want to know what you think."

Mackay and Duncan shook hands. Mrs Innes came in to say that supper would be in three minutes and would Duncan take his suitcase upstairs if he was staying the night. The tension was broken. Over soup and then plates of risotto, Dr Innes repeated to Duncan his plans for a public presentation of the stone in the Royal Museum in Edinburgh before handing it over to whatever authorities claimed it.

"I hope you'll be there for it, Duncan."

"It's the most exciting thing I can think of, Dad. Of course I will if you invite me. I'll be very proud – and I should say in front of witnesses how wrong I was about the other one." He looked at Morag. "Morag used to say I had a mind as closed as a mule's. She was quite right, and I'm trying to do better."

Dr Innes clicked his tongue and shook his head, but beamed in pleasure just the same. Morag wondered where this was leading: that last remark was an olive branch of sorts. Mackay steered the conversation to more sensitive ground.

"We've hardly touched on the politics of all this, Duncan. I haven't spoken to an MP for many weeks – not even my old friend Andy Wedderburn. Scotland's politicians are at daggers drawn – I think that's hardly an exaggeration. I wouldn't allot blame for that: some foolish actions have been taken, silly things said, and I'm sure that to a great extent they are victims of circumstances –"

" – which could have been avoided, but weren't," Duncan interjected.

"No doubt, as with many quarrels. Please be frank about what you're trying to do."

"It's about power, Dr Mackay, as of course you know," said Duncan. "The stone – my father's stone – has become the *casus belli*. Where it goes will determine who speaks definitively for Scotland, the MPs or the MSPs. It's as simple as that. And it would be true even if the stone had no palladian powers at all, or even if most of us didn't believe in them."

"I understand how strongly you all feel."

"Well, there can't be many others in Holyrood who do – perhaps not in Scotland – or who realise what they've done to us in Westminster. They hardly bother to vote for us any more. You know that. And the media don't care."

"It must be embittering."

"Oh, no, we're not bitter. Alarmed, rather. Please believe this. If Scotland's MPs are only ciphers, it's Scotland's loss, and it's the Union that's threatened."

213

"I wouldn't disagree with that," said Mackay.

"Anyway," said Duncan, calm returning to his voice, "that's why we persuaded the Prime Minister to insist on installing the stone where Scotland's MPs have their constitutional authority. And it's why we'll do everything we can to take it there and keep it there."

"Everything legal?" Morag asked.

"Yes."

Dr Innes coughed. "You're going to take away my stone, then," he said gravely, "before I've even seen it in daylight or shown it to the world?" Morag looked at him and saw that his eyes were smiling. "As you heard: we're planning to bring it to Edinburgh in a few days' time. Are you really going to stop me? Please tell me how."

"Dad – I want to be there in Edinburgh with you. Whatever happens afterwards, that must go ahead. That's why I'm here now."

"Oh? I wondered why you came at such short notice – apart from the pleasure it would give us."

"It was to tell you that you can't wait any longer. You must get it out of Macbeth's Castle at once."

"At once?"

"By tomorrow. Tomorrow morning. Can you?"

"Why?"

Duncan was looking anxiously at Morag.

"Why, Duncan?" She was frowning, suspicion written in her eyes. "It's in the only place where it's safe, isn't it? Safe from . . . politicians!" Her eyes narrowed. "All politicians."

He shook his head. "If we can get it to the Royal Museum and locked up there, it should be safe enough even till the twenty-ninth. Trust me. I can't explain now: but I promise it's not secure where it is any more." He was still looking at Morag. "You must take my word."

"How many coffees?" asked Mrs Innes. "Not for you, Morag, I know – one of those fancy teas instead, I suppose. Dr Mackay? Harry? Duncan?"

"I'll go and telephone Ian," said Dr Innes. "If we've to get going tomorrow, we'll need him and Tom and the pick-up truck and all that gear."

"I'll do the picnic this time, then," Mrs Innes remarked as she left the room for the kitchen. "For five? Six, then?"

"I've got a hired van with me," said Duncan to his father, "if it'll help. And a block and tackle, too, as it happens." He glanced sideways at Morag and saw that she was already exchanging looks with Mackay.

"Excellent!" Dr Innes said. "Much better than carrying it in the open on the pick-up."

Three vehicles reached their rendezvous in Collas village at ten the next morning and went on in convoy to the lay-by at the bottom of the track leading up Dunsinane Hill. Tom and Ian came in the Land Rover. Dr Mackay and Morag were passengers in Professor Innes's car. Duncan arrived by himself in the unmarked white van, Morag having politely declined his offer to join him. The day was sombre, with low cloud, a rising wind and the threat of rain: no one else was about. A few minutes passed as the party donned their wet-weather clothes.

In accordance with the latest amendments to the Land Reform Act in regard to rural access for all regardless of season, the gate had no padlock, and it was a simple matter for Tom and Ian to drive the Land Rover up the slope to Macbeth's Castle, leaving the van and the car by the road.

"If it was safe enough at Heathrow," Duncan said quietly to Morag, forestalling her question as they walked up behind the pick-up, "it'll be all right here."

"It's still on board, then?"

"On its way home, as I promised."

"You keep looking around, Duncan. What's going on?"

"Army training, I suppose?"

"You're expecting something, aren't you?"

"That's why I wanted to move as fast as we could."

"Would you be a little more open with me?"

"I'd rather not. Not yet."

They plodded on in silence in the footsteps of their elders, and found Tom and Ian at the top already assembling the lifting gear, a small derrick, above the entrance to the vault. Dr Innes gave each of the others a torch, conducted them inside and pointed to the wall concealing their objective. Tom and Ian joined them immediately, carrying mallets, cold chisels and crowbars, and quickly demolished enough of the wall first to allow Morag and Duncan to see inside and marvel, and then to be able to extract

215

the stone on a set of removers' wheels without damage. Quite soon the stone and the wheels were swinging together up to the surface in a nylon rope cradle.

For the first time it was close enough for Duncan to touch it, and Mackay saw that he was no less overcome by that experience than the professor had been three weeks before. He watched him turn and embrace his father spontaneously and warmly, sharing at last the rare excitement of his astonishing archaeological and historical discovery. Then Mackay observed Morag's face, too, bearing a wide smile of intense pleasure at seeing the two Inneses so reconciled and united again. It broadened even further when she caught Mackay beaming at her, aware of what she was thinking.

Tom brought planks from the pick-up and laid them across the grass so that the ancient throne could be wheeled gently across the bumpy ground to where the pick-up waited. While he and Duncan used the derrick to lift it onto a cushion of sacking on the back of the truck, Ian made his way below ground again with a trowel, a bucket of water and a heavy paper packet to effect some necessary restoration.

"We're walling up the inner vault again," Dr Innes explained to Mackay and Morag. "It's an archaeological site, and there may be more to come out of it. Perhaps you noticed – the stone seems to have been sitting on pieces of old leather which must be worth dating."

"About 1296," Morag said, "at a rough guess."

"No later, I imagine," agreed Dr Innes, chuckling.

"Besides," Mackay said a little uncomfortably, "I suppose we'd better cover our tracks."

"Certainly," said Innes, nodding at the stone. "In my view, this is Crown property and requires full protection."

The reconstruction complete and all evidence of interference cleared from the site, the Land Rover moved off through the castle earthworks and at walking pace downhill with Tom at the wheel. The other five followed close behind. Four hundred yards from the road there was a short flurry of rain. Then the wind increased sharply, bringing a perceptible lifting of the cloud base and some brightness to the day. A party of buzzards rose from the corpse of the ewe putrifying upside down in a ditch not far from the track. At that point Duncan's ears, ever alert, picked up a distant, familiar noise.

216

"We've to hurry," he said, searching round the sky.

"What is it?" Morag asked, trying to follow his gaze.

"There it is! A Lynx. They'll see us soon. Yes – now we're being watched – and photographed, too, I expect."

"Who is it?" his father asked, stopping.

The Land Rover proceeded while the little group paused to observe the helicopter hovering motionless a thousand feet up and about five hundred yards away.

"I don't know – the army, I'd imagine. Let's be quick. I think I've a plan. I'll explain as we walk. Please listen carefully."

Five minutes later they were at the road where Tom was quickly put in the picture. No watcher from the helicopter equipped with powerful binoculars could have failed to witness the large black block of meteorite being hoisted out of the back of the Land Rover and guided in its sling slowly towards the rear doors of the white van parked at right angles alongside. However, he would have noticed neither the simultaneous and surreptitious removal of the Land Rover's front passenger seat nor, his view obstructed by the van doors, the smooth switch in the direction in which the sling was moving. The Stone of Destiny was a large object but, covered with a sack, fitted neatly beside the Land Rover's driver.

"Good," said Duncan, closing the van doors. "Off you all go, please. Ian and Morag in the car too. They won't be interested in you, but keep together on the big roads just the same and get the thing to Chambers Street as fast as you can. I'll keep them guessing with the van as long as possible."

"And I'll just come with you in case you need help," said Morag. "I'll drive while you read a map – I've driven something very like that before."

Duncan looked at her, surprised. "Well, yes, I suppose you have. I'd be grateful."

"And I've got some chocolate for when you're hungry."

He said, as they closed the doors: "And I'll try to explain to you how . . . well, how the secret got out."

The lieutenant-colonel commanding 22 SAS was taking a direct and personal interest in what, for atavistic reasons he could not easily have explained, he had designated Operation Longshanks. He would fly up to Scotland if necessary, but for the present in his Herefordshire headquarters he was in close touch with the

SAS captain who had taken his team to Leuchars in Fife the previous evening. It was clear from the officer's report and from the picture relayed directly to him from the RAF Lynx as it followed the movements of the white van from a tactful distance, that there might never be a better time to strike. The van appeared to be trying to shake off the pursuit – as though the driver were aware of it – but Perthshire's trees had long lost their leaves and there was nowhere to hide in daylight, least of all in the traffic-free minor roads it seemed bent on following. Within ten minutes a second Lynx with troops on board would join the first one and it would simply be a question of choosing the moment. The colonel gave the order to move whenever it was opportune.

It was thus, about an hour after leaving Collas, on the narrow road which led west from the main Perth-to-Edinburgh dual-carriageway just north of Bridge of Earn, that Duncan and Morag encountered a road-block consisting of a single log. As the van drew to a halt, four armed and hooded commandos surrounded it, opened the doors and asked them to get out.

Duncan motioned to Morag to sit still. "Who's in command?" he asked.

"I'm in command," said one.

"Show me your authority."

"I don't have to. Please get out of the van. I don't want to use force." The captain signalled to his men. "Open the back doors, sergeant, and see what's in it."

They were not locked. A few seconds later, as to the captain's relief Duncan at last opened his door to get out, the sergeant returned.

"Nothing there, Sir, except a block and tackle and some spare wheels."

Leaving the van, Duncan looked up and down the road with a puzzled expression. "You have a police officer with you, of course," he said to the captain. "You can't do this sort of thing without one. You must know that."

The captain, recognising a military tone in Duncan's voice, looked at his face closely for the first time and said "Good God! I mean Good God, Sir! You're Major Innes, aren't you, Sir?"

Morag had got out as well, and Duncan sensed that she was listening closely.

"I was. Now I'm just an MP. You don't have to call me 'Sir'."

"I didn't expect to find you here, Sir. Marshall. Afghanistan, Sir, two-oh-oh-two."

"I remember. Where's your policeman, then, Captain Marshall?"

"Frankly, we didn't have time, Sir. You moved too fast for us. And if I may ask a question, Sir, why haven't you got the stone in there?"

"Your question is impertinent. What you are doing is illegal. And you haven't searched the van as well as you should. But I can overlook all those things. You're in touch with your CO?"

"Yes, Sir."

"Directly? Now?"

"Yes, Sir. It's Colonel – "

"Watch it! You don't have to identify him. I've a proposition to put to him. He'll like it. So will you. Get him on line."

Although Duncan's face was a mask, his eyes met Morag's and did not fail to detect the love there. She had lovely eyes, and he knew that for the present he could do no wrong in them.

When Sir Andrew McCallum heard on an early-morning news bulletin that the Stone of Destiny was in custody in the National Museum in Chambers Street, and that it would be making its first public appearance in the great hall there on the eve of Saint Andrew's Day, he immediately posted police officers at every outside door of that respected institution even before it had opened. His next action was personally to inform the First Minister of his accomplishment.

The First Minister, to whom ill-judged jubilation came readily, had difficulty in concealing his satisfaction on learning authoritatively that the stone was both located and within his reach. He was able to thank the Chief Constable curtly, for he still resented having been kept by him so long in the dark. But to those in Saint Andrew's House who were closest to him – Cadell his press officer, Millar his principal private secretary, and Morag McLeod his special adviser – his new air that morning of all-seeing wisdom and unimpeachable competence was nauseating. That self-satisfaction was no less deeply resented a little later in Bute House by his cabinet, whom characteristically he allowed to believe that he had himself approved the stone's temporary installation a conveniently short distance from Edinburgh Castle.

The cabinet agenda was already full that day. It included the discussion of covert plans for curtailing further the pretensions of COSLA, the convention of local authorities, who often provided the only serious political opposition to the executive in the social field; the draft Cruelty to Animals (Angling) Bill, a natural sequel to the Act to criminalise pheasant-rearing passed the previous year; a proposal to oblige restaurants to print duplicate menus in Gaelic; and the vexed question of paid paternity or maternity leave for single-sex couples. These were deeply controversial matters on which McNish found concentration unwontedly hard. He allowed a short comment on each subject to whoever wished to speak, and then closed the topic for a week on the grounds that the executive must more urgently attend to the impending ceremonies on the castle esplanade and in the parliament and, no less, to their likely repercussions on Holyrood's relations with Westminster.

The Scottish ministers were in their usual cleft stick. Their mistrust of McNish remained as profound as their loathing for each other. They suspected he was making all the personal political capital he could out of the affair of the stone, and would arrogate to himself all the glory available; but they realised equally that to point out the folly of crossing swords so openly with the Prime Minister in London would be to risk an instant stab in the back by one or more colleagues at the cabinet table.

"You're probably asking yourselves," McNish said with something like a smirk, for he guessed what was going through their minds, "how I intend to deal with any constitutional objections arising from what was said in the Queen's Speech and from the Bill which, as I understand it, the government are about to introduce in the House of Commons. Well, I've this to tell you. Shortly before I came here, my private office received a most generous offer from the Defence Secretary in London, proposing to stage an aerial display for us over the castle, and perhaps a fly-past, on Saint Andrew's Day. It's obvious that our position has been fully accepted, and that the Prime Minister is trying to make the best of it."

A murmur which might equally have been of dissent as of approval went round the table. The First Minister continued.

"I believe it would be prudent to be magnanimous in return. I've already given instructions for the erection on the esplanade

220

of as much of the public seating used for the festival tattoo as is practical in the time available. It's nearly winter, and for all the importance of the occasion we can't expect summer crowds: not more than a couple of thousand people. No tickets possible at such short notice, so seats will be first-come first-served. However, what I propose is this: openly to invite Scotland's MPs, from whom we've perhaps become a little estranged, to occupy reserved front seats on one side, opposite the press. Maybe they'll accept, maybe not, and frankly I don't care – but they won't be able to say we ignored them. And we might ask our MEPs too, if anyone knows who they are and how to get hold of them. Are there any comments?"

"Where shall we be?" asked the Justice Minister and the Minister for Single-Parent Families simultaneously, the latter forgetting how she had just been denied a lengthy discussion of the single-sex couples whom she considered to fall within her remit.

"The stone will arrive on a police trailer, and be on display in the middle of the esplanade, starting at eleven. It'll have its guard of honour, as I told parliament – the Royal Company of Archers. There'll be a rostrum and the usual red and gold chairs for all of us and a list of dignitaries my office is working on. We'll have the pipe band from the castle. I propose to make a speech. Perhaps the Moderator should say something as well – not too long. Then the fly-past and the aerial display: I don't know how much time that needs. Anyway, when it's over, the band will march off first down the hill, leading the stone. My plan is for the executive to follow it on foot. The opposition leaders and the rest of the MSPs will join the procession behind us. The MPs will stay where they are."

Ministers' faces brightened. Public sidelining and, with luck, humiliation of the Wimps would be an added bonus.

"The idea is for the Presiding Officer to receive us when we get to the Canongate. It's got to be an all-party occasion, although obviously the lead must come from me – well, from all of us here," he corrected himself with an expansive gesture. "I'll speak to him." A dark thought crossed his mind and his brow, not unnoticed. "We'll jump that bridge when we come to it." he added confusingly. "There are clearly a few details to be run over still."

"Suits and ties?" asked the Minister for Culture.

"Personally," McNish replied with a hint of self-righteousness, "under the circumstances I'll be in my kilt."

"Good idea!" exclaimed the Deputy First Minister, supported by nods from the others who remembered how ridiculous McNish had looked in it attending Tartan Day in New York in the spring.

The First Minister cast his eyes round the cabinet table, convinced that he was once more master of events. "You will agree, I hope," he said with a modesty everyone present could see through, "that there is something to be said for the bold approach to politics. If anyone wants to issue a press release, please would he or she clear it with Cadell? We must all try to sing – how shall I put it? – from the same song-sheet."

McNish concluded the meeting, dismissed the ministers and left Bute House in his car for the parliament. Rain drizzled over Edinburgh, but his mood was so sunny that he decided, despite his recent experience of the canteen's cuisine, to show his face there once more. As with many politicians who are neither much liked nor much admired, his appetite for a recognition he confused with adulation was almost bulimic. About thirty heads lifted gratifyingly as he entered, those of MSPs, their assistants and variegated parliamentary staff among them. To his dismay, however, one was that of Alasdair McNab seated alone at a table so placed that, when he left the canteen counter, it would be impossible to avoid a word with him, and difficult not to join him for the whole meal. Still, McNab sometimes had his uses. McNish would be making a statement about the Saint Andrew's Day plans in the chamber that afternoon immediately after Time for Reflection, and he could rely on McNab, when requested, at least to raise a related issue even though his choice of words was sometimes unfortunate. It would be helpful and entirely suitable for a backbencher to voice the chamber's appreciation of how the executive had handled the affair. The First Minister paid the small, heavily subsidised charge for what was billed as the dish of the day, pope's eye and mercat greens; helped himself to cutlery, some small coloured packets of salt and mustard, and a tumbler of water; and catching McNab's eye prepared to make the best of that unwelcome circumstance.

In the event, the proceedings in the chamber combined to dampen the First Minister's spirits – a normal and immediate retribution for irrational optimism in political life. An unhappy reaction from the opposition leaders might have been expected: if Saint Andrew's Day in the Old Town were to be the all-party occasion he claimed, it must be inappropriate for the twenty-two ministers with whom Scotland was burdened to march down the High Street at the very head of the procession. Jock Hamilton appealed to the Presiding Officer for a ruling, but found no comfort there.

"This is not a parliamentary matter," Mackay told the chamber. "For all I'm concerned, members may put on silly hats and cavort all the way to Ardnamurchan Point and back again, and do it in any order they please. Although it would no doubt meet the purpose of bringing the antics of parliamentarians to the attention of the public, it would still not be my affair. Mr Moncrieff?"

The leader of the Scottish Enlightenment Party stood up to announce that, although he had proposed the procession in the first place, he had not intended it to be an exercise in self-aggrandisement for the First Minister and his friends; and that none of his members would be taking part in it. For good measure, he put on record his objection to having the Stone of Destiny on the parliament's premises without the express consent of the Queen and her ministers.

Sensing that he had overstepped the acceptable prerogatives of office, McNish intervened to say that, if some members really felt so strongly about such trivial matters, he saw no reason why all the party leaders should not follow immediately behind him in the procession down the Royal Mile. Mrs Murray Stewart duly took the floor to express her disgust at being relegated to the rank and file, but the Presiding Officer, stating that the issue had taken up quite enough time, called Alasdair McNab as the final speaker.

And McNab, after paying fulsome tribute to the Scottish Executive for proving themselves worthy successors to a mixed bag of Scottish patriots and heroes – he mentioned Wallace, The Bruce, Montrose, Argyll, Bonnie Dundee, Rob Roy, William Paterson, Keir Hardie and Jock Stein – observed that he had been happy to oblige Mr McNish who had personally asked him to say what he had just said. Furthermore, he shared the First Minister's optimism that his steadfast leadership would bring new glory to "wir fairy-tale parliament." As jeering and catcalls mounted from the opposition benches and spread to the small row of spectators in the public gallery, the mercat greens which McNish had eaten in McNab's company less than an hour before began to rise in his gorge.

"Walter," said the Presiding Officer a little later, stopping Moncrieff outside the chamber and looking him sternly in the eye, "I think we both have the interests of Scotland, the Union and this parliament at heart."

"I don't doubt that, Douglas. The same worries, too."

"If that stone is brought here on Saint Andrew's Day we'll have a full-blown constitutional crisis on our hands. If it isn't, there'll be a political one."

"I think that sums it up perfectly. I'd say a political one's preferable."

"Probably it would be," Mackay agreed. "I believe you know more than I do."

"About –?"

"About what's in store. You must have a better reason than the one you gave for keeping away."

"Tell me how much you know first."

Mackay paused at this challenge. "Try this," he said carefully. "I know that, if they all come, fifty-nine Members of Parliament will be returning to the scene of their crime." He was gratifed by Moncrieff's look of astonishment. "I imagine that you and I are the only MSPs aware of that. So what do you know?"

Moncrieff considered how to reply.

"You have my word that I don't know in any detail what'll happen up at the castle next week," he said at last, "but I'm sure it won't be what anyone has in mind – McNish least of all. I don't want my party made to look stupider than necessary, and I'm glad you won't be there either. I hope it'll all turn out for the best, and that a constitutional crisis will be prevented. I can't say any more."

"Then I won't press you any more. But when it's all over you'll have to help me pick up the pieces."

11

B LACK, SHINING and magnificent, and sparkling to the flashes
of a hundred cameras, the Stone of Destiny sat high on a
velvet-covered wooden platform in the centre of the great, light
galleried hall of the Royal National Museum in Chambers Street.
Propped beside it were the two targes found in the same Perthshire
site. Red silk ropes held the large invited audience just out
of arm's reach of those extraordinary exhibits, and two of Sir
Andrew's police constables were posted not far off. The gathering
comprised numerous academics from Scotland's universities, the
directors of Britain's national museums, art collections and heritage institutions, highly-placed civil servants, church representatives, and senior figures from the Scottish Bar. There were many
politicians, too: well-kent faces from Scotland's local authorities
mingled with the half-recognised features of her representatives
in Holyrood and the unremembered ones from Westminster. The
media, of course, were there in force, and television cameras in
profusion. For three-quarters of an hour after the doors were
opened, this excited crowd jostled and surged round and round
the stone, staring in wonder, a hubbub of speculation.

Duncan had persuaded Campbell Macarthur and Andy
Wedderburn that the last two days of November would be too
important in Scotland's history to allow her MPs to obey the call
of the Chief Whips in the House of Commons, notwithstanding
the Government's need for its Scottish majority to carry an important vote on a supplementary budget. Their presence in Edinburgh
might not change that history, but it had to be established and,
in due course, proclaimed. To that extent, McNish had played
into their hands. They would certainly take their seats on the

esplanade next day, and the world would know it. In the meantime, Duncan had not found it hard to persuade his father to include them all in his invitation list to the first public exhibition of the palladium.

Although invited with his partner, the First Minister stayed away. His big day was to follow, and he knew he would be given no prominent part in the cultural preview. He was also fretting over the Presiding Officer's outright refusal either to be at the ceremony on the esplanade or personally to receive the stone into safe-keeping in Holyrood; and he ruminated over whether he could properly perform that latter function himself.

Dr Mackay and his wife, however, were present in the museum as Dr Innes's guests. So was Morag. She was there, absent from her desk, with McNish's express consent, for he agreed with her that some first-hand account of the proceedings in the museum might be useful to him when preparing his speech for the morrow. As she looked round the hall, she saw Janet Ross standing ten feet from her, and their eyes met. In neither case was recognition instant, for their single encounter had been under testing circumstances in Duncan's flat in Drummond Place. Each attempted a half smile, then their expressions froze, and both turned away.

"I had nothing whatever against that woman," Morag thought to herself, "– not until she betrayed Duncan." Out of the corner of her eye, she watched Janet's progress past the stone and round the hall, having a word here and there with MPs and other acquaintances before finding herself beside Duncan as though by chance. Whatever she asked him, his response was clearly unhelpful, negative and curt. Janet moved unhurriedly towards the main door, then disappeared through it into the street.

At noon, the museum's director asked for silence. Dr Innes, Tom and Ian joined the stone on the platform. The professor welcomed the company, expressed his pleasure in at last bringing the real Stone of Scone into the light of day, and disclosed where it had been hidden for more than seven centuries. He reminded his audience of the legend that here was the pillow on which, or by which, Jacob had rested and dreamed so long ago at Bethel in the land of Canaan. But he left it to his younger colleagues to recount their further researches and take their share of the credit. Ian, the geologist, was first. He related how a stony-iron meteorite shower of exactly the same rare composition had been recorded at Bethel, in all likelihood part of the rain of fire and brimstone which destroyed Sodom and Gomorrah, thus pinpointing the stone's origins. Tom followed. Carbon-dating of the targes had shown them to be a little over eleven hundred years old, consistent with the belief that they were of Dalriadic origin, and possibly used by Fergus, son of Erc, himself. He argued that this large block of meteorite had been carved for service as an altar by Saint Columba five hundred years earlier still, before its adaptation during the ninth century to form the coronation throne for the early Scottish kings. Dunsinane Hill, he concluded, was now an archaeological site of prime importance.

The press quickly sensed the excitement these startling revelations were generating among the academics. Here were all the elements of a good story – even beyond the historic magnitude of the stone's discovery and the priceless rarity of such an antiquity. As well as the topical association with the dark character of the Macbeths, there were the wickedness and sexual depravity of the cities of the plains, and the terrible vengeance of the Almighty. However, for parliamentary correspondents such as Ross Burton, the crux was the political sensitivity of its reappearance at that juncture. They had instantly marked the presence of Andy Wedderburn and other MPs at the occasion, and fully understood the strong feelings running among them in respect of the stone and the Scottish Executive's plans for it. Political combustion was in the wind, and they wondered how it would manifest itself.

When Dr Innes had enjoyed the congratulations and admiration of his university friends to the extent possible in a man of fundamental modesty, he was persuaded to give a short press conference. He protested vainly that there was surely nothing more to be said, and that Tom and Ian were the right people to answer all questions on archaeology or geology, but the press were having none of it.

"You'll have been consulted about the executive's plans for the stone, Dr Innes?" asked Jim Bell from the *Daily Record*. "Will you be at the castle tomorrow yourself, and do you think the parliament is a good place to put the stone now?"

"I wasn't consulted about any plans," the professor said, "but of course I've read about them. I'm sure they'll have been cleared by the Crown Office. And, yes, I've accepted the First Minister's invitation to watch his procession. It should be fun."

"But how do you feel about putting it in the parliament, Dr Innes?" Bell persisted. "After all, your son is a — "

"Ah, politics!" Dr Innes interrupted quickly. "We do our best to avoid talking about them in my family. Please don't draw me on that."

Ross Burton was allowed one more try. "Then, as a historian, Dr Innes, do you have any advice to offer the executive about where the stone should go – or even a view about where it shouldn't?"

Innes hesitated, then smiled. "Angels are said to have carried it here from the Land of Canaan. Maybe eagles will carry it away again. But it isn't for mere historians or antiquarians to comment on what eagles and angels do."

Morag was listening, and her cup was nearly full. Duncan had done what she had asked: his father was party to the plot.

It rained early on Saint Andrew's Day; but by mid-morning, despite a sharp wind, dry weather had brought a large crowd to Edinburgh Castle's broad esplanade. The public who arrived too late for seats on the stands filled the east end of the arena and spilled down Castlehill to the High Street, past the Heart of Midlothian and beyond.

They were cold, but as eleven o'clock approached the sun began to break through after its fashion over the Grassmarket, and spirits rose, encouraged by the first strains of bagpipes from inside the castle.

Sir Andrew McCallum was still taking no chances and had deployed a large squad of police officers to keep the populace well back from what they had come to see. The Stone of Destiny sat on a saltire-decked trailer in the centre of the arena, the blue and white flag admirably setting off its glistening black mass. The police vehicle which towed it from the museum was parked tactfully out of sight behind the batteries of television cameras which had been in place for an hour or more.

Now the reserved seats were filling up. The press were already in occupation of the front row assigned to them, Burton and his fellow parliamentary correspondents among them. On the opposite front row Scotland's MPs were arriving in twos and threes from their final briefing in the upstairs room in Deacon Brodie's Tavern, booked for the occasion by Maureen Findlay, the MP

228

for Cramond. Campbell Macarthur had asked them all to show the greatest restraint in the face of the provocation expected from McNish. They watched the first of the VIPs being shown to the long rows of red and gold chairs facing down the esplanade with their backs to the castle, protected by a white awning. Here were the Lord Provost and senior members of Edinburgh Council; the Moderator of the General Assembly of the Church of Scotland with the Bishop of Edinburgh and the leaders of other non-conforming churches; the Dean of the Faculty of Advocates, the Keeper of the Records of Scotland and the Lord Lyon King of Arms. Here was the Principal of Edinburgh University looking uncomfortable in the company of the notoriously gay comedian whom the students had recently elected Rector. Here were the Directors of the Museums and National Galleries of Scotland, the President of the National Trust for Scotland, and the Chairman of Historic Scotland himself, Sir Hew Cunynghame. Last to arrive was the new Lord Lieutenant, representing the Queen, to be seated not far from the special guests of the executive who included Dr and Mrs Innes and the team who had discovered the stone. Morag had come with them, at the professor's request. She looked at the rows of Scottish MPs, seeking out Duncan's face.

At the back of this distinguished audience, at his own insistence – in case, he said, of administrative problems – Major-General Sir Norman Brunstane sat with his wife. For the same reason the Chief Constable, Sir Andrew McCallum, sat near the front.

At three minutes to eleven came the thud of drums from behind the portcullis, then the whine of bagpipes, then the band itself, pipes a-skirl and kilts a-whirl, marching out into the sunlight, to halt beside the VIP seats, there to continue its repertoire while a detachment of the Royal Company of Archers proceeded almost in step from the castle gate to fall in some twenty-five yards downhill from the stone. The pipe-major threw his massive staff into the air, caught it, and let it drop six feet in his grasp; and there was silence. The scene was at last set for the nation's leaders to expose themselves to the warm plaudits of the people. A bugle sounded from the battlement above the gate. Led by William McNish and Jock Hamilton walking solemnly together, a hundred or so MSPs, prudently gloved and scarved, filed out of the castle to jostle for their places under the canopy in the front rows of chairs. Out of respect, perhaps, not a plaudit could be heard.

While the press, awake to any hint of disharmony, noted that neither the Presiding Officer nor any Member of the Scotch Enlightenment Party had appeared, the MPs watched the arrival of the flower of Holyrood with stony-faced dignity, silently damning their presumption and their impertinence. They saw McNish come forward to mount the little dais near the stone and stand there, his kilt four inches too long for him, letting his gaze range theatrically round the Edinburgh crowd before raising his face slowly towards the sun as though to seek inspiration from that quarter. Their emotions under challenge, they prepared to ride unprovoked whatever verbal humiliation he planned for them.

Yet McNish's posturing was less of a dramatic contrivance than it looked. He was savouring his moment. The audience forgotten, the Stone of Destiny pushed to the back of his mind, he was enjoying a waking vision which for a fortnight or more had merely haunted his dreams. It was of a statue of himself – the counterpart to the one of Donald Dewar erected a few years earlier outside the Royal Concert Hall in Glasgow and unveiled by the then British Prime Minister, no less. Not before he was dead, too, of course, but vandal-proof, and preferably somewhere on Calton Hill along with whoever they were up there already. A statue? No, a memorial! A monument! Or a wheel, like the London one. The McNish Wheel! How would he be remembered? How many "fathers" could Scotland have? He might consult the Minister for Single Parent Families about that, but circuitously, without revealing what was on his mind. His thoughts slid away again to the practicality of renaming the Salisbury Crags.

A sporadic burst of clapping from some supportive MSPs who feared, not without justice, that he had gone into a trance brought him out of his reverie. But then a new idea came to him. Wasn't there a well-known mountain in America decorated with the heads of the founding fathers of that nation? Why rename the crags? Why not reshape them? They were probably protected as a historic site, but it might be worth enquiring. Laws could be circumvented. And then, of course, the Makar, Scotland's laureate, would write a sonnet . . . or an ode. He smiled, prayed briefly that his wireless lapel microphone was switched on and functioning, and began to read out his speech.

He spoke of a parliament growing in stature; of a people with well-earned pride and confidence in their own government; of an executive, a leadership, at last capable of handling whatever challenges a stern Fate might throw at it. He spoke of purse-strings and apron-strings; and of those who failed to loosen either. His eye roving to the MPs seated on the benches to his right, he spoke of politicians who clung to the past, comparing them, much to their disadvantage, with those who represented the future. Then, sensing that he might already have lost the attention of most of his audience, and wisely deciding to omit a passage about his own passionate feelings on hearing of the stone's discovery, elected less sensibly to apostrophise that object directly and extempore.

"Great stone!" he cried. "Puissant guardian of the on-going destiny of Scotland! Today you are assured of a long-term relationship with the cream of Scotland's parliamentarians in a meaningful resting place in their midst. You, our majestic national palladium" – he had his usual two shots at it – "the symbol of our sovereignty, so long lost, so happily recovered!"

This was not what McNish did best. His words were at once extravagant, controvertible, banal, insincere and absurd. Detecting a distant drone, he raised his voice.

"Scotland has been awaiting your historic reappearance for exactly seven hundred years. Well, and a little bit more," he rambled.

But he had already gone on too long. Fly-pasts by their nature have to be timed to the second. The drone he heard was the final positioning manoeuvre of the Lincolnshire-based Red Arrows aerobatics team before their sensational death-defying display over Edinburgh Castle. His speech was drowned and the crowd, whose minds were anyway on other things, looked upwards thankfully to see the spectacle so many of them had come for.

Nine red and white Hawks tore out of the sun to the south of the esplanade, roared across the castle gateway in tight diamond-nine formation, fanned out as they pulled upwards over Leith Docks to stage a vast looping-the-loop embracing the entire city skyline, and then fell into close formation again to sweep over the esplanade's east end. McNish, still on his little dais, made an expansive though largely unnoticed gesture to the crowd as though to claim a ring-master's responsibility for the trick which they were cheering wildly; or possibly to exhibit the might of a Caesar able to provide circuses as easily as bread.

He heard, and misinterpreted, the cheering, but did not stay long in his place. From the west this time, over the castle itself, came the first of the Blue Eagles, the celebrated team of army helicopters whose dare-devil stunts had startled British air shows for three decades. In a few moments, while four Lynxes hovered in line abreast high above the half-moon battery, an Apache dropped downwards over the trailer bearing the stone, its chin-mounted cannon barrel sweeping menacingly around the arena in league with the pilot's line of site. This not only awed the crowd: it created a continuous, strong and bitterly cold downwash below – mercifully free of dust because of the earlier rain. McNish fled to his red and gold chair under the flapping canopy. Clutching their plumed caps, the Royal Archers retreated in disorder some thirty paces further from the stone they were guarding. All present who wore coats pulled them about themselves more closely than ever.

The stage set for their first trick, the four Lynxes flew off in a tight box formation to the south while the Apache snarled away to the north. Half a minute later, the Lynxes wheeled back toward the castle, rising to form a vertical diamond in the sky – to greet the Apache, which had turned simultaneously, heading toward them on an apparent collision course at a closing speed of more than two hundred miles an hour. The crowd held its breath, its normal practice when witnessing an act known as "threading the needle". Exactly overhead, the Apache passed cleanly and precisely through the hole in the diamond of Lynxes, leaving the crowd to gasp and cheer as the team broke and peeled away round the back of the castle rock.

The Prime Minister, thought McNish, had certainly pulled out all the stops. He might have got his timing a little wrong, but at this distance from Downing Street nothing could be absolutely perfect. Was the thing over? Should he resume his speech? There hadn't exactly been a fly-past, but there was nothing to complain about.

Neither consideration detained him long, for the noise of yet more engines could be heard, this time from an aircraft undoubtedly heavier than before and much higher in the sky. The public strained their eyes upwards and picked out an RAF Hercules approaching the middle of Edinburgh from its base in Wiltshire. Small dots were falling from it, which the *cognoscenti* on the esplanade recognised as the Red Devils, the British Army's free-fall parachute team which boasted an ability to land on a euro – or a sixpence, as an older expression had it.

At that point the morning's spectacular display turned into something entirely unexpected and, so far as the First Minister was concerned, unplanned and unwelcome.

One by one, each sky-diver's plunge was arrested by a red parachute. They swooped over the castle, slowing abruptly to land and dropping, a dozen in all, at the centre of the esplanade in a perfect circle round the flag-bedecked trailer bearing the Stone of Destiny. The crowd cheered and clapped: the parachutes were packed instantly into the team's equipment, and in little more than half a minute the trailer was protected by a wide, hand-held safety cordon, ready for what was to follow. Sir Andrew McCallum's policemen were swept back to the edges of the public seats and, in the east, to where the crowds were standing. And again the timing was perfect: a Chinook rose like a sea monster over the stands from somewhere near the Mound to position itself directly above the stone. Ropes cascaded from its open doors, and a dozen troops in black combat dress abseiled smoothly fifty feet down to the ground. Their commanding officer barked some rapid instructions and, before anyone on the esplanade could guess what was intended, the helicopter rotors began to turn faster, and the stone itself was rising into the air in a rope cradle and being carried off heavenward.

Scarcely three minutes had elapsed since the first Red Devil landed. No one in the public stands suspected anything was amiss. The crowd cheered as before, forgetting the chill of the day in their excitement. On the other hand the VIPs in the red and gold chairs, especially the MSPs, being better informed had risen to their feet in stunned amazement. However, even now the element of surprise of which the Special Services were such practised exponents was working for them. As the combined force of the sky-divers and the commando gathered smartly on the trailer, a second heavy-lift helicopter, a Merlin, loomed into sight and hearing, hovering towards the troops, rope ladders unrolling from its hatches. Here was how the cast would leave the stage. While the sky divers leapt for the rungs, sharper-eyed spectators must have noticed an apparently substantial package being lowered from the aircraft and installed on the trailer under the commanding officer's eye – just before he and the last of the troops swarmed on to the ladders to be borne gently into the sky.

At last, when any counter-action must be far too late, Scotland's First Minister found his voice.

"Stop them!" McNish shouted above the engines' noise. He turned to point an accusing finger at Sir Andrew McCallum, the Chief Constable. "Do something, man! Anything!"

Sir Andrew was at a loss. "What do you suggest, First Minister?" he roared back angrily. "A committee of enquiry? A joint report?"

"Don't be a fool!"

"Then perhaps General Brunstane has a howitzer?"

McNish waved wildly at the detachment of the Royal Company of Archers.

"Shoot!" he yelled.

A single arrow sped towards the still rising helicopter but flew wide of its mark. The high-ranking former army officer responsible for discharging it on the mere and dubious authority of a First Minister would certainly be called to account later at dinner in Archers Hall; but had made history in that, until that moment, since its appointment as the royal bodyguard for Scotland for King George the Fourth's visit in 1822, the Royal Company had not once engaged in a military action, nor had an archer drawn his bow in anger.

Watching the helicopters dipping out of sight again, the ministers of the Scottish Executive felt no sympathy for McNish in his panic and frustration, but necessarily shared his anguish. The shame of losing a second stone – for that was what had happened – would be theirs as well as his. Already MSPs from the opposition parties were physically distancing themselves from them, edging out of their places, anxious not to be associated with a public relations disaster of such an order. Jean Murray Stewart, who had earlier and skilfully inserted herself prominently in the front seats, mysteriously rematerialised two rows back. Maybe foul political play was behind it – the Enlightenment party had cunningly kept away – but somehow the opposition members were sure the executive had contrived to make a fool of them all. At a baser level, they knew that there would now be no procession down the Royal Mile to the cheers of the capital's populace. Yet their humiliation was not complete.

The aircraft mounting this memorable Saint Andrew's Day display over the capital had regrouped, not dispersed; and the fly-past promised by the Prime Minister and the Secretary of State for Defence now began. Running in southwards from the Firth of Forth came, first, the Red Arrows again, in a long but stupendous roll performed as a single wing, to a new and fervent round of public applause and enthusiasm. Close behind them, preceded by the almost sinister sound of thudding rotor blades, came the Blue Eagles in a wide "vic"-formation, escorting – almost carrying, it seemed – the two heavy-lift helicopters. The Stone of Scone, gleaming and hanging back at a slight angle in the slipstream, was clearly visible beneath the Chinook. The troops who had seized it were all safely on board the Merlin. On they flew, rising higher and higher over the Grassmarket, over the Meadows, out towards the Lammermuirs and the Borders. Meanwhile the Red Arrows, circling for the last time, sped in low with a gigantic roar from the direction of Arthur's Seat, releasing a thick triple trail of red, white and blue smoke behind them before embarking on a dizzy, helical climb to the skies. With their hands over their ears, the crowd watched the smoke billow patriotically over the esplanade and round the castle, before spiralling upwards in the aircrafts' wake into the inescapable rain clouds gathering above.

The air show was over. Somewhere above Peebles, the Blue Eagles dipped in salute and flew north to the RAF station at Leuchars. Inside the Merlin, the men noticed that the unusual tension exhibited by their colonel earlier was dissipating. By the time they crossed the Border he was himself again.

For the quarter-of-an-hour in which the aerial drama unfolded, Scotland's MPs sat still, silent and expressionless on their lowly front seats, observing the reconstitution of their political prospects with the deepest satisfaction. Their undemonstrative demeanour may have escaped the attention of the public, who did not know who they were, and of the executive and the MSPs, who did not care; but it did not go unnoticed on the press seats directly opposite, especially among the Scottish press. And the one certainty, shared alike by political editor, lobby correspondent, sketch-writer or common reporter, was that they had witnessed a highly-charged scene in which a needle battle for political ascendancy had been fought between Scotland's tribunes in Holyrood and Westminster. The Stone of Destiny, the symbol of their struggle, might be on its way to London; but no journalist made the mistake of supposing that it was the British Government, or the Queen, or "the English", who wanted it there. Since McNish's ostentatious arrogation of a power which belonged to the Crown, the schism, the gulf, the feud between Scottish MPs and MSPs had become common knowledge in the media. The only question had been how their rivalry would manifest itself, and how vividly. This was the answer. The very tranquillity of the Westminster members gave their game away. They had executed a *coup* of Macchiavellian subtlety, and their only false move was to keep their faces straight.

The TV cameras tracked along the ranks of the MPs recording a common gravitas and innocence unworthy of credence. There was Callum Geekie, MP for The Monros, offering what might have been a peppermint to the member for Inchcape Rock, Graham Fraser. There were a couple of the Glasgow Boys, Ian McWhirter (for Hornel) and Donald Mutwant Singh (for Lavery), looking upwards and seemingly gauging the probability of rain. Beside them Jennie Murray and Jessie Lambie (respectively for Rockall and Guthrie) affected to be comparing their diaries, and the political academic Ewan Cameron (Ailsa Craig) was explaining some technicality about Cannonball House to Duncan Innes (St Mary's Loch). However, that uniform façade of insouciance began to break when the MPs guessed it to be out of tune with the expectations of the public on the stands behind. Apart from an inaudible but histrionic argument developing between the First Minister and his colleagues, nothing of interest had happened in the arena for nearly five minutes, and the crowd, already cold and expecting soon to get wet, was restless. Following the lead from Campbell Macarthur the MPs began a slow hand-clap which quickly spread across the esplanade.

The media were not fooled, but saw that McNish was in something of a panic. His hair had become ruffled, and he could be seen pointing distractedly at the saltire-covered trailer where sat the large package delivered from the air and provocatively wrapped in the Union Flag. The Chief Constable with equal clarity could be seen forbidding whatever course of action the First Minister was recommending. Into this altercation strode Major-General Brunstane from the back row of red and gold chairs, his body language indicating forcefully that this was a matter for the army.

Sir Norman nodded towards the pipe band. The pipe-major called his band to attention; then, with a wave of his staff, elicited a series of mighty thumps from the drums before beginning the programme of inspiring Scottish marches that were to have taken the parade down the hill to Holyrood. A second signal from Sir Norman brought a sergeant and six kilted soldiers at the double from the castle gates. They ran to the trailer and carefully inspected the package on it. While the band started a third verse of *Scotland the Brave*, the sergeant marched up to the general and saluted.

"Is it a bomb?" This was McNish's question.

"No, Sir," said the sergeant addressing Sir Norman.

"There!" McNish said to McCallum.

"What is it, sergeant?" asked Sir Norman, formally rather than with any hint of curiosity.

"The stone, Sir. The one that was stolen."

"Thank you, sergeant. Take charge of it, would you?"

"Sir!"

The sergeant saluted again, turned and raised his hand to an unseen watcher posted on the castle battlements. An army truck instantly drove out of the gate. The trailer was promptly attached to its rear. The sergeant and his section fell in behind and shepherded it back inside.

Duncan looked across the arena to Morag. Only her lips moved, pursing then parting in a discreet kiss.

"First Minister," said Sir Norman, "I assure you I have no idea how that stone has come to be there, but I suspect one of your problems has been solved. I shall return it where it came from and place it properly under guard. The pipe band is available to play the lot of you down the High Street to the parliament if it's what you wish. But it's coming on to rain and we could call it a day."

He indicated bewildered spectators wearied of barracking who were leaving their stands unimpeded by Sir Andrew's policemen. Further off, the seatless spectators had enjoyed the air display but were thinning noticeably, unimpressed by the thought of politicians, however eminent, marching past them behind a stone, however extraordinary, in a cold drizzle, however normal.

237

Whatever the shortcomings of Edinburgh people, lack of proportion was not one of them.

For McNish, nemesis had overtaken hubris with depressing suddenness. He glared despairingly about the esplanade. The MPs talked together in small groups: no doubt they would soon be mocking him. Journalists and media people shook their heads at one another, none coming forward asking for his comments as they usually did. His ministers and members of his own party in mutinous mood waited for guidance. The rest of the MSPs, sullen, resentful and increasingly unruly, prepared to ignore it. As the pipe band launched into *Wae's Me for Prince Charlie*, McNish became aware of the chief press officer at his elbow.

"I think you should say something, Wullie," whispered Cadell. "You're still connected. That's the switch on your lapel."

"What the hell can I say? That I only lose one stone at a time?"

"Thank them for coming and tell them to go home."

"But they're going home."

"Well, make them think it was your idea."

McNish stepped out from under the canopy. Sir Norman signalled to the pipe-major who silenced the pipes at the next appropriate moment, two long minutes later during which the drizzle had turned to rain. Beginning to look sodden, his kilt dripping, the First Minister took a deep breath and switched on his microphone.

"Ladies and Gentlemen, this has been a great day for Scotland, a great day for the Scottish people, and a great day for the Scottish parliament . . ."

Rain turned to downpour. Disinclined to tarry, the VIPs dispersed quickly in the wake of the other spectators, those with umbrellas not so fast as the less fortunate. Dignitaries with official cars parked by the esplanade parapet waved urgently at their drivers. The Royal Archers had dismissed themselves. The press had gone. So had Scotland's MPs, led by Wedderburn and Macarthur down Castlehill and back to review developments in Deacon Brodie's Tavern, their planned rendezvous. Of the Members of the Scottish Parliament, the opposition parties broke and ran first.

". . . but it is not one for a parade."

"Exactly so," Sir Norman interrupted. "Pipe-major! You may stand your men down."

*　　　*　　　*

"Were ye up on the esplanade yesterday, Mr Burton? Ah heard it wis a great affair wi' the helicopters afore a'body got drookit."

"Aye, I was there. It was a marvellous air show, Maggie."

"Margaret, please, Mr Burton. Onyway if it went sae weel, why've they pit Mr McNish on the midden alang wi' a' the ithers?"

It was half past noon. The Presiding Officer had made the announcement to a full chamber, and the news that yet another First Minister was passing into obscurity had sped round the parliament buildings.

"You'll have heard about the stone."

"Oh, aye, that. They had tae cancel the procession. Is it yer usual?"

"No, I'll have a dram and a drop of water this time, Maggie. And you'll have watched the telly last night. And perhaps seen the *Record* this morning." He nursed no illusion that she read *The Herald*.

"Aye, they werena very nice aboot him." A measure of spirit drained out of a bulb below an upturned bottle of Teacher's into the glass she held. As ever, it looked discouragingly little.

"Make it a double, Maggie, please. Is that measure faulty?"

"There's the complaints box behind ye, Mr Burton, if ye'd care tae use it. The watter's beside ye."

"As I understand it, the cabinet decided it was all Oor Wullie's fault. He'd made a fool of them with his posturing, so they said they'd resign in a bunch unless he walked."

"So wha's gonny tak' his place?"

"It's for the Presiding Officer to designate somebody; and then for the parliament to agree if it wants to; and then for the Queen to make the appointment."

"Whit a palaver!"

"Who'd you choose, Maggie? It'll likely be from the same party as before unless they lose their majority; and they might, if the coalition falls apart. They're meeting now."

"Whit aboot that Mr McNab? He's an honest Glasgow man."

"Yes," said Ross Burton thoughtfully. "Maybe it's time he had a turn like everyone else, but I doubt he's ineligible. He was never on a council."

Burton was not giving the high priestess of the Pint o' Wine an entire account of what brought McNish down. The Scottish

Executive had been humiliated on Saint Andrew's Day, having had the Stone of Destiny snatched away in front of their eyes. They had felt affronted thereafter at having to forego leading a triumphant parade down the Royal Mile, not simply because of the rain; and furious at being robbed of a symbolic political victory over the Westminster members. And, had all other things been equal, these misfortunes might well have been enough to persuade them to oust the First Minister without delay and summarily from his post.

The chief factor that allowed McNish to stay in office and occupy his official residence in Bute House for one more night was still the mutual dislike and suspicion reigning along the rest of the cabinet table. There were lesser considerations as well, certainly. His deputy realised that news of her affair with a back-bench MSP was about to break in the press, so that she would be out of the running as his successor at least till the New Year – although, Heaven knew these days, when it came to scandal the public's immune system responded with ever-greater promptness. The Finance Minister, next in the pecking order, was unacceptable to their coalition partners. The Justice Minister, despite his talents, was considered over-ambitious by almost everyone in the parliament and had no strong following.

In the afternoon of Saint Andrew's Day, now in a dry suit and conscious of his precarious hold on authority, McNish convened a cabinet in Bute House and attempted to rally the executive, as was his habit, against Scotland's MPs. However, it was pointed out that he had personally invited them to be present at the castle with the clear and express intention of belittling them, and indeed had openly insulted them in his speech. So the First Minister tried to turn his ministers' indignation against the British govern-ment for an unprecedented breach of party solidarity. It was hard to distinguish, he claimed, between what had happened that morn-ing and the theft committed by Edward the First seven centuries earlier – although, he argued, this was more serious because that king had been palmed off with a fake. However, McNish's minis-ters knew better than to trust his historical judgment. The Lord Advocate remarked coldly that the First Minister seemed unaware of other outrages perpetrated by Edward, mentioning that in any case military activity other than civil defence was a reserved matter.

"And if the devolution settlement had been in place at the time," he added, "Edward the First would probably have been within his rights, too. *Mutatis mutandis*, of course."

"*Mew –?*" McNish hazarded.

"Forget it," said the law officer. As an *ex officio* Commissioner of the Regalia he still smarted over having been wilfully kept in ignorance of the fate of the stone. Anyway, he did not consider McNish's intellect worth wasting time on.

"What next?" the Enterprise Minister asked.

"Naturally I shall be putting out a statement to say where we stand."

"That'll be where *you* stand, will it, Wullie?"

However, no statement from the First Minister, nothing he might have said in the devastating interviews he exposed himself to that evening on television, could have saved his administration. The full story of the rivalry and bitterness between the two sets of Scottish politicians burst over his head as the pictures of the Westminster members he had tried publicly to degrade and marginalise crowded the nation's screens. Compared to the motley mob of MSPs, depicted damp, dispirited and running for cover, they appeared as a smart and presentable body of men and women who might even be trusted with the nation's future. The political narrative accompanying the dramatic shots of red, white and blue smoke wreathing Edinburgh Castle may have been speculative and circumstantial in its origins but it was acutely accurate in its conclusions – not least regarding McNish's acting beyond his competence and his failure to defuse a dangerous political and international crisis while there was still time. The seizing of the genuine Stone of Destiny from the castle esplanade was presented not as the deceitful and high-handed act of reprisal by London which McNish now claimed; but as a politically astute stroke engineered by honourable and patriotic Scottish MPs whose claim to speak and act for their electorate was as least as good as Holyrood's.

The following morning the press unexceptionally followed the same line: the MPs in Westminster – several of their names mentioned – had done no more than their duty in the face of searing provocation. There was no comfort for McNish anywhere, and now his cabinet too were sharing the heat. Political editors harked back to the Presiding Officer's words when McNish first proposed to install the stone in the parliament – warning against stirring unhappiness between nations. Who in the cabinet had counselled moderation?

Collective responsibility had often proved a fragile concept in the executive, but collective blame was more than they could stand if it could be pinned satisfactorily elsewhere. Mutual jealousies and personal difficulties ceased to count. By nine-o'clock, McNish could neither divide nor rule. There were no more sweeteners to be given to his party, no more extravagances to offer the parliament, and no more reshuffles with which to threaten his cabinet. On the insistence of Craig Millar, he sent a formal hand-written note to the Presiding Officer, so that the House could be officially informed. However, he took care through his press officer to let the media know first, in part as a last gesture of spite against Dr Mackay, in part to anticipate whatever twist his cabinet colleagues might hope to put on the story.

Some hours after Ross Burton had finished his glass of whisky in the Pint o' Wine in Holyrood, the Prime Minister called Andy Wedderburn to the cabinet room at Ten Downing Street.

"Andy – this man Moncrieff. What sort of a First Minister will he make? Another self-regarding buffoon?"

"It's confirmed, then? I only heard the old coalition had collapsed and he was trying to put another together. No – Walter's sound. Intelligent. Realist. Not into party politics too much, but he knows what's possible. You can do business with him."

"Well, that'll be a change."

"And support for his party is growing all the time up there. Mainly because everyone hates party politics, if you can understand that."

"I'm not surprised."

"Especially after yesterday," Wedderburn said with satisfaction. "The Enlightenment party stayed away and avoided the tarbrush."

"It was a neat operation. And Hamilton?"

"Jock's underweight and sometimes a little bit other-worldly, but he'll make a good enough deputy. I've been talking to Douglas Mackay – the Presiding Officer: he's an old friend. He moved quickly to designate Moncrieff, and he thinks it'll all hold together for a time."

"We've got to use that time cleverly."

242

"I agree. Before the constitution unravels any further."

"And before we lose any more votes, Andy. We needed your members yesterday. We lost by two."

"I'm sorry, Prime Minister. *Force majeure*, I'm afraid."

"Well, it's made your point with the parliamentary party in England."

"I've said it before – we're in this together. Your majority will be back down in London by tomorrow."

The Prime Minister coughed, glancing at his Cabinet Secretary. "It should be possible now to get two or three of your people back into the government, as well as yourself. We've been testing the water. Time for a bit of a reshuffle anyway. Matthew says it'll help build up their morale a bit. There's your Whip, for instance – a bright spark, Hartley says; and we need another woman. But of course that'll only be the start. We'll have to give them all something worthwhile to do – in all the other parties. A bit of control and responsibility for what happens at home. It all needs working out again. Everybody sees that."

Wedderburn nodded encouragingly. "And the stone, Prime Minister? Our MPs are anxious –"

"I've an Order in Council prepared. It's already secure in the abbey."

"There's some carpentry to be done under the chair," added the Cabinet Secretary. "The Dean wants it installed with as little fuss as possible, and before Christmas. An announcement afterwards, but no press."

"Yes," said the Prime Minister. "There'll have to be a short formal ceremony, but we thought it should only be for those who were closely involved. Your MPs, of course, if they want to."

"Moncrieff should be there – so long as the MSPs confirm his nomination, and they will. And the Presiding Officer."

"Very well. Give me a list. Would they come?"

In the Central Lobby on his way out of the House of Commons Duncan Innes encountered Janet Ross for the first time for more than two weeks. He wore an overcoat. She carried a sheaf of papers. There had been no communication between them since the first public appearance of the stone in the Royal Museum in Edinburgh. On the castle esplanade they had each taken pains to sit as far away from one another as possible. Now, welcome or not, and short of their mutually cutting one another, it was unavoidable.

"Hullo, Janet. Are you coming across the road with us all? It looks like the end of the chapter. You'll need a coat."

"No, Duncan, I've no time for all that. You'll excuse me." She made a step to pass him, but paused. "By the way, you should know that I'll be under Hartley now. Hartley Blackburn. The new Secretary of State for –"

"Under him?" Duncan raised his eyebrows.

"I mean I'll have my own Department," she said sharply.

"Ah! Good for you. Congratulations. You've begun a new chapter already."

"Yes."

"There's a general reshuffle, then?"

"That's the idea." Her eyes met his coldly. "Not before time."

The smile he returned concealed his relief that if her emotions were still involved it was with somebody else. He moved politely aside to let her pass, and made for Saint Stephen's Porch. Outside, through the chilly and overcast mid-December day he could see a familiar shape crossing the road ahead of him and hurrying past Saint Margaret's towards Westminster Abbey's north door.

"Campbell!" he called.

Campbell Macarthur stopped and turned. "Hullo, Duncan! It's working already! You said it would."

"Working?"

"The stone. The Prime Minister's reshuffle. We're in the government again. Three of us."

"Good! Janet was just telling me she –"

"Yes, she's one, and – well, Duncan, he's put me in the cabinet with Andy. No portfolio yet, but that can wait."

"Splendid, Campbell! Congratulations."

"The credit's yours, Duncan. We all know that. You were the inspiration. Look – there's Walter. And Wee Dougie, the Presiding Officer. And there's your father with them."

Duncan's gaze ranged round the few dozen people summoned for the occasion – most of the MPs who, if they ever dared break three months' silence, would scarcely be believed; Dr Mackay and the more eminent leaders of Walter Moncrieff's new Scottish administration; the team who unearthed the secret of Macbeth's Castle; the Dean and a busy swarm of abbey officials; technicians deploying the latest electronic security devices; even the colonel who planned and conducted the Special Services' *coup de main* at Edinburgh Castle. Something was lacking.

A hand slid into his, on cue. "Duncan," said Morag, "It's all wonderful. The only thing is, I've lost my job."

"Can I help? Young MP, male, requires lovely assistant, female, view to permanent relationship."

"That's a coincidence. Young woman seeks position with attractive male MP, view to long-term happiness."

"They ought to get together."

"They'd be mad not to."

EPILOGUE

As a news story, the installation of the authentic Stone of Destiny in Westminster Abbey was to sink – as the Prime Minister planned it should – under the greater political interest of the simultaneous pre-Christmas ministerial changes. The inclusion of Scottish MPs in the new London administration of course occupied the attention of the Scottish media. That there might have been a direct and significant connection between the two events passed unremarked either in programmes broadcast or in the public prints.

Those present at the ceremony, standing in a circle in the vicinity of King Edward's tomb, held a more profound view of what they were witnessing. King Edward's carved wooden coronation chair, built for him by Walter the Painter in 1298 at a cost of one hundred shillings, was at last to serve its purpose as a showcase for Scotland's true Stone of Destiny. The shelf under the seat had been removed and the recess below substantially deepened. The four lions on whose backs the chair rested stood a little higher from the base than before. Any who sat on it now would require an ample footstool for comfort, but its proportions were carefully preserved.

It was still empty. The black marble throne was brought forward on a low platform with rubber wheels and, after the Dean had pronounced some appropriate but barely-heard words over it, manoeuvred to where it could stand in safety behind brass rails until the next monarch was crowned. The wooden chair was then bodily lifted, placed over it and secured. No more needed to be done. No obstacle remained to impede the fulfilment of the ancient

246

prophecies. What new benefits the stone's presence there would bring to Scotland only time and her historians would tell.

Meanwhile, Lieutenant-Colonel Robert Corspatrick, Commanding Officer 22 SAS, the man who had personally planned, named and led Operation Longshanks, sat down in a nearby pew, leant back and closed his eyes. He could not have explained the keen and extraordinary sense of accomplishment he felt over what had been a relatively short, straightforward and risk-free task. All he knew was that his strange, nagging, ancestral voices were quiet at last.

The End